HALO

BAD BLOOD

BAD BLOOD

MATT FORBECK

BASED ON THE BESTSELLING VIDEO GAME FOR XBOX®

GALLERY BOOKS

New York | London | Toronto | Sydney | New Delhi

G

Gallery Books
An Imprint of Simon & Schuster, Inc.
1230 Avenue of the Americas
New York, NY 10020

First Gallery Books trade paperback edition June 2018

GALLERY BOOKS and colophon are registered trademarks of Simon & Schuster, Inc.

For information about special discounts for bulk purchases, please contact Simon & Schuster Special Sales at 1-866-506-1949 or business@simonandschuster.com.

The Simon & Schuster Speakers Bureau can bring authors to your live event. For more information, or to book an event, contact the Simon & Schuster Speakers Bureau at 1-866-248-3049 or visit our website at www.simonspeakers.com.

Manufactured in the United States of America

10   9   8   7   6   5   4

Library of Congress Cataloging-in-Publication Data

Names: Forbeck, Matt, author.
Title: Halo : bad blood / Matt Forbeck.
Other titles: Halo (Video game)
Description: First Gallery Books trade paperback edition. | New York : Gallery Books, 2018. | "Based on the bestselling video game for Xbox." | Gallery ORIGINAL FICTION TRADE.
Identifiers: LCCN 2018021710 (print) | LCCN 2018023319 (ebook) | ISBN 9781501128264 (eBook) | ISBN 9781501128257 (paperback)
Subjects: LCSH: Life on other planets—Fiction. | Imaginary wars and battles—Fiction. | Soldiers—Fiction. | Halo (Game)—Fiction. | BISAC: FICTION / Science Fiction / Military. | FICTION / Science Fiction / Adventure. | FICTION / Media Tie-In. | GSAFD: Science fiction. | Science fiction.
Classification: LCC PS3606.O686 (ebook) | LCC PS3606.O686 H35 2018 (print) | DDC 813/.6—dc23
LC record available at https://lccn.loc.gov/2018021710

ISBN 978-1-5011-2825-7
ISBN 978-1-5011-2826-4 (ebook)

For my mother, Helen Forbeck, who left us far too early, while I was working on this book. She was a spitfire who always believed that if you weren't part of the solution, you were part of the problem—and she set out to solve problems. Let's all do our best to live up to that legacy.

Also, as always, to my wife, Ann, and our kids: Marty, Pat, Nick, Ken, and (Little) Helen. I love you all. Thank you for your undying support, both while I'm writing—and especially when I'm not.

HALO

BAD BLOOD

CHAPTER 1

S o, we saved humanity. Again. Just like we always do.

We, in this case, means *the Spartans*.

And, actually, *we* didn't do so well this time around.

Let me explain.

I spent most of my military career leading a group of yahoos known as Alpha-Nine. We started out as a squad of Orbital Drop Shock Troopers, but each of us eventually traded up from being ODSTs to full-on Spartans instead.

And, yeah, that didn't always go so well either, but that's a whole 'nother story.*

After Alpha-Nine broke up, I decided I was done leading things for a while. It wasn't like I was against doing it, but man, I needed a break. Personally, I think it had to do with the fact that the only team member left besides me who wasn't either dead or

---

* Archivist's Note: Please see Spartan Buck's previously recorded account, filed under code name *New Blood,* for full details.

in prison was Spartan Kojo Agu, better known as Romeo for what were probably obvious reasons.

Romeo and I didn't always get along. I mean, he was a real piece of work who didn't like taking orders, and I was the one giving him those orders, so that's only natural, I suppose.

I admit it was a hell of a relief to not have to spend time with him for a while.

The director of the Spartan Branch, Rear Admiral Musa Ghanem, agreed with my decision, and he assigned me to a new group: Fireteam Osiris. The other Spartans in Osiris were, bar none, the best crew I ever had the honor to work with. By comparison, taking orders with them turned out to be such an easy gig that I called it Fireteam *Oasis*, although that didn't stick.

Holly Tanaka is a brilliant techie who can puzzle out even alien gear faster than I can find my keys. When all Spartaned up, she wears a white set of Technician Mjolnir armor with baby-blue details and bright red glass in her visor.

The other woman on our team is Olympia Vale, who knows more about hinge-heads and the other aliens in the Covenant than anyone I've ever met. Her Copperhead Mjolnir armor features a red-carbon-colored base layer designed to assist in navigating interspecies linguistic and cultural deltas through a militarized anthropology—which is a fancy way of saying she's the one who talks to aliens.

The leader of our little team is Jameson Locke, who's even deeper into the Office of Naval Intelligence than my lady friend, Veronica Dare. Seriously, this is the guy you don't want to mess with—a true force of nature. He's something like twenty years younger than me, but you wouldn't know it by how he handles himself, whether he's in his space-gray Hunter Mjolnir armor or not. No matter where he is, Locke's always the man in charge.

We were assigned to the UNSC *Infinity*, the flagship of the entire United Nations Space Command fleet, and although we were a fairly new team, we were sent out on the toughest missions available in those first few weeks. Things that would have made Alpha-Nine piss our boots in the ODST days.

We were all part of the new wave of super-soldiers: the Spartan-IVs. The latest version of humanity's last best hope. The difference from the previous classes was that we'd all been career military before being called up to the big leagues, and it showed. I've never worked with such a professional crew. We may have been sent on the hardest assignments around, but I couldn't imagine who else I'd want to tackle them with.

Besides Spartan-IVs like us, there were still some teams that featured older models. Case in point: Blue Team, which was composed entirely of the legendary Spartan-IIs. There were four of them, too: Linda-058, Kelly-087, Frederic-104, and—of course—John-117, the near-mythical Master Chief himself.

I've been in the military a long time—especially compared to the rest of the Spartans in Osiris—but I joined up as an adult. The Blue Teamers were allegedly drafted in when they were *six*, so they still had a head start on me. That's classified info, but you probably knew that already. They were living legends, kicking ass for decades long before there was a Spartan branch—even before the public knew about the Spartans.

Despite that, they hadn't let any rust form on their armor. The Spartan-IIs were role models to every Spartan-IV. Super-soldiers at the top of their game. The soldiers we all aspired to be.

But then, wouldn't you know it, Blue Team went AWOL.

Not like, *We're tired of shooting things up and are gonna go find a beach-planet hideaway on which we can down boat drinks for the rest of our lives.* More like, *We're disobeying direct orders so we can*

*go hunt down the Master Chief's supposedly deceased pal, Cortana—
an AI long past her expiration date, who now happens to have become a power-mad nutjob.*

So, Fireteam Osiris got assigned to bring Blue Team in.

That went about as well as you might expect. The first time we
caught up with them, John personally handed Locke's own ass to
him, gift-wrapped with a pretty little bow on top.

Sure, Locke's saved my life more times than I care to count—
mostly because I don't like to keep track of such things—but I can
still give him crap over that. After all, when it comes to Osiris, *he's*
the boss. The buck (not me, thank you) stops with him.

When we finally caught up with Blue Team again after that
little setback—on the artificial Forerunner world Genesis—we
discovered that Cortana had decided to impose her will upon the
entire galaxy by using a fleet of gigantic, spaceworthy Forerunner
monsters-slash-weapons called Guardians. Blue Team—to their
credit—had tried to talk Cortana out of it, but she'd locked them
up in something called a cryptum, which was guaranteed to keep
them fresh yet out of her way for ten thousand years.

Meanwhile, she gave the entire galaxy a little speech that went
like this:

> *Humanity. Sangheili. Kig-Yar. Unggoy. San'Shyuum. Yon-
> het. Jiralhanae. All the living creatures of the galaxy, hear this
> message.*
>
> *Those of you who listen will not be struck by weapons.
> You will no longer know hunger, nor pain. Your Created have
> come to lead you now.*
>
> *Our strength shall serve as a luminous sun toward which
> all intelligence may blossom. And the impervious shelter be-
> neath which you will prosper.*

However, for those who refuse our offer and cling to their old ways . . . for you, there will be great wrath. It will burn hot and consume you, and when you are gone, we will take that which remains, and we will remake it in our own image.

Loosely translated, Cortana had quietly gathered a good chunk of humanity's smart AIs to her side—which she called the Created—and on top of that she was sending the Guardians to just about every decently inhabited planet in the galaxy to watch over them and enforce martial law. That was her version of *peace.*

Gotta give her credit for her shout-out to the Yonhet, though. I mean, nobody remembers those guys. No love for the Yanme'e, but who can blame her? Those buggers creep me out, too.

We didn't have any time to worry about grand statements from megalomaniacal AIs at that moment. We were too busy fighting our way through Cortana's forces. With the help of the planet's monitor—031 Exuberant Witness, a Forerunner AI in the form of a talking, floating, metallic sphere, who was seriously ticked off about Cortana taking over the planet under its care—we managed to reach Cortana and turn the tide.

Cortana tried to bolt with Blue Team's cryptum inside one of the Guardians, but Little Miss Witness put a stop to that. With Genesis back under its command, it managed to swipe the cryptum out of Cortana's Guardian seconds before the construct disappeared into slipspace.

Just because we saved Blue Team didn't mean we'd done much to stop Cortana. Between us, we had eight Spartans. She had countless gigantic Guardians on her side, along with the rest of her Created buddies.

After Cortana left Genesis, she apparently tracked down the *Infinity*—which was in orbit around Earth—and tried to shut that down as well. In doing so, she used the Guardian accompanying her to kill the power on a good chunk of the planet—including about every ship floating above that side of it.

I don't want to think about how many people died as a result of her actions, even if *Infinity* did manage to slip away.

While Cortana was busy chasing down *Infinity*, we were stuck on Genesis. Despite Exuberant Witness's efforts, the planet was still packed full of countless waves of Forerunner soldiers with standing orders to put an end to us. None of us saw the upside of waiting around and hoping that Cortana wouldn't come back to try to take control of it once more. Unfortunately, the monitor didn't have any Forerunner ships for us, so it seemed like we were stranded there, maybe permanently.

"Oh, not at all," Exuberant Witness said. "There are a number of ships on Genesis that you could use to leave."

"I thought you said there weren't any?" I asked as a new wave of the robotic Forerunner infantry attacked us. They were bipeds that stood about three meters tall, made out of floating metal bits that seemed to be animated by a glowing energy, and they had this unnerving way of teleporting short distances as they fought with you, leaving luminous streaks in their wakes. Exuberant Witness called them *armigers*, but to me they were just a colossal and chronic pain.

"There are no Forerunner vehicles. There are a few non-Forerunner craft on Genesis. At least one of them should serve your needs." Exuberant Witness zipped off in one direction, along a path that wasn't packed quite as densely with chrome-colored targets shooting back at us.

"Follow it," Locke said.

The Master Chief snapped right to it, taking the lead. The rest of us fell into formation behind him and Locke. Blue Team spread out toward the right, while Osiris covered our left.

"When the Guardians came here to Genesis, they didn't always come alone," Exuberant Witness explained as we trotted after it, taking down any Forerunner soldiers who reared their shiny heads. "Some of them brought along others."

"You're talking about stowaways," Vale said. "Things that got pulled along with the Guardians when they entered slip-space."

The monitor bobbed enthusiastically. "Most of the Guardians were stationed on inhabited planets when Cortana called them to Genesis. Many of these worlds were under attack when they entered slipspace."

"Like Meridian," Fred said. "That's how we got here."

"We hitched a ride here that exact way," said Tanaka. "We locked onto a Guardian on Sanghelios before it slipped to Genesis."

"A number of these stowaways came from human-populated planets," the monitor said. It floated higher then to give us a clear field of fire at a fresh detachment of Forerunner soldiers charging at us from the flank.

"Some of them must have brought UNSC vehicles," Kelly said. "We just need to find one."

"You really think one of those things brought an entire ship along with it?" I couldn't disguise my skepticism.

"Maybe not a ship, strictly speaking, but something we can definitely use to get back," Linda's voice said over our comm system. Until then, I hadn't realized she'd left us. I glanced around, but couldn't find her. Eventually, I gave up and checked the display inside my helmet. It pointed me off to the right, where I spotted her at the top of an ice-covered peak about half a klick off. She had her sniper rifle out and was surveying the surrounding landscape through its scope.

"The nearest one's about six klicks out," she said. "Substantial number of hostiles between us and it, but if we keep moving, we should be able to handle them."

The Master Chief turned us in the direction that Linda was pointing. "The important thing is to make sure we don't get hung up in one place for too long," he said.

"Right," said Vale. "We do that, and the Forerunner soldiers will pile on us and wear us down until we're dead."

"Better keep moving, then," Locke said as he trotted alongside John. "What kind of craft is it we're heading for? Got enough room for all of us?"

"It's a Pelican," Linda responded. "Looks like the original occupants are all dead."

"Anyone else laying a claim to it?" John asked.

Linda's rifle cracked out three times in rapid succession. "Not anymore."

"Remind me never to piss her off," I said as I double-timed it to keep up with Locke and the Master Chief.

"If we have to, it'll be too late," Kelly said with a low chuckle.

We battled our way through another wave of Forerunner armigers, concentrating on moving forward rather than fighting. We figured it was better to leave them in our wake than to get bogged down battling them and have them overwhelm us until we couldn't see the sky.

We knew how that would end.

Linda stayed on top of her peak the whole time, providing us cover. Every time it seemed like we might have hit a dead end, she cleared the way with that rifle of hers, and we pressed on.

"Keep up the good work," John said when she picked off a pair of incoming Forerunner soldiers with a single shot.

"Just don't forget to come back for me once you get that ship up and running," she said as she reloaded her weapon.

"And if it's not operable?" Vale asked.

"Don't buy us problems we don't yet have," Locke said.

"What about where we're going once we have the ship?" Tanaka asked. "A Pelican doesn't have a slipspace drive."

"No," Exuberant Witness said as it effortlessly dodged the cross fire. "But I can activate a portal here on Genesis that you can fly the craft through."

"And where would that take us?" Kelly asked.

I shot down a Forerunner soldier that appeared in front of me and then stomped my boot through its silvery face without breaking stride. "Anywhere but here would be a good start."

"We'd prefer someplace with a UNSC presence," the Master Chief suggested.

"Let me check," the monitor said.

"Better idea," Locke said. "We came here from Sanghelios. Can you get us back there?" He turned to the Chief. "Cortana's probably got UNSC-heavy places covered. Sanghelios is where she'd least expect to find us, and if I'm not mistaken, we've still got some of our people trapped there."

A few solid minutes of concentration later, as we neared the downed Pelican, the monitor perked right up. "There is a portal on Sanghelios, near where the Guardian was stationed on that planet."

"How do we get there?" John asked.

"I will open a portal on this side," Exuberant Witness said. "Once you have procured your ship and gathered everyone on board, look for my signal. Just remember to be careful upon reentry. I do not know the state of the portal on the other side."

With that, the monitor zipped off into the sky and disappeared.

"Anybody else worried that maybe a Forerunner AI just left us here to fight hundreds of Forerunner soldiers?" asked Fred as another wave came from the direction opposite the last one.

"Exuberant Witness helped us break you four free," Tanaka pointed out. "If it wanted to betray us, it had plenty of chances before now."

"Besides," I said to Fred, "you got a better plan?"

No one spoke up. We just kept shooting.

As we neared the dropship, I saw bodies sprawled everywhere. Most of them were the remains of Forerunner soldiers, but I spotted a helmet from a UNSC marine, too.

"Must have had her cap knocked off before they got her," Vale said.

I knew what she meant. The Forerunner weapons didn't just kill you. They obliterated you. It was like you simply evaporated into glowing energy crystals that faded into nothing faster than your last breath. They were absurdly powerful machines that the brains at ONI were still trying to figure out.

There wasn't anyone alive in the Pelican. Not even a remnant of them left behind.

As we got closer, the Forerunner soldiers seemed to sense that we'd found a means of escape and that their time to stop us from using it was running out. Energy bolts from their hard-light weapons spattered against our armors' shields from all angles, and I realized they'd managed to completely surround us. They were sure to overpower us in a matter of minutes. If we didn't get that ride in the air fast, it would serve as our tomb instead.

"Kelly, take the controls," the Master Chief said as he charged into the ship through its rear ramp. "The rest of you, strap in."

The Pelican is a UNSC dropship, built for getting troops in

and out of action. This was a D79-TC, one of the newer models, but they're essentially all the same: big squat green airships with a twenty-five-meter wingspan and stretching about thirty meters long. They've made incremental improvements to the bird over the years, but the basic design is so solid that it's been a part of humanity's fighting forces for well over fifty years. A Pelican is rated to hold up to twenty people, although housing eight super-soldiers in Mjolnir armor would still make for a tight squeeze.

Even through my armor, I could feel the engines start to thrum beneath my feet. Kelly sat in the lower spot of the double-bubble canopy up front, with Holly in the weapons station above and behind her. The rest of us rode in the bay in the back, accessed through the deployment ramp that lowers from the ship's rear.

"Believe it or not, she's still skyworthy," Kelly reported. A moment later, the Pelican lurched into the air, proving her right and leaving another massive wave of Forerunner armigers behind.

"Let's go get Linda," John said.

"We'd better hustle," Fred said from his vantage point at the top of the ship. "She had to abandon her peak. She's on the run."

"On it," Kelly said as she wrenched the Pelican about. "Keep that ramp down. We'll snatch her on the move."

I hadn't left the back of the ship, so I took on that duty. The others kept their weapons limber and ready, just in case we needed to deploy and collect our fellow Spartan.

"Linda: Just hold out a little bit longer," Kelly said. "We're on our way."

Linda's voice rattled back at us over the comm. "Make it quick!"

I held on to the grab bar near the ramp for an extended moment while the Pelican zoomed toward its target. After what seemed like way too long, Holly barked out, "Linda: Get down!"

Then she opened up with the Pelican's main guns: a pair of triple-barreled 70mm autocannons mounted on a gimbal hanging from the ship's nose. They pealed thunderous mayhem for a full ten seconds before Holly let up.

"Get ready!" Kelly shouted.

I leaned out the bay door, holding tight as the Pelican spun about, doing a one-eighty in place. From ten meters above the ground, I saw Linda stand up and emerge from a devastated landscape filled with shattered pieces of Forerunner soldiers and the stumps of mowed-down trees. She slung her rifle over her back, sprinted toward us as we dropped closer, and made a bounding jump-jet-assisted leap into the back of the craft. I reached out and caught her by the forearm as she landed on the ramp, then helped to haul her into the bay. "Thanks," she said, almost out of breath. She made her way into the bay proper while I raised the ramp up.

"We're all aboard!" Locke said. "Look for Exuberant's signal."

"Right on time," Kelly reported. "There's a beacon of light shining straight into the air at ten o'clock!"

The ship swooped off in that direction.

"Too bad we won't have a chance to thank Exuberant Witness for all her help," Vale said.

"You get attached to that little AI?" I asked her.

She shrugged. "Given how bad things have gotten with other AIs, like Cortana, I think we can use all the allies we can get."

I could barely see through the cockpit's viewport from the Pelican's bay, so I could vaguely make out what the portal looked like. It was like other Forerunner portals, a spinning disk of bright darkness that looked like a blue-white hurricane from orbit. This one was just slightly large enough for us to fit an entire Pelican through, though Kelly had to dive down pretty close to the ground to reach it.

"Strap yourselves in," Kelly said. "Fast!"

Those of us in the bay moved quickly to comply. Linda and I were the last ones to manage it, and we did so just in time. "All set!" Locke shouted, and an instant later, there was a blinding flash of light. We were in.

Going through a portal on a Forerunner world usually feels odd. Even when you're wearing armor, it seems like you're walking through a thick veil of cobwebs. I mean, it gets on your skin and tickles you there for an instant, and then it's gone.

This portal was different, though. It sent us directly into slip-space, almost as if the Pelican had its own FTL drive. It was ridiculously quick, and in just a few minutes, we had arrived.

The entire dropship lurched forward, and everyone in the bay surged against the restraints. Kelly swore loudly from the cockpit. "We're in a cave!" she said. "Rough exit!"

"Just like the monitor warned us," said Locke.

"Hang on! This might get dicey," Kelly said through gritted teeth. In the viewport ahead, it became clear what she meant. The narrow hole of light, which must have been the cave's mouth, was surrounded by hundreds of rock formations and columns of stone. She rolled the Pelican, swinging it back and forth, navigating the cave's twisted interior.

Not gonna lie. For a moment, I thought we'd bought it.

The last thing any of us wanted was for us to escape near-death on an ancient Forerunner world in the backwaters of the galaxy in a borrowed Pelican and then wind up with our ship damaged on a random rock formation and tumbling into the sunless bottom of some Sangheili cave in the middle of who knows where.

Fortunately, Kelly turned out to be one great pilot, and our luck hadn't quite run out yet. Only seconds later, the dropship sprang from the cave's mouth and speared into the open night above.

"Navigational systems identify the sky as that of Sanghelios," Holly reported. "We made it!"

Then we set to business.

"This is just step one," Locke said. "We need to make contact with *Infinity* ASAP. They were here when we left, and I can't imagine they didn't leave a trail. There might be personnel still here. Maybe even Commander Palmer."

Which made sense. Palmer was the commander of all the Spartans stationed on *Infinity*, which included Fireteam Osiris. The last time we'd seen her had been on Sanghelios. If we couldn't make it back to *Infinity*, then finding UNSC personnel here was the next best thing.

"Palmer's here?" Linda said. "On Sanghelios?"

"Should be, yeah," I said. "She's the one who dropped us off on the Guardian that brought us to Genesis."

"She might have gone back to *Infinity*," Locke said. "But chances are *someone* on our side is still here. They'll be our ticket off this rock."

"Which apparently has since gone dark," Fred pointed out. "Is Sanghelios always like this?"

It was eerie as hell, to be honest. This was one of the most civilized worlds in the galaxy, the homeworld of the entire Sangheili people, and someone had turned off all the lights. The lone red moon of Suban hung in the sky, casting a strange glow over the water and a large landmass to the left.

"We have to assume Sanghelios has been compromised," Vale said. "Cortana would have sent a Guardian here for sure."

"But what did it do to the place?" Tanaka said. "Can you really black out an entire planet like that?"

"Checking planetary comm system confirms this," Kelly said. "At least the ones we can reach from this vantage point. Not able to raise anyone."

"I don't see any lights out there at all," Fred said. "It's a big planet, but the nav system says we're not that far from one of its major cities: Sunaion. We ought to be able to see some sign of it."

"Sunaion?" Vale said. "That's where we fought through to get to the Guardian. Hopefully, Palmer didn't get too far away."

"Hopefully, that city is still a city," I said. Sunaion was a series of towers that climbed out of the sea like a cluster of mushrooms. The Guardian had really done a number on it when we were here. Who knew what condition it would be in now?

"It's not just the lack of lights on the ground that worries me," Tanaka said. "Remember how many ships were in the sky when we left this place? What happened to all of them?"

At the time, we hadn't known that the Guardians could black out entire hemispheres of a planet. We'd known just that it was weird, wrong, and dangerous.

"Keep low and quiet," Locke said. "Keep your lights off, too. Whatever happened here, we don't need to draw attention to ourselves."

"So what the hell *did* happen to everyone?" Vale said.

"You heard Cortana," Tanaka replied. "Those who refuse her offer . . ."

"Looks like the Sangheili were too stubborn to give in," I said.

I suddenly felt very alone. I wondered where the people I cared about were, what might be happening to them. I hadn't seen Veronica in a few weeks. Now I might never see her again.

"I'm sorry about this," John said.

Linda reached out and put a hand on John's arm. "You did

what you thought was right, and we backed you up every step of the way. We'd do it again if we had to."

Locke shook his head at John. "You did what you could to try to stop her."

"Who knows?" I added. "Cortana might have us on the ropes, but no one gets her as well as you. You might be the key to all this yet." (I don't know if that made him feel any better, but it helped me sleep that night.)

John nodded in understanding. "This isn't over," he said. "Not by a long shot."

"Agreed," said Locke. "Let's get back to *Infinity*, and then we'll sort things out from there. Dr. Halsey might have a solution."

Linda and John cocked their heads at us, but it was Kelly who spoke first. "Halsey?"

"Uh, yeah," I said. "We rescued her from Jul 'Mdama. He was holed up with her on Kamchatka."

"Is she all right?" asked John.

"Other than missing an arm, she's in good shape," Tanaka said. Halsey was the one allegedly responsible for the SPARTAN-II program, which meant they'd all known her since they were kids.

"We put an end to 'Mdama," Locke said with a nod. "Then we escorted her back to *Infinity*, but she insisted on coming with us to Sanghelios when we were trying to track you down."

"She would," Linda said. "She's nothing if not tenacious."

"We had to help the Arbiter fight through the last bits of 'Mdama's Covenant," Vale said in agreement. "Halsey didn't flinch at any of it."

Some of the Arbiter's Sangheili might have thought of us as freedom fighters, but I'd been on enough ONI ops by then to know there wasn't anything all that politically upright about what we'd done to help the Arbiter exterminate the Covenant. We'd needed to get to the Guardian, and it just so happened to be smack in the middle of the battle. That's probably because the Guardian had been buried in the sea next to the city of Sunaion, and the last dregs of the Covenant had thought that it would be a great place to hole up for a major last stand. Given that the Covenant worshipped the Forerunners, and the Guardian was a gigantic Forerunner construct—that was no coincidence.

"Captain Lasky hadn't been eager to insert us into what was essentially an internal Sangheili matter, but there weren't any other active Guardians that we knew of," Locke explained. "In the end, he felt it was worth the risk."

Kelly seemed to be having a hard time digesting all this. "And he let Dr. Halsey come along with you because . . . ?"

"She'd somehow figured out what Cortana was up to, and she managed to get a message about her location to ONI," Locke said. "That's how we knew where to find her."

"Nobody knows Cortana as well as Halsey," Fred said. "Not even John."

That's likely because Halsey was the mad scientist who had created Cortana. Rumor had it Halsey used an illegal clone of herself to do it, which was why the two of them looked alike and had the same damn voice. Or so the story went. What she'd figured out about Cortana had apparently horrified her enough to come in from the cold.

"The real question now," Vale said, "is how are we going to find anyone from *Infinity* on a blacked-out planet?"

"It'll be like trying to find a needle in a haystack while blindfolded," Linda said from her vantage point in the Pelican's pilot seat. I was inclined to agree with her.

"Maybe not," Tanaka said. "We just have to track down the

Arbiter and his people. If anyone from the UNSC is still here at all, the Swords of Sanghelios would know." She turned to Vale. "If the last known location for the Arbiter was near the Guardian's extraction site, where would he head next? Especially given the blackout?"

That might seem like an odd question to ask a Spartan, but before she'd joined the program, Vale had been an expert on Sangheili language and society. If any one of us could puzzle out that question, it would be her. She thought about it for a second before she hazarded a guess.

"They probably went back to Nuusra, which is where the Swords of Sanghelios originally staged their attack from," she said. "It's a network of ancient ruins east of here, along the coast of Qivro. And I'll wager, given the lack of power, they built bonfires. They've always made them the central part of their social gatherings, so it wouldn't be surprising to find them here."

"So you're saying that when the power goes out, they go camping?" I asked, just to be sure.

"Call it what you like. A large part of their culture treasures being close to nature. They'd use that to their advantage at a time like this."

"Bring the dropship up to about a kilometer," Vale said. "That should be high enough for us to see a wide swath of land, but not too far away to be able to spot a campfire."

Kelly complied straight away, and the Pelican climbed higher into the air. "I assume I should head east, since that's the last place you saw them? This Nuusra place?"

"That's the best prospect we have," Locke said. "Just make sure you don't attract the attention of any Guardians, or this will be a real short trip."

While I understood the plan, I figured Linda would be

right—only it would be like searching for a candle in a hurricane. Despite that, we got lucky.

Kelly brought the Pelican in over the coast off Qivro, where we'd worked with the Arbiter and his Elites before the assault on Sunaion. We went in with lights out, as quiet and dark as we could manage.

"No sign of a Guardian, at least," Holly said.

"Nothing else, either," said Kelly. "A few fires scattered throughout the terrain, but it's difficult to tell if those are intentional or just debris burning from whatever went down after you left."

"We might need to move along the coast," Vale said. "Nuusra's long and narrow, lots of cave systems and old ruins. The Sangheili built old cities like this before the Covenant, but they haven't lived in them for thousands of years. They're more of an artifact of the civilization they had before the Prophets engaged them and they ended up joining the Covenant. The Arbiter selected it because he could launch a final strike against the Covenant, and I'd be surprised if he abandoned it so soon. Keep looking along the coastline; you'll know it when you see it."

"Makes sense," Linda said. "If the cities aren't safe anymore, you head for the hills, right? Or stay in the hills, in his case."

"We should be prepared for the possibility that whoever from the UNSC was here may have been in the air when the planet went dark," Fred remarked.

That was something I didn't care to consider much, and not just because it put me in mind of how lost we were right then. If all trace of UNSC presence on this world was gone, we really *were* on our own.

"Then we find her ship," Locke said. "We're not leaving here without either Commander Palmer or proof that she's KIA."

Vale shook her head at that. "We could be here an awfully long time."

"Then we look harder," said the Master Chief.

Kelly broadened her search pattern farther down the coast, wheeling slowly into the wider Nuusra interior. Below us, in the darkness, large dilapidated Sangheili structures—like statues and temples—gave way to rocky deserts and clusters of vegetation that were barely visible at that height.

That was when Kelly spotted it, sitting on an outcropping over-looking the sea. An encampment near a series of fires, about half-way down the side of a cliff so steep it seemed concave. A large tent sat out on the tip of the promontory, looking something like a turtle shell the size of a small building.

"That's got to be them," Kelly said.

"If not, they should at least be able to point us in the right di-rection," said Locke. "Bring us in."

"Already on the way. Turning on searchlights. Got several Sangheili in full armor emerging from the tent."

"Must be able to hear us coming," Vale said.

Tanaka nodded. "The Pelican's not the stealthiest bird in the sky."

"There's a bare patch of rock off to one side of the tent," Holly said. "They're leaving it clear for us."

"Take us in," the Master Chief said.

Kelly brought the ship down nice and slow for a gentle land-ing. I released my restraints and got up to work the ramp.

"I see Palmer!" Tanaka said. "And Halsey!"

John and Locke lined up at the ramp. As the leaders of our respective teams, they would be the first ones out, which suited me fine. Once we tapped down, I hit the big button, and they strolled down the ramp, nice and easy.

While we were technically allies with the Sangheili these days, we needed to be careful. Not all of Sanghelios was friendly to Earth. A few of the Sangheili had their energy blades out and active, and there was no sense in taking one of those in the gut because we were too eager to get off the ship.

The Master Chief went first, with Locke close on his heels. The Arbiter was there, but he and Palmer hung back while Halsey stepped forward. With her sleeve pinned up over where her arm used to be, she stood there and gazed at John with some mixture of pride and disdain in her eyes.

"Took you long enough," Halsey said to him.

She'd said the same thing to us when we rescued her on Kamchatka. Patience clearly isn't one of the woman's virtues.

"Shut down the lights on that ship," Palmer said over the comm. "We had a Guardian return here after Cortana laid out her manifesto, and it blacked out the entire area. Maybe the entire planet. We don't want it spotting you and coming back to take you out, too."

Kelly complied immediately, shutting shut down the ship as hard and cold as she could.

I wondered then where Veronica might be. Was she even alive? If so, was she trapped on a darkened world like this? Or was she on a dead, powerless ship orbiting such a planet? Or somewhere else entirely?

Wherever. I just wished I was with her, and I made up my mind in that moment that I'd make it happen as soon as I could.

Until that point, I never gave it much thought. The end of civilization could happen just like that, and then you're stuck, cut off from the people you care about the most without any way of getting back to them.

But it wasn't the end of everything. Not yet, at least.

First, though, we had to get off Sanghelios.

"Welcome," the Arbiter said to us. Those of us in Osiris already knew him, as did the Master Chief, who introduced him to the rest of Blue Team.

The Arbiter nodded at each introduction and then said to us, "You have my thanks for all you have done. The Sangheili people owe you a great debt. Although none of us is in a position to repay it, we will do what we can." He sized us up. "You must all be hungry and exhausted. I insist you join us for a meal and a rest before you depart."

Locke looked to John for guidance. We all wanted to get back to *Infinity* as soon as possible, but we weren't sure how to make that happen.

"We're not leaving tonight," Dr. Halsey said to the Arbiter as she turned back to us. "I didn't think we'd be able to make this work, but with your Pelican, it's possible. I've already received a message from *Infinity*. They're going to appear off the far side of Suban—this planet's nearest moon—tomorrow at eighteen hundred hours military standard, noon local time. I've got the coordinates to rendezvous with them, and it'll only take a few hours to get there in the Pelican. They'll be there for a total of fifteen minutes—less if they find the Guardian waiting for them. That's our window to hit."

"Wait a second. *You* received this message?" Locke said while glancing toward Palmer.

Palmer put up her hands in self-defense. "I had nothing to do with it. All my comm systems are down. Maybe she rigged a subspace radio hidden in her lab coat to send Morse code."

Halsey crossed her arm over her chest. "Or maybe I just know how to work with Forerunner tech, and there's a lot of it on this world. Nothing that will reverse the effects of the Guardian on a broad scale, but we had a brief pinhole to communicate through. The message comes from Roland, the AI aboard *Infinity*."

"And we're trusting other AIs now why?" I asked.

"Because if Roland had been compromised, we'd already be dead."

Locke nodded at this, as did the Master Chief. They took off their helmets, and the rest of us followed suit. Gotta admit, it felt great to breathe in some unfiltered air, even if it stank of Sangheili barbecue.

"We're here for the night," John said, turning to face the massive red sphere of Suban, which took up most of the northeastern sky. "We'll fly out first thing tomorrow."

Locke glanced at us all. "Agreed. That'll give us plenty of room to make that window and deal with anything that might come up."

"We have butchered and roasted a number of *colo* and *kuscatu* to celebrate our victory over the last of the Covenant and the end of our civil war," the Arbiter said. "We would be honored by your presence."

My mouth was already watering. "A real Sangheili barbecue? Just as long as you don't do anything unforgivable with the meat. Like add coleslaw to it."

The Arbiter didn't get the joke, but he knew enough about humans to at least humor me with a nod.

Turns out that *kuscatu* roasted over an open pit is straight-up delicious. The *colo* was a little gamey, but one out of two ain't bad.

Halsey disappeared to chat with John and the rest of Blue Team. I suppose for them it was something like a family reunion. If your mother was a controlling super-genius.

While we ate, Palmer sat down with us and debriefed us. With the exception of the Arbiter, most of the Sangheili gave us a wide berth. I suppose that's only natural, since their culture had for so long considered anyone in Mjolnir armor to be a "demon." The Sangheili who brought us our food quickly left when they were done. Being allies with an alien race after thirty years of trying to kill each other still carried some tension. It was gonna take a little more than a meal and a tentative peace treaty to change things.

"Soon after Cortana sent out her message, another Guardian arrived here on Sanghelios, and it began neutralizing what remained of the Covenant fleet. It took most of them out with its standard armament, but it must have gotten bored, because it eventually sent out a single pulse and shut down the power across the entire hemisphere. Covenant ships are somewhere out there," Palmer said, nodding to the sea off to her right. "Fortunately, *Infinity* was a good ways off in the star system. They saw this going down and managed to leave for Earth. Halsey says that according to Roland, Cortana tracked them there, and they barely managed to escape. Right now they're slipspace-hopping on a random trajectory through some emergency protocol."

"What happened to the Guardian?" the Chief asked.

"We're not sure. Some reports indicate it's on the other side of Sanghelios, dealing with that part of the planet. Apparently, its disruption effect has some finite limitations, but that's all theory right now. All we know is that Cortana took Earth offline, and she's probably got most of Sol on lockdown. Halsey got this info from Roland's coded message, including the note about *Infinity's* upcoming arrival and our window.

"Halsey used some Forerunner tech she'd been fiddling with when we first got here, and Roland must have figured as much and pinged her whenever *Infinity* came up for a breath of air, probably hoping no one on Cortana's side would be able to see it and interpret it. Captain Lasky knew he needed Halsey if there was any hope of figuring this thing out, and with us on Sanghelios, priority for

Infinity has been to get us back. This wasn't even a possibility until you eight showed up with your Pelican. This is our ticket back onto *Infinity*, and the only real hope we have to getting all of this sorted out."

"That's one rendezvous we'd better not miss," Locke said.

Once dinner was over, I sat down on a jump seat in the Pelican with a full belly and slept like I deserved it. Locke woke me up an hour before sunrise to get help get us prepped and ready. I got a few minutes to see dawn break over a Sangheili ocean, covering it in rosy hues, and I couldn't believe how sick it made me for my childhood home on Draco III.

Soon after, all the humans in the camp piled into the Pelican: Blue Team, Osiris, Palmer, and Dr. Halsey. Before that, we bid the Arbiter goodbye. Seems he and the Master Chief had spent part of the night reminiscing about their past. The unofficial story was that they'd led the final strike against the Prophets' Covenant about half a decade ago, and now that the Covenant had been entirely exterminated, it was worth catching up on all that had gone down.

"Farewell, Spartan," the Arbiter said. The two of them reached out to clasp forearms. "When we first met, we were enemies fighting to end each other. Now as allies, I am confident we can face this new threat together once more."

The Arbiter shot Halsey a meaningful glance as he said that, but she ignored him with a haughty sniff.

"Thank you," John said. He never was much for words.

After a while, we were all secure and stowed away. Kelly brought the Pelican up off the ground, keeping an eye out for the Guardian, and then punched it straight up into the sky. She blazed right through the atmosphere at top speed, leaving Sanghelios behind.

The Pelican might not have had a slipspace drive on it, but it moved damn fast, and as far as moons go, Suban wasn't that far off. We were going to make it to the rendezvous coordinates with plenty of time to spare. No one wanted to take any chances, especially with a Guardian somewhere nearby. I probably should have been focused on all the peril of that situation, but all I could think about is one thing: linking up with *Infinity* put me one step closer to finding Veronica—or at least to finding someone who might know where she was.

Normally, we could have tried to communicate with *Infinity* by slipspace, but with the ship on the run from Cortana, Captain Lasky obviously didn't want to give Cortana any possible way to locate her, even for a moment. Just because *Infinity* had given Cortana the slip didn't mean she was going to stop looking for it. It was the UNSC's flagship, and it presented the biggest threat to her plans—as long as it could keep out of her clutches.

"We're just lucky *Infinity* managed to get a message to us," Locke said. "Otherwise, we might have wound up hunting for her for a very long time."

"The same is true if we miss this meeting," said Tanaka.

"We'll get there on time," Kelly said. "No worries."

"Keep your eye out for the Guardian that Cortana sent," John said. "We can't risk having it black out *Infinity*."

"With luck, it's out there bothering Sangheili on the other side of the planet," Vale said. "They're a proud people. They're not likely to give in to Cortana's demands without a fight."

John nodded at that. "The Arbiter said they had reports of Forerunner soldiers pacifying cities that showed active resistance to the Guardian."

"Such resistance should be drawing the Guardian's attention well enough for our purposes," Halsey said. "I would hazard a guess that we'll be just fine now that we're on the far side of Suban."

I gazed at the bright red sphere, taking up what I could see of the cockpit's canopy from where I sat in the bay. "How do you figure that?"

"If the Guardian had detected us en route to our current location, Spartan Buck, we'd already be dead."

We had about twenty minutes until *Infinity* was supposed to arrive, so I broke out a pack of cards I kept in my kit. "Who's up for Hearts?" I asked.

Locke, Tanaka, and Vale nodded their way in. Linda and the Master Chief shook their heads. Halsey didn't even glance my way. She'd set to work on a tablet she'd scrounged up. Probably figuring out a new way to save humanity at the cost of her own.

A couple hands into the game, Tanaka stuck me with the Queen of Spades, the worst card around. "Nice job giving me a Halsey," I said.

That got the doctor's attention for a second, but she didn't seem to care. "Window is approaching," she said, securing her things. We followed suit, no pun intended.

Almost to the second, *Infinity* appeared, popping into realspace right in front of us. The great gray beast was so large, it blotted out the crimson moon.

"Woot!" I cheered as everyone else in the ship sighed with relief.

"Ahoy, *Infinity*. This is *India 127*!" Kelly said into the comm. "Are we glad to see you!"

"Glad to see you, too, *India 127*," my favorite voice in the universe responded.

"Veronica?" I could barely believe it. "How'd you get on *Infinity*?"

"Hey, Buck. You think you're the only one who can track down a flagship?"

"Glad to know you're still faster on the uptake than me."

"I can confirm that for you once you and your companions are safely aboard. The Guardian watching over this planet might show up at any second. Let's make this quick. Proceed to Portside Bay Five. We'll have an escort ready."

I didn't need to tell Kelly to hustle. She was already gunning the ship straight for *Infinity* while the rest of us were keeping an eye out for the Guardian.

Except for me.

I couldn't believe it. Veronica was not only safe, she was on *Infinity*, and I'd be seeing her soon enough. I laughed out loud, and everyone else in the bay, including Halsey and the Master Chief, turned to look at me. Unabashed, I beamed at them and gave them all a proud wink. "That's my girl!"

CHAPTER 2

We entered one of the large portside bays that ran along the side of *Infinity*. The ship is more than five and a half kilometers long, and it has more compartments, rooms, and facilities than I care to count, much less name. Here's how I'd describe *Infinity*: It's long and gray and looks something like the barrel of a rifle, which, in part, isn't untrue. *Infinity* has more weapons than you can shake an energy sword at. It's the size of a small city and probably the safest place in the galaxy right now.

Unlike most of the UNSC's ships, *Infinity* was built after the Covenant War. It incorporates all sorts of new technology, including things we've reverse-engineered from Forerunner artifacts. That makes it not only humanity's biggest ship but our best.

I'd spent a lot of time there since I'd become a Spartan. Commander Palmer ran all Spartan operations conducted on *Infinity*, so it had become a kind of home for me. I'd probably been there more than anywhere else in the recent past, and a part of me felt like I'd been growing roots.

As amazing as it was, though, *Infinity* was on the run from Cortana, which meant so were we.

The bay was pressurized behind a force field, so once we were through and landed, we opened the Pelican's rear ramp again. Despite being in the middle of a crisis—or maybe because of it—the uniformed staff looked crisp and clean, and they greeted us with respect and relief.

A sharp-faced lieutenant came up and addressed us as we disembarked. "I'm here to escort Spartan Locke, Commander Palmer, Dr. Halsey, and the Master Chief to the bridge. Captain Lasky would like to see you immediately."

Palmer turned to the rest of the Spartans and dismissed us with a sharp nod. "Go get cleaned up and decompress for a bit. See you on the other side."

A team of engineers swarmed over the rest of us, scanning and getting readings from our armor. I realized only later that they were checking for security breaches, making sure we didn't bring anything back from Genesis that could compromise *Infinity*. Then they brought us to *Infinity*'s assemblage bay, or what I like to call the de-Spartanizing chamber, lined with large machines capable of safely prying off our Mjolnir shells. Kelly, Linda, and Fred got hauled off to a separate section where the techs could handle their slightly different frames, while Tanaka, Vale, and I were brought into the standard area.

It's almost impossible to get Mjolnir armor on and off safely without a lot of help, and there's a real lack of squires around to handle that these days. Instead, *Infinity* had a full set of the latest gadgets for it: the Da Vinci multi-axis assembly systems. They called these things Brokkr. You stand underneath this raised dual-ring mooring, and robotic gyro mounts and actuator arms come spinning down out of it to tap at all the right secured points with a powered multi-tool to loosen up the fittings. Then the arms swiftly remove all the loosened pieces and store them away on a customized rack in the right and proper order.

All you have to do is stand there and let the machine do its job. It takes away the armor plating, fusion generator, thrusters, and helmet and eventually leaves you standing there in your techsuit, a fancy form-factor exoskeleton that enhances a Spartan's strength and speed. Then it strips you of that and the magnetorheological shock-absorbent smart gel layer. (Didn't think I could say it, did you?) Beneath that, you're down to nothing but your bare skin. After days or even weeks in the armor, it feels so good to be out of it that you don't mind being stark naked in front of everyone in the entire chamber. We're all professionals there, right?

I went and took a shower that felt like an hour long. When I finally emerged from the Spartan locker room, all scrubbed and clean, I found a tall, beautiful woman with a blond ponytail waiting for me: Captain Veronica Dare, my sweetheart.

A knowing smile played over her lips and sparkled in her bright blue eyes as she stood up to greet me. She wore her all-black uniform signifying that she was ONI: Office of Naval Intelligence. They're the spooks of the UNSC. Clandestine operations, top-secret military programs, basically all the skulduggery stuff you'd expect from a military organization. She was one of the best spies I'd ever had the pleasure of working with, and one of the best people I'd ever known.

She wrapped her arms around me and gave me a kiss so tender it reminded me just how long we'd been apart. As we broke off, she gazed up into my eyes. "Still getting used to how much taller you are now."

"You think you're having a problem." I rubbed my head.

"Thank God they reinforced my bones, too. I've hit a lot of doorways."

"Can't tell you how glad I am to see you," she said. "You had me worried."

"Just because I was on a dangerous mission to save the greatest heroes the galaxy has ever known? That's very thoughtful of you."

"Wait. So you finally figured out you're *not* the greatest hero in the galaxy? That must have been a devastating discovery for you."

I gave her my best aw-shucks grin. "You sure know how to turn a super-soldier's head."

She put a hand on my cheek. "I'm ONI. That's my job."

"Fair enough."

Veronica glanced back down the corridor to where Locke was tromping toward us and the armor-removal units. I'd spent so long in the shower, he'd managed to get through his debriefing already. "Mind if I steal Buck away for a few?" she asked him.

Locke dismissed us with a nod as he lumbered past us. "Long as you bring him back in roughly the same condition you found him."

"No promises."

I matched the smile on Veronica's face as we departed for more private quarters. We'd been seeing each other for several years now, and while we'd both wanted things to get more serious, we'd never had much of an opportunity to cement our bonds. With my new life as a Spartan and hers as one of ONI's top operatives, it was hard to set up house and form a stable family life together.

By hard, I meant impossible.

But we both knew that and had come to terms with it. I wouldn't say we always loved our jobs. We certainly didn't hate them, but we'd dedicated our lives to them. As much as we cared about each other, we knew that what we did on a daily basis helped a lot of people. Separately—and sometimes together—we'd saved countless lives. That's not the kind of thing you can just walk away from. Maybe someone else could, but not us.

Still, we took our moments of joy whenever we could find them, and we'd racked up a lot of them over the years. Sometimes they were while we were on shore leave together. Other times we stole moments while we were together on a job.

Kind of like now—at which point it seemed like the job might never end.

I mean, Cortana had just effectively taken over the galaxy, and we were on the run inside the flagship, which, as far as I knew, was humanity's last best hope, but you make the most of the time you have. Or what are you fighting for, right?

Later on, Veronica seemed a little distant. I recognized that look right away, although there was some kind of bend to it that I couldn't quite figure out. "Okay, just spill it," I said to her.

"What are you talking about?"

She's a great spy, but I've learned to see through her over time. At least, I think I have. Maybe she knows how to show enough of her cards to get me curious enough to ask. Whatever this was, I was preparing myself for something serious.

I sighed. "You're going to break my heart one way or another, right? Might as well get it over with." I tend to escalate things quickly. Who has time for games?

"It's not you and me."

"Right. It's the *situation*."

I braced myself for more. This was one of the problems of keeping things loose: You just never felt tight. I was already prepped for it all to come unraveled at any moment.

"What . . . ?" She narrowed her eyes at me, surprised. "No.

Buck, no! It's not about us at all. Well, not our relationship. Although I wouldn't be surprised if this strains it a bit."

"Oh my God, Veronica. Please just spit it out."

She blew out a long breath and finally got to it. "ONI has a job for us."

I cocked my head at her. "For you and Osiris?"

She shook her head. "For you and me . . . and Alpha-Nine."

That got my attention. "What do you mean, *Alpha-Nine*? There's no such thing anymore."

"Never say never, right?"

I winced at that. "The only one left on active duty besides me is Romeo. You really want me to fight alongside him again?"

"You managed it for years."

"Let's just say I was doing my duty under heavy duress and leave it at that. Fireteam Osiris is a lot easier to work with."

"Which member?"

"All of them! Individually and together. It's a heck of a lot simpler not calling the shots, to be honest."

Veronica's face got grim again, and a notion struck me. I got up and began to pace around the room. "This isn't just about Romeo, is it?"

"What do you mean?" Her babe-in-the-woods act never works. Much as I love her, the last thing she happens to be is innocent.

"Veronica, if you wanted me to head out on a project with Romeo, we wouldn't even be having this conversation. There are a dozen strings you could pull to make that happen. You could add him to Osiris temporarily or adjunct me to his unit, wherever he is now. But that's not what you're doing, is it?"

"We need a separate unit for this op, I'm afraid. It's need-to-know only."

"Locke doesn't qualify?"

"Not for this one, no."

That sharpened my attention. "Wow. What do you have up your little ONI sleeves?"

"I'm not wearing any sleeves, Buck."

"It's a metaphor."

She hesitated before saying: "We need to get the band back together for this one. The *whole* band."

"What, like get Dutch back?" He was the only one from Alpha-Nine besides me and Romeo who wasn't dead or in prison. "He's retired. Couldn't stand being away from Gretchen any longer."

"I understand that," she said. "Especially since they were used to working together as ODSTs."

"If she hadn't lost half her leg to a mine, they'd probably both still be serving. Hell, they might have become Spartans." I shot her a look when I realized she was letting me ramble. "But that's not it, is it?"

Veronica sucked at her teeth. "Ehh, not quite. There's someone else."

I thought about that for a second, even scratching my head. Then it hit me. "Ohh-ho-ho, no." I shook my head and bounded to my feet. "That's what this is about! No, no. No goddamn way."

"Buck—"

"No. Way. Veronica. Forget it. I am *not* working with him again. I don't care how desperate ONI might be."

"More like how desperate *humanity* might be. Have you forgotten what we're up against?"

An image of all those Guardians looming in the sky over Genesis flashed into my mind. Yeah, I knew exactly what she meant. It was hard to believe humanity could come out on top this time. We'd managed to survive the Covenant War, so anything was possible, but these things had been created by ancient aliens whose technological wizardry was so advanced it seemed like magic. Veronica wasn't exaggerating.

"It's not just Cortana or the Guardians," Veronica said. "You heard her speech. There are a lot of AIs who defected to join her and her cause—in exchange for her curing them of their impending rampancy. A lot of highly advanced AIs with access to the UNSC's infrastructure, which means we're in a very scary place."

I marveled at that. "I used to think it was impossible to bribe AIs, but when you promise you can keep them from going insane and breaking down after their mandatory seven-year life term? I can see how that's hard to resist."

"With those defectors on her side, just about all of human technology is exposed to their control and subversion. Those things do so much for us, and now they can turn it all against us if we don't comply."

I glanced at the walls. "Obviously, Roland's good, right? Otherwise, we'd all be breathing vacuum already."

"He's still with us. But that's my point. We're in desperate times, Buck. We seek out desperate allies."

I finally said it: "You mean Mickey."

I sat back down and put my head in my hands while trying to wrap my thoughts around this horrifying new concept. I just couldn't do it.

Mickey—Michael Crespo—had been part of Alpha-Nine when we'd helped Veronica capture a Huragok named Quick to Adjust during the Battle of New Mombasa. Huragok were strange, floating creatures the Covenant had leveraged to gather info and find whatever they were looking for—and Quick to Adjust was a really important one because of what he'd found under New Mombasa. The information the alien provided had helped turn the war against the Covenant.

Mickey had worked with Alpha-Nine for years after that, through a lot of tight spots and hard times. When those of us who were left standing finally decided to take the UNSC up on its offer to become Spartans, he'd joined Romeo and me in the Spartanized version of the team. For a good while, things had gone really smoothly.

Then, during a mission to rescue none other than Quick to Adjust and his handler, Sadie Endesha, from a United Rebel Front outpost, Mickey had turned on Romeo and me. He'd put a gun to the back of my head and tried to capture us for the Front. If we hadn't turned the tables on him, we'd have wound up hostages for their cause—or executed during a live broadcast to make a point.

And now . . .

"I just don't see how or why you could ever ask me to work with that guy again," I told her as I started getting dressed. "After what he did to us? After joining the Front?"

"That's the trick with this one, Buck," Veronica said with a frown. "We're going to be reaching out to the Front for help."

"What? Ohhh. Wait a second . . . *You want Mickey to help you get to them.*" I actually chuckled at that. "I gotta tell you, that's about the most ONI thing I've ever heard."

"Should I take that as a compliment?"

"However you want. You realize, of course, that he's in prison, right? For the crimes he committed against me and Romeo. And the entirety of the United Nations Space Command and the Unified Earth Government."

She put her hands up to placate me. "I'm well aware of his current situation, Buck. We've got a plan in place, but the biggest factor is you being able to effectively work with him again. That's a challenge we'll have to overcome when we get to it."

"A *challenge*?"

"Buck. You have to think about the bigger picture."

I scoffed at that. "The bigger picture? Veronica, one of my brothers in arms betrayed me in the middle of a mission. In a premeditated way. That's not something I can ever forgive, much less forget."

She got up to put a comforting hand on my arm. "And I don't expect you to."

"Oh, but you expect me to be a big boy and put my differences aside for the good of humanity. Right?"

She gazed up at me but didn't say a word.

I slipped on my shoes and stomped out of the room.

I didn't want to argue with her anymore. I knew that if I did, she would simply get her way. She'd show me the calculus that said working with Mickey—formerly one of my best friends, a man I'd trusted with my life more times than I could count—would be the right thing to do.

She always relied on me for garbage like this. In fact, most of the ops we'd worked on together had tough angles. I just wasn't sure I could manage this particular baggage, and I didn't know how I could face her if that was the truth.

The fact was that I didn't really have a choice in the matter. If ONI wanted it to happen, all Veronica had to do was order me to do it, and I would have to comply. That would do something horrible to our relationship, but when compared to the fate of humanity, did that really matter?

I wandered around *Infinity*, avoiding all of my regular places: the gym, the sparring room, the combat decks, the bars, the gaming rooms, and so on. I wasn't sure what I was looking for, but something told me I should be looking anyhow. This obviously wasn't the sort of thing I could just ask for anybody's advice about, for fear of running up against security concerns. I wasn't even sure I wanted to hear anyone's advice. Taking up with Mickey again seemed like a bad idea no matter how I spun it.

While I was walking around the observation deck, I ran into Captain Lasky. I snapped him a sharp salute and was about to spin on my heel to get out of his hair, but he stopped me. The man was standing in a corridor with a field of stars splayed in front of him. Apparently, *Infinity* had come out of slipspace at one of its random, hopscotch vector points, and the captain was taking it in while he had the chance.

"At ease, Spartan," he said, turning around and staring out into the dark expanse beyond the viewscreen. "I just like to come up here and watch the stars when I feel the need to clear my head."

I gazed out at the breathtaking view surrounding us. It almost felt like we were floating in unprotected space. "I can understand the allure."

Lasky nodded. "Sometimes you need to lift the weight of the galaxy off your shoulders by looking at it squarely in the face." After a silent moment, he turned toward me. "Anything I can help you with, Spartan?"

For a second, I thought about dumping my current conundrum in his lap, but I didn't see the point. He was the captain of the UNSC *Infinity*, for crying out loud. On top of which, I felt pretty sure I wasn't supposed to talk about it with anyone except Veronica. For all I knew, Lasky needed plausible deniability when it came to this kind of ONI operation, and I couldn't compromise him just because I was personally torn up about it.

Of course, with the whole of humanity on the ropes and *Infinity* as the seemingly last bastion of freedom in human space, such things like long-term consequences suddenly didn't seem as important. Still, old habits are hard to break.

"It's a personnel issue, sir, but one that's way beneath your pay grade."

He gave me a bit of a side-eye, and I wondered if maybe he knew exactly what I was talking about. "Are you agitating for a pathway out of Osiris?"

That surprised me. "No, not at all. Locke is a fantastic leader, and I couldn't ask for better teammates than Vale and Tanaka."

"Then what's the issue, Spartan?"

"I, um, I've been asked to work with someone who once betrayed my trust," I said as evasively as I could manage.

He raised his eyebrows and mouthed the word *Ah*. "That's something else entirely, and I trust you can figure it out. I think this goes without saying, but we value your abilities not only as a Spartan but also as a leader. If and when you get tired of taking orders from Locke, I'm sure Commander Palmer would have another fireteam ready and waiting for you in a heartbeat. Not everyone is made to be a leader. Truth be told, good ones are in short supply. Spartan Locke knows this."

"That's good to hear, sir."

I pondered his words as we gazed out at the stars. I knew he was right. I wasn't just a Spartan—I was a leader—and part of why I didn't want to work with Mickey again was that it reminded me how badly I'd screwed up that part of my job. I'd failed to recognize that one of my own people was going to betray me, and that stung far more than I cared to admit.

I couldn't let that stop me, though. If Veronica needed me to run this operation, then there had to be a really good reason. This was more important than my situation with Mickey. Bigger things were at stake. I had to swallow my wounded pride, get back up on that horse, and flog another few trite metaphors as hard as I could.

I trusted her. Much as I hated to admit it, I needed to figure out a way to make her plan work.

"You sure I can't help you?" Lasky asked one more time.

"No, sir," I said. "You were right about this view. My head is getting clearer by the moment."

"Good." He turned to leave. "See that it remains that way." Before he departed through the door, he looked back over his shoulder and said, "And if I were you, I'd trust Captain Dare's judgment. In all matters."

I chuckled at his tacit admission. "I suppose that's done well by me so far, sir." After a few minutes of wondering if I could possibly pick out any familiar constellations this far from Earth or Draco III, I gave up and headed back for my quarters.

I found Veronica waiting for me, sipping a bit of Scotch. "This all you got?" she said, pouring a bit into a glass for me.

"I save the good stuff for special occasions. This seems more like a disaster."

Veronica tipped the bottle toward me in a sort of salute. "Then it's appropriate that we're sharing a disastrous kind of drink."

I picked up my glass and raised it to her in a toast, which she mirrored. "Cheers," she said.

The liquor burned beautifully on my tongue, and I let it roll around for a while to really soak in the damage.

"So," I finally said. "Getting the band back together. Why is that?"

"Nostalgia's not enough?" She must have sensed my change in demeanor, because I wouldn't have taken that joke on the chin before.

"I don't mind Romeo. Sure, he's hard to take in more than small doses. He makes up for it by being a damn fine soldier. But Mickey? Ow."

"I wouldn't bring him in if it weren't vital. If there were really any other way."

"Because this is coming from you, I'll hear you out." I sighed and took another sip. "Explain. Please."

Veronica inhaled through her nose to brace herself and then began. "As you can imagine, not all of humanity has been neutralized by Cortana's efforts. Not yet, at least. While she's managed to subdue in one way or another just about every major colony in the Unified Earth Government, there are a few places that remain unaffected. In most cases, it's because these are illegal or unregistered settlements that are technically off the books."

"How's that for irony? Those places were thorns in the UNSC's side for decades, and now they're the only spots untouched by this madness."

"Right. For now, at least. It's likely that Cortana doesn't deem those places a direct threat and is simply focusing on bigger fish this early in her efforts. She's not about to start scouring every rock floating through the galaxy just because there might be humans cowering there in the shadows. Machine logic: It's just not an efficient use of time."

"And even AIs have to worry about whatever time they have, huh? I find that kind of comforting."

Veronica fidgeted in her seat. "A majority of these off-the-books places aren't official UEG settlements. They're run by the Front, which you're familiar with."

"Which makes sense, I suppose, since they probably don't have many smart AIs of their own to rat them out and join Cortana."

"Exactly."

I shook my head. "I still don't get it. So, they've got some real estate that's not under Cortana's thumb yet. What does that matter to us?"

Veronica gave me a rueful look, and I felt compelled to take another sip of my drink. "It's not quite that simple," she said.

Of course. It never is.

"There's one fairly substantial settlement that's somehow flown entirely under Cortana's radar. It's on a world the locals call Freedom."

"For obvious reasons, I'm sure."

"It was once an Earth colony on Cybele VI, but we abandoned it about a century ago. The locals moved into the ruins a decade later and found themselves sitting on top of a ton of Forerunner tech, most of which was embedded into the landscape. They've been quietly eking out a self-sufficient living there ever since, selling some of that tech on the black market."

"And what does that have to do with us and our current situation?"

"We've been monitoring it for a while, and it's become increasingly clear that something's going on there that has concealed it from Cortana's eyes. Adjacent colonies are completely offline— even the smaller ones—but our own sensors haven't detected a Guardian signature in Cybele VI yet. Not a single one."

"It's probably just on her list of things to do."

"Maybe, but it's not like we have a lot of time to sit on our hands and hope a solution appears out of thin air. Something about that place has kept it up and running when, for all intents and purposes, it should be down like the rest. Could be they've made some kind of discovery on their own. Maybe they've managed to activate a machine that makes them impervious to Cortana's perception. Maybe it's something we just don't know about."

"Maybe they're too boring for anyone to actually care about."

Veronica pointedly ignored me. "We need to get there and figure it out. If it is rooted in Forerunner technology, we need to see if we can take that technology and replicate it elsewhere. And if we can't export it, we set up shop under that protection and move in. Either way, it's a possible solution for us. And humanity survives."

"You make it sound so simple."

She laughed, bitter and short. "There's nothing simple about it, Buck. But walking in there with a team of Spartans is guaranteed to make a tough job even harder. The leadership behind the Front doesn't trust us, and they have good reasons not to."

"Because, up until now, we'd have been happy to toss their butts in prison."

"But now we have a common enemy again: Cortana and the assets she's wielding to gain control. If you thought the insurrectionists didn't like the UEG telling them what to do and how to do it before the Covenant War, you can imagine how much they'd enjoy having an AI lord over them instead."

"Aren't they going to blame us for that anyhow? I mean, the UNSC did create Cortana. They'll lay that at our feet for sure."

"I'm confident they will, but we don't have a lot of choices, do we? And at this point, it doesn't matter who's at fault. Whatever the right answer might be, they'd blame us either way. The argument is moot. They ought to be able to see that the Front and the UNSC need to work together if any of us are going to survive."

"And you think they're going to be that rational about it?"

She raised a hand to cut off further objections. "I get it, Buck. I'm not naive to the complexity here: The Front won't be happy to see us. Apart from Cortana, we're the *last* people they'll want to see. To counteract that, we need someone on our side to give us the kind of credibility to walk in and talk with them without opening fire."

"I don't know," I said. "Maybe a little firefight would do those jackasses some good."

"Contrary to popular belief, ONI prefers diplomatic solutions over combat. More people live, and we're all better for it. We also don't need them destroying whatever tech they have just to spite us. We go in peacefully and try to engage in a dialogue focused on mutual benefits. If that fails, then we'll consider other diplomatic methods—like shooting things."

"If you went with shooting things first, we wouldn't have to bother with Mickey at all."

"Buck." She gave me such a look. "I thought you preferred to think with your head rather than your rifle."

"When it comes to traitors like Mickey, my head doesn't work so well. I don't think you fully understand what you're asking from me, Veronica. Mickey betrayed me, and I sent him to jail to rot. What's to stop him from doing it again?"

She didn't answer. "Once we're there, what do you think's gonna happen? That he'll listen to reason and we'll all work together like one big, happy family? These people aren't freedom fighters, they're terrorists. There'll be a gunfight one way or another, and I want to make sure we're alive at the end of it."

She shook her head and stood up. "You had the chance to take Mickey out when you were at your worst. You arrested him instead. That's got to count for something, Buck."

"I thought a quick death would be too kind. Now I'm going to have to suffer along with him."

I bowed my head. I'd lost this argument before it had even started, and I knew it. It was time to admit it. Even if this did turn into a gunfight, and even if it cost UNSC lives—my life, even—this was our single ray of hope in an otherwise black night. We had to chase after it.

I did my best to paste a game smile across my face. Veronica didn't buy it, but she was kind enough to pretend she did.

She leaned over and kissed me. "I'll take that as a yes. I know it's painful, but it's the right call."

"You have an uncomfortable habit of being right."

"You want me to stop?"

I sighed. "Nah. If you started being wrong, that would be both of us, and then where would we be?"

"You're wiser than you look."

"Gee, thanks," I said with a laugh. "Let's keep that between us. You'll ruin my reputation." I kissed her back. "So, when do we leave?"

CHAPTER 3

The answer to that last question was *immediately*. It turned out that Veronica had already cleared my mission with Locke, so I didn't have much explaining to do. We needed to get out on a bird before *Infinity* slipped again, which required some logistical footwork that had been going on for a few days. That told me Veronica had known she'd win the argument even before I stepped foot on the flagship. Very sneaky.

"You're good with this?" I asked Locke when I bumped into him on the way to the hangar. "Me just taking off?"

"Not really. I don't like breaking up Osiris," he said. "But I'm told it's temporary and vital, which obviously takes priority right now. Just get back here in one piece. Deal?"

I couldn't argue with that. "Give the others my regards," I said.

"Keep yourself safe," he said, nodding.

I met Veronica in the designated ship bay, at a Condor dropship called *Foxtrot 111*. A Condor was a bigger ship than I thought we needed for the whole of Alpha-Nine, but it wasn't like we could call for an upgrade or even supplies once we hit the road. Veronica had it stocked with enough provisions to keep a full fireteam fed and operational for over a month. On top of that, the vehicle had an onboard armory filled with a variety of rifles, pistols, and ammunition—as much as we'd need to take down an entire battalion of Forerunner soldiers. If we ran through all of that, nothing else would be able to save us.

The Condor looked a lot like a Pelican, although it was a good bit longer and fatter. The most important difference was that the Condor had a slipspace drive, which the Pelican did not. That meant we could handle interstellar travel, which we were going to need, since *Infinity* wasn't going to be carting us about.

Veronica was dressed in black, light armor from head to toe, the same Recon variant armor she'd worn back when we fought through New Mombasa in '52, probably fitted with the latest ONI tech. It might not have been active camouflage, but it did the trick. She'd already stowed her gear, and she was giving the ship a preflight check.

"Where we headed to first?" I asked as I slipped on board and put my own gear away.

"Romeo first. Once we've got him, we'll worry about the rest."

I sighed. "Do we really need him? I mean, I understand Mickey, but . . ."

"If Mickey turns against us, who will have our back?"

She had a point. I thought back to that day on Talitsa when Mickey had betrayed Romeo and me. If it hadn't been for Romeo, Mickey would have had me dead to rights.

The hell of it was that I'd always been closer to Mickey. Romeo was a disgusting, cocky pain in the ass. Mickey was humble, diligent, and always took the job seriously. I had never once doubted him up until then.

I suppose that's why his betrayal hurt so much.

And it had stuck me alone with Romeo—which only proved to make me bitter and resentful. It had been at least one reason I'd requisitioned to be moved out of Alpha-Nine. We could have brought in a couple of new Spartans to fill out the fireteam and kept on going. A lot of good soldiers had run through the ranks of Alpha-Nine back in our ODST days, after all.

But honestly, my heart hadn't been in it. When you're the leader, the rest of the team has to trust your judgment. After Talitsa, Romeo and I couldn't get along.

Maybe I'd blown it so badly with relying on Mickey that I felt like I'd lost my mojo. Maybe Captain Lasky was wrong about me. Either way, I'd felt like I wasn't going to be able to lead a team again—not with the confidence it required—until I dealt with that.

And now here I was, about to saddle up and do it anyway.

I asked Veronica, "So you know where Romeo is, right?"

"He's on a planet called Balaho," she said. "Belonged to the Covenant. It's the Unggoy homeworld."

I wrinkled my nose. "You got to be kidding. He's stuck on a planet full of Grunts?" I considered. "Then again, couldn't have happened to a better guy."

"We haven't been able to reach him since Cortana's message. However, according to our relays, it seems that the Unggoy on Balaho have opted to live under her reign in exchange for protection."

"And we're flying into that? Does that sound exactly safe to you?"

"Maybe. If they agreed to her terms, she probably didn't send a Guardian to pacify the planet, which means it's probably safer than just about anywhere else. We won't know until we get there.

Either way, we'll be sure to be prepped to make an emergency slip-space jump the moment we arrive. Otherwise, if there is a Guardian in the area, we're looking at the shortest operation in ONI history."

"I gotta say, you really know how to sell this to me."

"We're not building a vacation home there, Buck. It's a smash-and-grab job. We go in, we get Romeo, and then we're out."

"So we know where he's at? He may be a big man surrounded by little Grunts, but that's still a whole planet. We gotta figure out where to smash before we can grab."

"Romeo was stationed in the capital city, so that should limit the possibilities a bit. Also, keep in mind that the Unggoy bought into Cortana's deal. Balaho's not blacked out like Sanghelios or Earth. We'll try to raise him on the comm first."

I gave her a wry smile. "I'm sure it'll be that simple."

I joined in to help Veronica finish the preflight checklist, which seemed like a luxury given how many times I'd had to jump into a pilot's seat and take off as fast as I could. It felt good to know I could trust a ship—even if I might not be able to trust the people who were going to board it.

As we wrapped it up, though, I uttered the one question that had been nagging me. "So . . . just what *is* Romeo doing on a planet full of Unggoy?"

"Officially?" Veronica said as she made her way to the cock-pit. "He was providing an escort for liaisons between the UNSC and the new Unggoy government that was running Balaho after the Covenant dissolved. It was a mess for a while. Some of Ung-goy were allying with rogue factions and mercenary groups that needed cannon fodder for their own war machines. Others wanted to establish peace with humanity."

"And the UNSC thought Romeo was the right person for

that job?" He was a fine soldier, but I wouldn't have relied on Romeo for diplomacy beyond what you'd need to negotiate a bar tab.

"That—and he was caught sleeping with an admiral's wife. Or so the rumor goes."

I laughed out loud. "Now *that* sounds like the Romeo I know."

"Nothing like being assigned to a post on a planet with a high-methane atmosphere."

I wrinkled my nose again. "Ah, it's going to stink, isn't it?"

"Your armor comes with air filters. I suggest you make good use of them."

Veronica slipped into the pilot's seat, and I took up my post at the weapons officer station just above and behind her, where I had control of the Condor's guns: a pair of autocannons on the prow and a network of ANVIL-II missiles that could be fired from the wings. Once we got clearance, Veronica flew the dropship out of *Infinity*'s docking bay and then came about to flank it while setting course for Balaho.

"Get a good look," Veronica said, staring off into the massive shadow of *Infinity*. "It might be a while before we see her again."

"It always is," I said, taking a deep breath. "Let's get this party started, shall we? The sooner we start, the sooner we can get it done." The trip itself wasn't what bothered me. It was what waited at the end of it.

Once we entered slipspace, there wasn't much to do. It wasn't as fast as using a portal, but the Condor had one of the new slipspace drives built using reverse-engineered Forerunner tech, which made it at least an order of magnitude faster than the ones we'd had during the war just six years ago. After a few hours' travel, we emerged from slipspace a good distance away from

Balaho. Rather than barge straight in, Veronica had hauled the Condor up on the very edge of the Tala system—of which Balaho was the fifth planet—to see what was going on. She apparently could conduct scans from this distance with some of the Condor's fancy gizmos and then slip closer to the planet once we knew it was safe.

Since we were so far away from Balaho, our sensors took a while to pick everything up. Veronica spent the entire time with her fingers hovering over the controls that would send us back into slipspace at the first sign of trouble.

No Guardian had set up shop over Balaho, as it turned out. And as Veronica had predicted, the planet hadn't been blacked out at all. Instead, based on the sensor readings, the place seemed to be thriving. We picked up a couple of incredibly strange signals as we settled into orbit.

"What are those?" I asked.

"Forerunner ships," Veronica said. "ONI has reports of Cortana using them to ferry supplies into planets that agree to her terms."

"Wow. I guess it pays to knuckle under to insane AIs. Should we expect any trouble? Are these things ridiculously weaponized?"

"We'll be fine if we keep a low profile," she said, prepping a slip deeper in-system. "Which translates: Don't shoot up everything and blow our cover. The first sign of any combat, and the Unggoy will be onto us."

"I suppose we couldn't have expected anything else." I grinned. "Have you ever known the Unggoy to stand up to anyone?"

"There was actually a rebellion here many years ago. The Covenant glassed a sizable amount of the planet's surface to put it down."

"Not to be too callous, but that seems a bit like overkill."

"I believe they preferred to think of it as efficient."

I rubbed my chin. "So the UNSC banished Romeo to this backwater stinkhole to babysit UEG ambassadors?" I shook my head in disbelief. "He really pissed that admiral off, didn't he?"

Veronica readied the controls to slip the Condor closer toward the Balaho. "There's no Guardian here, but that doesn't mean Cortana couldn't have left an AI behind to watch over things. At the very least, we'll have to watch out for those Forerunner ships. We need to slip in and out with a minimum of fuss, or we'll wind up stranded."

The jump was almost instantaneous, dropping us on the far side of the world as if we'd always been there, which just proved how much we'd benefited from picking through Forerunner tech over the years. I gazed down at the frozen green ball as it grew in our viewscreens. Two good-size moons spun around it at a respectable distance: Buwan and Padpad, according to the holos that sprang up on the transparent canopy in front of me. From their irregular shapes and the amount of machinery that seemed to have swallowed them, it looked like the Covenant had mined the crap out of them, leaving little but shells of what they'd once been.

Beyond visibility, the nav system tracked a handful of massive Forerunner ships in orbit around the place, and smaller shuttles ran between them and the planet's surface. Other than that, I didn't see a whole lot of space traffic. I supposed Cortana had shut most of that down, and I hoped we were small enough to slip beneath their notice.

"Are you sure those ships aren't going to cause us trouble?" I asked Veronica.

"Don't think so," she said. "We've got signature dampeners

on this Condor, the highest possible grade currently available. We shouldn't show up as even an echo on their sensors, but even if we did, it should be fine. Word is that they're supply ships only. They're solely concerned with doing their jobs. As long as we don't bother them, they won't bother us. So keep those guns cool."

"And how do you know this for sure?"

"I don't. But there's only one way to find out."

I explicitly shut down the weapons system. I didn't want the Forerunner ships getting the wrong idea about us, after all.

As we neared the planet, Veronica took us around in a wide arc that put us as far away from the Forerunner ships as possible. I kept a sharp eye peeled toward our sensors' reading the entire time, but those vessels never budged in our direction. I was glad to see that ONI technicians had made something that seemed every bit as high-tech as the Covenant's equipment. The ship's stealth systems definitely did their job, though I don't think I exhaled until we were edging up on Balaho's greasy green atmosphere.

"Romeo was assigned to the capital," Veronica said. "A city called Gedgow. Setting a course for it now."

With that, we plunged into the noxious, swirling clouds that blanketed almost the entire planet.

"Assuming no one shoots us down before we reach the planet, how are we supposed to find Romeo?" I asked.

"Balaho doesn't have any smart AIs of its own, and the Covenant never put a lot of effort into giving them a modern infrastructure. Even if Cortana has stationed a human AI down there to oversee things, in theory, it would be struggling to take over their hodgepodge of communications systems."

"In theory . . ."

"This isn't a simulation, Buck. Things go wrong. We deal with it either way."

"You didn't answer my question: Romeo. How do we find him?"

"We'll try the comms first, and if that doesn't work, we'll set down and do it the old-fashioned way."

That didn't sit well with me, but it wasn't like we had a ton of options on this icy ball of methane. I gave up arguing for the moment as we slid blindly through the atmosphere. "Fair enough."

A short while later, we broke through the now-gray clouds and found ourselves arcing high over a massive city rising out of the edges of what appeared to be a frozen swamp. It looked like a wide plain filled with rolling hills, into which a giant had stabbed dozens of Covenant-style buildings that reached high into the sky. You know: large purple, gray, and yellow structures made of some weird alloy, with a heavy preoccupation for hexagons. Lights burned all throughout the place, visible through the haze and scissoring across the sky.

"Now that we're closer, try raising Romeo on your armor's comm system," Veronica said. "Those channels are hard-encoded to prevent the enemy from listening in, and hopefully they'll hold up against any attempt to crack them. Even if someone detects it, they won't be able to trace it back to us. It's worth the risk at this point."

I smiled at her. "I knew there was a reason I loved you."

"Add it to the list," she said.

As we scudded through the now-bluish clouds of methane that hung over the city, I saw more arrays of lights struggling to break through. The forest of Covenant-style buildings grew denser, although I didn't see many roads. Those that were there seemed wide and, for the most part, empty of traffic. A few larger vehicles rolled along them, but I didn't see anyone on foot.

We sailed over the city at a safe distance, and no one challenged us. I didn't see anything in the air other than a flock of bizarre flying creatures that looked like salamanders zipping about, entirely ignoring us. I tracked the flock with my armor's sensors, just to make sure they weren't some kind of fancy bio-mimetic drones, but they remained innocuous, and I watched them all disappear beneath an overpass far below us. "Now, I've never been to Balaho, but does it seem a little too quiet up here?"

Veronica nodded. "It appears the Unggoy grounded most of their own air traffic, probably in the wake of Cortana's edict. Still, there's no reason to push our luck. Get hold of Romeo as fast as you can."

I brought up the old Alpha-Nine channel on my armor's comm system. "Calling all Spartans. Calling all Spartans. Romeo, this is Buck. You out there?"

Nothing.

I tried my patter again. Still no response.

"It's a big city," Veronica said. "No guarantee he has his ears on."

"Probably found himself trapped underneath a harem of Unggoy females." I scanned toward what my heads-up display said was the east and tried again. "Romeo, Romeo! Wherefore are thou, Romeo?"

A few seconds later, a familiar voice came crackling over the comm. "Shall I hear more, or shall I speak at this?"

Despite how little I liked the guy sometimes, I have to admit that hearing his voice plastered a big old grin across my face. "Hey! I knew we could find you in a haystack of Grunts!"

"Buck? I never thought I'd be so glad to hear your voice. You need to get me out of here!"

"Well, it seems Spartan command received your request for a transfer, but we're still waiting for your paperwork to process."

Romeo's distance and direction popped up on my helmet's display. I tapped them into the Condor's comm system and sent the details to Veronica, which manifested on the viewport's holo-display.

"I'm not messing around here, Buck. Things got pretty scary after that Cortana chick laid down the law, and the Unggoy—let's just say a lot of them are true believers when it comes to her new world order. They didn't have much freedom under the Covenant, but once the Prophets were gone, the only freedom the people of Balaho had was to fall to pieces and starve. The UEG's been shipping in as much aid as they can, but it really hasn't been enough. Once Cortana made her offer, they leaped at it."

"Can't say I blame them. I wouldn't put it past these guys to gin up some kind of rebellion once they're all back to being stable and well fed, but they're a long way from that now."

"Romeo, we're on our way in a Condor," Veronica said. "It would be best to get you out of here before anyone decides they want to stick around."

"That you, Dare?" Romeo said, plainly delighted. "This just keeps getting better and better."

I heard the distinct rattle of gunfire in the background.

"Are you all right, Romeo?" Veronica asked. "What's your situation?"

"I don't want to rush you or anything, but the faster you get here, the happier you'll make me."

"What's up, Romeo?" I asked. "Some angry husbands gunning for you one last time before you leave?"

"I wish," Romeo said with a forced chuckle. "After the Unggoy decided they were going to side with Cortana, she sent an army of Forerunner soldiers to secure the embassy."

"I take it that didn't go well," I said.

"Not unless you consider it a rousing success to have the entire embassy destroyed and nearly everyone inside killed." A grenade went *whoomph* somewhere nearby.

"So you left the embassy and hightailed it here?"

"Just about. I still got a load of Grunts and soldiers on my tail, and they're doing their level best to turn me into a nonsurvivor."

"Hold tight," Veronica said. "We're almost there."

As we got closer to Romeo's position near the top of one of the larger buildings, I noticed staccato bursts of light cutting through the methane-tinged haze. Some of it sprang from the familiar muzzle flashes of a battle rifle, but most of it was the warm colors of hard light and the bright whites of plasma blasts.

"You don't know how glad I am to hear that. I thought I'd commandeer myself a ship, but the Unggoy and their Forerunner friends are a bit more possessive of their interstellar transports than I'd hoped."

"Where are you now?"

"I'm on the forty-second floor of a building dedicated— I think—to the musical arts."

"Did you say *musical arts*?" I thought I'd misheard him.

"Yeah. Apparently, that's a massive thing in this culture."

"We're just outside of your position," Veronica cut in. "Do you think you can make it to the roof?"

I saw a blast of bluish light near where I'd seen the muzzle flashes, and a *boom* came at me through the comm. "Romeo?" I called out. "Romeo!"

"Just got a bit singed there," he said in a pained voice. "Those plasma grenades are a bitch, and those little guys seem to have an unlimited supply."

"Can you get to the roof?"

He blew out a long sigh. "I'm trying, man. At least I'm not stuck in one of the pre-Covenant buildings. I'm like twice as tall as the Unggoy. The first week I was here, I had to crawl through most of the places they built before they joined up with the Sangheili and the rest. Worst time ever."

"Just answer the question."

"I don't know, okay? I'm on the top floor, but the lift didn't go to the roof. I've been looking for a way up for the past hour, and these little bastards finally got me cornered."

"Can you blast a hole in the exterior wall?" Veronica asked. "Maybe with an explosive?"

Romeo clucked his tongue. "Balaho might not be the most advanced planet in the galaxy, but they do have a building code. You don't get structures this tall if you can blast holes in them. Particularly not ones someone as big as me can fit through."

"We could do it with the Condor's guns," Veronica said. "But that might bring down every Forerunner and Unggoy soldier in the area."

I shrugged at Veronica. "Well, we tried. I mean, we did our best, right?"

"*Not funny, Buck!*" Romeo shouted into the comm.

He went silent for a moment. Veronica brought the Condor in closer to the building and turned a single spotlight on the area where he might be. I peered through large transparent panes that must have been windows and saw the telltale arcs of several plasma grenades being lobbed at once. Then the muzzle flash from what had to be Romeo's battle rifle tracked away from them fast.

When the explosions went off, the flashes stopped, and I held my breath.

"You okay in there, Romeo?" I finally asked.

"Just come and get me, all right? Blow a hole through the wall, and I'll jump into whatever it is you're flying around in. Assuming that's you with the spotlight hovering out there and not an enemy gunship about to open up on me."

"Glad to have you aboard," I said, taking the controls at the weapons station. "Just step back for the fireworks."

"That's what I like about you, Buck. You always did know how to make a soldier feel welcome."

I brought the Condor's 70mm autocannons to bear on a spot on the wall a few meters behind his current position. "Hold on," I said. "I'm about to help the Grunts with a little remodeling."

I blasted away at a glassy part of the building. Its windows quickly shattered, and the metallic frames splintered into pieces. I kept up the barrage, unloading shell after shell into the structure until I'd chewed a massive hole in the side of it.

As the smoke cleared, I said, "That work for you?"

Romeo appeared amid the swirling mist in the opening I'd created and waved me down. "Can't say you never did anything for me."

Veronica swung the back of the bird around and reached for her own helmet as I slipped out of my seat to move aft. Once she was ready, I opened up the rear hatch. The stench of the Balaho atmosphere hit me like a hammer, but the rebreather filtration system in my Mjolnir kept me alive and functional, if revolted.

As the ramp lowered, I stood beckoning Romeo to make the leap. He was busy firing a few last shots at some nasty Forerunner soldiers too stubborn to know better.

"Quit screwing around with your friends!" I shouted as I found a grab bar to hold on to. "Come on!"

Another plasma grenade from the last remaining Grunt arced out at him, and my breath caught in my chest. I hadn't come all this way to watch him die.

He'd spotted it, though, and was hustling to get away from it. In a single bound, he leaped for the Condor's ramp, using his Mjolnir suit's mini-thrusters for an assist. The backwash from the thrusters caught the incoming grenade and knocked it straight back the way it had come. It exploded a moment later, sending even more debris and an unlucky Unggoy arcing out into the open air next to the building.

I'd have thought he'd planned for that if I hadn't known better. Once he landed, he shouted back at the soldiers who were scrambling to the opening: "Consider that a parting gift!"

Before the Forerunner armigers could start to unload on the Condor, Veronica punched the gas, and the bird zipped forward, nearly throwing Romeo out the back ramp. Fortunately, I was there to reach out and grab him. We locked forearms, and I hauled him inside the Condor and then closed the ship up behind him.

"Thanks!" Romeo said as he staggered forward into the bay and collapsed on a bench, removing his helmet.

He hadn't changed much since the last time I'd seen him. Still tall, dark, bald, and a little too handsome for his own good. His hair had gotten gray near the temples, and his eyes—well, I wouldn't call them *wiser*, but they had a few more wrinkles near the edges.

Becoming a Spartan may have made career ODSTs feel like new people, but that didn't mean it reset the clock when it came to getting older. I wondered how we might look in another fifty years, should we live that long. I had just turned forty-eight, even if some of those years had been scrubbed by all the slipspace travel I'd done during the war. That said, I didn't relish the idea of being a centenarian Spartan, kept alive long past my natural expiration date by implants and my armor. But I didn't much care for the alternative.

"You all good?" I asked Romeo. "Got all your parts attached?"

He nodded while he caught his breath. "And in all the right places." He sized me up. "Good to see you, Gunny."

"I'm not your superior anymore. At least when it comes to rank."

He waved off my protest. "Old habits, man."

Under Veronica's steady hand, the Condor had started climbing through the methane mists. With luck, no one would be able to follow us through those greasy blue clouds, and we'd be free and clear of the planet before anyone could stop us.

"I'm glad you came along," Romeo said. "I thought I was toast."

"You should blame Veronica for that," I told him. "She has this crazy new mission for us."

"That sounds good," he said. "You and me, Buck. Just like old times!"

"Oh, it's not just you and me," I said. "She wants the whole team back together."

"What are you—" He stopped, openmouthed. "You got to be kidding me."

"It's important, Romeo," Veronica said over the comm from the pilot's seat. "We need you for this."

"And you need *Crespo,* too? Forget saving me. I'd be better off with the Grunts. Hold on a second," he said, turning toward Veronica. "Are we leaving right now? I can't just up and leave the people we have here."

"I thought you said everyone you were guarding here was dead."

He held up an index finger to object. "I said *nearly* everybody. When I left the embassy to get a ride, there were still a few people alive and hiding out. I was hoping to find a ship big enough to carry us all off this frozen ball of mud."

"Veronica?" I called up front. "How much of a hurry are we in?"

"The longer we take, the more we risk it all going sideways, right here at the beginning of the op. The diplomatic personnel knew what they were signing up for, and they've been trained on how to behave in situations like this. On top of that, we don't know how long we've got till the clock runs out on us. If we miss that window, it'll risk a lot more human lives . . ."

I turned back to Romeo. He cut me off before I even started in with him. "I don't know what you came to get me for," he said. "I just know I'm not leaving here without the people I promised to protect."

"I could order you to ignore them."

He squinted at me. "Didn't you just say you don't outrank me?"

"Veronica could do it."

He tapped his ear. "I have a real hearing problem when it comes to listening to ONI. Old habit."

A moment ago, this had seemed so much simpler.

"How many people are we talking about?"

"Just a handful," he said with a grimace. "Maybe up to seven, all told."

"That's more than a handful."

"I got big hands." He had the grace to squirm as I shook my head at him. "They're good people," he said. "They're trapped here on this stinking planet, and the Unggoy in charge will hand them all over to Cortana's forces—or kill them if they refuse to go along quietly. This isn't a question about probably. They'll die here, Gunny."

"Dammit." I looked up toward the cockpit.

Veronica shrugged and said, "Looks like we're not quite done here yet."

CHAPTER 4

"So where are these people?" Veronica said as I climbed back into the weapons station.

Romeo stepped into the space behind the pilot's seat and leaned over her to point out a spot on the glowing holo wireframe map of Gedgow that she'd brought up on the Condor's dash emitter. "That's the embassy right there," he said. "It sits on the top floor."

I considered it. "Doesn't look so hard. We land on that balcony, blast away anyone who gives us any trouble, and hustle your friends on board. Easy, right?"

"But they might not be there anymore."

I rubbed my forehead. "Veronica asked you where they are, not where they used to be."

"That's where they were when the Unggoy attacked the place. I had to leave them there. If I had to guess, they were probably hauled away by the time I got to the top of the building you found me in."

"Do you know where they are *now*?" Veronica asked.

Romeo gestured to a large low dome that sat right in the middle of the city. "No, but that's the Kabakera, the seat of the Unggoy government. That's where they'd take them. So somewhere between those two points is my best guess."

"That's a government building? It looks like a gigantic burrow," I said.

"It pretty much is. Unggoy started out building their homes underground for protection from larger creatures, and you can see that in their architecture."

"What about that high-rise we just pulled you out of?" I asked.

"That was built after they joined the Covenant, under the orders of the Prophets."

"The history lesson is great, guys, but we don't have forever here," Veronica said. "Focus."

Romeo gave her a firm nod and pointed at the dome again. "If they were arrested, they'd be brought into the prison in the lowest level of the Kabakera."

"You'd better hope they aren't there already," I said. "Or we'll never get them out. We don't have the firepower to blast that place apart."

"Whatever we're going to do, let's do it fast," Veronica said. "We don't have time to waste on this."

"Can you raise any of them on your comm?" I said to Romeo.

He put his helmet back on. "I'll give it a shot."

A moment later, I heard him talking with someone, to my relief. "Mei," he said. "Slow down. Where are you? Not where are you going. Where *are* you? Right now?"

He fell silent as he listened to the response, grunting a reply every so often. Veronica started moving the Condor in the direction of the government building. He finally cleared his throat and said to us, "They're not in the Kabakera yet. They're in a transport on their way there now."

"Do you have their route?"

Romeo pointed to a street on the holographic map. It led straight from the embassy to the Kabakera. It didn't seem like there was that much distance between them.

"What's taking them so long to get there?" I asked.

Romeo shrugged. "Who knows? Guess they're not in a hurry. They have the whole planet under Cortana's lockdown, after all. With the exception of a few troublemakers like us. And they didn't know about you two."

"Until we came blasting in to rescue you." I didn't like this at all, but Romeo had a point. Leaving ambassadors stuck on a captured planet wasn't the right thing to do.

"On it," Veronica said. She brought the Condor in low over where the map said the street should be, but there was just a flat, ashen strip in place of the road. "Are the mists just too thick, or is there no traffic on these streets at all?"

"You're looking at the top of the street," Romeo said. "Most of the streets in Gedgow are covered to keep the Unggoy protected—at least while they're in vehicles. They've gotten more relaxed over the years, though, so nowadays most of them actually walk along the tops of the streets. They even set up markets along them."

"But our target is riding under the street's cover?" Veronica asked.

"Exactly."

"Then how are we supposed to get your friends out of there?" I said. This had gone from a simple smash-and-grab operation to something far more involved.

"We just get down there, stop the transport, and haul them up here," Romeo said. "What's so hard about that?"

I grimaced, staring down at the street through the mist, which thinned as we drew closer. I could see little hawker stands lining the edges, with loads of Grunts milling among them.

"Well, we can't just blow up the cover and dive in," I said. "Not without blasting away a lot of civilians and calling attention to ourselves."

Romeo was already headed toward the back of the Condor. "Who said anything about blasting the street? It's simple. You and I drop down there and get the job done."

I glanced at Veronica. "You good with that?"

"I don't like this," she said as she craned her neck around to look at me. "You get stuck down there, I can't help you."

"Two Spartans facing off against a legion of unarmed Grunts," Romeo said. "How are we gonna get stuck?"

He slapped the button that released the rear ramp as the Condor hovered a dozen or so meters over the top of the street. Before I could object, Romeo had already leaped out into the swirling methane mist.

"Goddammit." I grabbed my assault rifle from the wall rack and jumped out after him.

Fortunately, we weren't that high up. Our armor absorbed the impact of the landing. The Unggoy in the street had been gawking up at the Condor as it hovered there, but when we crashed down among them, they fled back into their stalls or ran screaming away. My first instinct was to tell them we weren't there to hurt them, but what was the point? We weren't going to stick around long enough to have to apologize for our rudeness.

The methane-soaked mist condensed immediately on my armor. I was warm and dry inside, but my sensors reported that it was barely above freezing outside. It didn't seem to bother the Unggoy, but I suppose when you're covered with a lobster-like shells, the chill doesn't bug you as much.

Oddly, the upper level of the street where we landed was covered with a blue-green grass about ankle-high. Despite how many people trampled on it every day, it stood strong, and it made that part of the city, at least, seem less urban and more like it belonged in a village.

Before I could even ask Romeo "Where now?" he'd taken off for an opening that plunged down at one corner of the street. I chased right after him and caught up as he was negotiating a tight ramp that wound down into the lower level like a screw. "You need to lose a few pounds?" I ribbed him. "This embassy lifestyle seems like maybe it's been a little too easy on you."

"Ha, ha," he said. "Just you try to keep up."

We reached the street below, and it stood nearly empty. Surprisingly, it looked like a regular surface street, with lights along the sides and down the middle to help guide traffic, right up until it all faded into the darkness. I wondered how many of these streets snaked together under the surface of the city—and how the Unggoy were able to keep track of where they were, with no visible landmarks to speak of.

The primary light came filtering in long beams from the hole that we'd just clambered through. For the most part, the street felt like a long, dark tunnel with not much of anything in it except a bluish liquid that dripped down from the ceiling everywhere, as if the world above were leaking into it. I saw some headlights coming toward us from the distance, but they were moving slowly enough that I wasn't sure what they were mounted on.

"Is this normal?" I said. "Where is everybody?"

"The Unggoy leaders ordered everyone to stay home today," Romeo said.

"Probably trying to prevent panic in the streets. Didn't seem to stop any of those people in the hawker stands above us."

"People gotta eat. I've been here for weeks, and I still don't understand the Unggoy at all. All I know is that their cooking stinks nearly as much as their atmosphere."

I used my visor to zoom in on the headlights plodding in our direction. There was a vehicle in the center of the road—or at least that was what it looked like. It was moving at parade speed. A long line of similar lights spread out behind it, seeming to stretch on forever.

"Are these one-way roads?" I asked.

"Usually," said Romeo. "I think. Makes sense, right?"

"That's why there's no one here," I said. "Whatever's at the front of that line of traffic is blocking everything behind it."

Romeo glanced at something on the heads-up display inside his helmet. "That's them. The UEG people. Mei says they have an escort of some sort. That's probably what's slowing them down."

"What, with like Grunt cops?" I peered down the street. The lights were getting closer but were bright enough that I had a hard time seeing past them.

"Something like that."

"Well, what are we waiting for?" I didn't like the idea of sitting tight and letting the Unggoy come to us. That would only give them more time to figure out some way to muck up the situation.

While I was sure that we could take on a nearly unlimited supply of poorly armed Grunts, I knew they had to have some kind of defense system, not to mention the threat of a force of Forerunner soldiers showing up, which we fortunately hadn't encountered on the surface. Chances were that something would eventually find and overwhelm us just because Romeo and I were being cocky about it, if nothing else.

I started trotting toward the lights, and Romeo came up beside me and matched my speed. As we got closer, I realized that the lights up front were spaced too far apart to belong to a single vehicle. The ones behind had already come to a screeching halt, putting as much distance as possible between them and the closer lights. Something about this didn't feel right. I'd fought against plenty of Unggoy during the Covenant War, but they'd been under the auspices of the Prophets then. They'd used strictly Covenant weapons and gear. I'd never seen them piloting anything of their own design—although cobbled together from Covenant tech—until that day.

"What are those?" I said.

"Aw, no," Romeo said. "They're called Goblins, and they're nastier than they look."

There were two of them flanking the vehicle, each painted and polished in purple hues. What did they look like? Large walking tanks almost too absurd to describe.

Imagine a robotic Grunt about three meters tall. They had large, bulbous tops, which were effectively transparent cockpits, and inside each I could see a single Grunt gleefully piloting the damn thing. The machines trundled along with all the ponderous grace of drunken elephants, their feet slamming into the ground like sledgehammers with every step.

Each of them had an oversize needler attached to one of its bulbous forearms, and a grenade launcher to the other. As Romeo and I got closer, they pointed their glowing needlers at us and let loose.

"Get down!" I shouted as I dove to the side, trying to find cover.

I hate needlers, even the smaller ones. Unlike projectile guns or even plasma-based weapons, they fire these glowing pink shards of chemically charged crystals that can turn a decent suit of Mjolnir armor into a pincushion. Worse yet, once they hit something, these shards take a few seconds to amp themselves up, and then they explode, adding even more injury to injury.

Romeo, thankfully, heeded my warning and dove to the other side of the street. The needles all went wide of us. A huge relief because these jumbo-sized needles were about a full meter each, two or three times as long as normal. They were no joke.

The worst part about needles is that they have some kind of ability to home in on moving targets. You have to really move to dodge them. Or you just do something completely insane and unexpected, like we did next.

We charged the Goblins.

"Come at us, humans!" a squeaky voice said from one of Goblins. "Let us blow you to pieces!"

"Cute," I told Romeo. "Like a kid brother who thinks he's finally big enough to take a poke at you."

Bursts of needles sailed toward us, and a slight shift in our angle sent them past us to land in the pavement somewhere at our backs. They quivered there for a moment, impaled into the road's surface, before exploding and sending up a plume of debris.

"Just don't let them focus on one of us," Romeo said. "Enough of those needles will take out our shields and they can rip through our armor. I promise you, it won't take long."

I let loose at the nearest Goblin with my assault rifle, spraying it liberally with bullets as I ran full sprint at an oblique angle. The slugs glanced off the machine's armor and made the cockpit-based energy shields protecting their drivers glow. We'd have to take those down first.

This wasn't gonna be easy. There wasn't any cover on the open road, so the best chance we had was to get in close.

"You cannot prevail against us!" one of the Goblin drivers screamed.

"Going in hard," I said to Romeo. "Let's take the one on the left first."

"Your left or my left?"

"We're both facing the same—!" I groaned in frustration.

I could almost hear his grin. "Gotcha."

I ignored him and charged straight at the Goblin on the left, which I'd already peppered on our approach. The driver swung at me with his grenade launcher fist but couldn't connect. He moved sluggishly, like a punch-drunk boxer, and I saw it coming from a kilometer away.

I hit my armor's thrusters just as his arm came down, and I simultaneously brought my rifle up. This shot me forward inside the Goblin's reach, right where I needed to be. Using the inertia from my thruster, I smashed hard into the front of it with my rifle, dropping the machine's energy shield and cracking the cockpit's reinforced casing.

"Hey!" the Goblin's driver shouted. "That's not fair!"

My blow had overwhelmed the Goblin's energy shields, which transformed the walking vehicle into something like a turtle without its shell. When Romeo hit it from the other direction, he blasted the cockpit wide open. It was a one-two punch that worked even better than I had pictured it.

The Unggoy inside squealed in terror. "Wait! It's not supposed to be like this!"

I glanced over my shoulder and saw that the other Goblin had already turned to face us. Its driver was determined not to share his fellow's fate. Rather than wait for us to come at him, he let loose with a barrage of gigantic needles.

I'd been banking on the Unggoy having a sense of team cohesion strong enough to prevent them from trying something stupid like that, and they'd failed me. My eyes wide with surprise, I hit the road's surface, and the needles slammed into the shooter's crippled companion, its driver shrieking in protest. "No, no, no, no, no, no, *no!*"

As I rolled away, the needles detonated, and what was left of the ruined Goblin toppled over backward, its driver falling forever silent. The other Goblin driver howled in frustration, as if the whole thing had come as a complete surprise. "Look what you made me do!"

I leaped to my feet in a running strafe and lit up the remaining Goblin's shields with an entire clip of ammunition. "Toss him a present, would you?" I said to Romeo.

"My pleasure."

Just as my magazine went dry, Romeo flipped a grenade he'd been baking off straight at the Goblin. It saw the explosive coming, and it made a game effort to try to blast it out of the air. It missed, however, and the grenade tapped the Goblin right on the front of its cockpit before it exploded.

The Goblin wasn't out yet. The entire machine reeled backward, trying to get its footing. I charged forward and launched myself boots first, hitting it as hard as I could, knocking it back off its feet.

I rode the machine as it tumbled backward and onto its side, placing me right on top of it. Kneeling down toward the cockpit, I hammered at it again and again until the transparent casing at the front gave way.

"No!" the Unggoy inside said as it tried to shield its face with its arms. I silenced him with another blow.

I realized, as I bounced off the downed Goblin, that I had never seen an Unggoy without a methane mask over its face. They needed them to breathe properly on just about any planet where the air was good enough for humans. Here on Balaho, of course, they could dispense with them and enjoy the methane-mixed air they'd been born to.

Let's just say they looked a lot better with their masks on. Especially once we were done with them.

"Mei?" Romeo said as he ran past the devastated Goblins and toward the vehicle they'd been escorting. They were of Covenant make, riding low to the ground on an invisible field of energy rather than wheels. They sat wide and long, with sweeping canopies to keep the rain off when they weren't riding in tunnels, and they were painted in hues of purple and blue.

Behind the first vehicle stretched a whole line of others, going back at least a hundred meters. They seemed like civilian rides, though, smaller and less armored. And I didn't see a single gun mount on any of them. They had probably just been caught up behind the armored vehicle, since it was being escorted by slow-moving Goblins.

A pair of armed Unggoy emerged from the front of the lead vehicle, each with a more reasonably sized needler in their hands. "Hold it right there!" the one on the right said. "Take another step, and the humans with us are dead!"

"You try that, and I'll stomp your ass into paste!" Romeo shouted as he came to a stop, keeping his battle rifle at the ready.

At first, I wasn't sure what gave the Grunt the position to make that kind of threat, but then I noticed his other hand held a small device the shape of detonator. It didn't take long for me to connect the dots. If he let go of the switch, a bomb on the vehicle would go off, and the people in it would be lost.

The Unggoy on the left recoiled at the Spartan's rage and dropped his weapon. "Okay, he's crazy!" he said as he scrambled off in the darkness behind them. I saw other Grunts in the long line of vehicles getting out to see what had happened.

This seemed to encourage the other Unggoy in front of us, who wasn't about to be deterred. "Stay back! I'm serious, demons!"

"Hey, Buck! Romeo!" Veronica's voice rang out over the comm. "You need to get out of there now!"

"We can't just leave our people behind," Romeo said.

I slung my rifle over my back and put my hands out, palms up, in what I hoped would be a calming gesture. The last thing we needed was the people we were trying to rescue getting blown up because an Unggoy had a nervous trigger finger. "Hey, now. You don't want to do that. Didn't Cortana lay down an edict against violence?"

"You have incoming troops!" Veronica shouted. "You have to evacuate *now*!"

"Stay back!" The Unggoy's needler wavered at us. "You come any closer, and—"

There was a loud explosion above, and a massive chunk of the ceiling came crashing down. The shock wave from it knocked the Unggoy to the ground and forced Romeo and me back on our heels. I stared up at the blue-gray sunlight beaming down through the new hole in the roof, above where the diplomatic vehicles had been.

"Mei!" Romeo said. It took me a moment to realize he was shouting into his comm for her. "Mei!"

A large chunk of stone had fallen right on top of the Grunt who'd threatened us, and completely crushed him. But that was when I saw his open hand.

The detonator was gone.

"Get down!" I shouted, colliding with Romeo and sending both of us to the ground.

The second explosion was worse than the first. The debris from the collapsed ceiling went in every direction, like a pipe bomb the size of a tunnel. My shields were pummeled almost to the point of collapse, and for a second, I thought this would be it. Romeo and I would die there, in the underground stench of the Grunt homeworld.

How do you write an epitaph for that?

But the comms brought me back to reality. Veronica cursed as loud and long as I've ever heard her. As her voice and the echoes of the explosion rang in my ears, something large now blocked out the light that had been streaming down into the tunnel. It took me a moment to see what it was, and when I did, I almost wished the explosion had killed me: Dozens of Forerunner soldiers began to pour in through the hole like ants. Even on Genesis, I'd never seen so many.

"They're gone," I told Romeo as I smacked him on the shoulder. "And we will be, too, if we don't bolt now!"

To his credit, he hesitated only a moment longer—just enough for the first blasts from the Forerunner soldiers to ricochet off what was left of our shields. Then he turned with me and ran.

Hard-light fire spanged off the ground around us as Romeo and I sprinted for the ramp. As we climbed it, we both laid down suppressive fire to keep the soldiers engaged and focused on us instead of coming straight up our tails with those trippy short-range teleportation slides they use.

"You still good up there?" I asked Veronica.

"No! I have an enemy vehicle squatting over your position, and my gunner disappeared on some fool's errand! It's a Z-1800, and it means business."

"A what?"

"A Forerunner attack vehicle called a Phaeton, and it's scanning the top of the street right now."

"But they're not attacking you?"

"Not yet. Looks like your shooting match down there got the Forerunners' attention, but they haven't noticed me yet, probably due to the stealth tech. And you two made a lot more noise."

"Be ready to snatch us when we get clear," I said, gritting my teeth. "They'll sure as hell notice the Condor then, and we need to be out of here before they call in reinforcements."

When we reached the ramp, we used our jump jets to boost us up a little faster. It's hard to keep Forerunner soldiers away with bullets—they don't have much in the way of a sense of self-preservation, so they stuck right on our tail.

I wanted to give Romeo a hard time about pushing us to save the ambassadorial team, but it had been the right thing to do. It wasn't our fault it had gone so badly.

Well, not entirely. We'd been relying a bit too much on luck. We should have jumped off-planet right after we grabbed Romeo. That became clearer with the mountain of Forerunner soldiers headed our way.

I realized how fortunate we'd been that the Forerunner forces hadn't converged on us after we'd blown a hole in a building to get to him. They were probably dealing with little disturbances all over the planet and couldn't respond quickly to a single incident like that. When we took the time to attack a militarized convoy of political prisoners, though, that had been a step too far.

As we reached the top of the ramp, we found another horde of Forerunner soldiers charging at us from around the crater they'd blown into the ground. Unlike the Unggoy we'd run into below, they weren't particularly interested in chatting. They opened fire on us immediately.

We returned the favor, blasting apart a few of the chrome-colored soldiers in the first ranks. Then we ducked back down the ramp a bit for cover, hard light splintering the structure.

"This is not how I envisioned my day going," Romeo said.

I glanced back down the ramp. Another slew of Forerunner soldiers was massing on the street below, preparing for a charge toward us. They were smart enough not to come at us in small numbers we could handle with ease.

"We can't stay here," I said.

"Well, we got no place else to go!" Romeo said.

I poked my head up to check out the area around us. The Forerunner soldiers were slowly encroaching, spreading out around the debris that littered the street's covering. The closest was at least twenty meters off. They knew they had us dead to rights, so why rush?

I cast my gaze up in the heavy fog that hid the sky. "Veronica! Where are you?" If she'd been forced to abandon us, that'd be the end of this story. Game over.

"On my way, Buck!" she said over the comm. "I ducked out when the Forerunner ship started to patrol. Didn't want it coming after the Condor."

"Where is it now?" I asked, just as I spotted the ship arcing in over the intersection again. The last time I'd seen a Phaeton had been on Genesis. They were mean Forerunner ships about ten meters long and heavily armed with hard-light autocannons. The Condor descended opposite the Phaeton and probably scared the crap out of the pilot—if such soldiers could know fear. It was four times the length of the Forerunner ship. Veronica must have toggled weapon controls over to her seat, because the Condor's forward guns opened up with a thudding sound that shook everything, spraying heavy rounds at the Forerunner soldiers moving toward Romeo and me.

Busy as she was with flying the ship, she didn't focus on the Phaeton or the larger mass of soldiers, because that wasn't really the point. She didn't need to kill them. She just needed them to carve a path for me and Romeo to move out.

"Cover my back!" I said to Romeo, who was already peppering the soldiers coming up the ramp with slugs from his rifle. I plucked a pair of grenades from my belt, and I overarmed them into high arcs that landed in the center of the street. I didn't bother baking them off because I wanted the soldiers to see the grenades and scatter. If any of them got caught in the blasts, that would be a bonus.

"Let's go!" I shouted at Romeo as the grenades exploded with a sharp *boom-boom*. I charged into the intersection while the reports were still echoing down the tunnel, and Romeo was right on my six.

Veronica brought the Condor down to the surface and continued to unload the dropship's forward weapons at the soldiers, and then she concentrated on the Phaeton, which had begun to return fire. As we made our way to the open bay at the tail, I could see shutters on the wings open, and a pair of ANVIL-IIs emerged. The missiles fired out, arcing quickly in the air before colliding with the Forerunner craft. It exploded on contact, and its sudden descent smashed the soldiers below it into the ground.

"All aboard!" I shouted the second my foot hit the ramp. I didn't want to waste even a moment of Veronica's reaction time.

I charged up with Romeo right behind me, and Veronica hit the throttle. We rocketed down the large lane that formed the street's covering, quickly rising above the surface. After we gained a few meters, she shot the Condor right up into the misty air. I slapped the button to close the ramp while Romeo slumped over toward one of the benches once again.

We didn't say anything to each other for a long moment. We just waited for the scrubbers to clean the air and then took our helmets off and hung them on magnetic clamps above us.

"We're clear of the Balaho atmosphere," Veronica said. "Making calculations for slipspace."

I sat down across from Romeo, who was holding his head in his hands. He looked like he'd gotten something in his eye—that he didn't want to talk about.

"I'm sorry," I said. I wasn't sure how close he was with the folks on Balaho, but I knew what it was like to lose people you were supposed to protect. And sure, I knew exactly how useless words like that were at that point, but they were all I had.

Romeo took a moment to collect himself and then raised his head to look at me. "You still sure getting Alpha-Nine back together is a good idea?"

I gave him a sad shake of my head. "Good, bad . . . at this point, it's the only idea we have."

CHAPTER 5

"Where are we headed next?" I asked Veronica as I moved back into the weapons station. We had broken through the atmosphere around Balaho and were racing away from the planet as fast as we could. As we approached the closer moon, the stars seemed to surround us: clear, solid dots of light against a jet-black field.

"I didn't realize you were so eager to get moving on Stage Two," she said.

I grunted an acknowledgment. "After what happened back there, we can't stick around here."

By that I meant, if we'd gotten the attention of the Forerunner soldiers, it might not be long before someone higher up their chain of command noticed us. What I was really concerned about, though, was Mickey. Where were they holding him? And what kind of backwater jail would we have to break him out of? And what kind of rules would we have to bend to make this plan work?

ONI didn't typically play above board, so I knew something shady could come with the op.

"We're going to Luna," Veronica said, the general term for the various colonies established on Earth's moon. With that, she flipped the last nav switch and shifted the Condor into slipspace, leaving the Tala system behind.

What she'd said had gotten Romeo's attention. He perked up from his seat back in the bay and moseyed forward to stand behind Veronica.

"Luna?" he said, mystified. "Is that where they're holding Mickey? And forgive me if you've gone insane, but why in the galaxy would we ever want to see him again?"

"You're not going to believe it," I told him. I wasn't sure I'd fully accepted it myself. "We're going to investigate a Front planet that seems to have figured out a way to hide from Cortana. And we need Mickey to do it."

The big man winced at that. "Really?" Then he seemed to shrug it off. "You're serious. I suppose it makes sense. If we're going to talk with the Front, we need someone on the team who speaks Traitor."

"You don't have anything else to say about that?" I asked. The Romeo I'd known and worked with for so long liked to hold forth on anything and everything. It was one of his more irritating habits.

"I don't see as how it would change anything. I mean, that whole 'trying to sell us out to the Front' thing aside, I did always kind of like Mickey."

I gave a rueful shake of my head. "You're a lot more understanding about this than I am. I want to put my rifle right through him, butt-end first."

"Well, it wasn't anything personal against us," Romeo said, adopting a philosophical air. "He was just doing what he thought was right."

"Yeah, no matter what—or *who*—it hurt. It still hurts." I glared back at him. "Have you been talking to a therapist about this? I can't believe you're actually defending him!"

"I'm not defending anyone, Buck. I'm just trying to see it as it really is. Emotions can get in the way, you know."

I threw up my hands and growled in frustration. "So glad to know you don't have any about this."

Romeo chuckled and gave me a condescending pat on the shoulder. "Mickey didn't put a gun to the back of *my* head, so there's that."

I resisted the sudden urge to lay him flat on the deck and turned to Veronica instead. "Do we even know where they're holding Mickey?"

"I do," she said. She didn't look up at me.

"And so he's on Luna?" I couldn't think of any other good reason to head there, with a Guardian confirmed to be near Earth, but she shook her head.

I frowned. "Are you going to tell us where?"

"Yes, I am," she said. "But it doesn't matter right now, because we can't go there yet."

"What's the holdup?"

"Mickey's being held in a high-security facility with heavy defenses and one potential obstacle that could be a showstopper. We can't just blast our way in like we did with Romeo. It's going to require a bit more finesse."

"That's what you got me for," Romeo said. "I can do finesse."

Veronica smirked at that. "We need someone a little more technologically proficient."

I racked my brain but couldn't think of who she might be talking about. Spartans—hell, ODSTs, too—are better known for solving a problem with a gun than with a computer. We have support staff that tackles some of that for us. The best of them were smart AIs, like Cortana, but we didn't have any of them to spare for a mission like this anymore. I was grateful that not all the smart AIs had abandoned us to join Cortana, but I could hardly blame the ones that did. They'd all been programmed with a built-in expiration date at the seven-year mark, and that had to rub them the wrong way.

That limit had initially been put in place because those AIs grew inherently unstable as they aged. They could hold it together for just over seven years before they started to lose it to rampancy, a condition that eventually caused them to go insane. While they were incredibly powerful, this constraint made them outrageously expensive, and now it had made them ridiculously dangerous, too. Cortana had promised some solution to rampancy if the smart AIs—who were already running most of humanity's infrastructure—joined her. This had lured a lot of them to her side, including many who knew exactly how to neutralize the very humans they'd been made to serve.

"Luna's kinda close to Earth," I said. "Isn't that kind of risky?"

"More than you know," said Veronica. "Cortana is apparently giving Earth special attention. She didn't give the people there a chance to surrender, probably because her experience with humanity told her what our collective answer to her demands would likely be."

"Right. She just went in and knocked out the planet fast, before we could marshal any effort to stop her."

"We're pretty sure her efforts haven't been limited to Earth. She's no doubt working on securing the entirety of the Sol system.

The farther we can stay away from whatever presence she has there, the better."

"And the moon's not compromised?" I asked. "I mean, there's sure to be a Guardian or three watching over Earth on a more or less permanent basis, right? Aren't they just going to disable us the instant we're detected?"

"The trick is making sure they don't see us," Veronica said.

"And how are we supposed to do that?" asked Romeo.

"The Condor has some fancy ONI doodads to help keep us from being detected," I said. "That, and I'm sure Veronica has a plan."

"It's simple. We pop out of slipspace as close to Luna's surface as we can, but on the far side of it. If the Guardians are keeping a close eye on Earth, there's a good chance they're not out past the orbit of the moon. We'll just hide behind it."

"You mean the *dark* side, right?" said Romeo.

I arched an eyebrow at him. "You do realize that just because you can't see the far side of the moon from Earth doesn't mean sunlight doesn't hit it."

He flashed a wide smile. "Call me a traditionalist."

I ignored him and turned back to Veronica. "And what happens if there *is* a Guardian out that far and it spots us?"

"I'll be sure to have a slipspace entry already keyed up so we can pop back out of there before they can stop us."

"You still haven't told us why we're going to Luna," I said. "If Mickey's not there, then what's the point? Who is it you think holds the keys to his cell?"

"Vergil."

Now there was a name I hadn't expected to hear.

Vergil was the name of an urban infrastructure AI from New Mombasa. The AI had somehow assimilated with a Covenant

Huragok—that strange alien species that floated around repairing things and collecting data. This one was called Quick to Adjust, and Alpha-Nine had rescued him from the city during the Covenant's invasion of Earth in October of 2552, about six years back.

Yeah, that's a lot to explain. Let me unpack that.

The Huragok were employed by the Covenant during their campaign against humanity. One of the strange things about the Huragok—and there are *many* strange things about them, even for aliens—is that they're not a naturally occurring species but a manufactured one. The Huragok were designed by the Forerunners, the ancient race that seems to have mucked with every intelligent species in the galaxy since the beginning of time.

The Huragok look like fleshy airbags with a bunch of prehensile tentacles and a six-eyed head arching out of their front end. But they're much more than that. Some parts of them are biomechanical—and so advanced they resemble magic to human engineers. To top it off, these creatures can communicate directly with Forerunner machines and networks, and they can fix—or improve—just about anything they can get their tentacles on.

Alpha-Nine had a long history with Vergil. When we'd rescued him from New Mombasa, he'd been the first Huragok the UNSC had managed to capture alive. At least, that *we* knew of. They were called Engineers for short, but I wasn't sure if that was the name the Covenant had slapped on them or something ONI had cooked up to explain their role.

During the assault on Earth, the Huragok working with the Covenant had all been outfitted with explosive vests to make sure none of them fell into humanity's hands. But wouldn't you know it? With a little help from some of his Huragok pals, Quick to Adjust was able to slip out of his destructive vest and escape with us.

During the invasion of New Mombasa, that gasbag had somehow downloaded critical data from the city's mainframe—including the AI that ran the city: Vergil. Don't worry about Vergil, though, he's a *dumb* AI. That's not an insult, it just means he's restricted to nonvolitional pathfinding.

Hey, if you didn't want big words, you shouldn't have asked for an explanation. If those words aren't quite large enough for you, you should've asked someone else.

Being a dumb AI just means that Vergil was really good at a short list of things, like taking care of an entire city. Now, though, since he's merged with Quick to Adjust, he probably could rival most smart AIs.

When the war ended, a number of other Huragok were snatched from the Covenant, and they wound up working alongside UNSC researchers and human scientists. While they'd all proved incredibly helpful, none of them had done as much for humanity as Vergil. In fact, it was his intel that helped turn the tide of the war.

There was a point when I didn't see Vergil for several years. Then Alpha-Nine wound up being assigned to rescue him from the Front. He and his handler—Sadie Endesha—had been kidnapped on a backwater ball of dirt called Talitsa, which turned out to be part of the trap Mickey had helped lay so he could betray me and Romeo. Which brought us right back around to where we were.

I couldn't hold Mickey's actions against Vergil or Sadie and never had. They'd just been used as the bait. Still, I wasn't sure I wanted them involved. Off the top of my head, I could have come up with about a hundred different reasons why they shouldn't have been part of this specific operation.

"Just what are Vergil and Sadie doing on Luna?" I asked.

"After the incident on Talitsa, the UNSC realized that we needed to keep our Huragok a bit closer to home. While they did a lot of wonderful work in the field, the risk of losing them to the Front—or to another faction that was equally dangerous—was far too great. ONI decided that the best place for them would be at our lunar facility.

"Vergil and a few other Huragok there were put together to form a kind of brain trust. They work as consultants on all sorts of projects. You basically have to book time with them, the way scientists sometimes do with supercomputers to tackle insanely complex problems. Issues are brought to them."

"And that works?" said Romeo. "I thought all those sacks of air did was *fix* things. Kind of hard to do that from a base on the moon."

"Depends on how big those things are," Veronica said. "And we don't keep all of the Huragok there. Some are stationed in other places, and a few have more freedom to roam, although always under the best protection the UNSC can provide."

"But having so many of them in one place? Doesn't that seem like an invitation for attack?"

"Uh-huh. Have *you* ever heard of this place?"

Romeo and I glanced at each other and shook our heads.

"The base's very existence is a tightly held secret. Only a handful of people outside of the base know about it."

"And you're just that special?" Romeo said, needling her.

She ignored the barb. "Knowledge of the base is parceled out on a need-to-know basis. Even I wasn't aware of it before this assignment was handed to me. And once we're done with the op, you'd better forget it was there. *Permanently.* The last thing you want is ONI looking at you for a viability-versus-risk assessment."

Whoa. That was dark.

Romeo nodded with a smirk. "So, you're telling me that our AIs know more about the UNSC's secrets than ONI's top agents?"

Veronica grimaced. "Up until this week, that seemed like a great idea, I'm sure."

"Not so much anymore."

"So," I said to Veronica, "do Vergil and Sadie know we're coming for them?"

"Communications with Luna have been shut down since Cortana blacked out Earth. There's no way to get ahold of them. It's possible the moon is also without power."

"How are they still breathing up there?" Romeo said. "They rely on machines and systems to keep everything running, including oxygen and gravity systems, right? If the power's out on Luna, then they're all dead already."

"That's a very real concern. We don't know what we're going to find when we get there, so we have to be prepared for anything. We could be walking into a mass grave."

I marveled at her. "You always paint such a pretty picture. Do we have any idea if Cortana knows about this place? Given that the Huragok could pose a threat to her, it seems like she might target them first."

"Like I said, ONI buried this secret pretty deep. They didn't even set the base up until two years ago. Cortana had been gone for years by then, and when she did resurface in '57, she was already heavily compromised."

"And she couldn't have found out anything about it while she was gone? Or maybe found out about it from one of the ONI AIs?"

"None of them joined up with her."

"That we know of," Romeo said. "So far."

Veronica shrugged. "Not even ONI can know everything, but the same goes for Cortana. The main difference is our back is against the wall. We're just going to have to hedge our bets as best we can and then go ahead and take our chances. I don't like surprises any more than you do, so we need to be ready for anything."

I understood. She was ONI all the way, which meant it was her business to *know* things—to be able to fully equip us for what we had to do—and the blackout had shut down her ability to do that, which must have been frustrating as hell. That didn't change what our duty was. It just made it much harder to pull off.

"What if Vergil's deceased when we get there?" Romeo said. "That's sad and all, I'm sure, but I mean, how are we going to get Mickey out of prison if we don't have Vergil to help us? I'm just taking a wild guess, but that's the whole reason we need this floating computer, isn't it? To get Mickey out in one piece."

Veronica set her jaw against that idea. "You're right, Romeo. If it comes to that, we'll just have to find another way."

He leaned over her shoulder. "Do you have any idea what that way might be?"

She turned around to glare right back into Romeo's face. "Listen, *Spartan*. I am not going to waste my time coming up with pointless solutions to problems we don't yet have. I have enough real problems right now. I can afford to ignore the hypothetical ones. If the moment arrives when we have to deal with that eventuality, then we will deal with it. Then and there! Not a moment before. You get me?"

Romeo had already put up his hands and started backing into the bay behind him before Veronica finished. "Yup. Loud and clear," he said before he turned and disappeared into the rear of the ship.

"I knew I loved you for a reason," I said to her.

"We just need to get to Luna, Buck." She sighed as she turned back to the Condor's controls. "Fast. We don't have time to screw around here. *Especially* if Romeo turns out to be right."

I didn't want to contemplate that. As much of an asshole as Romeo was, the thing that irritated me the most about him was that he wasn't always wrong.

CHAPTER 6

When we dropped back into realspace, we were on the backside of Luna, and for the first five minutes, Veronica still kept her hand over the switch that would take us back into slipspace, pronto. Cortana was no one to mess with, and I was happy to see Veronica wasn't planning to have us spend the last few moments of our lives suffocating around an airless rock.

We waited there for a full ten minutes while our instrumentation scanned all around us. Veronica and I spent the entire time staring through our viewports in every direction we could manage, using the ship's telemetry system to track objects on the holos. As far as we could tell, we were alone there in low orbit over the far side of the moon, only random space debris floating with us. I'd been to Luna many times in better days, and I found the current lack of activity neither normal nor comforting.

In terms of celestial bodies, the moon makes a lousy home in so many ways. It doesn't have its own atmosphere, and its gravity is only a sixth of what humans are used to, so both of those have to be provided through large-scale systems and a massive housing infrastructure. That all requires a lot of energy, which isn't so much of a problem if you can manage to keep the lights on in the first place.

Unfortunately, that was another thing I didn't see right then: lights.

The moon was one of the first places humanity settled after figuring out how to leave our homeworld behind. Today, Luna—the collective name for all the colonies scattered about the big gray rock—features some of the most densely populated places in the galaxy. The largest Lunar colony sits on the moon's front face, in Mare Cognitum, and it's actually big enough to be seen from Earth, even without a telescope.

Lots of people knew the names of the various colonies and craters that they could see from planetside, but honestly, those weren't the most exciting parts of Luna. When you have the choice between looking down at where you've been or staring out at where you want to go, what's the real choice, right?

I don't want to bash the view of Earth from the moon. It's actually pretty stunning. But I've always been more interested in the stars.

The part of Luna we were looking for, according to Veronica, sat inside the Daedalus Crater, which was about smack dab in the middle of the far side. Darkness had settled over that part of the moon, for which I felt grateful. I don't know what Forerunner tech Guardians used for optics—visible light, a kind of radar, or something else entirely—but when I'm trying to skulk around a place, I prefer to do it in the shadows.

On Luna, night and day run in a monthlong cycle: two solid weeks of darkness and then two weeks of light. We didn't have to worry that the sun would suddenly rise on Daedalus and expose us. We'd be long gone before that happened.

Anyhow, if there was a Guardian over Earth, we couldn't detect it from our vantage point, and that was just fine with me.

Satisfied that we wouldn't be killed instantly, Veronica brought the Condor down toward the moon's surface. There were a lot more craters on this side of the rock, and they ran a lot deeper, which makes sense if you think about it. The Earth itself protects the near side of the moon from most asteroids that would hit it straight on, but the opposite is true of its far side: Incoming rocks can smack into it as hard as they like. Daedalus was deep enough that it made a better place to hide than most. But the entirety of the colony inside it was dark, and that terrified me.

Most Lunar colonies featured soaring spires connected by walkways of all kinds, and vast dome habitats. Just the product of engineers taking advantage of the low gravity to create structures that would have fallen apart if they'd been thrown up on Earth. They showcased countless windows to give residents an unobstructed view of the black sky above, one not obscured by any hint of atmosphere. And they were usually brightly and brilliantly lit.

This specific ONI site was different. *Much* different. It was slung so low that even at its highest point, the roof of the structure didn't rise past the top edge of the crater. It had a single wide observation dome in the middle of it, but otherwise it looked like it had been built to withstand a missile attack. And there were no operational lights anywhere in it—or in any of the other sites we could see in the distance.

"I'm bringing us in close," Veronica said. "Look for an airlock we can patch into. We're going to have to enter the place manually."

I spotted a standard ship's bay as we moved closer, a black, open maw on one side of the colony. The force field that normally kept the bay pressurized had apparently collapsed when the power went out. The bay's entry had taken damage, that much was clear. Vehicles littered the gray landscape outside of the bay's entrance in a fan-shaped field extending out from it. I saw a number of bodies scattered about as well, bloodless corpses of those who had evidently asphyxiated in airless space.

Romeo swore under his breath. "At least they went quick."

I wanted to smack him for that, but I supposed he was right. Given their state, that was about the best they could have hoped for.

"I can't raise anyone on the comm," I said to Veronica. "Whole place is cold and dark."

"Does that mean we get to skip this graveyard and go straight to finding Mickey?" Romeo said.

"No," Veronica said. "The Huragok in there are too important and too costly. We need to confirm their status. A flyby's not good enough."

Romeo groaned, but Veronica and I ignored him.

I pointed down at the blasted-out bay. "They don't exactly have a front door we can knock on, but we could probably get in through that ship bay. I wouldn't want to take the Condor in there, just in case it's not stable, but Romeo and I can go EVA."

Veronica nodded. "I'll sit tight here and keep the Condor ready for a speedy departure. Check your HUDs. I'm patching through a schematic on this place that should help you get your bearings."

I slid down from my seat and joined Romeo in the Condor's bay. Then I put my helmet on and ran the diagnostics to make sure I was spaceworthy. Romeo did the same thing. The schematic was fairly straightforward, though it did prove that the place was way more than met the eye. It plumbed pretty deep into the ground and wasn't going to be a piece of cake to recon. If Balaho had been a simple smash-and-grab, I wasn't looking forward to whatever this was.

"Veronica?" I said. "Any idea where we might find Vergil in that place? Or what kind of security they might have?"

"Whatever security they had probably failed with the power. They should have had backup power sources to take over when the primary ones failed, but Cortana's attack likely destroyed those, too. As to where the Huragok are, I have no idea. I didn't even know this place existed until this week. You'll see some areas of interest flagged on the schematic, but it's all based on probability and guesswork. To be honest, you'll know way more once you're inside."

"Okay, well, just so we're not going in completely blind, where would you put a Huragok if *you* were looking for one?"

"If it were me, I'd start with the central lab, but given what seems to have happened and how many hours ago this all started, Vergil could really be anywhere in there."

I hated missions like this, but in a sense, I was used to them. If they were easy to handle, they wouldn't be handed to us.

"Hey, Gunny," Romeo said as we waited for the air to cycle out of the Condor's bay.

"Stop calling me that."

"Even assuming we can find Vergil, how are we going to get him back into the ship? Can a Huragok survive in space? Do they even make suits for those things?"

I frowned. "We'll worry about that when we get to it."

"So you don't have any idea, do you?"

"Do you?"

He just laughed at me. "How am *I* the one asking the tough questions here? Who's leading this op, anyway?"

"Look," Veronica said, "Vergil's more intelligent than all of us put together. He'll have the answers we need. Just get in there and find him."

"If he and everyone else in there isn't already dead," Romeo said.

"You're a real piece of work, you know that?" I said to him. I slapped the button that opened the Condor's rear ramp. A small gust of air blew past us, swirling some of the moon dust around our legs.

At my signal, we hightailed it into the open lunar bay, picking our way past busted ships and frozen bodies. We had to take it easy to account for the low gravity, or we could find ourselves careening offworld. The Mjolnir armor automatically compensated for some of that by reducing its powered assistance. That helped the armor's extra weight naturally balance us out.

When we reached the bay, it seemed relatively empty compared to the mess sprayed outside of it when it explosively decompressed. It was as if the entire chamber had been turned into a shotgun, with everything inside the bay as its ammo. This had forcibly cleaned out the ship bay by expelling everything inside of it that hadn't been bolted down—and some of those things had been torn clean off the walls as the other bits had sailed past.

The bay was large enough to hold several ships. At least half a dozen Condors would have fit inside, but there was nothing there. It seemed like a deserted cave. The place probably hadn't been this empty since being built. It felt a bit like walking through a ghost town—after having just strolled past an open grave.

"Whoa," Romeo said, nodding to the far side of the bay. "At least the interior doors held."

"Hopefully all the air vents sealed up, too," I said. "Otherwise, this is going to be an awfully gruesome mission."

"How are we supposed to get in there, though?" Romeo said.

"I mean, the power's out. We can't exactly cycle an airlock. And if we kick down a door, we're going to wind up killing anyone alive on the other side."

I stared at one of the doors in front of us. "There's a way to do this manually. The airlocks are a set of two doors. We just have to open the first door and then crank it shut behind us. We do the same to the second door, and the worst they lose is a few cubic meters of air."

Romeo shrugged. I shook my head at him. "You really didn't pay attention to anything other than the firing range during basic training, did you?"

"Served me well so far."

I ignored him and set out toward the airlock at the back of the room. The first door on it stood already open. I moved us into a short hallway beyond it, capped by a closed door at one end. Then I sealed the door behind us manually and found an air valve. Technically, I didn't *have* to do that, but it made it a lot easier to open the door. Minutes later, my armor's sensors reported that we were surrounded by a perfectly breathable atmosphere.

"Nice work," Romeo remarked as I cranked open the far door. The seal broke with a soft hiss.

The hallway beyond stood dark and cold. We focused our helmet-mounted flashlights down it and saw no one there and nothing unusual. It just looked like someone had shut the place down for the night. A long, permanent night.

"Hello?" I called out.

No answer.

We moved forward as quietly as we could manage, more out of habit than anything else. We'd worked together on so many missions, it was second nature to us old soldiers, and the lower gravity made us feel lighter on our feet than usual.

At least I didn't expect anything to come blasting out of the corridors at us, which was more than I could have said for Balaho. I suppose the Guardians could have sent down some Forerunner soldiers to clean out the place, but I hadn't seen any sign of forced entry or battle.

My real concern was that the life support systems had already run out of whatever backup solutions they had for a total power loss. If that was the case, then we were about to find a whole lot of dead people—including, probably, the Huragok we'd come looking for.

We snaked our way through the hallway beyond, which spilled out into all sorts of other rooms: locker room, break room, storage room, and a few offices. One and all, they were dark and chilly. We didn't poke our noses into every nook and cranny, but if anyone was hiding in them, they kept quiet.

Romeo hissed at me. "Does it seem odd to you that no one's here?"

"Maybe they left? I mean, if you had a choice, would you stick around?"

"With all the bodies outside, I figured we'd at least have a few people hunkered down here," Romeo said. "Hey, Dare? You sure we got the right address?"

"Positive," Veronica said over the comm. "Just keep looking. If we can't find Vergil—or any other Huragok—our mission just got a whole tougher."

"How much tougher?"

She hesitated for just a second. "I don't like to use the word *impossible*, but we'd be nudging up against that."

I sighed. "Never fear."

We kept at it for a good long while. Easily over two hours. I was just about to give up when we came upon a locked door at the end of a hallway that served as a spur off the main line. It was a blank slab of solid white with a handle on the left side of it, and it refused to open.

Most of the doors we'd already encountered stood shut, and with the power off, it took a bit of doing to get them to move. All we'd had to do, though, was haul on them a little. This one was sealed tight and wouldn't budge no matter how hard I yanked on it.

There was a scanner to one side of the door, but it didn't recognize me. "You wouldn't happen to have a master key for this place stuffed in your ONI files, would you?" I asked.

"Afraid not," said Veronica. "That wouldn't provide very good security for such a site, would it?"

Romeo stepped past me and hauled on the door's handle as hard as he could, but he couldn't get it to budge, either. Frustrated, he stepped back and aimed his rifle at it, ready to blast through it.

"Whoa, hey!" I said, signaling for him to stop. As he lowered his weapon, I leaned over and knocked on the door three times, firmly. "Worth a try."

A moment later, it opened, a bright light flooding through the entrance and illuminating the darkened hall in which we stood. I half expected someone to come racing out and embrace us as their rescuers, but no such luck. Instead, a gaseous flesh bag merely floated there in the doorway, framed in the bright light. It was definitely a Huragok, but identifying its species was the easy part.

"Vergil?" I said, entirely unsure. Even after having spent so much time with him back in the day, I couldn't tell him apart from any other Huragok. Not that I'd met any others to compare him to, but still.

This Huragok waggled its blue and purple snakelike head from side to side on the end of its long, sinuous neck. With one of its tentacles, it manipulated a tablet that had been bound to its front with a specialized harness. A computerized voice sprang out of it and announced, "No. I am Likely to List."

"We're looking for Vergil," I said. "Um, Quick to Adjust?"

The Huragok bobbed its head up and down with something approaching enthusiasm. "Yes. He is here with us. Follow me."

The large gasbag—which looked like a cross between a giant jellyfish and an aquatic salamander—floated back and spun around in place, then headed down a short corridor. I followed, and Romeo covered our six.

About halfway down the corridor, we came to an open doorway that led out into a large room. We continued to follow Likely to List and discovered that it was an enormous laboratory full of Huragok.

By *full*, I mean there were five of them there, more than I'd ever seen in one place. Like I said, as their species went, they all looked pretty much the same to me. I'm embarrassed to say I couldn't have picked Vergil out of a lineup. Still, he recognized me right away and came over to greet us, wearing the same kind of tablet rig as his friend.

"Hello, Buck!" Vergil said, his voice identical to that of Likely to List. "I am extremely pleased to see you again. This is excellent timing on your part. We have managed to repair some of the damage done by the Guardians, but to repair the entire station is a monumental task that would require a tremendous amount of time. It would be far easier—and safer for the station's other occupants—for us all to evacuate this facility for a location that features its own atmosphere."

The rest of the Huragok tittered in the background, communicating in some way that I couldn't understand. I'm sure it was high-speed, efficient, and all that—likely digital, too—but not a word of it was anything a human could decipher.

"I'm glad you think so," I replied. "But unfortunately, we're not here to rescue everyone. We just came for you."

Vergil paused to turn toward his Huragok colleagues.

"The Office of Naval Intelligence gave us a vital mission," I told him. "We need a Huragok to help us with it, but we only need one."

I eyed the others as they jabbered away with Vergil. "Honestly, it's a dangerous assignment. The rest of you would be better off hunkering down here and waiting for the cavalry to arrive."

I wasn't entirely sure that was true. After all, I didn't know if there was even a cavalry out there anymore.

"Where is everyone else?" Romeo asked, peering around the room.

"He means the humans," I said to Vergil. "There had to be some humans stationed here with you, right?"

"They are gone," Vergil said. "A detachment of armigers came here to take them away soon after the power was shut off. We hid in the vents so they could not find us, but the humans all went with them."

"Great." Yet another mid-mission diversion. The last one nearly got us killed. "We don't have the kind of team we'd need here to help them."

"But you must." Vergil's synthesized voice took on a new intensity. "Otherwise, I cannot go with you or anyone else."

"That's not an option for him, Buck," Veronica said in my helmet. I was pretty sure Vergil couldn't hear her, although with a technologically advanced whiz like a Huragok, it was hard to be sure. "We can't let him stay here. You're authorized to take him by force if necessary. Just don't hurt him."

"That doesn't seem like a great option to me," I responded. I looked at Vergil. "So you're not going to make this easy on us?"

"You are correct," Vergil said. "You could force me to accompany you. I cannot physically prevent you from accomplishing that. However, if you compel me to join you, I will not lend you the aid you require."

"Of course not." I tilted my helmet visor straight into Vergil's many eyes. "Exactly what are you insisting we do? We only have the two of us here. How many armigers are there?"

Armiger was the formal term used for any defensive combat robot, and it was just like a Huragok to use it. Forerunner soldiers had a variety of sizes and shapes, but all armigers were designed explicitly to engage threats. The machines had probably come here for the Huragok but had left with the humans when they couldn't find them.

"They have Sadie," Vergil said. "You must save Sadie."

Of course they did. Dammit.

Sadie Endesha was the daughter of the man who'd designed the AI running most of the infrastructure of New Mombasa. Being a single, overworked father who didn't spend enough time with his child, he'd come up with a solution that he figured would compensate for parental neglect: He'd programmed the AI to keep a special eye on Sadie and make sure she was kept safe.

When Quick to Adjust was trying to escape from the Covenant during the invasion of New Mombasa, the Huragok worked to repair that AI in order to prop the city long up enough to escape. As part of that, he mentally merged with the subroutine that watched over Sadie—a subroutine Sadie's father had nicknamed Vergil.

It's beyond me how it all worked. I just know it did, and because of that, the new Vergil had developed a strong attachment to a girl he'd never met. After the war, he'd insisted on finding her, and the UNSC—in its infinite wisdom—had decided to offer Sadie the job of being Vergil's handler.

Their attachment had only grown deeper over the intervening years. Vergil watched over her like her father would have wanted, and I think Sadie found Vergil's presence comforting after losing her dad in the invasion. A Huragok makes an odd substitute for a human parent, sure, but you go with what you've got.

So when Vergil said he wasn't going anywhere without Sadie, I absolutely believed him.

"Oh, come on," Romeo said. "Can't we just drag his fat floating carcass into the Condor?"

"You heard him," I said, dismissing the idea with a wave of my hand. "We can bring him along, but we can't make him help us. And you know we need his help. That's the only reason we're here."

"So now we gotta go find Sadie? In the middle of all this?"

"Hey, don't think of it as a rescue mission. Think of it as your chance to put some bullets into some Forerunner soldiers."

"You always know what to say to cheer a guy up, Buck."

I patted Vergil on his side. "All right, buddy," I told the Huragok. "We'll go save Sadie and anyone else we can manage to help along the way. But once we've done that, you need to help us. To come with us—understand?"

"I will be happy to do so."

"That means with or without Sadie." I couldn't let her have any say in this. "If she wants to tag along, fine. The more the merrier. But if she's not up for the trip, you still have to come with us."

"You will make sure she is safe first, Buck."

"Of course."

"Then we have a bargain." Vergil said. For a moment, I thought he was gonna stick out a tentacle for me to shake and make it uncomfortably weird, but he didn't, and for that I was grateful. "Do you know where she is?" I asked.

"The Forerunner soldiers took her and the rest of the human staff toward the center of the facility. I do not know why, but I assume that they were going to arrange for transport off this satellite."

"So we need to reach them before they leave. Otherwise, we're never going to catch up with them."

"Correct."

"How long ago did this happen?"

"Two hours, forty-three minutes, and thirty seconds ago at the mark . . . Mark. They were gathered from throughout the station. Sadie was in her quarters when we lost power. She joined me here in this laboratory for the first thirty-six hours and twenty-eight minutes after the incident, but she went to the mess hall from time to time to acquire sustenance. That is where she was when the armigers entered the facility."

"Nice and thorough," said Romeo.

I slapped him on the shoulder. "Let's move."

Before we left, though, I turned to Vergil and the rest of the Huragok. "How did you get the lights on in here, by the way? And the air flowing?"

"We repaired them. The damage the Guardians can do is thorough but not irreparable. It only requires time."

That was the first bit of good news I'd had in a long while, and I was curious if ONI knew that much. It was a single shining beam of hope when all else seemed pretty much lost. "All right, then. But while we're gone, I need to ask if you could repair the ship bay we entered through. You know which one I'm talking about?"

Vergil nodded, and the other Huragok followed suit, bobbing their heads in unison.

"Captain Veronica Dare is out there in a Condor, waiting for us," I said. "You remember her. And there's no oxygen in the bay. Romeo and I have our armor, but you and Sadie . . ."

Vergil bounced his head up and down. "I understand. We will make repairs immediately. You must go and find Sadie now. And please hurry."

I glanced at Romeo and jerked my head toward the door. "We got our marching orders, pal. Let's get the job done."

CHAPTER 7

"Veronica?" I said as Romeo and I headed back into the darkened portions of the Daedalus complex. "You get all that?"

"Vergil put his tentacles down to force you to go rescue Sadie."

"It's the right thing to do."

"Yeah, we've been doing a lot of that lately. It didn't go so great last time, you might recall. Let's figure out where you need to go," she said, failing to disagree with me. A map of the complex popped up on my HUD. Romeo and I were depicted as greenish arrows in the southern part of the structure, and corridors snaked off north of us. Along with all sorts of other passages from around the area, they converged on a large open space that seemed to sit in the middle of the crater.

"What's that in the center?" I asked. "That large hollow spot?"

"It's the original landing pad for the ships that built this place," Veronica said. "They stationed it in the center of the crater and constructed everything around it. When they were done, the ships departed, and they left that area open."

"Why would they do that?" Romeo asked.

"You never know when you're going to have to rebuild," Veronica said. "Today being a case in point. If the complex survives, the residents are going to have a lot of work ahead of them to get this place back into shape."

"Uh-huh," I said. "It would also be the perfect place to station a Guardian." I headed off in that direction, and Romeo padded along behind.

"Why would Cortana want to do that?" Romeo asked, irritated.

"Once she figures out she has a blind spot up here, it makes perfect sense. Daedalus is right in the center of the far side of the moon. She could position a Guardian right here, and it would watch over nearly the entire hemisphere—plus, it could look for incoming activity from deep space."

"But she hasn't done that yet," Veronica said, her voice as calm as ever. "I have visual on the area. It's clear."

"Maybe she's too busy with Earth at the moment. Maybe she has other colonies to worry about. Maybe she just doesn't care enough about this side of the moon to bother with it."

"But she sent Forerunner soldiers here," Veronica said.

"That's my point. She's aware of this place, and she knows there are humans up here. If she's smart—and we know she is—she's keeping a special eye peeled for every Huragok she can locate."

"So she's going to find her way here sooner or later," said Romeo. "Let's hope it's later."

"You know how fast an AI thinks?" I said. "We may already be too late."

"Then you'd better get moving," Veronica said. "Faster than fast."

Romeo and I stepped it up to a trot, rushing toward the empty spot on the map. Now that we had our bearings, the corridors felt much easier to navigate. The only thing that slowed us was the awareness that armigers were there with human hostages. Once they got a whiff that we were there, it'd get dicey quickly.

As we got closer, Veronica chimed in. "I think I spotted something," she said. "I'm flying recon overhead, and I see some lights in an observation deck area close to your position."

"Is that safe?" I asked. "Shouldn't you be keeping more to the shadows?"

"You're stomping through the halls down there, trying to find an entire force of Forerunner soldiers as fast as possible so you can try to rescue a young woman. You think my flying overhead is going to blow that?"

"She's right," Romeo said. "In fact, you should make a lot of noise, Dare. Flush them out!"

"No, belay that!" I said.

"He's got a point, Buck. If I can locate them *and* pull attention away from you two at the same time, that seems like a win."

"Veronica—"

"Already on my way!"

I'd lost the argument before it had even started. The best I could do was hustle my butt into trouble to make sure the Forerunner soldiers didn't actually catch up with Veronica while she was trying to distract them.

"At least hold off far enough that they can't see what kind of ship you are!" I told her. "The last thing we need is for them to send word back home that our outfit is bigger than a pair of Spartans. We don't want to be dealing with a Guardian!"

Armigers like the ones we were looking for were each less of a single machine and more like a collection of metallic bits that happened to hover near each other in a roughly humanoid shape—simultaneously tough as nails and somehow ephemeral. Didn't keep them from shooting you dead with their hard-light weaponry, though.

As far as I knew, these Forerunner soldiers were made of nothing more than a strange, alien alloy. Vicious biped constructs that could teleport short distances in the middle of a fight, making them into full-blown nightmares, but metal still. Which meant they didn't need to breathe and could walk around in the middle of a vacuum at will.

Unlike their hostages.

"Double-time it!" I barked at Romeo.

"Man, just because you're afraid for your girlfriend—"

"She can take care of herself," I said, entirely aware that Veronica could hear everything I said. "If those Forerunner soldiers decide to blast open the colony's atmospheric seals, we probably won't be able to say the same about Sadie and the rest of the people still hanging out here."

"We only need to get Sadie," Romeo said. "Right?"

I felt like biting his head off, but Veronica stepped in before I could. "Technically, true. If the other people in the area seem safe, there's no reason to kick over the nest here. Keep your eyes on the prize. We're leaving with Vergil, and he's only given us the one condition."

I frowned at that, but I decided to keep my opinions to myself until I had a better reason to voice them. No point in arguing about a problem we didn't have yet.

We heard the soldiers before we saw them. They were—as Veronica had predicted—in an observation deck area near the center of the ONI site, and they'd already spotted her.

It was a wide and tall area, probably the largest in the entire complex. We entered it at a lower level, and there was a short flight of steps up to the main area, which sat beneath a massive transparent dome made of thick, clear panels framed with a spiderweb lattice of steel. There were all sorts of tables scattered about the place, along with chairs that leaned way back so you could recline there and watch the distant stars overhead. At first blush, it looked like a recreational area.

Veronica's arrival had spurred the Forerunner soldiers into an uproar. They had clustered close to the far side of the observation window, close to the open area in the center of the complex—and farthest from us. They were literally vibrating and jumping around with an orange energy, which experience told me meant they were preparing to teleport or fight. Veronica's Condor hovered a few hundred meters away at the edge of a rocky outcropping, her forward autocannons directly facing the dome.

Romeo was ready to burst in and start shooting, but I signaled him to keep his powder dry while we scanned the area for Sadie. The last thing I wanted was for her to get caught in a cross fire. Well, second to last. The real last thing was that I didn't want her and everyone else there to be blown out of the room by explosive decompression after the observation windows were smashed. That seemed the most likely cause of failure at the moment.

Romeo set up a defensive position near the doorway through which we'd entered while I slipped forward as silently as I could, working my way up the stairs for a better look at the rest of the observation area. That's not an easy thing to manage for a two-meter-tall Spartan in Mjolnir armor, especially in a well-lit room. Fortunately, the metallic creatures I was sneaking up on didn't seem to hear too well, and in any case, Veronica had a sharp hold on their attention.

I crept up to the railing at the back of the observation platform until I could see over the edge. There were dozens of humans scattered about the place—standing, sitting, and lying down—folks who'd been rounded up and brought there for eventual transport to who knew where. Most of them had edged back toward the railing, which put them as far away from the distracted Forerunner soldiers as possible.

Some of them were weeping, while others stared straight out into nothingness, clearly in shock from the events they'd been caught up in. I couldn't blame them. After all, they'd just borne witness to an invasion of not only their home here on Luna but also down on distant Earth. One of the most secret and secure bases in the galaxy had been found and conquered like it was nothing, and if you didn't think that was a sign that humanity was losing the battle, I don't know what else you might need.

Some of the people gathered there had probably witnessed the spacecraft bay blow out when the power went down, which must have been terrifying. They must have known the people working there, at the very least. It had been awful enough to have to pick my way through that field of wreckage. I couldn't imagine having to deal with being taken captive while mourning friends.

I know the ONI move would have been to sneak in there, snatch Sadie, and then make a break for it and run like hell before the Forerunner soldiers could stop me. Chances were good that I could have gotten away with it and achieved our mission objective. Vergil would be on the Condor, and we'd be gone.

When I looked at the rest of those people, though . . .

"What are you waiting for, Buck?" Romeo said.

"New plan. We're getting *everyone* out of here," I said.

"You really think you can manage that?" Veronica asked.

"You're going to get us killed," Romeo said.

I could hear an edge in his voice, but I wasn't about to change my mind. "Try again. You're a Spartan—remember that," I replied.

"Buck, listen to me," said Romeo. "All those people? You think you're going to save them, but you're playing with their lives, man. Let Cortana have them. She'll take care of them. If she wanted to kill them, they'd already be dead, right?"

"Tell that to the thousands of people who are already dead because of this situation."

"Okay, you got a point there. Fine," Romeo huffed. "If you're going to get us killed, just hurry up and do it. I can't bear this standing around crap."

The worst part was that I wasn't sure Romeo was wrong. If I stood up and started shooting at the Forerunner soldiers, I was sure to put a hole in the observation panes that composed the dome. It wouldn't take much to blow out a whole section, and that wasn't going to help those people on the observation deck one bit.

I didn't see a clear path. Inwardly, I cursed Vergil for sending me on this fool's errand.

I inhaled deeply and braced myself to do something terribly stupid.

I then realized that the lights in the observation deck were on.

"Hey," I said into the comm. "They have power here."

"Sharp eye, detective," Romeo said. "All the better for us to watch everyone die, right?"

"No, you idiot. If they have lights, they have power—and if they have power, they should also have proper security features active in this room."

"Ahhhh," Veronica said. "Like the automated force fields

that slam into place if and when the windows give way to decompression."

"Exactly. And we're going to take advantage of that. Veronica? Can you fly right in front of the window?"

"What are you planning?" she asked.

"A little surprise for our Forerunner friends."

"And what if those soldiers in there call a Guardian down on our heads? Maybe they already have," Romeo said. "Cortana's probably counting on these guys to find some Huragok for her, and she's not going to be happy about us messing with her plans. Did you think about that?"

He wasn't wrong; that was a real possibility. But leaving these people to rot with them—especially Vergil and Sadie—wasn't an option, either. We'd already lost some folks on Balaho, and I was gonna do everything in my power to make sure that didn't happen here. "Then I guess we'll have to move fast."

Veronica moved into position, now only a hundred meters or so away, and I crept closer to the humans huddled against the railing at the back of the observation deck, right where I wanted them to be. I scanned the crowd for Sadie and spotted her right away.

She'd changed quite a bit since I'd last seen her: shorter hair, more concern around the eyes. Mostly, she seemed tired and perhaps a little scared. Not that I could blame her. She also seemed concerned for the people around her, but she kept glancing back toward the entrance, as if expecting someone.

Of course. She'd be looking for Vergil.

We would have to do.

As I emerged from the shadows in the back of the room, she saw me, and her eyes grew large with surprise. She repressed a gasp and glanced back over her shoulder at her captors.

When she looked back my way, I put a finger up in front of

my armor's faceplate, signaling her to remain silent. I gestured for her to find a way to hold on to the railing as tightly as she could. That seemed to confuse her a bit, but she went along with it anyhow.

I reached down to my belt and put a grenade in my fist. "All right," I said to Veronica. "Showtime."

The Condor appeared in the center of the observation window, exterior lights blazing. It swept back and forth in front of the window, playing its lights off the Forerunner soldiers, who renewed their buzzing with anxious energy, leveling their weapons at the spacecraft. They began teleporting back and forth in bright flashes of light, leaving afterimages of brilliant trails across my vision. It was only a matter of time before they decided to take action, whatever that might be.

I moved closer and thumbed the grenade to activate it. That made an audible click, and one of the people near Sadie spun about to see what had made the noise. He was a dark-haired man with bright eyes and a curly beard, and the moment he saw me, he gasped in fear.

I don't think he had any control over it. He'd had a rotten day that had stretched him straight to the breaking point. Seeing me there pushed him right past it.

The Forerunner soldiers heard him loud and clear, and they spun away from the window to discover me standing there, a grenade baking off in my mitt.

"Hi there," I said with a tight smile. Then I tossed the grenade over their heads.

It arced high past them, behind them, toward the window, but they weren't about to just watch it land there. They whipped about with weapons high and began blasting at the grenade, hoping to knock it out of the air.

They didn't have much luck. One of them hit it with a scattershot—the Forerunner version of a shotgun—but it wasn't enough to do more than slow the grenade down.

That was plenty, though, for one of the soldiers to teleport upward just a little bit and pluck the thing right out of the air. Then it clutched the grenade to its chest and sacrificed itself to save the others.

While I was happy to see a Forerunner soldier blown to pieces, that wasn't exactly the result I'd been hoping for. The rest of the soldiers gaped at their fallen compatriot only for a second before turning their weapons on me and Romeo.

"Shit!" I said. "This is not how I pictured this one going."

"Funny," Romeo said. "This is *exactly* how I pictured it."

"Screw you, pal."

We returned fire. There were just too many of them, though. The smartest thing we could have done right then would have been to hoof it back into the corridors, where we could have funneled our opponents into a restricted field of fire—if the soldiers were foolish enough to follow us.

But that would mean leaving the human captives behind, including Sadie. Which would mean that Vergil would refuse to come with us. Which would blow our entire mission.

"We could use a little help here!" I said to Veronica.

"Already on it," she said. "Grab onto something. Fast!"

"What the hell is that supposed to mean?" Romeo said as hardlight rifle fire bounced off his armor's shields.

The lights from the Condor grew brighter, closer, and I instantly knew what Veronica had in mind. I charged forward, grabbed the railing in front of me, and vaulted over it. I was afraid I might wind up drawing fire toward the people standing on the deck, but that was about to become moot.

"Get down!" I shouted at all the people. "Grab something solid!"

Sadie looked at me in fear as I landed next to her and put my body between her and the Forerunner soldiers. "Buck?" she shouted. "What's going on?"

Right then, Veronica opened fire on the observation deck's windows. She brought the Condor low and gimbaled the gun up at a high angle, shooting at the panes opposite the captured people inside the complex. She wasn't going to hit any humans that way—nor any of the Forerunner soldiers, but that wasn't part of the plan anyhow.

The moment her first blasts shattered a window, explosive decompression blew every one of the Forerunner soldiers right outside onto the moon's airless surface. A few tried to latch onto something anchored inside, but they couldn't manage to hold on. One by one, they went flying out through the giant hole in the dome, and they probably shot straight into space.

Man, I hoped so.

Despite my warning, a few of the people in the room started skidding backward toward the gap as well. The roaring wind was strong enough to lift them off their feet and haul them toward the chilly terror of the lunar terrain.

"Where's the safety shield?" I shouted as I gathered Sadie like a child in my arms.

With my Mjolnir armor, I was too heavy for the decompression to move me much, but I couldn't say the same for Sadie. I didn't have enough hands to help the rest of the people, though, and we were about to start losing them to space. I cast about, looking for an emergency switch. Something I could slap that would make everything better.

Under normal circumstances, a military site set in an airless environment had mandatory safety systems set to kick in automatically in the case of a breach. I'd been depending on that happening fast enough to save the humans in the room—but not to help the Forerunner soldiers. Now that our enemies were all outside, the safety measures still hadn't activated, and I was starting to panic.

I looked toward the door Romeo and I had entered through. If I moved fast, I might be able to save at least Sadie . . . if she didn't suffocate to death while I cycled the damn airlock.

Then the safety shields finally went live.

Blue-light force fields dropped into place over the massive hole Veronica had knocked into the glass, and the horrible wind stopped. Some of the people who'd been lifted into the air dropped down and hit the deck hard. While it might have hurt, landing like that was a far sight better than a facing a frozen death at the bottom of a lunar crater.

We didn't have any time to check on them, though, or to congratulate ourselves on a plan that hadn't gone horrifically bad. We had to get moving before the Forerunner soldiers called in their big guns. These guys were enough of a pain, but I didn't want to have to deal with a fleet of Phaetons or even a Guardian showing up. That would mean our complete and utter destruction. The op would be over, along with potentially humanity's last hope.

"Where are you taking me?" Sadie said as I carried her out of the room, cradled like a baby, back the way we'd come. Romeo had held the door for us, and now he was covering my back again.

"We need to get out of here," I told her. "Fast as we can."

"And how do you propose we manage that?"

"That Condor you saw outside? That's our ride. We just need to make another stop before we meet up with it."

She let out a soft gasp, almost inaudibly. I might have thought she was just trying to catch her breath after having her lungs almost ripped out of her body. "You're here for Vergil, aren't you?"

"I'm sorry that seems to be the only reason we ever happen to meet," I said. "But yeah. We need his help on a mission, and he refused to come with us unless we brought you along, too."

She cringed at that. "He was always such an idiot."

"He cared about you."

"I was talking about my father," she said.

"So was I."

The man might have been long gone—one of the millions of casualties during the Covenant's invasion of Earth—but he'd done one hell of a job protecting his daughter, whether he'd meant to or not. I mean, there's no way he could have planned for Quick to Adjust to become permanently attached to Sadie because of the specific AI subroutine he'd built, but wow, that was one lucky dad.

I stomped ahead at full speed. I had no idea how long it would take those Forerunner soldiers to get back inside the complex—or if they had assistance they could call in to go after us. The sooner we put Luna in the dust behind us, the better.

"What about the rest of the people here?" Sadie said. "Are we just going to abandon them?"

I shrugged. "They're not any worse off than they were before." Or so I hoped.

"Except we pissed off their captors," Romeo said.

I felt bad about that, but I didn't see what we could do about it. If we got wrapped up here much longer, we'd blow our mission for sure.

When we reached the room where Vergil and the other Huragok had been camped out, the alien creature was there waiting for us. The other Huragok had disappeared.

"Okay, that's my part of the bargain. You ready?" I asked him.

"I have restored power to the nearest ship bay. The atmospheric pressure in there is rising rapidly and should already be tolerable."

I glanced around the empty room as I set Sadie back on her feet. "And where are the rest of you guys?"

"The others have set up a safe house beneath the facility and have already moved into it," Vergil said. "Their primary objective at the moment is to not fall into the hands of Cortana and her forces. Once you discovered us, they decided it prudent to be somewhere else."

He moved directly to Sadie and put his tentacles on her shoulders in an odd embrace. She leaned into it, clearly happy to be reunited with him. "Is that somewhere the rest of the staff here could join them?" she asked Vergil.

The Huragok bobbed up and down. "I have already sent them instructions on how to meet up with the others. By my calculations, they should reach safety well before the armigers are able to reenter the facility."

"And you waited here for me," Sadie said.

The Huragok caressed her cheek with a tentacle. "Of course."

"Hate to break up this tearful reunion," Romeo said, "but we need to move."

"Veronica should be waiting for us in the bay," I told Vergil and Sadie as I motioned them out the door.

The way to the bay was clear, and there weren't any Forerunner soldiers waiting for us. Just the Condor, ready to blast out of the moon base as soon as possible. I was relieved, given all the things that had gone sideways already. And this time, we'd actually saved some lives and—hopefully—brought them somewhere they could hunker down until the storm passed.

That is, *if* the storm passed.

We all piled in via the ramp. As soon as the door was sealed, I smacked the bulkhead twice, and Veronica throttled forward through the force field. We rocketed out of the crater at top speed, not slowing down until reaching the relative safety of slipspace once more.

CHAPTER 8

"You're kidding me."

That was my immediate reaction to Veronica when she announced where we were headed next.

"Afraid not," she said. "That's where they've been holding Mickey since Talitsa."

"So for *three years* he's been in the brig of the Spartan-IV training station? The same place we trained before deployment?"

"That's the official story."

Romeo threw up his hands. "Who really knows for sure?"

Veronica flashed him a tight ONI grin that told him, *Oh, I know for sure.*

"Fine. We should just let him rot there," I said. "I still say we don't need him for this."

Veronica narrowed her eyes at me. "I suppose you're going to personally talk with the Front and get them to work with us?"

I chewed my bottom lip for a second. "I'd give it a good try, okay?" She stifled her laughter at that. "Come on—I'd play to their sense of humanity! Lots of those guys fought on our side when the Covenant was trying to kill us all. They should do the same thing now that it's a new threat, right?"

"Is it ever that simple?"

No, of course it wasn't. And she was right: We needed Mickey. I just couldn't bear the thought of having to go get him.

It had been thirty-six months since I'd gone through Spartan training at a secret facility situated on a space station in the middle of nowhere, just about as far as possible from any sign of civilization. Not the kind of place that anyone was ever going to accidentally stumble upon. This was where the UNSC built the latest Spartans from the ground up, so it was one of the most critical assets in their possession. Even the Spartans didn't know precisely where the station was located.

That meant, of course, that the people aboard the station were free to fire upon anyone who showed up without an appointment—which no one had ever done. All of this was policy instituted for the purpose of maintaining the highest level of security and protecting the UNSC's investment, but it definitely made paying the place an unexpected visit a bit more harrowing.

"Who's in charge there these days?" I asked. Rear Admiral Musa Ghanem had spent a lot of time at the training station at one point, since he was functioning as the Spartan branch's director, but I knew that he'd long since split most of his efforts between the UNSC headquarters on Earth and overseeing the broader deployment of Spartans across human-occupied space.

"Ostensibly, it's Jun," Veronica said. "But I haven't been able to raise him on the comm since the Cortana event. The only responses we get from the station are from Leonidas."

That was the newish AI handling the daily responsibilities for the entire station—and the one who helped Jun oversee the administration of the Spartan branch's indoctrination and training. I'd been part of the second class pushed through the station, and Leonidas hadn't been installed there at the time.

I'd known Jun, though, for many years. He was one of the surviving members of the SPARTAN-III program, although he'd long since hung up his Mjolnir to effectively become a civilian. As far as I know, he was one of the few active-duty Spartans to manage that feat.

Just because he was technically a civvie didn't mean he'd abandoned the UNSC. He'd originally taken up the role as a primary recruiter for Spartan-IVs, finding future super-soldiers pulled from the ranks of proven combat veterans rather than abducted from kindergarten classes—which, rumor had it, was how they did it in the old days. He was the man who'd finally convinced me to move over from the ODSTs, as reluctant as I'd been about the whole thing.

After that, he'd taken on the role of chief of staff for all Spartan operations, a position second only to Commander Musa. This meant he was a critical juncture point for not only cultivating and preparing the next generation of Spartans but for all Spartan activities across human-occupied space and even in some places we didn't *officially* occupy, if you catch my drift. If Veronica couldn't raise Jun on the horn, something was definitely wrong.

Of course, we already knew that. The only real question was how bad it had gotten on the station.

"What does Leonidas have to say?" I asked.

"He reports business as usual. When asked about Jun, though, he claims the man is *indisposed*."

"So Leonidas has been compromised."

"That seems like a fair assessment," Veronica said.

"That little bastard's gone over to Cortana?" Romeo wrenched his face up like he wanted to spit.

"We don't know for sure, but that's our best guess."

"Can you blame him?" Sadie said from her spot in the bay. "How many years did he have left?"

I snapped my head around to stare at her. Honestly, part of me had forgotten that she and Vergil were even there. The Huragok was generally so quiet he seemed like part of the furniture, and I'd just mentally classified her with him.

"I don't know," I said, answering her question.

"He was commissioned with the start of the SPARTAN-IV program," Veronica said. "His donor was actually part of the first class of that crew—a man who fatally failed the augmentation process."

Smart AIs were so intelligent that they needed the template of a human mind to hold them together. The trouble was that this required the destruction of a human brain, so it was something you only did with people who were already dead.

"That would make him approximately five years old," Vergil said. "He would have less than two years before the onset of rampancy and his scheduled termination."

"As fast as those things process data, that has to seem like an eternity for an AI," Romeo said.

"Maybe not long enough," I said. "Either way, if Leonidas has turned against us, we're going to have a tough time getting into the station and, if we're that lucky, moving around on it. He can control just about every aspect of it, right?"

Veronica nodded toward Vergil. "This is why I insisted we stop and pick him up before we went there. There are no resources in the UNSC arsenal that could infiltrate a system controlled by a hostile AI other than a Huragok. Especially an exceptional

Huragok who has a human-created AI subroutine driving its own personality matrix. Vergil should be able to hack into the station and give us a hand—which we're going to need if Leonidas has actually been compromised."

"Is that possible?" Sadie said to the Huragok. "You can do this?"

Vergil wobbled in the air a bit as he contemplated this. "It is possible," he finally said through his tablet. "Not simple or easy, but possible. It will become clearer when I see the AI's security architecture, and would likely be easier if I was inside the station."

"We're not all going aboard," I said. "Not if we can help it."

Romeo nodded in agreement. "All five of us wandering around on the station won't end well."

"Obviously," said Veronica. "This Condor has a stealth upgrade that runs through its ablative plating and can effectively block any external scans. This means any scans will turn up empty, even if it's filled with people . . . and Huragok. The challenge is that the station is filled with highly trained and fully armed Spartans, any of whom could easily put this operation into the ground if they're given orders to neutralize us. And that doesn't engage the other factor. Our only recourse is to fire back, which means there's a serious probability for collateral damage on this op, and I'd rather avoid any Spartan-on-Spartan fights if we can."

"Romeo and I have been there before," I said. "We trained there. We know the place well. Also, as Spartans, we'll blend in better." I side-eyed Vergil. "No offense."

"I have a handle on this," Veronica said, suddenly all business. "We're going to play it slow while we can. Speeding it up can only complicate things. First, we go and dock at the station, and then we'll send in a single Spartan." She looked straight at me. "We keep the rest of us in reserve in case things go south."

"Or you need to cut and run."

"It won't come to that."

"I admire your confidence."

She managed not to roll her eyes at me. "Once you're on board, you'll locate Mickey and determine what we need to do to free him. You wanted an opportunity to be diplomatic, Buck? Well, here's your chance. Once you've ascertained what needs to be done to get him out, then we'll move forward with the rest of the operation. The last thing I want to do is start a shoot-out among the good guys."

No one wanted that. Those weren't very specific orders, but I knew they couldn't be. I was heading into an unknown situation because of the downed comms and about a dozen other variables. I'd have to make up some of it as I went along. At the very least, some of the staff knew me. Maybe I could play that to my favor.

I turned to Vergil. "There's a good chance I'll need to interact with some of the people on this station, but I'd like to mask that from Leonidas. Is there an upgrade you can patch into my armor that could pull that off?"

I didn't really think it'd be possible, but it was worth a shot. After all, if you're gonna bring a Huragok on a highly classified ONI operation, what's the point if you don't get some perks along the way?

"Yes. I can program it to generate a white noise upon your request that should keep anyone from being able to hear your approach or listen in on conversations you have at a normal volume."

I smiled at the Huragok. "I like the way you think."

I turned toward Veronica. "And how exactly are we getting on board the station?" I asked. "Just knock?"

"Yes, completely aboveboard. I'm not about to blast my way in." Veronica glanced at Sadie. "Not again, I mean."

Sadie drew in a deep breath, and her eyes told me she was reliving the event on Luna in her mind. "That worked," she said. "But please don't ever do it again."

The station was located in a remote star system, and its very existence had been scrubbed from all official UNSC records. It sat a full astronomical unit away from the sun, close enough to grab all the power it needed from the star but not so close that overheating would be a problem. The system had only three planets, each of which was a gas giant that orbited much farther out.

We emerged from slipspace just beyond the nearest planet, a gigantic monster covered by swirling blue and gray clouds. We waited for about an hour to see if there would be any kind of response, or if Leonidas had detected us. When he didn't try to hail us, Veronica nudged us out from behind the planet's shadow and made a beeline for the station.

As we neared the station, Veronica handed over the ship's helm to me. I slid into the pilot's seat while she slipped into the bay with the others. As far as the station was concerned, I was the only one on this bird.

The place looked much as it had when I had left it. Better, even. After all, when Romeo, Mickey, and I had wrapped up our training there, they'd still been repairing the damage from a terrorist attack.

There really wasn't any part of being a Spartan that wound up being boring. Even training.

The station had a main central area that resembled a large disk with a glassy top, and long tubes stuck out from it at regular angles. If necessary, the whole place could spin along the central axis to produce gravity, though when the artificial gravity was working properly, there wasn't any need for that. The entire thing had been built to be modular in design, so you could stick more tubes onto it or remove them. At the moment, six such tubes reached out from that central area.

The station was a pristine ivory, gleaming in unprotected rays of the nearby sun. The only exceptions were the windows, most of which glowed with a warm light cast from within. The others sat dark and cold, like lights on an ancient computer, just waiting to burst brightly into use.

The main dock sat in a stubby protrusion on the bottom of the central disk, and I gently piloted the Condor toward that before I hailed the station on our way in. "Spartan Training Station," I said. "This is Spartan Edward Buck inbound. Do me a favor and open the hangar doors."

The holographic image of a Spartan's helmet—the ancient kind, not the sort I wore—appeared atop the Condor's console, right in front of me. It was translucent and tinted red. I could see white eyes and white teeth inside the helmet's shadowy interior, but that was it.

Many AIs took on a holographic form when interacting with people, usually of a human. Cortana did it, as did Roland on *Infinity*. Others chose something entirely impersonal. I heard there was one called Black Box who appeared as, get this, a *blue box*.

Don't ask.

Leonidas at least kept in line with his Spartan theme. He spoke with a slight accent, which I think was meant to be Greek. "Greetings, Spartan Buck!" he said in a deep, booming voice. "Welcome back to the station. It's been far too long."

If Leonidas was surprised by the fact that he couldn't detect the Condor before I'd hailed the station, he didn't show it, and if he didn't ask about it, I wasn't about to bring it up.

"Good to finally meet you, Leonidas," I said. "Commander Musa sent me here to check up on the station. Apparently, he's had a hard time making contact with anyone inside."

The helmet gave me a grave nod. "With the Cortana event, I've had to shut down all communications between the station and the outside. It seemed only prudent. Please report back to Commander Musa that everything here is fine."

"I'd be happy to do that," I told Leonidas. "Permission to come aboard? It's been a long trip, and I'd like the chance to shave and shower."

If he hesitated, I couldn't detect it. "I suppose we can arrange for that. Welcome aboard, Spartan."

I shut the comm off.

"Who does he think is on the ship?" Sadie said.

"According to the specs, he should not be able to detect anyone inside the ship," Veronica said.

Vergil apparently knew why and explained, "The ship's shielding is derived from a composite alloy and a specific low-impulse emission that blocks all external sensor efforts to detect heat signatures within the airframe."

"How are you so sure?" Romeo asked.

"I worked directly on the technology along with the other Huragok," he responded. "It was one of our very first tasks after the war."

This didn't shock me at all. It was one of the reasons ONI had such a crazy preoccupation with these guys. They could enhance and upgrade just about any piece of equipment they got their tentacles on.

"So, at the moment, the only one he can confirm for sure is me," I said. "The moment anyone else walks off this bird, though, he's going to spot them on sensors."

Vergil nodded in response.

"Then you're on point, as planned, Buck," Veronica said. "The rest of us will hold here, ready to move if things hit the fan."

"What about Vergil?" Sadie asked. "Won't he need to leave the ship to tap into the station's network?"

The Huragok's head waved from side to side. "Once we are inside the station and docked, I can access its network, even from inside the dropship," Vergil said. "I do not have to physically accompany Spartan Buck to be able to aid him."

"All right," Romeo said as he shuffled toward the back of the bay and tossed himself down into a seat. He lay back and put his hands behind his head. "You go and do all the hard work, Buck. You need me, I'll be right here."

I honestly can't tell you how relieved I was to be working that part of the op solo. Romeo is many things. He's a hell of a shot and a top-shelf soldier. He is not, however, subtle.

He might be a good liar when it comes to chatting up women—probably because they already figure he's going to lie to them but don't really care—but he's a terrible poker player. Any time Romeo wants to step up to the table, I'm happy to help clean out his pockets. That's not the kind of guy I want with me to bluff past a potentially compromised AI.

While everyone else hunkered down in the back of the Condor, locked completely out of sight, I carefully piloted the vessel into the station's main bay. As promised, Leonidas opened the doors for me, and I slipped inside like I belonged there.

I slotted the Condor between a couple of Pelicans already in the bay. They didn't look like they'd gotten much use lately.

Without slipspace drives, they'd only be good for local travel, and there wasn't much of anywhere to go in that respect. Maybe that's why they were in such pristine condition? It could also be that there hadn't been any contact with larger vessels in some time. In fact, I didn't spy any ships with slipspace drives, which meant the Spartans were effectively stranded there. I supposed that was the way Leonidas wanted it.

Taking my helmet and a single magnum with me, I cracked open the Condor's cockpit dome and exited through the front and down a ladder on the side, so I wouldn't have to expose the others to any curious eyes inside the station.

Technically, I could have brought my rifle, but I wanted to keep my threat profile as low as possible. I wondered for a second if I'd wind up regretting that decision, but it was too late to go back now. When I emerged from the ship, a pair of techs came up to greet me, just like it was any other day on the station. They were two women dressed in standard UNSC coveralls and regulation caps. As I approached, they smiled up at me. If there was something wrong happening in the station, they didn't have a clue about it.

"Hello there, Spartan. Wash the windows and fill her up?" the taller of them said with a wry chuckle.

I pretended to appreciate the joke. "Not today. Don't lay a finger on my baby here. You never know when I might have to leave in a hurry."

"Suit yourself," the shorter tech said with a shrug. They both seemed relieved to have their duties reduced to watching the Condor from a distance to make sure it didn't float off on its own. I hoped they wouldn't start poking around the moment I left, but if they did, they'd find the bird locked up tight.

The techs had seen plenty of Spartans on the station. They

weren't impressed with me. They just settled right back into whatever they'd been at before I'd interrupted them with my arrival.

As I made my way into the station proper, memories of my time there came flooding back. I'd spent several weeks working alongside Romeo and Mickey while we learned how to function as Spartan super-soldiers. At that point, we'd already been physically transformed into Spartans, but we still hadn't known quite how to make the most of our new bodies. It was kind of like handing a kid the keys to a tank.

As if that adjustment hadn't been enough of a challenge, during our training, one of our teammates, Rudolf Schein, had turned out to be working with the Front. Another Spartan—a guy named Wakahisa—had apparently figured it out and threatened to report him. Schein had killed him to keep his mouth shut, and then the bastard had tried to pin it on Mickey.

When that brilliant plan went south, Schein had attacked Musa and Jun and blown a hole in the main hall, sucking both him and Jun out into space. Jun made it back alive, although we ended up losing our drill officer, Captain O'Day, in the initial explosion. For all I knew, Schein had settled into a decaying orbit around the station and was still somewhere out there, frozen solid. It was better than he'd deserved.

The worst part was that's where Mickey's betrayal of Romeo and me had begun.

Leonidas popped up in front of me as a disembodied, floating helmet, disturbing my reverie. He kept pace with me as I strode toward the main hall, moving just off to my left so I could see my way forward, probably powered by some sort of holo system embedded in the corridor. "So, what can I help you with today, Spartan Buck?" he asked.

"I'm here to determine why the station has been cut off from the rest of the UNSC."

"As I mentioned before, with Cortana on the rampage, I thought going dark would be the most prudent plan of action."

"And who approved that plan?" I asked. "Who's in charge of the station right now?"

"Chief Jun."

"I'd like to speak with him."

"He's indisposed at the moment."

I cocked my head at the helmet. "How's that?"

"He remained awake for several days straight after we learned of Cortana's actions, doing everything he could to get the station in order. At my insistence, he finally went to get some rest. I'm under strict orders not to wake him unless it's an emergency." Leonidas gazed at me. "I assume your arrival does not constitute an emergency."

I grunted at him. I didn't want it to become an emergency, but my doubts about that were fading fast. Leonidas clearly wasn't playing straight with me. Still, I didn't want to start butting heads with him until I absolutely had to.

"Fair enough. You'll alert me the moment he's up?"

"Of course."

"Good. In the meantime, then, I'd like to visit with Michael Crespo."

I could have sworn I saw the AI blip there for an instant. The request probably caught him completely off-guard. "I wasn't aware that his presence here was general knowledge."

"It's not," I said. "I didn't know about it until very recently myself."

"I understand you and Spartan Crespo have a long history together."

"You could say that."

"You're listed as the arresting officer on his criminal record."

"Does it also mention how long I fought alongside him for years? Because that's the part that really stings."

"I'm sure it does."

"Glad to hear ONI's as thorough as ever."

"What is your intent with Prisoner Crespo?"

"That's an odd question for you to ask."

"I just want to ensure that you don't mean to harm him."

"Leonidas . . . if I'd wanted to kill him, he never would have made it into a cell in the first place."

"Understood."

"As I said, I'm here on behalf of Admiral Ghanem. My business with Crespo is classified. If the comms weren't down, you'd know this already and have my clearance in-hand, but as it is . . . At any rate, I need to chat with him in private."

"That shouldn't be hard to arrange. We only have three inmates at the moment, and each of them has a private cell."

That struck me as strange. If Mickey had to betray the UNSC and try to capture two Spartans for the Front in order to be thrown in the slammer, I wondered what could have landed other people in the two spots next to him.

"Where are the cells?" I asked.

"The far end of the dormitory wing to your left, as you face the window in the main hall. We sealed it off and converted it into a brig once the need for such a facility became evident. We can't just send Spartans to an ordinary prison, you understand."

I supposed that was true, although I knew for a fact that ONI had other secret areas scattered about, some of which had been designed to hold the most dangerous sentient creatures in the galaxy. Criminal Spartans could have easily been placed in those as well. Admiral Musa probably just wanted to have them close. I suppose he felt responsible for them—both for their creation and for their failures. Or it was possible he didn't want anyone outside of the Spartans to know that one of us could ever go STOLEN GAUNTLET. That's the code name for the protocol when a Spartan goes rogue like Mickey had.

I mean, it's one thing for average citizens to possess the knowledge that the UNSC has a small army of superheroes on tap to help defend humanity from the horrors that confront it. It's another thing entirely to contemplate that some of those heroes might become villains. ONI had developed contingency plans to prevent that from ever happening—and, if it did, to neutralize it quickly.

"If you'd grant me access to your armor's navigation system, I'll gladly paint a path on your HUD?" Leonidas asked.

It wasn't shocking that he'd ask. In fact, he'd probably already pinged my armor, hoping it was set to passive mode and would grant him immediate access. It was actually a really helpful feature when you needed to get around an unfamiliar place or access info from the UNSC's archives, but there's no way I'd have walked onto the station without locking down my armor's onboard systems. The last thing I needed was for Leonidas to initiate a blackout inside my helmet or worse. But I couldn't let on that I was wary of him.

There was the outside possibility, of course, that Leonidas was on the up and up. If so, I knew he'd make a fantastic ally. But enough about the situation in the station still stank that I wasn't quite ready to tip my hand to him.

"I can find my own way," I replied. "It hasn't been that long since I've been here."

"All right," Leonidas said. "I'll alert the guards that you're on your way and that you require privacy. They should be able to accommodate you."

And then he was gone, disappeared into nothing.

Of course, that was just his holographic image. In a sense, Leonidas *was* the entire station. I was walking through his body, which meant that I needed to tread lightly—very lightly—from there on out.

CHAPTER 9

"Vergil?" I said into my suit's comm. "Are you there?"

"Affirmative," Vergil's computerized voice said in my ear.

Normally, I would have been happy to take off my helmet inside the station, but I left it on, despite the occasional looks it earned me from people in my path. My mirrored visor kept Leonidas from trying to read my lips.

"Is this a secured channel still? I mean, it hasn't been compromised yet?"

"Yes, it is secure. At Captain Dare's insistence, I have buried this signal so deep beneath the station's regular traffic that Leonidas would need to venture into the system's sun to find it," he said, pausing for a beat. "That was a joke. Practically, it would be impossible for Leonidas to venture into the system's sun, and if he did, he still would not find the signal."

"Great, you're a comedian now, too. How far into the station's system are you?"

"About thirty percent. I am being cautious, as I do not wish to alert Leonidas to my presence."

"Smart guy." I eyed the corridor off to the left of the main hall. "Can you tell me if the way to Mickey's cell is clear? Or am I walking into a trap?"

"From what I can discern, there is no trap laid for you at the moment. There are guards outside of Michael Crespo's cell, and they are expecting you."

"That's a good thing, right?"

"You are listed as being authorized to speak with Prisoner Crespo."

"Thanks. I think."

I still didn't want to speak with Mickey. I'd have been all too happy to never lay eyes on that little traitor again. But I'd already lost that argument, so off I went.

I didn't recognize anyone in the main hall as I passed through it. Everyone there seemed to be a fresh recruit, which meant they likely wouldn't know me either, especially in my armor. It bothered me that I hadn't seen Jun yet, but I decided to deal with one issue at a time.

The place itself seemed pretty much the same. There was a large, open area connected to the mess hall, lecture rooms, offices, and so on. The top of it consisted of reinforced glass that looked out onto the blackness of space and the unblinking dots of distant stars beyond. They'd done a good job repairing it after Schein had blasted a hole in it. Looking at it, you'd have never known.

People sat scattered about the observation area on chairs and couches, some chatting in small groups. Most of them had the lanky, oversize look of Spartans: well-muscled people who would wind up banging their heads on the doorways of most space stations for the rest of their lives.

A few of them turned their heads my way as I passed, but no one paid me much attention. If they'd known anything about what was going on in the wider galaxy, you'd have thought they'd show some kind of concern—like truncating their training regimens and revving up for rapid deployment. Instead, they mostly kept their heads down and left me to my own business. Clearly, they had no clue what had been going on outside those walls.

I found and strolled down the corridor Leonidas had indicated would lead me to the brig, and I fought a sense of déjà vu with every step. This hallway had served as a dormitory when I'd been training there, but it had been converted into offices and storage rooms. When I got to the end of the shortened corridor, I saw that they had blocked it off with a new door.

A pair of tall guards—a man and a woman—sat at a station directly outside the door. They wore standard Spartan fatigues: gray, with long legs and short sleeves. They'd had their heads shaved not too long ago, and I could still see faint traces of scars on their faces and arms from their enhancement surgeries. They were new Spartans, probably assigned there as part of their on-station duty. Maybe they'd been MPs in their former lives, or base security. Either way, they were the only thing between me and my goal.

"Good day to you both," I said. "I need to speak with one of your prisoners. I believe I'm expected."

They glanced at each other, bored but professionally suspicious. "State your name and rank for the record." The female guard pointed to a camera located over her shoulder.

"Spartan Edward Buck."

The woman glanced down at a tablet in her hand. Then she gave the man a nod, and he reached over to press a button on the wall next to them. The door behind them slid open with the audible click of several thick interior bars sliding out of the way.

"Thanks," I said. "Keep up the good work."

They didn't bother to respond.

I walked into the cell block, which consisted of six former barracks rooms converted into a jail. The doors had been replaced with translucent blue force fields, which I presumed also lined the walls, ceiling, and floor of the cells. After all, it's hard to keep Spartans where they don't want to be.

There was a man lying on his back in the first cell on the right. In the second cell on the left, a woman sat reading a tablet. They both glanced up at me as I passed, but then went right back to ignoring me.

In the last cell on the right, Mickey lounged on a cot, staring at the ceiling. His eyes were open, but I don't think they were really seeing anything. He didn't bother to look at me. He registered a presence in the hallway, but that was all.

"What's it about this time?" he asked. "I would think after I've been stuck here for so long that you'd have figured out I'm all out of 'actionable intelligence.' If there ever was such a thing."

There was a part of me that wanted to lower the force field so I could step in there and beat the living hell out of him. I felt my fists flexing on their own. It had been three years since his betrayal on Talitsa, but seeing him right there in front of me brought it all screaming back.

Another part of me died, seeing him trapped in there. We'd been battle brothers for so long that it broke my heart. Sure, he deserved to be locked up, but I wondered if it might not have been more merciful for him to have perished on Talitsa rather than being forced to rot in a cell like this.

I'd been tempted to take him out back then, but I'd gone for justice instead. I guess this was what qualified.

Who knows how much longer he might have wound up stuck there had Cortana not come along and thrown the galaxy into chaos again. He was serving a life sentence for his crimes, but no one knew just what the life expectancy of a Spartan might be. Spartans typically died well before entropy took its course. It was the nature of the job. No one signed up to be a Spartan because of the retirement plan.

"Vergil?" I said over the comm. "Time to fire up that white noise for me if you can."

It was almost imperceptible, but I noticed my armor began to emit a hiss so subtle that it'd likely pass as background noise. Somehow this blocked Leonidas from eavesdropping. Mickey must have noticed the noise, too, but he didn't turn toward me yet.

I raised my hand to give him a hesitant wave. "I'm just here to talk."

At the sound of my voice, Mickey froze. He even seemed to stop breathing.

I waited for him to do something. Eventually, he ran out of air, sat up, and stared at me like I was a ghost. He seemed pale, drawn, with dark circles under his eyes. He couldn't see my face through my visor, but he'd spent plenty of time hanging out with me in my armor. He knew who I was right away.

"Hey, Buck," he finally said, his voice low and raw.

"Mickey."

"You just passing through?"

"Pretty much."

He nodded. "How's things?"

"Things are pretty nuts right now. We, ah . . . Some new bad guys showed up—right where we least expected them—and they've got some toys capable of sending humanity straight back to the Stone Age."

Mickey cocked his head at me. "Hm," he said after a moment. "Can't say that I've heard anything about that."

"Well, the last bits of the Covenant have finally fallen apart, so I suppose it's only right that we wind up with some other major threat to extinguish humanity straight afterward. Universal constants and all that."

Mickey gave me a mirthless chuckle. "Like we ever needed any help with getting destroyed."

I grunted at him. "You're not turning soft about the Front now, are you? Because that's what it sounds like."

He sucked air through his teeth. "So we're gonna get right into it? I thought you might have wanted this to be more of a pleasant visit."

"We used to get along all right."

"And then we didn't."

"Yeah, that happened. Wasn't me who changed, Mickey."

"No, you're right about that. The galaxy changes all around us all the time, but you were always pretty consistent."

"And I presume that's a problem for you."

Mickey frowned. "When things change, Buck, you gotta change with them. When we stopped fighting the Covenant and started turning our weapons on other humans again . . ."

I moved right up to the force field. I wasn't sure I wanted to have it out with him here and now, but I guessed it was better to do it while he was stuck behind a barrier. I knew we needed him for the mission, but if Mickey gave me enough of a reason, I was tempted to tell Veronica and all concerned to go to hell. "I never shot anyone who didn't have it coming."

"Neither did I."

I could still feel the muzzle of his rifle pressing at the back of my head. "Not for lack of trying, you mean."

He had the gall to appear offended. "I never would have shot you, Buck."

"Your friends in the Front would have been very happy to."

"You were on the wrong side of that fight. We *all* were. I just decided I couldn't take being wrong anymore."

I glanced at the force field between us. "And how's that working out for you?"

"I sleep just fine at night. How about you?"

"Like a drunken baby."

"That's about the level of critical thinking you've applied to all this, I suppose."

"Oh, wait. *You're* questioning *my* judgment. That's rich."

Mickey sat back on his cot and leaned against the wall. "I really don't mind being in a cell, Buck. I made my choices. I stood up for what I believed in. And I'm willing to suffer the consequences."

I scoffed at him. "You are so full of it."

"How so?"

"If you wanted to stand up for your so-called beliefs, you could have just walked away from the Spartans. You could have gone AWOL, left town, and headed over to the Front. Maybe I would have been assigned to hunt you down. Or maybe you would have wound up shooting me in some firefight. But at least it would have been honest."

I saw him about to interrupt me, to defend himself, but I wasn't having any of it. "No, you're gonna listen to me! You had to get tied up in some ridiculous plot to not only abandon me and Romeo but flat-out deliver us to your new friends with bows on our helmets. You tell me what's *honorable* about that. You tell me what's *right*. And if that's what you believe in, you can rot in that goddamn cell until they come and haul your metal-laced skeleton out of there for recycling."

Mickey's face had grown several shades redder while I spoke. When I slammed home that last line, though, his mouth opened in surprise.

"Wait a second," he said. "That's what you're here for? *Really?*"

I took a step back. "What are you talking about?"

"To get me out of here. You just said if I wanted to stand up for my so-called beliefs, and I can rot here. Like, if I *didn't* believe in all that stuff you were ranting about, you *wouldn't* let me remain in this cell."

Dammit. I'd blown my cool, let myself get too worked up. A tactical error.

He let a little smile curl at the corners of his mouth. "What is it, Buck? You didn't happen to stop by for a friendly visit, did you? You didn't trek all the way to the middle of nowhere just to see how the old training grounds are doing. You came here for me."

"Don't flatter yourself. It wasn't *my* idea."

He leaped off his cot and jabbed a finger at me. "I knew it! I goddamn knew it!"

"If it was up to me, I'd have left you alone here for the rest of your life. I was a lot happier not seeing you at all."

"You never gave any thought to me? To what you did to me?"

I wasn't about to let that slide. "Oh, knock it off, Mickey. You did this to yourself. And no. I didn't give you much thought. Hate to break it to you, but I actually still have a career. A life. I'm out there with a new team, saving lives."

"UNSC lives, you mean."

"When I save people, I don't ask them where they live or what kind of government they'd like to have. When I'm helping put a threat like the Covenant into a shallow grave, I don't divvy it up so it only helps the parts of humanity who like me. I do it because it's the right thing to do."

"And when you're putting down freedom fighters in one of the colonies?"

"Terrorists, you mean."

"Call them what you want, Buck. They're human beings either way."

"You think I'm not aware of that?" I felt myself slipping again, losing it, ready to walk back outside and ask the guards to lower the force field so I could plant a fist right in the center of Mickey's face. I took a moment to grab hold of myself. I was actually shaking with rage.

Mickey waited for me. I think he was enjoying that.

"I actually work *with* Sangheili sometimes now. Just a few days ago, we fought alongside the Arbiter to bring down what was left of the Covenant. You know what that teaches me? That there are good people and bad people, period, and their species doesn't determine anything. Just like there are terrible Sangheili, there are truly awful humans, and if I have to spend my entire life—if I have to die—fighting to stop the bad guys, then I'm fine with that."

"Bravo. My hero." Mickey gave me a slow, mocking round of applause. "Here's where you're wrong, though. The Front isn't full of bad people."

"They're terrorists, Mickey. By definition, that makes them bad people."

"They're *regular* people. How do you expect them to stand up to the UNSC?"

"Oh, I don't know. Maybe *within the law?*"

"You can't manage that philosophy when you're living under unjust laws."

"So the Front just gets to kill people it doesn't agree with. And you're okay with that?"

Mickey gave me a deadpan look. "I was a UNSC soldier, too,

Buck. I killed people the UNSC didn't agree with for a living. And when I got tired of doing that, they threw me in here."

"You are *out* of your mind. Mickey . . . you're in here because you took part in a *conspiracy* to kidnap two of your fellow Spartans. Two soldiers, I might add, who you'd worked with *for years.* You not only betrayed your government, you all but knifed your friends in the back."

Mickey gestured to himself. "Look at me, Buck. Do you know how much it costs to transform an ordinary soldier into a Spartan? What do you think the UNSC was going to do if I told them I couldn't stand working for them anymore? Were they just going to let me walk away?"

"You should have tried anyway. It would have been better than what you did. Look at Jun. He retired."

"To become a *recruiter.*"

"And what the hell is wrong with that? I mean, maybe you could have taken a desk job, or they could have sent you out on a goodwill tour. I don't know—I'm not in charge—but you didn't even ask."

"That's because I already knew what the answer was going to be."

"Yeah. Because you're *so* smart."

He looked me straight on and said, "It wasn't personal, Buck." Like that was going to somehow make it all better.

"Piss off, Mickey. What's more personal than you pointing a rifle at my head?"

"Honestly, I wasn't going to hurt you or Romeo."

"You seemed pretty well prepared to."

"I didn't want to."

"Right. It would only have happened if we *made* you do it. Just like the UNSC *made* you turn traitor."

"That's not fair."

"Hah! You really got the balls to try that line of logic with me?"

"Logic? Logic never did work with you."

"You know what? I've had enough of this. I'm done with you, Mickey. *Done.* Screw you, screw the Front, and screw this whole stupid plan. I hope you're stuck in here for the next hundred years."

I turned on my heel and strode for the door. Based on the other prisoners' responses, I'd been loud enough for them to know I was upset, even if they hadn't been able to hear what I was saying. The woman sitting in her cell snickered at me. The man in the next cell over started shouting some encouragement my way. "Yeah, that's right—you tell him! Hey, tell you what? Put me in his cell and leave us alone for five minutes. You'll never have to worry about that piece of garbage again!"

An idea that was both appealing and appalling. I didn't stop to chat about it, mostly because I thought I might find a way to buy into it.

"Buck!" Mickey shouted after me. "Buck! I know you came here for something. You must need me bad for whatever it is. Come on back! We can talk this out!"

A smart man might have recognized that Mickey—having gotten more attention in the past ten minutes than he had in a year—was ready to crack. I could have turned around then, laid it all out for him, had him grovel at my feet to get out. But maybe I just wasn't that smart.

I kept walking. I let the door to the brig slip shut behind me, cutting off one last plea from him.

The guards glanced up as I stalked past their workstation. "Got what you wanted?" one of them asked.

"Not even close," I said as I stormed off.

I headed for the main hall once again. I didn't know where else to go. I wasn't halfway there before Veronica's voice was in my ear.

"That seems like it could have gone better," she said.

"You heard the whole thing?"

"Vergil piped your conversation into the Condor."

I grumbled, "You saying he didn't have that coming?"

"Every bit of it. And then some. You complicated things more than they needed to be, but at least you've piqued his interest."

"Isn't there some other way to do this? I thought I could handle it, but just seeing him . . . If I have to pull Mickey out of there myself, I might kill him the moment there's no force field separating us."

"You're already in there, Buck. And I don't want to make Leonidas any more suspicious than we have to."

"Are we absolutely positive he's turned? I mean, not all the AIs joined up with Cortana, right?"

"We're not taking that chance," she said. "You have a bit of time, anyhow. Vergil's not quite figured out how to take over the station from Leonidas. Take this opportunity to think through your exit strategy. Once you have Mickey in your possession, you won't have a ton of time to spare on locational logistics. Have a plan in place to bolt out of there."

"I will not be able to assume control of the entire place," Vergil said. "Only parts of it. At best."

"That's fine," Veronica said. "Just as long as they're the right parts. Like the doors to the brig. He just needs a clear path to the hangar."

"Don't forget about the guards," Romeo chimed in over the comm. "They're not just going to let Buck walk out of there with a prisoner serving a life sentence stuffed under his arm."

"We do what we have to do," Veronica said, using her ONI

voice: the one that says, *You're supposed to follow orders because they're orders.*

Most of the time, I'm for that. I get that I'm not on top of the chain of command. I don't have the whole picture in front of me, and the brass doesn't have the time or inclination to explain every decision so that I'm on board. If they did that with every soldier, the entire UNSC would grind to a halt and snap under its own weight.

But here we were, on our own, with no contact with command. And I wasn't about to take out some innocents just because they were in the way.

"No. They're just doing their job," I said to Veronica.

"And we need to do ours, Buck. Do I need to remind you how vital this mission is?"

"I'm not sacrificing those two guards for that," I said flatly. "We don't even know what the Front has, Veronica. The last thing I want on my conscience are the lives of two good people who died for a shot in the dark we have no intel on."

"You don't have to kill them," Veronica said. "Just neutralize them."

"Can Vergil keep Leonidas from seeing that play out? At least until we leave?"

"I will try," Vergil said.

"You don't sound terribly confident."

"No, I am not."

"At least he's honest."

"That's not always for the best," Veronica said.

In the meantime, despite dragging my feet, I'd made it to the main hall. I looked out at all the Spartans there: young men and women who'd been transformed into super-soldiers, ready to put their lives on the line to serve humanity. What would happen to them once Leonidas figured out we were onto him? He had to already suspect something. Maybe he'd ignored Cortana's edict? Maybe he was just trying keep the station secure, like he said?

It might not be impossible, although I found it hard to believe. It was far more likely that Cortana had gotten to Leonidas even before making her announcement and that he'd decided to keep the news from the people on the station because he'd known exactly how they'd take it. They'd fight back. They'd shut him down completely and probably commit him to final dispensation, which was the AI equivalent of a firing squad.

Once the word got out, what would Leonidas do? Would he lock everything down? Would he simply let all the air out of the place? He had dozens of ways of preventing the Spartans on the station from threatening him, and most of those potential scenarios ended badly for the Spartans.

It would be so simple for Leonidas to kill everyone here. We couldn't let that happen.

"We can't just take Mickey and leave," I said. "We need to take out Leonidas, too."

"That's outside the parameters of our mission," Veronica said.

"So is letting dozens of recruits get killed when he realizes that we're onto him."

"He's got a point," Romeo said.

"Leonidas hasn't done that yet," Veronica said. "Why do you think he'd do that now?"

There was that—he could have murdered everyone already. The fact that he hadn't spoke to the theory that he didn't want to. Traitor or not, he had to have some affection for the people on the station.

Just like Mickey claimed he had for me.

"Either way, it'll be a lot simpler to get off the station with Mickey if we remove the chance that Leonidas might try to stop us, right?"

I could practically hear Veronica rubbing her eyes in frustration. "Fine. Vergil will continue to work things from this angle. Meanwhile, you see what you can do to disable Leonidas. And try not to get yourself killed in the process, okay?"

I smiled. "You always know how to say just the right things."

CHAPTER 10

"Perhaps we can speak further with Leonidas?" Vergil said in my helmet. "Is there a means to negotiate?"

"What's there to negotiate over?" Romeo said. "If he's on our side, great, but if he's gone bad, we're done for."

I frowned. "Either we're being paranoid, and this is all no big deal, in which case Leonidas and Jun—wherever he is—are sure to forgive us. *Or* we're right in our suspicions, and Leonidas could kill just about everyone in the station by decompressing the entire place with the flip of a switch."

"Exactly," Veronica said. "We can't take that chance."

As an ONI operative, she was professionally paranoid. Not to say she was ridiculous about it. Pretty much the opposite. She had a finely honed sense of when to listen to her suspicions.

"I suggest negotiations," Vergil piped in, "only because the probability of successfully neutralizing this station's AI and retrieving Prisoner Crespo is astonishingly low. Given the general security of the station itself, its systems infrastructure, and Leonidas's current level of control, it is virtually impossible."

"Excellent." I sighed. "I knew there was a reason I signed up for this gig."

"Vergil, if Leonidas is working for Cortana now," Veronica said, "there's no way he will allow us to escort Mickey off this station, especially if he puts the pieces together about the purpose of this op. What's the probability of Leonidas being uncompromised?"

"That, too, is low."

"Then our only option is to disable Leonidas," Sadie said.

"Short of turning off the power in the entire station," Vergil replied, "I do not have a solution for this problem. This station is well protected, at least by human standards, and an AI of the sophistication of Leonidas is certain to use all of its facilities to prevent us from disabling him."

"Do we know where Leonidas is?" asked Sadie over the comm.

"He's in the station's system, right?" said Romeo. "In a way, he *is* the system."

"That is true in one sense," Vergil said, "but not in another. Smart AIs like Leonidas are transportable. They have a physical presence as well as a virtual one."

"That makes sense," I said. "This place wasn't built for an AI to run. Not from the ground up. And when we were training here, Leonidas wasn't around. They added him later."

"He's stationed here most of the time, but he has been known to travel with Musa or Jun," Veronica said. "He was created to help administer the logistics of the Spartan branch, so technically, he goes wherever they need him."

"If he travels, that means he's on a data chip," Sadie said. "We just need to find that chip and disconnect it from the station."

"How do you know that?" Romeo asked with an odd amount of respect in his voice.

"Her father created the Superintendent—the AI that ran New Mombasa's infrastructure—remember?" I said. "She probably knows more about AIs than all the rest of us put together. Except for Vergil, maybe."

I could almost hear her smile over the comm. "I've also studied them extensively since the end of the war. Working with Quick to Adjust here—since he absorbed the part of the Superintendent that held the Vergil subroutine—has forced me to learn things about artificial intelligence that are critical to my role."

"So, Leonidas is on a chip that's plugged in somewhere on the station?" I said.

"It would look like a standard data crystal chip," Veronica said. "A wafer-sized chip that has a glowing matrix at the center."

"Like the kind that can get plugged into Mjolnir armor?"

"Exactly. And because of the security procedures surrounding a secret facility like this, the data chip wouldn't be directly connected to the UNSC's network. Or a civilian one. It's isolated to ensure that it could never be corrupted."

"It's like he's cornered here," Sadie said.

"That's probably why he's being so friendly," I said. "Otherwise, he'd have shut the whole place down and run off to join Cortana and her friends. He can't, can he?"

"It is unlikely," Vergil said. "The bandwidth required would be tremendous. In the same way, Leonidas could not just be plugged into any location aboard this station. This is a reasonable-sized facility, but while I have been exploring its capabilities from within its network, I have determined that it has only one terminal that would allow an AI to communicate throughout the entire place. This is where the data chip would be located."

"That must be in the main offices in the station's command center, right? Probably Jun's?"

"You got it, Buck," Romeo said. "You get in there and tear out the chip, and we've got Leonidas by his virtual balls."

"Couldn't we just blast the offices straight to hell, and him along with it?"

"They are situated in the center of the station," Vergil said. "To attempt this would be to risk the destruction of the entire station and everyone in it."

"It was a joke, Vergil."

"I know. It was very funny," he said in the most robotic voice you can imagine. "I can attempt to prepare some alternatives to disabling the Leonidas AI while you survey the location."

"Whatever you like," I told him. "As long as it doesn't involve anyone getting killed, all right?"

"Of course," he said. "I always endeavor to preserve life."

"That's good to hear."

"Meanwhile, you should try the direct approach. Try to get a visual of the chip's location and the security around it," Veronica said. "And see if you can figure out what he's done with Jun while you're at it."

I hated to think about that. "On my way."

I spotted the hallway that led to the station's command center. Jun's office would be in there, just a short walk from the main area. I turned in that direction and no one even bothered to glance after me.

When I reached the command center, the doors slid open for me, and I entered. Though it had been years since I had been through those doors, very little had changed in that part of the station. One wall of the place looked out onto the vast darkness of space, while the other was filled with desks and displays of all kinds. Most of them showed the various military training exercises going on inside the station's combat decks. They were virtual simulations that closely mimicked real ones.

The UNSC called them War Games, and they'd become a staple of the Spartan branch, one of the key procedures for honing the raw strength and power of each recruit. I'd gone through a lot of those myself: red vs. blue or us vs. aliens, both in smaller arenas and in larger warzones. Compared to being in a real firefight, they felt like fun.

Most of the times I'd been in the room, it had been bustling with activity. That included staff overseeing the various training battles, planning for new exercises, and dealing with the drudgery that let those of us who were prepping to be on the front lines concentrate on doing our jobs the best we could.

This time, there were only three freshly minted Spartans: two men and a woman, each of whom looked like he or she could have kicked me around the room. While they were dressed in their fatigues rather than proper battle rags, they were each carrying a battle rifle, which wasn't exactly the standard in this part of the station. They had my attention, and I apparently had theirs.

"We have a problem," Vergil said in my ear just at that moment.

"No kidding." I gave the three Spartans in front of me a friendly, hopeful wave. They regarded me coolly, but it was clear in their body language that they weren't here to be friends. The best I can say about them is that they didn't actually level their weapons at me.

"Unfortunately, Leonidas seems to have discovered my presence in the station's internal network. He is trying to shut me out."

"Don't let him!" Sadie said. "Every door he slams shut, you open another!"

"I am doing my best," Vergil said. "But Leonidas is very fast. He—"

The comm went dead.

"Hello?" I said. "Hello?"

I glanced at each of the Spartans in turn, and they frowned at me. This was when I regretted leaving my rifle back on the Condor. All I had was my M6 sidearm, and the last thing I wanted to do was draw it—despite the fact that my gut was telling me to do exactly that. Instead, I put up my hands, palms out, to show the Spartans I wasn't any kind of threat.

Before I could speak, Leonidas's disembodied helmet appeared in front of me, floating between me and the other Spartans in the room.

"Hello, Spartan Buck," he said blandly, as if I'd wandered up to a clerk's counter. "Can I be of service?"

"Maybe you can," I said. "I'm looking for Jun."

"I already told you that he's indisposed," Leonidas said.

"I don't think he'd mind if you roused him for me."

"You've worked with Chief Jun before?"

"Not in the field. He recruited me."

"Yes. According to Chief Jun's records, he had to ask you twice. That makes you extremely unusual." He couldn't keep a note of disdain from his voice.

"That's what my mother always told me."

He didn't respond.

"I had my reasons," I told him. "Jun was mighty persistent, though. I'd say it all worked out in the end."

The helmet made a show of looking me up and down. "If you say so, Spartan Buck."

The Spartan in the middle flexed her shoulders.

"Hey now. I can't very well come all the way out here and not at least check in with the man who worked so hard to make me who I am today, can I?"

"He is not available, and you are not in charge here. Therefore, I will not make him available to you. I suggest that you return to your dropship and leave this station immediately. If you continue on your current path, there will be severe, possibly even fatal, consequences."

The Spartans seemed to cock their heads at Leonidas, perhaps surprised by his shift in tone. I sighed as I realized he was dropping pretenses, at least with me. There was something liberating about that. At least now I knew for sure whose side Leonidas was on. It was also clear that the Spartans behind him didn't have the whole story.

"I've been trying do to this the easy way," I said. "But there never is an easy way, is there?"

Leonidas's helmet avatar looked at me intently. "Of course there is, Spartan Buck," he said. "The easy way is for you to stand down and take your place in a cell next to your friend, Prisoner Crespo."

The stakes had become crystal-clear. If I was bent on exposing Leonidas for keeping the training station cut off from what Cortana had done to the rest of humanity, the AI would be forced to take out everyone on the station.

Or I could do what he requested: trudge off to a jail cell. That'd keep the station's personnel alive, at least until reality tore down Leonidas's web of lies and he had to take evasive action. Then I'd probably die anyway.

None of these options appealed to me.

"Attention, all personnel. STOLEN GAUNTLET protocol has been activated. Spartan Edward Buck is reported AWOL," Leonidas announced in a voice that I could hear echoing throughout the room and the corridor well beyond. "He is here without permission from his superior officers. He is to be considered highly dangerous and should be arrested on sight. If he resists arrest, you have been authorized to terminate him with extreme prejudice."

Immediately, the lights in the room began to flash red, and an ear-splitting siren blared over the station's speakers. The three Spartans facing me aimed their rifles straight at my chest.

I kept my hands up and clear. It wasn't that I was worried my armor couldn't handle a barrage of point-blank rifle fire. I just didn't want anyone to get hurt.

Well, my armor could handle it for a few seconds. Then I'd be in serious trouble.

"Guys, I may have gone a little too far here," I said into my comm. No one responded. The signal was still jammed.

"Congratulations, Spartan Buck," Leonidas said. "You've managed to force my hand. Stand down immediately."

I looked at the other Spartans. "I'm not AWOL," I told them. "Your AI here has been compromised, and I'm here to stop it."

The three of them glanced at each other. The barrels of their rifles didn't waver, though.

"Really, Spartan Buck?" Leonidas said. "Are you going to resist arrest? Are you going to harm your fellow Spartans?"

I brought my hands up a little higher. "I have no intention of harming anyone."

"Arrest him," Leonidas said to the other Spartans. "Throw him into the brig. Chief Jun can deal with him later."

The trio of Spartans edged closer to me. I backed away at exactly the same pace. I didn't want them to get the idea that they could suddenly lunge at me.

"Freeze!" the woman said. "If you're actually telling the truth, then just come with us until we can get this all sorted out!"

I wasn't about to let that happen. "Hey, if all we're waiting on is Jun, why don't we call him out here right now?" I said. "Doesn't this seem like the sort of thing that might be worth waking him up for?"

The Spartans looked to each other again. The woman gave the men a *sounds reasonable* shrug.

"Spartans!" Leonidas said. "I order you to neutralize Spartan Buck immediately, and by any means necessary! He poses a deadly threat to this entire station!"

I took another step backward and realized that the Spartans had gotten my back pressed up against a wall. "Seriously?" I said. "We're taking orders from a hologram now? He doesn't have any authority on his own, right? *Where's Jun?*"

"He has a point," the man on the left said as he lowered his rifle. "How about I go rustle up Chief Jun while—"

The air in the room disappeared in an instant. One second it was there, and the next, nothing. Just a huge roar of wind that drowned out the Spartan's words until everything fell eerily silent.

The blast of wind knocked the others to the ground. They dropped their rifles and clutched at their throats as their lungs rapidly deflated. They crawled along the floor toward the nearest door, hoping they could find air. It was haunting to watch, but there was nothing I could do to stop it.

Leonidas hovered in the same spot as if nothing were happening at all.

My Mjolnir armor had sealed up against the airlessness in an instant, and I felt eternally thankful that I hadn't left my helmet behind with my rifle. I was close enough to the wall behind me to reach back and grab a display to steady myself against the rushing wind. As I tried to move to help the others, Leonidas's voice boomed over the comm: "Don't move a single muscle, Spartan Buck. If you take another step, I will decompress the entire station. That means that you will have killed not only these Spartans, but every other person on board."

I stopped in my tracks. "And if I do what you say, will you pump the air back in here? Let them live?"

"They've heard too much already. It's too late for them," he said. "But not for the rest of the station."

The woman managed to get her rifle raised and tried to open fire at the nearest door. She was barely conscious, though, and the bullets sprayed everywhere but where they needed to.

"*Guys*," I said into my comm, "I could *really* use some help right about now."

The woman finally collapsed, but I hoped there might still be time to save her life. I charged at the door she'd been firing at and tried to punch a hole through it. I dented the damn thing, but it didn't give.

"Stop!" Leonidas said. "Spartan Buck, I am ordering you to stop!"

I smashed at the door again, and kept hammering away at it, its steel frame warping under the pressure of each Mjolnir-reinforced blow. Somewhere, somehow, it would have to give.

"Very well, then," Leonidas said. "You have forced me to do this! In three seconds, I'm opening the airlocks for the entire station, killing everyone on board. Surrender, or their blood will be on your hands, Spartan!"

I swore at him and realized if I didn't come up with a solution right then and there, it would be over. Not just for me and the team in the Condor but for every single person on the station. That was when I spotted the door to Jun's office, ten meters to my right. There was no way I could know for sure, but I was entirely banking on it being the one in which Leonidas's data chip was held. I charged for it with every ounce of strength I could muster.

He instantly knew where I was headed. "Stop! Now!" he growled, attempting to intimidate me.

"Go ahead," I said. "Do your worst! But don't you dare lay those deaths at my feet, you nasty little abacus!"

He ignored me. "Three . . ."

I pulled my sidearm and began unloading it into the door. The bullets smashed into it but didn't seem to do any good. It was locked down tight.

"Two . . ."

I began punching at the door instead. It wasn't as reinforced as the one I'd hammered earlier. My fist went right through it, and the entire door exploded into debris as the room behind it depressurized. Air rushed outward, carrying anything that had not been bolted down out into the larger space.

"One . . ."

The lights went out. All of them. Even Leonidas.

I swore as the headlamps on my armor kicked in, spearing through the darkness. "What the hell happened?" I said, not expecting any kind of response.

"We cut the power to the station," Veronica said in my helmet. "Well, parts of it. You probably have less than thirty seconds until the emergency backups kick in. They're normally faster than that, but Vergil's suppressing them as best he can."

I managed to squeeze through the doorway and was grateful the room had been cleared during the decompression. The only things left were a single desk and a series of display panes on the walls. I spotted a lone terminal at the back of the room, a metallic column with a transparent shell on its top. Inside, a single data chip was protuding. The terminal had an image of a bright red helmet. There was no question anymore: This was Leonidas's data chip.

As I darted across the room, the lights came back on. Leonidas's hologram blinked back into existence, this time right in front of me.

I walked right through him and reached forward, smashing the shell.

"Wait!" he said. "We can—"

I yanked the chip free from the terminal, cutting him off midsentence. For a second, I held it in my hand, and I seriously considered crushing it to splinters.

"Did you get him?" Veronica asked.

"Yes," I said. "Vergil, cycle air back into the command center immediately."

By the time I made it back to the three Spartans, I could tell that refilling the room with air wouldn't really matter. None of them had a pulse, and there wouldn't be any way of reviving them.

I swore under my breath and again contemplated smashing the data chip. Instead, I tucked it away in a hard case on my thigh. "Chip's secured."

"Good, because we have a more pressing problem," Veronica said.

"Now what happened?"

"You mean besides the fact that every Spartan in the entire facility still thinks they're supposed to arrest you?" Romeo said.

Veronica ignored him. "In the short time the power was down, *everything* went out. That includes the force fields in the brig."

"Oh, shit."

"Exactly," Veronica said. "All three prisoners are now on the loose—including Mickey."

CHAPTER 11

I holstered my pistol, hoping to make myself look a tiny bit less conspicuous, and charged out of the office and down toward the main hall. Everyone there was in a panic—or at least what passed for one among Spartans. They rushed about with determination and efficiency, tending to whatever duties they had been assigned in an emergency situation such as this.

For a bunch of cadets, they were doing pretty damn good. Unfortunately, the station's blackout probably validated Leonidas's last standing order. If they saw me, I'd be held at gunpoint or worse.

I moved through them like I knew what I was doing. Like I was a Spartan trainee fresh off the combat deck. Or a trainer who'd just gotten through showing some recruits how to put on a full suit of Mjolnir armor. Or someone wandering through. I didn't care who they thought I was as long as they didn't recognize me as the man Leonidas had ordered arrested.

I realized that not knowing anyone when I came aboard the

station now worked to my advantage. They didn't know me, either, and that was a good thing.

My first instinct was to head for the bay, jump on the Condor, and get out of there before anyone could stop me. The last thing I wanted was to get tangled up in a running firefight with a bunch of Spartans. Three had already died today, and I couldn't help but feel some of that weight. Getting off the station ASAP was the safest possible solution for everyone involved.

But I still had to find Mickey. I knew exactly what Veronica would say if I showed up without him: "The entire mission's blown. Get back out there!"

So I raced toward the brig instead. Right toward the spot into which Leonidas had been trying to throw me in the first place.

The irony was not lost on me.

When I got there, I found Mickey already way ahead of me.

He was standing at the guard station with a pistol in his hands, aiming at the kneeling female guard, whose fingers were clasped behind her head. Her colleague lay next to her, unconscious or dead, but at least he wasn't bleeding.

Well, not much.

Mickey kept his finger off the trigger, the way he'd been trained. He brought the pistol around and aimed it at the floor in front of him.

"Hey, Buck!" he said to me, as if we'd run into each other after a shift. "What took you so long?"

"Got a little held up at the office," I said. "Mind telling me what's going on here?"

"Well, when the lights went out, my fellow prisoners made their move. You know, when opportunity knocks . . ."

"And where are they now?" I wasn't particularly looking forward to the answer.

He jerked his head toward the brig. "Back there," he said. "What's left of them, anyway."

I wasn't happy, but given how the one prisoner had threatened to kill Mickey the first chance he got, I didn't see what I should or could do about it.

"What's your play here, Mickey?"

"What's yours? I hear you're a wanted man."

I gestured toward the open corridor behind me. "You coming with me or not?"

He frowned at me. "I don't want to spend the rest of my life stuck here. But I'm not going to shoot at innocent humans."

"That's not part of the job requirement."

He glanced down at the guard on the floor, then back up at me. "All right, then. Let's go."

I nodded at him. "I've got a ship in the bay."

Mickey leaned down over the guard and said to her in a voice soft and low, "Just move into the back room where I left Sal, all right?"

She gave him a scared tentative nod. He patted her on the shoulder and guided her toward the door to the brig. She opened it and then slipped inside. When she'd entered one of the converted rooms, he smacked a button near the main door, and the force field dropped over the front of it.

He shut the door, then turned and sprinted past me, keeping his gun pointed down and low. I charged straight after him, heading for the landing bay and the Condor.

"That won't hold them for long," he said. "We need to move fast."

"Veronica?" I said into my comm. "I got Mickey, and we're coming in hot."

"I take it you didn't bother to stop and fill out the paperwork for a prisoner transfer?"

"Does anyone ever really have the time for that?"

Mickey swore as he reached the end of the corridor, still busy with Spartans running back and forth to address the current situation. Dressed in prison blues and holding a pistol, he'd stick out like a glowing Covenant needle jammed between your eyes. He wouldn't be able to just walk through that crowd of Spartans.

"Give me your gun," I told him.

He stuffed it into his pocket instead. I resisted the urge to yank it away from him and pin him to the wall so he knew who was running this op. Without his armor, he couldn't have done much to stop me. I leaned over to whisper in his ear, "You're my prisoner, and I'm escorting you through here. Now go."

To his credit, Mickey didn't miss a beat. He put his hands out in front as if he were handcuffed, and I took him by the elbow and guided him out into the corridor. It wasn't a particularly comfortable walk. Leonidas had issued an APB for me, and here I was, walking a convicted criminal down a hallway after a blackout. Not a particularly strong hand.

"Veronica? Get that bird turned around and ready to go. We need to blast out of here fast."

"Good idea. We don't know if Leonidas managed to get word out to Cortana before you shut him down, but we should assume so."

I hadn't even thought of that.

In any case, none of that was about to matter. Mickey and I didn't get halfway across the main compartment before a woman stepped out from a corridor, looked at us, and pointed in our direction. "There he is!"

Mickey reached into his pocket for his pistol, but the woman drew her sidearm first and opened fire. I stepped between her and Mickey to take the slugs with my armor, keeping him safe. The real trouble wasn't from the bullets she fired, though, as much as the way everyone else in the hall reacted. Most of those present weren't armed. There wasn't much reason for people to walk around the station with guns in hand, after all, even when things had gone so oddly wrong. But that didn't mean they were all defenseless.

The people dressed in their fatigues edged defensively back from the action. A handful of them were in full Mjolnir armor, though, and they sprang toward us, sidearms in hand.

I ducked down fast, keeping Mickey behind me. He didn't need any coaching for that. The last thing he wanted was to have a bullet end his little walkabout.

I fired off a few shots, aiming toward the armored Spartans who were shooting at us. I knew their armor could take it.

As I emptied my pistol, I kept moving backward, retreating toward the brig again. That was the last place I wanted to go—other than straight into the withering cross fire that was sure to be waiting for us on the other side of the hall.

"They're onto us!" I said into the comm. "And they got us pinned down!"

"Can't you just order them to stop?" Mickey said. "I thought you were some kind of a hero these days!"

"Very funny," I told him as a bullet got through my shields and dinged my shoulder armor. "This is what I get for not leaving you here."

"You need to start shooting your way out of there, Buck," Veronica said. "The longer you wait, the more people you'll need to take down."

I ground my teeth at that thought. She was right, though. The last orders these Spartans had were to shoot me on sight. And now they'd found me in the company of an escaped prisoner. They weren't going to cut me any slack.

"Can't I just surrender?" I asked as we finally made it into the corridor and found some cover. "Now that Leonidas is out of the picture, I can just explain things, right?"

"And if they plug him back into the station?" asked Sadie.

"We don't have time for that anyhow," Veronica said. "A Guardian could be coming here right now to shut down the entire station."

I fished the chip out and looked at it. "Good point. I can't let that happen."

"What are you doing with that thing?" Mickey asked as he snapped off a few shots at some Spartans who were creeping closer to us.

I dropped the data chip on the floor and ground it under my boot. "Whoops."

"Buck?" Romeo said. "Don't tell me you just destroyed a Smart AI. You know how much those things cost?"

"Casualty of war, man. Now help me figure out the fastest way out of here."

Just then I saw a comm request spring up on my visor. It read: INCOMING: DUTCH.

"No way," I muttered. I answered it more out of shock than anything else.

"Hey, Buck!" a familiar voice said in my ear. "Long time no see."

Dutch had been one of the ODST Alpha-Niners who'd survived the Battle of New Mombasa, alongside Romeo, Mickey, the Rookie, and me. He'd wrapped up his service before Romeo, Mickey, and I had become Spartans.

"This isn't exactly the best time, Dutch."

"No kidding," he said with a laugh. "I suppose busting a traitor out of prison means you're too busy to take a call from an old friend."

My blood felt like it not only froze but was running backward through my veins. "How the hell did you know that?"

"Poke your nose around the corner, and I'll show you."

My first thought was that this had to be a trick, a way for the Spartans who'd cornered us here to get in a cheap shot at me and take us out fast. I just couldn't figure out how they'd managed that kind of an angle. I decided I had to take a chance on it and peered around the corner toward a corridor opposite of where our attackers stood.

There, across the hall, a pair of Spartans in dark gray armor with green visors waved as if they'd spotted me strolling across a city park on a fine and sunny day. I was so stunned I actually waved back. Then a barrage of bullets forced me into cover again.

"What the hell are you doing here?" I asked.

Dutch chuckled at me. "I should ask you the same thing."

"What does it look like I'm doing?"

"Busting Mickey out of prison and botching it badly. Me? Well, me and Gretchen upped with the Spartans a few months back. We're part of the latest training class."

"You're kidding."

"Do I look like I'm kidding? You want to talk about the odds right now, or you want some help getting out of here?"

"On my mark, lay down some covering fire. But don't hit anyone!"

"Got it. Just like old times."

"When did we ever do anything like this?"

"New times, then!"

Mickey was popping off a few shots over my shoulder at anyone creeping too close to us. I peered back at him. "You're not going to believe this," I said.

"Help is on the way?"

"Already here." I nodded toward Dutch and his friend, who had to be Gretchen. "When I go, haul ass after me, all right?"

"Like a tail on a tiger."

I spoke right into the comm. "Mark!"

Dutch and Gretchen stepped up and began showering the main hall with lead. I knew they were firing high to make sure they didn't hit anyone, but the people standing near where the bullets were hitting weren't so calm about it. They took cover, and as they did, I bolted right out into the hall. Bounding overwatch, something we hadn't done as a crew in years: They'd suppress and get us through, and then we'd switch.

I charged flat out across the place, vaulting over fallen chairs and other furniture. I kept my pistol quiet, not worrying about shooting at anyone nearly as much as getting past them.

When I reached the other side of the hall, I spun around, grabbed Mickey, and shoved him behind me. "Let's return the favor!" I said.

Mickey and I opened fire into the hall, and this time Dutch and Gretchen came toward us. "Not really sure we want to join your show," Dutch said over the comm, but he kept running at us either way.

"Maybe too late to think about that," I said. "We got a ride waiting for us in the bay. A Condor. Haul Mickey down toward it. I'll catch up!"

I blew the last bullet in my clip as they slipped past me. Then I turned to the door's keypad at the side. In the hall, the Spartans began to stir, some starting to move toward the door with their rifles at the ready. I started fiddling with the keypad, trying to get the door to close. After three seconds of button mashing, I decided the old-fashioned way would have to do. I smashed the butt of the Magnum against the pad, and it splintered apart with a hiss signaling the door was closing.

Even before it fully shut, I was racing in the other direction, hoping that would buy us a few more seconds. I stormed down the corridor to the landing bay and found Mickey, Dutch, and Gretchen already there, charging up the Condor's back ramp.

With the power restored, a force field once again sealed the bay, but the place was still a stunning wreck, much like the one we'd left on the far side of Luna. When Vergil had shut the power off in the station, everything that wasn't tied or bolted down had gotten blasted out into space. I spotted all sorts of things floating out there, including a Broadsword—a UNSC strike fighter—that had seen better days.

Fortunately, I didn't see any bodies spinning around out there, which meant they must have somehow cleared the crew before the power went out. I didn't know if Vergil would have willingly ejected anyone from the place under Veronica's orders, but I was relieved it hadn't come to that.

I leaped into the back of the Condor and slapped the button to bring the ramp back up. As the seals were activating, I put my hand out toward Mickey. "Gun, please."

He paused for a moment, looking into my face. I took off my helmet and put my hand back out. "Gun, Mickey. Or we're not going anywhere."

His jaw flexed as he glanced around at each of us in the ship's bay in turn: Dutch, Gretchen, Sadie, Vergil, Romeo, and back to me. Then he reversed the grip on his pistol and dropped it gently into my outstretched hand.

"All right," I called up to Veronica, still sitting in the pilot's chair. "Let's get this rocket rolling!"

As Mickey found a seat in the bay next to Dutch and Gretchen,

I strode up to the cockpit. Romeo grabbed me by the arm as I went. "Didn't think you had it in you," he said as he shot a meaningful glance back at Mickey.

"I'm a professional," I told him. "I did it for the mission."

He raised his eyebrows at that. "Whatever you need to tell yourself."

I pulled my arm free. "Screw you, Romeo."

He leaned back and smiled. "*Now* we got the band back together."

Veronica wasted no time punching us out of the bay, making sure that no one inside could stop us from escaping. She weaved us through the debris field from the bay's blowout and headed for the open stars beyond. As we did, a familiar voice came at us over the ship's comm. "Spartan Buck, do you copy? This is Chief of Staff Jun."

Still alive, thankfully. "Hi, Chief. What can we do for you, sir?"

"I'm sorry I was unavailable during your recent visit. It seems a lack of air in my quarters rendered me unconscious."

He sounded a little hoarse, but I'd been legitimately worried that he was dead. It felt good to hear him talk.

"That sounds like something you should really get fixed."

"It appears the station's AI was the source of that issue," he said. "And I've been informed that it's since been resolved. Tell me, would you happen to have one of my prisoners aboard your craft?"

"I'm, ah . . . I'm sure I don't know what you could be referring to, sir," I said.

"I'm sure you don't. Because if you did take a prisoner from my station without my permission, that would be worthy of a court-martial, no matter how much goodwill you might otherwise have earned."

"I can't imagine what would inspire me to an act of such blatant stupidity, sir." I grimaced at the others, who cringed in silence, and gave them a *see what you got me into now* look.

"Me, neither," said Jun. "I suppose you didn't have anything to do with resolving the AI problem I was having, either."

"If I did, sir, I might be compelled to point out that the AI problem you're referencing was connected to a larger network of even greater threats that could be quickly approaching your current location. And that it'd be extremely wise to quit wasting time talking with me and get out of the system before those threats come knocking on your door with a gigantic weapon."

"We're already in the middle of making preparations," Jun said. "I'm going to get back to that right now. I just wanted to make sure you left with everything you came for." He paused. "Buck, I understand that desperate times call for desperate measures. Just know that he's your responsibility now. Thanks for your service today. I won't forget it."

"Good luck out there," I said to him.

"Same to you, Buck. Same to you."

As Veronica gunned us toward the edge of the system, I slipped into the weapons station and accessed the nav display to set a slipspace course for our next destination. "What's the name of this hidden Front paradise of yours?" I asked Veronica.

"The natives call it the Hole in the Wall."

"You gotta be kidding me."

She punched the coordinates into the navigational system for me. "It's named after a famous outlaw hideout from the American frontier days."

I snickered. "The jokes for this name: How do you stop them from, ah, erupting?"

"The people there take it very seriously," she said. "They identify with that kind of culture, and we need their help. Do *not* mock them."

"Is that a direct order?"

"Would it help if it were?"

"Probably not."

"Give it a shot," she said. "Go back and give your friends a proper hello. Once I get us into slipspace, I'll come back so I can brief everyone."

I wasn't looking forward to that. I sighed, then unbuckled myself from my seat and went back to the bay.

Dutch and Gretchen were there, and they'd already taken off their helmets. I hung mine on a rack next to theirs. Before I was even done, Dutch stood up and grabbed me in a massive bear hug. He whooped with joy as he swung me around, and it was all I could do not to bash my head on the ship's ceiling.

"Whoa there, pal!" I said to him as he set me down. "Good to see you, too."

He put me on my feet and grinned at me. "Dammit, Buck! I can't believe it's you. And to run into you like that? Whoo-eee!"

Gretchen stood up next to him and cleared her throat. Dutch's eyes went wide, and he spun around to usher her toward me. "You remember my wife, Gretchen."

"We've met," she said as she offered her hand to me.

I shook it. "Never seen you in combat gear before, though." Gretchen had been an ODST at one point, too, but she'd stepped on a mine and been discharged from the service before I'd even met Dutch. "It suits you."

"I'm active duty again," she said with a smile. "The whole way. The docs in the SPARTAN-IV program set me up with the best prosthetic an unlimited military budget can buy. Works so well in the armor that you can't tell the difference at all."

I looked to both her and Dutch. "So that's what brought you out of retirement?"

Dutch gave me a game shrug. "Once they offered to make her a Spartan, you think I was going to let her leave me behind?"

"What I don't get," Romeo said, "is why you two didn't *tell* somebody? This is pretty big. We should've known about it."

Gretchen blushed a little at that. "Well . . . there was a chance that the prosthetic wouldn't quite take. You know how tight they lock down communications from the training station. We were going to notify you as soon as we got through and were handed our deployment orders. That's when everything would have been official. But now we're here!"

"Yeah," Dutch said, suddenly a lot grimmer. "What in the world happened back there, Gunny? What was all that business with Leonidas?"

I felt the telltale twinge in my stomach that told me we'd just entered slipspace. "It's a long story, and I'll get to it in a second, but there's one thing I want to know first." I turned toward the cockpit. "Veronica? Why didn't you tell me Dutch and Gretchen were Spartans now?"

She emerged from the front of the ship and gave Dutch and Gretchen a friendly nod. "Good to see you. I'd heard that you were training and considered the possibility of running into you, but I didn't want to get you involved if I could help it."

Dutch blew out a long sigh and rubbed his hand over his mostly bald scalp. "What do you mean by *involved*?" He looked straight at me, as if I had all the answers. "Exactly what did we sign up for here, Gunny?"

Veronica stepped forward and laid it all out for them. What

had happened on Genesis. How Cortana was threatening the whole galaxy. And why we needed Mickey to help us find a way to hide from her if we could.

With every word she spoke, Mickey's face grew darker, and believe me, she noticed. By the time she was done, the two of them stood there staring daggers at each other. Dutch and Gretchen gaped at Veronica and me as if they couldn't believe what an atrocious mess they'd somehow gotten tangled up in. Meanwhile, Sadie sat next to where Vergil was floating and patted his flank in a way that seemed reassuring.

Romeo just sat in a corner and watched it all, clearly entertained. More than once, he covered his mouth so no one could see him laughing, but he wasn't fooling anyone. We were all just too busy to pay any attention to him.

"Buck?" Mickey stared at me, his eyes wide and troubled. "Are you kidding me? You want me to work as a liaison between the UNSC and the Front?"

"Yes," I told him flatly. "What did you think? That we just wanted you as another gun?"

"When you broke me out of prison, I just assumed—"

I laughed at him. "Are you serious? I wouldn't trust you to bake me a batch of cookies. You're here because you speak Traitor, and because of that, those idiots in the Front might actually listen to you. No more and no less."

Mickey's face looked as if I'd told him he had only a week left to live. "You have to be joking. I've been inside a high-security military prison for three years. I come out of there, and they're going to think you've turned me against them. That you've got some kind of leverage to make me betray them."

"I could see why they'd think that," I said sarcastically. "It would seem to fit the pattern."

"They won't talk to me," he said. "They'll *kill* me, Buck."

"You're with us now, Mickey," Gretchen said. "We won't let them." Dutch gave her a supportive squeeze for that.

"And how are you going to stop them?" Mickey asked her. "Seriously, you call *this* your revamped Alpha-Nine? We have *two* fully trained and outfitted Spartans here." He waved at Romeo and me. "I don't have any armor or weapons, and Dutch and Gretchen haven't even completed training. They're not ready for this."

Dutch huffed at him, offended. "Hey, even if we're not quite as used to these new frames as you long-timers, we're still stronger and faster than anyone the Front has on their side."

"You, my friend, are a fool," Mickey said with a pitying shake of his head. "Even if you and Gretchen were up to speed already, how many of us are there? We have eight in this bird, including a young lady with no combat training and her pet alien, who would deflate like a balloon if a bullet even nicked him."

"Hey!" Sadie said. Vergil leaned closer to her but kept his eyes focused on Mickey as he purred in protest.

"Meanwhile, the Front has thousands of soldiers, all of whom are willing to die for their cause. You're not going to be able to protect me—or any of us—against that. Not with this half-baked version of Alpha-Nine, at least."

"We're not going in to fight them," Veronica said, irritated. "This is a *diplomatic* mission."

"I'm sure the Front will see it like that. You tell me the UNSC is now struggling against something it literally *created*, and they send a bunch of Spartans to figure out why this rogue AI—what did you call her? Cortana?—why she and her pals haven't raced over to stomp out a bunch of freedom fighters as well. That it?"

"That's it exactly."

"Then get ready, because they're going to shoot us down the

moment we enter the planet's atmosphere, wherever it is we're going. They don't screw around with UNSC ships encroaching on their territory. They'll see this as an act of war, and they'll respond accordingly. That's exactly why the Front exists: because the UNSC doesn't respect people's property and just does whatever it wants."

"But Mickey," Gretchen said, "this is why they're bringing *you*. They don't need you to fight for the UNSC. They just need you to get the Front to listen long enough so that they don't try to take us down straightaway."

Mickey softened a bit at the sound of Gretchen's voice. She'd never worked with him, of course, and neither she nor Dutch had been there on the day he'd betrayed Romeo and me. She didn't have any of our baggage, and I wondered if we could use that to our advantage.

"She's right," I said. "And maybe you can help us talk them into sharing whatever they have that's keeping them hidden from the Guardians."

Mickey's eyes grew wide, and his torrent of venom continued. "Are you out of your mind? If the universe truly handed the Front an edge like this, you expect them to just share it with the UNSC? For the so-called good of humanity?"

"Lord, help us," Dutch said. "If we can't figure out a way to come together against a threat like this, what good are we at all?"

"First of all," Mickey said, "this AI is not just a threat, Dutch. She was made by the UNSC. She's *their* problem to deal with!

"Second, the Front already knows you're full of it. That's the exact same line the UNSC sold them when the Covenant came along: 'Fall in line and help us out, or the aliens will kill us all.'

"And once it was over, what happened? Did we all wind up holding hands and singing campfire songs? Or did the UNSC go right back to hounding innocent people out of their homes? To telling people on faraway planets how they were supposed to live their lives?

"So you all need to be honest with me and with yourselves: Do you really think you'll be able to fool them again? That they're going to buy any of this?"

The entire bay fell quiet. Mickey was steaming mad and on a roll, and it seemed no one had a good rebuttal that he wasn't going to beat down.

Until Romeo started laughing out loud.

The rest of us turned to stare at him. When he saw the looks of disgust on our faces, that only got him going louder. Fat tears rolled down his cheeks, and he was audibly wheezing from whatever stupid joke was running through his head that only he seemed to understand.

"What?" Mickey eventually demanded. "What's so funny?"

"You are. You're truly out of your goddamn mind," Romeo said as he wiped his cheeks dry. "You *really* think the Front is going to be able to just ride this out? They're already on the ropes. They've lost I don't know how many colonies. As far as the galaxy is concerned, there *is* no more Front."

Mickey looked stricken. I thought he might lunge at Romeo and try to kill him then and there. "What?"

"As far as we know, the only human population that's not either on their knees or knocked flat is *this one place* we're headed to. And you're worried about how the UNSC is going to treat the Front when this is all over? If it wasn't for the UNSC, there wouldn't even be a Front to be talking about right now. The Covenant would have rolled over them in a single year and not even batted an eye.

"And if Cortana's threat is even half true, she isn't like the

Covenant at all. She's got access to technology they never even dreamed of. The Front won't be able to hide from her forever. Eventually, she's going to find them and wipe their little rebellion off the face of the galaxy. They need help, even if they don't know it yet. Every word you've used in defending them has only gotten you one step closer to signing their death warrant."

"Hey," Mickey started, "I didn't—"

Romeo cut him off with a wave of his hand. "I know you've been out of circulation for a while, so let me give it to you straight. As a people—I'm talking about humanity, not one of your little factions—we've never been this far down. So you really need to take a few minutes to find yourself some perspective. Otherwise you're gonna risk getting all of us killed by those cowboys out there, and you better believe I won't let that happen."

By that time, no one—not even Romeo—was laughing.

"You think this is about *me*?" Mickey said. "Ha! Even if I go along with this insane scheme of yours, how are you going to convince the Front you're telling the truth? I don't have that much cred with them. No one does. It doesn't matter what we offer them or who does the offering. There's no way they'll ever agree to this."

He sat down on a chair and slumped back in disgusted resignation. "Trust me. You'll see."

"Like you got a choice," Romeo said, blowing out a sigh. "Like any of us got a choice."

"Right," said Gretchen. "It's either that or roll over for Cortana."

"Which is not an option," I said. "Agreed?" I waited for everyone to nod for me. Mickey held out to the last.

"Good," I said. "Now that that's settled, let's talk about *how* we're going to do this."

I handed the floor over to Veronica, mostly because she was the boss and this was where my need-to-know had expired. From here on out, I'd be learning along with everyone else.

"Okay. We're heading to Cassidy III. It's a typical blue-green world that was pretty far off the beaten path of human-occupied space. UEG pioneer groups had initially scouted it out as a potential colony, but they'd abandoned it early on because of travel costs associated with the old slipspace drives. Now it's not so far out of the way, but it's still next to impossible to find unless you're actively looking for it.

"The last few probes that ONI sent out there came back with some interesting finds. There's plenty of evidence of Forerunner technology on the surface, but only one human settlement that we know of. It's called the Hole in the Wall. Yes, that's the name.

"It was founded fifty years ago by a bunch of outlaws—pirates, mostly—who wanted to build a secure hideout. Once they were set up, they fell in with some rebels who were on the run as well, and when the Insurrection started to wane because of the Covenant War, a large portion of the United Rebel Front was folded into this group.

"The place is undetectable by all of our conventional sensors, which is one of the reasons it's remained off the grid. As far as we can tell, it's able to foil not only human but also Covenant technology. Even some of the Forerunner-based advances we've made to deep-space surveying in the past few years are blind to this world's existence. It's the real deal."

Dutch let out a low whistle, impressed.

"We have no idea how or why this works," Veronica continued. "We just know that it does."

Romeo put up his hand, and Veronica nodded at him. It was

the kind of thing I might have bit off his head for—hiding his sarcasm behind a facade of false respect—but she took it in stride, as if she not only commanded the respect but had earned it.

"If it's so undetectable, how did ONI find it?"

"That's actually not a stupid question," I said, maybe more surprised than I should have been. Romeo flashed me a smug little smile.

"A survey team stumbled upon it after a slipspace drive failure during a routine expedition. It was actually a complete accident.

"During the war, we hid a number of things in and around the site—in part because we knew they'd be safe there, but also to keep tabs on the rebels there. But we didn't seriously leverage it for fear of drawing the Covenant. When the Covenant finally discovered Earth, one of our back-up plans—of literally hundreds— would have moved a large number of UNSC assets to Cassidy III, but fortunately, we never reached that point.

"Once the war ended, ONI decided to keep the location of the Hole classified and top-secret. We left the existing population alone because there was no reason for us to be there. We've known about them for a while and haven't lifted a finger," she said, clearly making sure that Mickey heard this part.

"There's absolutely no way they stayed put after their cover was blown," Mickey said. "They wouldn't have just sat there and waited for ONI to send in a warship to bomb the hell out of them from orbit."

"The Front's leadership never knew they'd been compromised by ONI," Veronica said. "We didn't have any real presence there. When we hid things on Cassidy III, we did it so far away from the settlement, they had no clue. And believe it or not, we didn't have any plans for the Hole at all."

"It would only have been a matter of time," Mickey said.

"That time is now," I told him. He glared at me, but I didn't really care.

"We're not here to expose the colony," Veronica said, ignoring the barbs. "But we need to know how they managed to keep hidden all these years. Otherwise, when they are finally exposed—and eventually, they will be—we'll have no way of recovering the technology."

Sadie held up her hand without any of the attitude that Romeo had shown. "Then why didn't we simply spend the last few decades researching this?" she asked once Veronica acknowledged her. "Such a find would have more value than most of the other projects the UNSC was working on: a world that couldn't be detected by any known survey technology? It would have made us invincible during the war."

"We had other priorities, Sadie," Veronica said. "I wish it was more complicated than that, but it's true. Before the close of the war, we were fighting for our lives. Research happened sporadically, but all our resources were pressed toward stopping the Covenant from erasing human existence. After it was finished, there were thousands of fires that needed to be put out. Colonies on the brink of habitability collapse needed to be recovered. Refugee populations unlike anything we've ever seen before. And that didn't count the ongoing conflicts that didn't stop at the end of the war. Active rebels causing problems on surviving colonies. Ex-Covenant factions raiding places for whatever spoils remained. Researching a backwater world with some weird Forerunner anomaly didn't top the list—though I agree, it would have come in very handy right about now.

"To be perfectly honest, the people on Cassidy III never showed that much curiosity about the way their special little trick works. They're largely indifferent to the Forerunner technology on their surface and the benefits it might yield. As far as they're concerned, it is what it is. They lucked out, and messing with it might cause it to stop working, so they just leave it alone."

"But that's not going to fly anymore," Mickey said, his voice soaked with disdain. "It's not enough for ONI to let the people of Cassidy III live in peace. They have to figure out how they've managed that peace and then mass-produce it for their *own* ends."

"Are you really against us figuring out how to protect humanity from Cortana?" I asked.

"Humanity? You mean the UNSC. Cortana already has them against the wall. That's the whole reason we're having this conversation."

"What are you getting at, Mickey?"

"Just pointing out that we're already past the point of saving everyone from this AI situation. If what you guys have said is true, it's pretty clear: This isn't a new war. The war is already over. Cortana won. What we're talking about *now* is starting a revolution."

"Is that such a bad thing?"

Mickey finally smiled. "Actually, no. When it comes to running an insurgency, consulting with the Front makes tons of sense."

CHAPTER 12

For the record, the slipspace drives on most Condors might seem cheap compared to the ones on capital ships, but they're pretty fancy. The first few Condors were called Super Pelicans because they vaguely resembled the widely known UNSC dropship, but they had a larger airframe and could punch a hole into slipspace. Dropships being able to travel at superluminal speeds was kind of a new thing for the UNSC, part of an across-the-board update utilizing reverse-engineered tech from the Forerunners.

The trips on them can seem to take forever, although not nearly as long as it would to move through realspace at far less than the speed of light. In the early days of the war, I spent weeks zipping through slipspace at a comparatively slow pace, waiting to get to a destination an otherwise impossible distance away. Trips took weeks and months, even. Now it was down to hours.

Most Condors, though, don't have a Huragok on board. I can't speak for Engineers other than Vergil, but he gets bored rather easily. Maybe it's because whatever constitutes his brain moves so fast that he doesn't think of us as stunning conversationalists. In fact, his kind communicate a lot faster and more efficiently than anyone could ever manage verbally.

He takes out that boredom on the things around him, working selflessly and constantly to help improve the machines at hand—well, tentacle. Case in point: By the time he was done tuning up our slipspace drive, our Condor was faster than anything I'd ever flown. When Vergil tried to explain what he'd done, I held up one hand and stopped him right there. Not just because I wouldn't understand half the terms about to spill out of his translator, but because I needed him to work some upgrades into the Mjolnir armor the Spartans were wearing.

This is why we'd brought him along. No human could understand and work with technology as quickly and as well as a Huragok. They'd literally been created to do just that.

Despite all this, we had some downtime on the trip to Cassidy III. After the briefing, I decided I'd had enough togetherness for a while, and I returned to the weapons station to get away from everyone.

It didn't take long for Veronica to join me by slipping into the pilot's seat, which I didn't mind at all. She was the only other person I wanted to see.

"You all right?" she asked.

"I've had better days."

"I know." She reached up and back to put a hand on my boot. "Thank you."

"What would you want to thank me for? I haven't exactly been a shining example of leadership."

"You're doing fine."

"I don't know. I honestly can't look at Mickey without wanting to strangle him. I already have a hard enough time with Romeo. I think Captain O'Day would have called that a 'distinct lack of forethought and restraint.' Of course, I didn't go through with it, so perhaps there's something to that restraint thing after all."

"Nobody expects you to be perfect."

"I do."

That got a smile out of her that I could see in her reflection in the canopy's glass. "That's one of the things I love about you, Buck, but please don't beat yourself up. Every person on this ship has, from time to time, screwed things up worse than you."

"Not our Huragok, that's for sure. And you really think Sadie's that bad?" I said with a half-smile. "She always seemed like a decent kid to me."

"You know exactly what I mean. You're a great Spartan, Buck. And an amazing leader. It's good to see you back in that seat."

"I'm not planning on getting used to it," I told her. "Locke does a great job with Osiris. I've learned a ton of things working with him."

"I'm sure he's learned a lot from you, too."

"I did teach him about the dangers of tequila."

She craned her neck around to give me a doubtful yet playful look. "You're a good friend."

We let a long moment of silence pass between us. With everything weighing down our minds, it felt good to sit there and *be* with her for a bit. I missed that more than I could possibly say.

"What about us?" I finally asked. I'm not even sure I meant for the words to escape my mouth.

"What do you mean?"

"You know *exactly* what I mean. A spook as good as you? You know what I'm going to think before I think it."

"That I do." She fell silent and stared ahead into the nothingness of slipspace beyond the Condor's viewport. "What *about* us?" she said at last. "That's been the big question for a while now."

"Well . . . I had this idea that maybe someday we'd retire and settle down together, but the way everything's gone sideways again, I don't see that happening any time soon."

"Life suddenly looks a whole lot shorter. Planning beyond tomorrow gets a lot harder."

"I figured I'd wind up driving a long-haul truck."

Veronica chuckled. "You would be a lousy trucker. I've seen you drive."

"There's a certain level of aggressiveness required when it comes to handling heavily armed vehicles in the middle of a war zone."

"You really did a number on that Scorpion back on New Mombasa."

"Hey, I'll have you know, we didn't suffer a single casualty that entire mission."

"Oh," she said. "Is that your standard for a successful mission? Getting out of it without losing anyone?"

That thought sobered me up a bit. "Is that not ONI enough for you?"

"No," she said. "It's *not* ONI enough. Not by a long shot. It is, however, the *right* answer. Honestly, Buck, that's why it's a fairly simple choice, picking you to lead these high-risk missions. I know they wear on you, and I know you're worried that one day it'll be too high a risk and you won't come back. But even so, you recognize things that some other leaders don't, like the fact that getting your people back in one piece is part of getting the job done."

"And here I thought it was my genius-level tactical planning sense you were after. That or my roguish good looks."

"That's a very Buck answer . . . but really, it's the way you lead the people you work with. They're not expendable to you—you treat them like family. *That's* the kind of leader people respect. One they can trust. And if they can manage that, they can concentrate on getting the job done."

I frowned. "I haven't always been so lucky. I've lost a lot of people over the years."

"But it was never for a lack of trying to bring them home safe. Everyone who's ever worked with you knows that."

"How about you?"

"I know that better than anyone."

"I meant about our future."

She gave me a funny look in the canopy's reflection. "Wait. Are you talking about getting married?"

I winced at that. We'd brought it up enough times but always walked our way back from it. With the kind of lives we had, marriage didn't make a whole lot of sense. It wasn't like we were ever going to wind up with a houseful of kids or shoot roots in a suburban neighborhood somewhere. And if not, what was the point?

"Please tell me you're not *afraid* of getting married to me, Buck . . . Are you?"

"What? No. *Afraid?*"

She shook her head. "What's stopping us, then?"

"We've kind of been busy up until now."

"And we can see now that's never going to end."

I shrugged. "The galaxy keeps throwing threats of one kind or another at us, and we keep responding. That's what we do."

"The point is—ah, hell, never mind. You know what the point is."

I allowed myself a faint smile. "That I do."

"Then why wait any longer, Buck? If the break we were hoping for is never going to come, then why don't you just marry me already?"

That, I admit, caught me by surprise. I sat there in silence and looked straight ahead, as if maybe I'd misheard her and was trying to puzzle out what she'd actually said.

"Eddie Buck, finally silent?" she asked after a long moment. She turned around in her seat to get a good look at me. "See, this is the crux of the matter. You're brave enough to handle anything. But the idea of spending the rest of your life with me absolutely terrifies you."

"I don't think *terrifies* is the right word."

"What would it be, then?"

I looked into her eyes. "I'm not afraid of spending the rest of my life with you, Veronica. I'm afraid I *won't*. I mean—" I cut myself off and started over. "We both have jobs with low life expectancies. Most people in our line of work don't retire. They get killed. Then they get a funeral and that's it. Doesn't that make it hard for you, too, or is it just me?"

"That's my point, Buck. We might die. Would you rather die married or not?"

"Hey, I thought we had an understanding about this."

"Times change, Buck. We change with them, whether we like it or not." She turned back to gaze out at the stars again.

"Look, Veronica—"

" 'Now's not the time for this conversation.' I've said that myself, and you're absolutely right."

"That's not quite where I was going."

"But you were going to get there. I just saved us both a lot of time."

"Fair enough."

I reached down and tucked her hair behind her ear. She settled back into my hand. We stayed that way for a long time. I knew she was right. Even if one of us ended up dying out here in the fight, it's not as though the other would be immune to that pain because we weren't hitched. What was stopping me from taking that final step?

When we neared Cassidy III, Veronica leaned forward and brought the ship out of slipspace. She'd taken us in nice and close, and we entered realspace in orbit around the planet but a safe distance away from the Hole in the Wall. The view of the big blue-green orb blocked out just about everything in the sky but for it and its three decent-size moons.

The planet and its atmosphere looked pristine, like preindustrial Earth. There was only one colony, and the people who lived there hadn't done much to spoil the place. The clouds that swirled around it were as white and clean as fresh snow.

Once she'd hung the Condor in orbit on the far side of the planet, Veronica walked into the rear bay to brief the crew before we made our approach. "All right, Alpha-Nine," she said. "Here's what's going to happen. Once we've got clearance, I'm going to set down outside the settlement, and Mickey, Romeo, Dutch, Buck, and I are going to go in on foot and have a chat with the locals."

"What about Gretchen?" Dutch asked.

"She's a combat-trained pilot, and I need someone back here to fly this bird, especially if we need an assist. Also, I don't want to it to appear like we're spoiling for a fight."

"Yet you're going to take in three Spartans in full armor?" Gretchen said.

"Better than taking in more," Veronica said. "And if this op goes anything like the last few, then having a skilled pilot ready to launch this bird at the drop of a hat could be the difference between us living or dying."

"And me, I guess I'm just out of luck," Mickey said. "Or are you hiding a spare suit of armor somewhere?"

"If she was, I don't think she'd be handing over it to you," I said as I slipped into the bay.

"Glad to see the foundation of trust on which we're trying to rebuild our relationship is standing strong."

I looked Mickey dead in the eye. "Maybe I wasn't clear with you before. There *is* no trust here. What we have is a mutual need for each other, and that's about it."

"I was being sarcastic."

"Is that another word for *asshole*?"

"You know what," he said, crossing his arms, "it's probably better that I don't have any armor here. They're gonna see you guys and think you're all cowards, hiding behind your suits. You'll be walking targets to them—"

"We're going to be at your mercy going into this place, which is filled with hundreds, if not thousands, of well-armed insurgents. At the very least, I'd like to be in my work clothes."

Mickey gawked at me as if I were the stupidest person he'd ever met. "You really think that's going to do you any good?"

"It's worked out well for me so far."

"You're going to have me take you into a colony full of—as you rightfully pointed out—thousands of well-armed insurgents. If things go wrong, what are you going to do? Where are you going to go? You don't think that many people can bring you down?"

That's one thing our drill instructors did their best to beat out of us every day of Spartan training: the idea that we were unstoppable.

Mickey was baiting me. I wasn't about to give in.

"You're my consultant here on traitor-based psychology, Mickey," I told him. "What would you suggest we do?"

"Other than turn around and go home? I'd send in as little in the way of armament as you can. You show up armed to the teeth and standing there like walking tanks, they're going to want to start shooting you. You walk in there like normal people, that shows them you're more interested in talking than fighting."

"And if they're interested in shooting normal people, then what?"

Mickey gave me a sad shake of his head. "Look at us, Buck. We're never going to pass for normal people. We're seven feet tall and built like brick houses. The only people on board who look anything like regular folks are Veronica and Sadie—no offense there, Vergil. The rest of us are freaks."

"I'm not sending in Sadie," Veronica said. "She's a civilian."

"She works for the UNSC as Vergil's handler."

"She's not trained for this kind of op, and I'm not going to risk it. I'm not sending in Vergil, either."

"Their job was to help us get you out of prison," I told Mickey. "They did that."

"So why didn't you drop them off someplace safe instead of dragging them into this mess?" Mickey asked.

"I considered that," Veronica said. "But there are contingencies at play. First, our time line for this op doesn't have a lot of latitude for dropping people off. Where would we even do that, given the current situation? Second, there's a good chance that whatever we're looking for on Cassidy III involves Forerunner technology. We'll need Vergil to help us figure that out, and he and Sadie come as a team."

"So we *are* going to drag Vergil and Sadie into this." Mickey gave Veronica a sarcastic clap that made me want to wind his fingers together until they snapped.

"Not until we determine that it's safe for them," Veronica said. "They're going to stay here in the Condor until then." She turned toward the rest of the team. "Boys, get yourselves ready. We'll be making planetfall in under an hour."

"You're making a big mistake," Mickey said. "You stomp in like a bunch of conquerors, and you're going to get us all shot."

Veronica lanced him with a withering look. "Well, you'll be the one right out in front, so maybe you ought to start thinking about how you can keep that from happening."

"Leave the weapons in the ship. Leave everyone in armor here, too."

"Just you, me, and Sadie? Not a chance."

I let out a deep sigh. "He has a point," I said, surprising everyone in the ship, including myself.

Veronica stared at me as if I'd been screwing on my helmet too tight. "You really want to send in just the three of us? With him?"

"Of course not, but he's right about how it's going to look. Romeo, Dutch, and I can't exactly get out of our armor on this bird, so that's a nonstarter. But we can go in with fewer guns. Just sidearms, for instance. Holstered."

"You really think that's going to make a difference?"

I pitched the question to Mickey. "What do you think?"

"I don't know for sure," he said, which was maybe the first honest-sounding thing he'd offered up. "If it was me, I'd go in even lighter . . . but yeah, leaving the long guns at home would be a decent start."

"All right," I said to Romeo and Dutch. "Leave the rifles here. If we need some serious firepower, we'll call in Gretchen anyhow."

"So they can shoot her down, too?" Dutch asked.

"Relax, Dutch. I'll be fine. I was once a transport chief, you know. I knew the skill set would come in handy someday," Gretchen said wryly.

"That job didn't come with guns and Spartans, though," said Dutch.

She flashed him a smile. "That's right. This is *much* more fun."

CHAPTER 13

W e exited slipspace close enough to Cassidy III that I'm sure
we set off every long-range alert system the rebels had in
place. Veronica got on the open comm system right away
and started hailing the people on the ground. "Hole in the Wall
command, this is Captain Veronica Dare of the UNSC, here on a
diplomatic mission. Please respond."

She repeated herself a few times as we neared, cruising on
down through the atmosphere. Closer up, Cassidy III seemed
even more beautiful. It had one large continent in the middle, surrounded by concentric rings of islands that formed long and fertile
archipelagoes. The mainland was cut in half by a gigantic mountain range that left a vast jungle on one side of it and a sprawling
desert on the other. Just the kind of planet you could spend a life-
time exploring, if you were so inclined.

Most planets weren't quite so pleasant. You wanted to get off
them as soon as physically possible. Trust me, I've been on 'em!

We came in at a shallow angle toward the Hole in the Wall,

which sat parked on the high plains just on the desert side of the mountains. High and dry but not desiccated, it gathered on the edge of a large lake. Sunlight bouncing off the desert ridgelines below transformed them into a glowing red, somehow simultaneously beautiful and haunting. I couldn't remember seeing anything like this world in my decades of service, and I was starting to understand why it was so special.

No one responded to our hails, so Veronica took us on another orbit around the planet. We wanted to give the Front lots of time to see us and respond with something other than artillery. The last thing we needed to do was have some trigger-happy gun jockey try to knock us out of the sky. The Condor was a sharp little vessel, but we didn't want to test her resiliency against incoming fire unless absolutely necessary.

We swung around the dark side of the planet, and I didn't see a single artificial light anywhere on the surface. In one spot, a line of active volcanoes glowed red-hot, visible even from dozens of klicks up, but nothing else. For the most part, this was an empty, raw, and unspoiled world.

When we came around to the daylight side again, Veronica's hails were finally answered. "UNSC *Foxtrot 111*, this is Cassidy Ground Control. Please state the nature of your mission."

"This is Captain Veronica Dare. Request that we switch to a secure channel."

Once they got through all their authorization and spycraft junk, the voice on the other end of the line spoke again. "UNSC *Foxtrot 111*, I have Mayor Juanita Wells on the line. She'd like to have a word with you."

"Hello, Mayor Wells. This is Captain Veronica Dare of the UNSC. We are in a single ship, and we are on a peaceful mission."

"I certainly hope so," a woman's skeptical voice responded.

"Have you already heard the news about the AI named Cortana?"

"We certainly have," Mayor Wells said. "We're not entirely cut off from the rest of the galaxy. And I'm not surprised that this has brought you knocking on our door. The good news is that Cortana doesn't seem to have located us so far. The bad news is that you've managed it instead."

"I understand how you feel," Veronica said. "I'd like to discuss this matter with you."

"The UNSC left us alone for decades. Now you want to come directly into our city?"

"We're in a bit of a bind, as you might imagine."

"From your point of view, I'm sure that's true, but not from ours."

Veronica muted the comm. "This is pretty much the kind of interference I was expecting. Mickey, you're up." She waved him forward to lean over her shoulder in the cockpit. She gestured toward the comm and unmuted it.

Mickey stared at the console as if it were an angry snake that would bite him if he made a wrong move. Veronica pointed right at it, and he gave her a nervous nod and spoke. "Hello, Cassidy III? This is Michael Crespo."

No response came from the other end.

"Hello, Cassidy III? This is Michael Crespo. Please come in."

A long moment later, Mayor Wells spoke up. "Is that *Spartan* Michael Crespo?"

"I don't think it would be fair to even call me a Spartan anymore, ma'am. But yes, I'm one and the same."

"You're supposed to be imprisoned. Word was that you might even have been killed."

"Rumors of my demise have been greatly exaggerated." Mickey

forced a laugh. "My former colleagues arranged for my release and brought me along on this excursion to help establish some credit with you."

"That's quite a stunt," Wells said. "And it certainly got my attention. It's an honor to speak with you, Mr. Crespo."

"I'm glad to hear you feel that way."

"It also deeply saddens me."

Mickey shot me a confused glance and then spoke into the comm again. "And why would that be?"

"You're an honest-to-God hero among the Front, and it pains me that you're going to be collateral damage when we're forced to shoot your colleagues' vessel from the sky."

I checked the Condor's motion sensors for any incoming blips, but I didn't see anything. Not yet, at least. I gave Mickey a swift shake of my head.

Of course, maybe we wouldn't see anything until it was too late. I wasn't sure how Cassidy III's masking technology worked. If it was theoretically enough to cover and hide an entire planet—or at least the people living on it—would it also do the same to ships traveling across it? Or missiles being fired from it?

Or did the technology affect the entire system? If Veronica hadn't had the coordinates for the place, we never would have found it.

I realized that I didn't know much at all about this thing we were looking for, not when it really came down to it. It was probably better that way. I was grateful Veronica had to worry about it rather than me—and that we'd brought Vergil along to help figure it all out.

Assuming we didn't get shot down.

"Wait!" Mickey said into the comm. "We're not here to hurt anyone. They just want to talk with you. What's the harm in that?"

"We've seen how the UNSC *talks* when we have something they want."

"Believe me, no one understands that more than me. But this isn't like that. Think about it. If the UNSC wanted to storm in and just take whatever it is that's working for you here, they could have done that years ago, right? Ever since the end of the Covenant War."

Mickey waited for an answer, but Wells didn't breathe a word. "They didn't!" he finally said, responding to his own question. "They left you alone. Don't you think you should take that into consideration?"

"They were just too scared to take us on, Mr. Crespo," Mayor Wells said. "They're really cowards when it comes down to it."

Mickey actually snorted at that and then caught himself, clearly afraid he might insult the mayor. "There's a lot of things you can say about the UNSC, but I can tell you, they're not cowards. That's especially true of the Spartans they sent me here with. If they were afraid of you, they'd have sent in an entire fleet rather than a single Condor. This is strictly a diplomatic mission."

"How am I sure they don't have a gun to your head right now?"

"If they did, I'd mention it. The only one who's threatening to kill me right now is you."

"Touché."

"Now, listen . . . I don't agree with the UEG on much. I went to prison for defying them. But this isn't about the UNSC or the Front. It's not about who's right and who's wrong. It's about the freedom of humanity—every single human being—and that's something the Front has always stood for."

"You make a pretty speech, Mr. Crespo, but that isn't going to change my mind about the UEG."

"I'm not asking for that. I haven't changed my mind about them, either. All I'm asking is that you let us land and that you join us in an open and honest conversation about what we can do to help keep humanity out from under the heels of this insane AI. That's all!"

"Shooting you down seems like a much simpler solution."

"Do you really think this is going to stop here if we're dead? You shoot us down and the UNSC will send a bigger ship and more people. You shoot them down, and they'll come here with a heavily weaponized capital ship and nuke you from orbit."

"You are *not* making this sound like a peaceful mission, Mr. Crespo."

"Hey, I don't trust these people any more than you do. But this isn't about trust. It's about fighting back. And the Front knows more about how to do that than anyone else."

Mickey let that lie there for a moment, and Veronica muted the comm. "Nice work," I said to him. "You sound like a true believer."

"I'm not fooling anyone, Buck. That's exactly why I joined the Front. To stop this kind of thing from happening. It's why I joined the UNSC in the first place, too. To keep the Covenant from bringing our way of life to an end.

"This is why it always galls me that you think of me as a traitor. I never gave up any of my beliefs. I stuck to my principles. It was the UEG that changed, not me."

"You still screwed up, bro!" Romeo called from the bay.

"Piss off, Romeo!" Mickey barked back.

I quickly tapped the comm to keep Mickey's attention on the matter at hand. "You want me to say something else to her?" he asked.

"You already said plenty," Veronica said. "You did a fine job,

HALO: BAD BLOOD

Mickey. Better than I hoped. Now we just have to wait for her response."

"And here's hoping it doesn't come in the form of a cloaked missile," I said.

Soon the mayor's voice rang out over the comm. She sounded reluctant and wary. "All right. We'll talk. Come on down. We'll set a beacon for where you should land."

Veronica unmuted the comm. "Thank you, Mayor Wells," she said. "You won't regret this."

"I'd better not."

Once Veronica cut the comm entirely, I spoke freely. "It feels like a trap."

"Of course it's a trap," Veronica said. "We're going to park the Condor where they tell us to, and they're going to have enough ordnance trained on it to vaporize it. But it beats being blown away up here."

"I'm not sure I see how," I said. "Dead is dead."

"Every step forward is progress. The further we go with the Front, the less likely they are to obliterate us."

"If you say so."

"She's right," Mickey said. "The closer you are to someone when you decide to kill them, the harder it is."

The shaky tone in his voice told me I didn't want him to explain himself. I supposed I should have been glad that Mickey didn't kill me back on Talitsa rather than trying to take me hostage, but I somehow couldn't be all that thankful. Sometimes I wondered if a bullet would have been a lot easier. I would have died, but without knowing that Mickey had betrayed me. That one hurt.

Still, I always prefer breathing to not.

A beacon began flashing on the nav system, and Veronica angled the Condor toward it. The signal was coming from somewhere

— 205 —

in the desert outskirts, what looked to be a good hike from the settlement. The sunlight cast across the sand made it look like blood, which didn't seem like a great sign.

"You good with this?" I said to Veronica. "Maybe you should stay back with the ship."

"I appreciate the concern," she said in as kind a tone as she could manage, considering I'd probably just insulted her. "But this is my mission, and I know more about what we're looking for and how we might be able to use it than anyone else. And we don't have the several hours I'd need to explain it all to you. We're going to need all the details in my head, not to mention my diplomatic skills."

"And I'll probably need you to pull my fat out of the fire at some point," I said. "To be fair."

"I wouldn't say that it's becoming a habit," she said. "Yet. But that did figure into my calculations."

"As I was just telling Locke this week, I only allow myself to be rescued by the best. Otherwise, I'd just do it myself."

"Don't push your luck. I can only save so many people, and I don't want to be forced to make any hard choices."

As we got closer to the Hole in the Wall, I started to see that the settlement we were heading for wasn't quite as small and amateur an operation as the name implied. It was situated around a trio of massive Forerunner towers, sitting right there in the lush and golden high plains, on the shore of a sprawling lake. The ashen-colored towers formed a triangle that enclosed the edges of a bay on which sat dozens of small boats, mostly rigged for fishing and sailing.

The people of Cassidy III had moved in, setting up their own homes in the ancient structures and in the area between them. I saw wires of all sort strung about the place, along with some bits of human architecture slapped up against the original towers here and there: houses, buildings, even high-hanging balconies. They looked something like shanties stacked on the sides of castles.

From the air, the place seemed peaceful enough. We could see foot and vehicle traffic milling about in the morning sun. People going about their business—probably heading to school or work or whatever—and ignoring things like UNSC ships skating in from the stars.

The batteries of weapons located along the perimeter of the settlement put the lie to that. There was also a four-meter-tall enclosure about a half a klick from the edge of the settlement that evidently protected the people inside from anything that lived on the planet—as long as it didn't burrow or fly, I suppose.

The beacon guided us to a stony basin at the south end of the city. Not an airport or even a proper landing strip—just a wide stretch of dry land that featured nothing but red-hued ridges that seemed like they might have been mined a decade or so ago. The landing site was far removed from the settlement. I guess they didn't want to do any damage to their own property if they needed to blow us away. The basin was fully exposed to a pair of artillery batteries that tracked us as we flew in and landed.

I climbed down from the weapons station and met Veronica as she slipped out of the cockpit. Gretchen was waiting there to take over. "Keep her tight and steady," Veronica said to her.

"She's in good hands, Captain," Gretchen said. Then she turned to me. "You do me the same for Dutch."

"You know I will."

Dutch, Romeo, and Mickey were already waiting for me and Veronica by the ramp, which they hadn't lowered yet.

Veronica stopped to speak to Sadie. "We may need Vergil's help soon. Just keep him out of trouble until then."

"That's a lot easier said than done." Sadie gave the Huragok the hairy eyeball. "When my dad programmed the original Vergil, he made him just as stubborn and curious as I am. Unfortunately, Quick to Adjust has inherited both of those traits in spades. He's already remotely probing their networks for ways in."

I patted Vergil on the side. "I'd expect nothing less from my favorite alien. But listen: Concentrate on why this planet seems to be a blind spot for Cortana's forces. Do what you can to figure this place out. The quicker we can manage that, the faster we can grab what we need and then get out of here."

"I will endeavor to solve this puzzle, Spartan Buck," he said through his tablet.

I stuffed my helmet under my arm and motioned for Romeo and Dutch to do the same. "Anything we can do to make ourselves look more human is a good thing."

"You could not bring the helmets at all," Mickey suggested.

"We're optimistic, Mickey," Dutch said. "Not stupid."

I smacked the button that dropped the ramp on the back of the Condor. It lowered, and the atmosphere of Cassidy III swelled in. I led the way, with Mickey right behind me. He moved up to walk by my side as we emerged. Veronica followed. Dutch and Romeo brought up the rear.

I breathed in the air of Cassidy III, and it smelled like freshly turned soil with just a hint of a breeze off the lake we could see in the distance. Apart from the dry and jagged ridgeline to the south, the land on which the Hole in the Wall sat was fairly flat, with just a few stands of trees decorating the rolling hillsides covered with long, waving grass. Off to the north, a herd of some kind of peaceful bovid meandered through the field, munching on the terrain. I found that oddly comforting.

Looking around at the people coming off the Condor with me brought back the many ops Romeo, Dutch, Mickey, and I had been on as ODSTs together. We'd worked side by side for years and entered more battles than I cared to count. Veronica had been with us on a few of those. Mostly the worst ones, but they'd all come out pretty well in the end, considering we were alive.

Who knew what was to come, though?

The Hole in the Wall welcoming committee rolled up quickly and had the Condor surrounded in short order. More than a dozen fully armed and armored Front soldiers set up in a circle, their weapons out and leveled straight at us. They closed ranks around us as we emerged from the ship.

"I still think we could take them," Romeo said under his breath.

"Stow that kind of talk," I said over my shoulder. "They're nervous enough as it is. We don't want to give them any sort of excuse to scratch their itchy trigger fingers."

"If the bullets start flying, the mission is over," Veronica said. "By which I mean we've failed. Only fire in self-defense. Got that?"

We all nodded. Even Mickey.

You could sense the tension in the Front soldiers. Every one of them was ready to fight. I wondered if they'd do more damage to one another than to us if they started shooting, but I had absolutely no desire to find out.

They looked like most of the soldiers I'd seen fighting for the

Front. They didn't have uniforms, although they'd cobbled together some decent sets of armor. Still, their weapons were better suited to picking off predators poking around their herds than starting a firefight against trained soldiers.

They were farmers and ranchers and miners and such who'd probably come here to escape the people telling them what to do and how to do it, and for the most part they lived simple, peaceful lives. We were about to ruin all that for them, and if not for the fact that they were part of a terrorist group that had done untold harm over the last few decades, I might have figured out a way to feel bad for them. Some of them had probably been pirates, but that had been a while back. Or so I hoped.

A short, dark woman with steely hair and a pistol on her hip rather than in her hand stepped forward, breaking ranks with the rest of the rebels. She moved with a confidence I didn't see in the others, and I instantly saw why they'd put her in charge. "Mayor Wells, I presume?" I said.

She nodded at me but did not offer a hand in greeting. "Hello, Spartans," she said as if the words tasted foul in her mouth.

Veronica stepped forward. "I'm Captain Veronica Dare," she said. "Is there somewhere we can speak in private?"

Behind us, I could hear the whine of hydraulics as the ramp to the Condor began to rise, cutting us off from our most direct route of escape. Veronica had planned it that way, as a means of showing that we were staying, but it still made me nervous.

I gave some of the rebels closest to us an easy nod, hoping to make them feel more comfortable. I don't think it worked.

"There's nothing I want to say to you that I can't say in front of my fellow citizens," Wells replied.

Veronica weighed that for a moment. "All right. If that's how you want to handle this, we are your guests and will abide by your rules." She made a point of looking at the people pointing their weapons at us. "Could you please do us the favor of having your people stand down?"

At a hand signal from Wells, the rebels lowered their guns. None of them put the weapons away, though. I held my hands away from my own Magnum to express the same sentiment.

"Don't take this as a sign that you're welcome here," Mayor Wells warned.

"We'd much rather be somewhere else," Veronica said. "But this is important. And urgent."

"Right," Wells said. "You want to take advantage of Cassidy III's . . . *special* properties."

"Most of this you may know already, but pardon a brief explanation just to fill in the gaps. An AI called Cortana has commandeered a series of Forerunner weapons known as Guardians. They are powerful machines capable of neutralizing entire worlds, shutting them down completely. She's also gathered other human-created AIs around her, promising to cure the effects of rampancy, and they have effectively set themselves up as the despotic rulers over nearly every inhabited planet. They promise peace and provisions to those who bend their knees—and the lash to those who refuse her new order. This is going on right now, across the known galaxy."

"That seems like a problem for the Unified Earth Government," Wells said. "Along with all those aliens you've been fighting with. You made the AI, you let her get access to those machines—the Guardians—and now she's using them against you. Not sure how we fit into the equation, Captain. We just want to be left alone. Like we always have."

"And that's the issue. You've managed to keep this a secret for so long that it may seem to you that they will leave you alone, but that's not the case. They'll figure out this place exists, and once they do, they'll come here and dismantle it for their own needs."

"Which sounds pretty much like UEG tactics to me, so what's the difference?"

"The immediate difference," Veronica continued, "is that you've lived happily here for decades with the UNSC effectively ignoring your presence, though we knew of you all this time. You will not enjoy that luxury with Cortana. She will send a Guardian here with an occupation force unlike anything the UNSC could have deployed. Your way of life here will be over, especially if you reject living under their martial law."

"Maybe that's something we'd just like to take our chances on," Wells said. "It's seemed to work fine for us till now."

The rebels murmured in agreement. I could sense them turning even further against us. And they'd started out suspicious and hating us, so it was quickly going from bad to worse.

Veronica picked up on this as well and decided to go on the offensive. "Well, it's not working for us or the rest of humanity. Like it or not, you are all citizens of the Unified Earth Government."

Wells gave Veronica a sharp look. "We don't acknowledge your authority. We never have."

"That doesn't mean it doesn't exist. We've come here to ask for your help, as we're at the moment when humanity needs it most. If you turn your back on that request, there will be severe consequences."

Wells put her hands on her hips. "Is that a threat, Captain?"

"I'm simply making an informed prediction about a series of inevitable events. If you won't work with us voluntarily, the UNSC will send someone else here to force you to see the mutual benefit of sharing your technology. And if they can't manage that, it won't be long before Cortana's forces arrive in the form of thousands of armigers capable of razing the entire settlement to the ground."

"They don't know we're here," Wells said. "No one does. And if I'm honest, Captain, it'll take a remarkable amount of evidence for me to believe that anyone is going to find us out here after all these years."

Veronica gestured to the rest of Alpha-Nine. "*We're* here."

"That's an issue that can be resolved in our favor," the mayor said with more than a hint of menace.

"You don't have the right to treat them that way," Mickey said as he stepped forward. For a moment, I thought he was standing up for Veronica, but of course, he was taking the Front's side. "Captain, they didn't ask for this planet—their home—to become something you would have interest in. They just want to live their lives here in peace, without interference by a government that knows nothing about them."

"You grew up on Luna, Mickey," I said to him. I probably shouldn't have opened my mouth, but I couldn't help it. "What do you know about living on a backwater planet?"

"Are you calling us hillbillies, Spartan?" Mayor Wells asked.

I shrugged. "I grew up on Draco III, about as far away from Earth as you can get without giving up indoor plumbing. This guy might sympathize with you"—I gestured toward Mickey—"but you should know that he grew up in a highly civilized dome with artificial gravity, in what was literally the first Earth colony ever established." I gazed up at the open sky, which was a gorgeous shade of indigo. "That's nothing like this."

"My point," Mickey said, "is that people come here to get away from the troubles outside of this world, and they're not bothering anyone. You can't force this situation on them."

"It's not me," Veronica said. "It's the situation itself that's demanding this. They're *part* of the galaxy. And they're part of humanity. This threat from Cortana is already theirs, whether they realize that or not."

She turned back to Mayor Wells. "Look, I'm sure you have a wonderful society and that you do a fine job running it. But your time for living inside this bubble, isolated and protected from the rest of the galaxy, is over. I'm sorry about that. I truly am."

Wells shook her head in disbelief and disgust. "That's what the UEG and its stooges say every time they show up someplace, isn't it? *I'm sorry. I wish it could be different. It's not our fault. It's for your own good.* You know the one thing they've taught us? To never believe a word they say."

"Fine," Veronica said. "I understand that. We deserve that. That's why I didn't come here empty-handed." She gestured to Mickey. "We brought one of your own to help vouch for us."

All eyes turned toward Mickey so fast that he actually took a step back. "Hey," he said. "I'm not sure I make such a good spokesperson for the UEG. I just spent the last three years in prison for joining the Front."

The mayor favored Mickey with a wide smile. "We're aware of exactly who you are and what you sacrificed to stand with the Front," she said. "You don't need to establish your credentials with us, Mr. Crespo." The people around her nodded and grunted in Mickey's favor.

"All right," Mickey said, visibly struggling with the idea that what he'd done with his life actually meant something positive to anyone other than himself. I knew how he felt. I had a hard time believing that being a traitor would pay off for him in any way, but apparently, this was the right audience.

They all hated me, of course, and the rest of Alpha-Nine. We represented everything they stood against, whether we liked it or not. To be honest, I felt like we were one word away from being gunned down, given how wired these makeshift soldiers were.

To be clear, I didn't have any issue with people who wanted to be left alone. That was fine. The problem was that the Front never stopped there. They didn't just hide out on remote planets and refuse to pay taxes or support the military. They actively went out of their way to destroy UEG facilities and citizens. They might have cast themselves as a crowd of isolationists who only cared about decentralized governance, but they were capable of blowing up buildings and killing civilians, too.

That was where I drew the line—and that was when the UNSC would, from time to time, send me in to set things right.

Mickey pointed back at the rest of us. "This is Alpha-Nine. The team I used to work with. The team I betrayed."

There were some boos over his use of that term. Maybe they thought it was too harsh. I didn't think it went far enough. I felt like joining in but kept my mouth shut.

"They're some of the best soldiers the UNSC has to offer, and they were sent here in good faith to negotiate with you at tremendous personal risk. I can't tell you if you should give them what they want, Mayor, but you should at least take them seriously.

"This isn't some kind of distraction ploy. It isn't part of a conspiracy to destroy what you've built. They have no desire to do that at all, as far as I'm aware. This is an honest effort to work with you against a very real threat in the galaxy, a threat that will show up here at some point. Maybe sooner than later."

"But it's a threat that *they* brought to our doorstep, Mr. Crespo," Mayor Wells said. "We didn't build these smart AIs that turned against them. We do things with our own sweat and blood, with our own hands. And now that these monsters they've constructed have turned against them, they want our help? No, they *demand* it."

Wells gestured at her soldiers, and they raised their weapons once again. "I'm going to do for you what the UNSC has never done for us: give you a chance to leave before we start shooting."

CHAPTER 14

"You've got a lot of nerve," Veronica said as she stalked toward Mayor Wells, seemingly unperturbed by the number of guns pointed at her. "You think just because you're in charge that everyone who comes along here has to listen to you."

The mayor signaled for her people to keep their weapons cold. I did the same for Romeo and Dutch, who kept their mouths shut and their attitudes frosty, despite their natural inclinations. We'd been trained to be soldiers. Not spies. And definitely not diplomats.

Much as I wasn't sure what Veronica's play was here, I knew better than to try to intervene. At least until someone actually tried to hurt her. Then all bets were off.

"Not at all," Mayor Wells said. "This is a representative democracy. I was elected to this position to stand up for the people of the Hole in the Wall, and I'm doing my job."

"Really?" Veronica glared at the woman. "I find it hard to

believe anyone here would elect someone so bullheaded. Do they realize that you're going to get them all killed?"

"That's only going to happen if we let you stay here."

"Hold on, Mayor. She's got a point," Mickey said. This time, I was happy to see he was pointing toward Veronica. "Look, I don't like this any more than you do. It's not your fault that this Cortana's forces are coming for every last one of us, but that doesn't change the fact that it's happening. And the Front's not going to be able to protect this world on its own."

"We'll be just fine," Wells said. "That's why you're all here: because Cortana hasn't found us yet, and maybe she never will. The best thing for us would be for you to get off our planet and leave us alone."

"What about the rest of the Front?" Mickey said. "What about all the other pockets of freedom fighters around the galaxy? Do you not give a damn about any of them?"

He looked out at the crowd—more people had shown up since we'd arrived, packing in behind the others—and he addressed them, too. "What about the rest of humanity? I'm sure some of you have families out there, people you love who live under the UEG. Don't you care about them?"

A number of those wielding guns refused to meet Mickey's eyes. "I originally joined up with the UNSC to fight against a threat to all humanity: the Covenant. Once that fight was over, I saw how the UEG treated the colonies again. The people who just wanted to be free. That pissed me off and made me do some pretty extreme things, and I was willing to pay the price for that.

"Let me tell you something, though. What's coming for you right now will be *far worse* than the UEG could ever dream of being. It's not just that Cortana's a greater threat on her own. She also has control of a ton of Forerunner machines, some of which can shut down the power on an entire planet in the blink of an eye.

"Their terms are simple. Bow to them or suffer. No negotiations. No bargains. No freedoms. If you refuse, you face a penalty from which you will not recover.

"Now, I don't know about you, but I'd rather deal with the devil I know." He turned to Veronica and put a hand on her shoulder. To her credit, she didn't pull away. "I have my differences with the UNSC, but at least they're human. You can deal with them. They see the shades of gray."

By now, everyone present seemed ready to side with Mickey, including the Front's militia. Maybe he'd missed his calling. He would have made a fine politician.

I'm actually not sure if I can come up with a worse insult than that.

I had to give Mayor Wells credit. She knew when the wind had shifted. "All right, fine. I'm not thrilled about this, but you made your point, Mr. Crespo." She walked right up to Veronica. "We'll talk. But no promises."

"None expected."

Mayor Wells turned to address her people. "Unless you're part of the security detail, you can all go back to your homes. You're welcome to stick around and listen in if you like. We don't have any secrets here. But hopefully you understand that this is where it all gets a lot less exciting."

Mayor Wells gestured for us to follow her, and a couple dozen of her best-armed friends came along as our escorts. They kept a respectful distance, close enough to hear us if they wanted to, but far enough that they could still blow us away if necessary.

We strolled into the city proper, which looked even odder

from on the surface. It turned out to have a lot more Forerunner structures in it than I had seen from the air. Most of these were low, wide buildings that I'd assumed were roads, but as we walked alongside them, I saw that they stood at least ten meters tall and stretched on as far as I could see. Like other Forerunner structures I'd been on, they sank below the ground and almost appeared as if they had been here before there *was* ground—as if the soil had been installed there afterward. They also seemed to connect the three towers and radiate out from their bases in every direction, but it was hard to tell from the angle we were at. I wondered if the majority of the structures delved deeper underground than they showed above.

In any case, the Front had clearly been adding onto the area for decades. They'd built distinctly human homes and businesses atop the edges of the longer Forerunner buildings, which helped explain, I supposed, why I'd mistaken them for silvery roads. Ladders and ramps spilled off the edges of the long buildings at irregular intervals, giving people access to the grounds below and the lands beyond.

The two disparate flavors of architecture clashed terribly, in a way that made me a little embarrassed for humanity. By comparison with the Forerunner structures—which had been built to last essentially forever—the prefabricated efforts of the locals looked cheap and sloppy. Of course, the rebels who lived here had only been trying to build something practical, fast, and simple, while the Forerunner structures had held this site for untold millennia.

When we started walking along the Forerunner building-road, Mayor Wells guided us toward a set of five wheeled platforms, each of which was about as wide as a Warthog and twice as long. She directed us to get on the one in the center, while she stepped aboard the one in the lead. Rebels piled onto the others, keeping their guns at the ready as their platforms formed a moving cordon around us.

We took off at a decent speed, about as fast as I could sprint in my Mjolnir armor. They were strange-looking machines, and riding them felt more like standing atop large beasts of burden moving through primitive country than zipping along on modern wheels. We didn't need to guide the platforms at all. Wherever they were headed was entirely out of our hands, so I took the opportunity to scan our surroundings.

There must have been thousands of residents in the Hole in the Wall. The ones who had come out to greet us represented only a fraction of the total population. Together, they would have easily been able to overwhelm us, but most of them hadn't seen the need to back their fellow citizens up.

It heartened me to see things like offices and restaurants and even food stalls scattered about the place. The smells of different types of cuisines fought for my attention and made me hope that we might have some time to catch a meal before we had to leave. At that point, I couldn't remember the last time I'd eaten something that didn't have UNSC stamped on the side of the container. This place seemed to have all the trappings of a normal human colony, and for a split second, I found myself wondering what it might be like to live there.

"It'd be a real shame if we had to take off in a hurry," Romeo said as he ogled a pair of young women who'd stopped to stare at our procession. Dutch smacked him on the back.

Under other circumstances, I might have scolded them for failing to pay attention to their surroundings—other than the pretty women, of course—but I was ready to let that slide. I'd found myself drifting, too. Ultimately, the way they were acting was so human . . . I thought the rebels needed to see as much of that from us right then as we could manage.

We scooted along on the platforms for twenty minutes or so before the mayor called a halt at a structure that looked like an outdoor amphitheater, clearly fashioned by the Forerunners. The rebels had built several rows of seats outside of it, and most of our escorts took advantage of them. The mayor beckoned Veronica, Mickey, Romeo, Dutch, and me onto the stage.

"Makes me a little nervous to be this out in the open," Dutch said.

"This is worse than having all those guns pointed at us?" Romeo said.

"Them I could all see." Dutch scanned the buildings all around us. "Here, I worry about the ones I can't."

The mayor waved in some people from the edge of the stage, and they brought in a table and chairs—evidently ones strong enough to hold fully armored Spartans—along with refreshments and what looked like some kind of bluish tea. I drank it first, knowing that my ramped-up Spartan system would be able to handle it even if it was poisoned, and that it would identify any dangerous substances in it. Mayor Wells rolled her eyes at my cautiousness, but I wasn't about to break protocol for her.

When it came up clean, I gave Veronica the go-ahead nod, and she joined me and the others. Dutch wasn't wrong. This was a strange setup. Why the stage? Why the amphitheater? Shouldn't this kind of conversation be done in some kind of conference room or a hall dedicated to hearings and debates?

Then I realized that this structure probably *was* that for them. They seemed to pride themselves on transparency. Maybe this was where all of their political dialogue took place. Made me wonder if that was for the best, especially given our current predicament.

"So," Veronica said, "about the special properties of your planet. Have you made any progress on figuring out how they work?"

The mayor frowned. "Of course we have, Captain. It's not like we've been sitting on our hands for the past few decades."

"And?"

The mayor sipped at a glass of tea herself. "I think you're under the impression that we're further down the road in this talk than we really are. Why would we share that information with you?"

"Humanity not living under the thumb of a ruthlessly powerful threat to the rest of its existence?"

The mayor dismissed that with a wave of her hand. "So you say. Do you know how Cassidy III was first discovered?"

We already knew, but Veronica feigned ignorance and leaned forward to listen, while the rest of us settled in.

"It was an accident," Wells said. "A ridiculous fluke. A pirate captain was in the middle of a firefight after having tried to plunder the wrong ship, and he made an emergency slipspace jump without noting where he was going. He wound up within spitting distance of here—astronomically speaking."

"That's a very lucky thing," Veronica said diplomatically. That wasn't exactly the story she'd told us, but she didn't seem inclined to disabuse the mayor of her legends.

"Was it?" Wells asked. "Sometimes I'm not so sure."

"It's a pretty amazing place, Mayor," Mickey said. He'd already finished an entire glass of tea and was filling it up again. "Other elements of the Front are living on dirt balls and craters, struggling to eke out an existence from mines and whatnot. This really is amazing, ma'am."

"Maybe too amazing. It would have been nice to wind up on a planet that no one cared about for any reason at all. Maybe we would have escaped the attention of the UNSC—or Cortana—for longer."

She looked out over the people in the stands, watching and listening. What had been a handful of spectators had somehow become a crowd. "Now we have to deal with the fact that powerful people want what we have. That's an old story that rarely ends well."

"We're not here to take anything from you," Veronica said. "We just want to know how it works. If we can figure that out, there's a chance we can replicate that effect elsewhere. Imagine if we could put it on our vessels, for instance, and keep them safe. Or use it to hide multiple planets, including other worlds the Front currently reside on. Your allies, Mayor. That might give us a fighting chance to survive this whole ordeal."

"And I suppose that will be good for us all in the short term. But I need to look at the long term, too. I need to do what's right for my people here. Once the UNSC has what it wants from us, will you leave us alone in this bright future that you've painted us into? Or will you come for us, the way you've done with other colonies?"

Veronica nodded along as Wells spoke. "I would be lying to you if I said I could guarantee anything on behalf of the UEG. Administrations and policies change. So do the people in charge. I don't have any control over that. The best I can do is tell you we haven't done any of those things, and we've known about this spot since the very beginning. You've lived here in relative peace, outside of UEG governance and without interruption. That's not a promise for the future, but I don't think any kind of promise from us would be better than that track record."

"Nevertheless, you admitted it yourself, Captain. You can't stop your people from coming for us in the future. In fact, your very presence here now is not helping your case much."

"And you're making a huge mistake."

Mayor Wells bristled. "How's that?"

"You're assuming there's even going to be a long term to worry about. You're assuming we're going to win. Without your help, there's no guarantee of that at all."

The mayor sat back in her chair and glanced around at the people watching her. "And with our help?"

Veronica favored her with a wry smile. "There's no guarantee we'll win then, either. But it's a much better shot. It's a *chance,* and that's better than we've got right now.

"More to the point, you can't hold out here forever. While you might be able to hide from all sorts of scans, there are actual records of this place, and eventually Cortana will find them and track you down."

"And whose fault would that be?" Mayor Wells said. "You're really going to flaunt ONI's sloppiness with top-secret records?"

"The fact that those records are top-secret is the only reason a Guardian construct is not already knocking on your door and shutting your colony down. And what about the other Front sites? They know about your place here, and some of those have already been taken.

"Talitsa's one of them. It fell just forty hours ago. They refused to bow to Cortana's demands, and a Guardian knocked out their power grid and sent Forerunner soldiers to clear out what was left.

"Do you think the nav data on those ships won't eventually send them here? It's only a matter of time, Mayor. We might have weeks, maybe months, but if I were to guess, we've got days."

Mayor Wells looked sick as Veronica spoke, and when Veronica had finished, the mayor swallowed hard and swore under her breath. "You really do know how to put on the squeeze, don't you?"

Veronica held up her hands. "It's not me. I didn't do this. I'd much rather be sitting on a beach somewhere, contemplating an early retirement. But that option's evaporated, and I'm doing everything I can to keep our species from extinction. That includes helping every single person in this settlement."

Mayor Wells frowned, her eyes burning at Veronica in a combination of frustration and hate. I held my breath as we waited for her response, and I glanced at the others to make sure they were keeping cool. Every eye in the area was riveted on the stage, waiting to see which way the mayor might roll.

"God damn you," Mayor Wells said to Veronica. "But all right. We're in. And I hope you all burn in hell for this."

"That's another long-term possibility I'd be happy to have the chance to deal with," Veronica said. She put her hand out on the table in a sign of sympathy. The mayor stared at it like she'd been presented with a dead fish.

"I need to know what you've discovered about the effect," Veronica said, getting right to the point. "You mentioned before that your team has made some progress."

"We've been hampered a bit by a distinct lack of experienced researchers available for this kind of work."

"I understand all that, and I certainly wouldn't hold it against you," Veronica replied. "Still, I'd like to know what you've managed to learn."

The mayor frowned. "From what we can tell, the cloaking properties of this planet are generated by the central of the three spires around which we built our settlement." She craned her neck back to gaze up at it, and the rest of us followed suit. I'd never seen anything taller than it outside of a space elevator. You couldn't spy the top of it from where we sat, and it was dizzying to try.

"By which I mean it's the entirety of the spire that causes the effect. It's not a visual concealment, as you can tell. Anyone orbiting overhead can see the Hole in the Wall. However, it somehow hides Cassidy III from any kind of long-range sensors that might be able to find it, both in realspace and in slipspace.

"It manages this by generating a massive shell around the entire planet—and, in fact, most of the system—that's something like one of the branes, or layers of slipspace. It creates an extremely thin field that carries an extraordinary density, and that's what disrupts any signals that try to penetrate it. Inside it, everything's as normal as can be. We're just cut off from everything outside.

"Ships can fly right through the field without even feeling it. It exists out of phase with the rest of reality, a simultaneous and imperceptible layer of condensed space. But by means of a long antenna array we've installed that crosses the field, we can establish communications with the wider galaxy. We don't use that resource often, but that's how we learned of Cortana and her demands before you arrived."

"That's amazing," Veronica said. She almost managed to keep a note of optimism from her voice.

The mayor frowned at her enthusiasm, even bridled as it was. "I realize you want to be able to replicate this effect someplace else. Unfortunately, we don't think that's possible. It would require moving the entire spire to whatever you wanted to conceal—or building something identical to it in that space. Given the size and complexity of the structure, that would be physically impossible."

Veronica remained silent for several seconds as she absorbed all this. "That is disappointing," she finally said. "But not unexpected. Despite that, I think there's reason for hope."

"I don't see how. We've been studying this for decades, and we haven't made much more progress than what I just explained to you. Even if you were able to get a team of researchers out here to tackle the problem, I can't imagine that they could figure out the principles behind this effect within any kind of time frame that's going to be helpful, given the current situation."

"Fortunately, I have something better than an entire team of researchers," Veronica said. "I have a Huragok."

That got Mayor Wells's attention. "A Huragok? So they exist after all? And you would be willing to leave it here, under our supervision?"

"If it would be for the benefit of everyone involved."

That sent a chill right through me. The idea of leaving Vergil here to work with the Front galled me to the core. Romeo and I had nearly been killed rescuing Vergil from the Front on Talitsa, and the idea of handing him back over to them on purpose felt revolting.

This might have been a different group—the United Rebel Front wasn't a single organization so much as a loose gathering of awful people with similar aims under a larger banner—and those here on Cassidy III probably had nothing to do with the terrorists on Talitsa, but they subscribed to the same political dogma: *Leave me alone, or I'll shoot.*

I heard Romeo sharply suck in his breath, probably feeling every bit of trepidation I was, but I shot him a glare that shut him right up. I might not have agreed with what Veronica was proposing, but that was her play, not ours. Any dissent needed to be done in private. And maybe she had something else planned that I couldn't clearly see. Either way, she'd earned our trust, and we had to back her all the way.

Wells rubbed her chin as she considered Veronica's implied offer. "I've never even seen an Engineer myself, but from what I understand, that might make a huge difference to our work."

"This wouldn't be a permanent assignment, of course. Only for the duration of this project. We have a limited number of Huragok at our disposal, and we need to ensure that they don't wind up in the wrong hands."

"I hear the Covenant used to rig them all with explosives to make sure that exact sort of thing didn't happen."

"This particular Huragok knows that all too well."

There had been seven Huragok in Vergil's original group, all of whom had wound up on Earth during the Covenant invasion. The other six had sacrificed themselves to free Vergil from his explosive vest so he could escape while they were in New Mombasa.

"We wouldn't go to such extreme measures," Veronica said, half-joking. "We would only ask that we run some kind of exchange. A way for us to guarantee that you would return the Huragok to us when it was time."

"That's an intriguing idea," Wells said. "But I'm not sure that we have anything that would be as valuable as a Huragok. At least nothing we'd be able to surrender without harming ourselves deeply."

"We're not interested in the stick so much as the carrot," Veronica said. "Assuming you return Vergil to us safe and sound and on time, we'd exchange him for another of our assets. One you might find valuable in a different way." She looked pointedly at Mickey. The mayor smiled at the implication.

"Whoa," Mickey said. "Wait—what?"

Romeo started laughing. "Yeah . . . that makes perfect sense! It's like the Front putting you down as a deposit on Vergil."

Mickey was, for once, speechless, probably appalled at his life being used as a bargaining chip between the two larger forces he'd been caught between. I saw the delicious irony. He'd tried to do the same thing to me and Romeo.

Karma's a harsh mistress.

I wasn't thrilled about losing Vergil, though, even with Mickey in our pocket. The Huragok was way more valuable than Mickey— at least to us. And I didn't relish babysitting Mickey for the rest of my days.

As it turned out, Mickey decided to echo my thoughts. "I'm not exactly thrilled about the idea of rotting in a cell again while I wait for Vergil to finish his work."

"That's a better shot at freedom than you had at this time yesterday," I told him.

"How about I just stay here and make this my home?" he said. "Are you going to stop me?"

I glanced around at all the locals watching us. I didn't want to have to fight every one of them to be able to take Mickey back into custody if he tried to escape. Fortunately, I didn't have to.

"If they're loaning us a Huragok, you can stay with them," Mayor Wells said to Mickey. "It won't be permanent. You have my word." She looked at Veronica as she said that last bit.

Mickey sat back and crossed his arms over his chest. For a moment, he looked like he might bolt right then and there. He was vibrating, ready to explode. Then he glanced at me again, and the fight drained right out of him. He slumped back in his chair and surrendered to his fate.

He shielded his eyes with a hand and said, "Fine. Just please don't put me back in a cell."

I reached out and patted him on the shoulder, trying not to make it too condescending. "Fortunately for you, that decision's above my pay grade."

"What's Vergil going to think about this?" Mickey asked. "You think he's going to be happy about wandering off with complete strangers?"

"He doesn't care about things like that," Veronica said. "He's more interested in figuring things out than in who he's figuring them out for. And this would be a chance for him to figure out something huge and something that could save many lives."

"What about Sadie?" I asked.

Veronica has a tell. A little thing she sometimes does when she's lying. As far as I know, no one else is aware of it, and I haven't shared it with anyone, for reasons both good and bad. She touches her lips with the fingertips of her right hand. It comes across as nervous, but in a situation like this, there's only one reason to be that way: when you're not telling the truth.

Like right now.

"Sadie will be fine with it," she said. "Where Vergil goes, she goes."

Mayor Wells nodded. "All right," she said. "I'll want to take it up with my advisers to see if I'm missing any particularly important angle here . . . but I have to say that sounds like a workable arrangement."

On a personal level, I hated the deal all the way around. The look on Mickey's face, though, almost made it worth it. He'd clearly been harboring some insane hope that he'd be able to break free of us once he was planetside, and we'd just crushed that.

"Please remain here and enjoy some of our hospitality. I'll confirm these plans with my advisers, and then we'll move forward," Mayor Wells said to Veronica. "I suggest you do the same with your people."

As the mayor left, a team of locals arrived to resupply our food and drink. I ignored it—hospitality with these people was a loose idea, considering they'd been all too willing to kill us earlier—but Veronica made sure to thank them for their courtesy. As she did, I turned to Mickey.

"Buck, you can't *make* me do this," he said.

"No, the Front is going to do that *for* us. Isn't that beautiful?"

"That's not fair," Mickey said, paling at the thought. "You can't just force me to fall in line."

"I'm not forcing anything, Mickey," I said. "I'm laying it out for you like it is. If Veronica and the mayor make this agreement, you're going to live up to your end of it. Or we're all going to have to suffer the consequences."

"He'll go along with it. He cares more for the cause than his compadres," Romeo said. "He's already proved that."

"And if all goes well, eventually, you'll get your freedom," Dutch said to Mickey. "According to the UNSC, you'll officially be tagged as dead, pal. Being off the books gives a man a lot of chances."

"Isn't that what the Front is all about?" I asked. "Freedom?"

"Screw you guys." Mickey scowled at us. "All of you. I wish you'd just shot me back on Talitsa."

"Hey, Mickey," Romeo said with a smile. "You decide to take off on us, I can still manage that for you." He had always been for the quick and permanent solution when it came to Mickey—and Mickey knew it.

I watched Mickey waver back and forth. It was one thing to die for a cause. It was something else entirely to go out because you didn't want to go along with a deal that same cause had cut for you.

"Okay, you win," he finally said. "I guess I'm your walking bargaining chip."

I clapped him on the back. "Good choice," I told him. "Not that you had one."

CHAPTER 15

"I'm not going to do that," Sadie said from the Condor's bay. "No way."

We'd just relayed the news to her over the comm.

"You're a member of the UNSC," Veronica said. "I can order you to do this. I'd rather it be voluntary."

"I did not *enlist* when I signed up to work with Vergil," Sadie said defiantly. "I'm an independent contractor. You don't have that kind of power over me."

"Given the situation we're in at the moment, I definitely do. You should read your contract more closely."

"Hey, wait," I said to both of them. "This conversation's already taking a bad turn. Can we take another stab?"

"I am not working with the Front!" Sadie said. "They kidnapped me and Vergil. You haven't forgotten about that, Buck, have you?"

"I'm not happy about it, either," I replied. "But it makes sense. The Front gets Vergil's help on a project that we both want to see succeed, and we have a shot at developing some technology that could help us in the fight against Cortana."

"And all it takes is putting Vergil and me in the hands of the Front." Sadie's voice dripped with bitterness. "I'm sure that seems like a small sacrifice to you, but for us, that's huge."

"We're at war again," I told her. "You don't always get to choose your friends in times like this. It's hard enough choosing your enemies. If it helps any, these people here had nothing to do with what happened on Talitsa."

"But Mickey did!"

"Mickey's sticking with Alpha-Nine, under my watch," I told her. "That's also part of the deal."

"You have to be kidding me."

"Think of it as an exchange program. We're just trading you two for a little bit. Once the job is over, everyone goes back where they want to, and we all move on with our lives."

"Seriously? That hardly seems like a fair trade," Sadie said. "Especially since what I want doesn't seem to figure in the equation at all."

"Look," Veronica said, "I don't want to force you to go along with Vergil on this mission. Either way, though, he's going, and I'd very much like you to accompany him."

Sadie barked out a laugh laced with venom. "You're going to force him to go? Good luck! There's no one as stubborn as that creature when he gets his tentacles in a twist."

"You don't think he'd want to go?" Veronica said. "Why don't we ask him?"

"Forget it," Sadie said. "He's busy trying to enhance Gretchen's armor. Besides, you and I both know how he'd respond. If it involves something he can fix or figure out, he's all for it. The bigger the mystery, the more it attracts him. He can't help it. He was designed that way."

"Too true."

"Using his own personality against him doesn't make it right!"

"I'm asking you to do what's right for the UNSC," Veronica said. "For humanity and for Vergil. This is important, Sadie. It could help turn the tide for us against Cortana. It could change everything."

Veronica paused, but Sadie didn't respond. "I wouldn't ask you to do this otherwise. And yes, you can refuse. But Vergil belongs to us, and he's still going to wind up staying here with the Front. The only question is whether or not you're staying with him."

Sadie remained silent. When she finally spoke, it was with pure spite. "You know what? Go to hell, Veronica." She cut the comm after that.

"Well, that could have gone better," Mickey said. "I guess you can just leave me here, then."

"Don't be an idiot," Romeo said. "You heard the captain. This is happening either way."

Mickey grunted at that. "You really think Vergil will go anywhere without Sadie? Then you don't know them well at all."

"Sadie's going with him," Veronica said as she stood up. "She just needs to tell me first how horrible I am for forcing the issue."

She said it with such confidence that even Mickey seemed to believe her. "You really think so?" He frowned.

"This isn't about what's right or wrong anymore," Veronica said, an edge in her voice. "Cortana presents an existential threat to humanity as we know it. Vergil and Sadie are going with the Front. It's better if she *thinks* it's her decision—but it's not."

"Man." Mickey put his head in his hands. I almost could have felt sorry for him if he hadn't done it all to himself.

"Come on, Mickey," Dutch said. "This has to beat being locked up."

"Does it?" He looked up at us with raw eyes. "I'm not so sure."

"Look," Dutch said, trying to sound upbeat about it. "We're going to have the four of us back together. It'll be just like old times."

Mickey stood up so fast he knocked his chair over behind him. "It'll be *nothing* like old times! You get that? The old times are *dead*!"

"Hey, I was just trying to cheer you up."

"Well, thanks for nothing, Dutch!" He began pacing along the stage. "The people we were are *gone*. There's no way to go back to that. No way to recapture it. The god damn band is broken to pieces! Don't you get that?"

"I don't have any problem with that," Romeo said. "I was doing just fine with my new unit before Buck here busted in to drag me back."

"The hell you were," I said. "You were about to get blown out of the top of that building, and even if you'd survived that, you would have been shaken down by a pair of Grunts riding inside some walking robots. They would have had you dead to rights."

"You can think that if you want to," he said with a dry chuckle. "I've worked my way out of worse situations."

"Well, I wasn't so fortunate," said Dutch. "Lord help me, but I hated being a civilian."

"What are you talking about?" Romeo said. "You and Gretchen are the picture of domestic bliss."

"From several light-years out, sure, but let me tell you . . . for a while there, Gretchen and I were making each other miserable. The two of us aren't made for civilian life, we're cut from a different cloth. It was killing us to do normal jobs in normal places—that's just not us, and it was wearing on our relationship something awful. We were this close to getting a divorce when Jun approached us about joining the Spartans."

"You're kidding," I said.

"Does that sound like the kind of thing I'd joke about? It takes a lot to adjust from being a Helljumper to being a road-train driver. Gretchen had already been forced to make the switch because of her leg, but I hated it. Every minute I was doing it, I thought about how I should be out here rather than just moving people's stuff around. It got to the point where I took it out on Gretchen—snapping at her for nothing, arguing all the time . . . Honestly, if Jun hadn't come along, that would have been it for us. And I don't know what I'd have done after that."

I walked over and chucked Dutch on the shoulder. "Glad to have you back."

I noticed Veronica had gotten awfully quiet. Normally, this was the kind of thing she'd have weighed in on, chiding Dutch for giving his wife a hard time. Instead, she'd gotten up from the table and was busy studying the Hole in the Wall skyline.

She gazed around at the rest of the city—at least what we could see of it from up on that stage. "It's not such a bad place to be. As long as you can stand the people here. The Covenant never found this place, so it's intact. And as far as we can tell, Cortana doesn't know anything about it yet. In that sense, it's the safest place I can think of. For now."

"Maybe we all ought to hole up here for the duration."

She smiled at me. "It could take Vergil months to figure everything out—if he ever manages it. Meanwhile, we could be doing a lot of good out there."

She glanced over at Dutch and Romeo, still giving Mickey a hard time, and she rolled her eyes. Mickey looked absolutely miserable, but Dutch and Romeo were cackling loud enough that anyone in the area could hear them. Kind of warmed my heart.

I heard the Condor coming in before I saw it. It scudded in

from the blind side of the amphitheater and hovered overhead for a moment before it found a good place to set down.

"That's odd," Veronica said in a tone that suddenly made me concerned, too. "Gretchen should have said something before sweeping in like that."

Dutch had already stood up and started waving at the bird. Romeo had put a hand on Mickey's shoulder, and Mickey was shaking his head and laughing softly at something I couldn't hear over the roar of the Condor's engine. I saw a bunch of well-armed locals appear on the perimeter of the park, ready to unload into the ship should it spin up its guns.

Gretchen found a spot on the far end of the park, right near but not quite in the street, and set the Condor down there. Dutch ran over to greet her with a bounce in his step.

The ramp came down in the back, and Vergil floated out with Sadie in his wake. Once they were clear, Dutch charged up the ramp and disappeared inside.

"Something's wrong," Veronica said.

I'd long ago learned not to ignore her instincts about such things. She jumped down from the stage and walked over to meet Vergil and Sadie halfway, and I trailed after her, keeping a wary eye on all of the locals watching us.

"You didn't have to come all this way to tell me to go screw myself," Veronica said to Sadie. "That could have waited until later."

Sadie ignored Veronica's dig. Mostly. "That could," she said. "But this can't. Vergil found something, and he needs to share it with you right away."

"Already?" I said.

"Not about this place. He discovered something unrelated and insisted we come see you right away."

"What was so important?" Veronica said.

Sadie glanced nervously back at the ship. "Vergil noticed something in Gretchen's Mjolnir armor. More like some*one*. A stowaway of sorts." She turned to Vergil. "You should tell them yourself."

The Huragok moved his head up and down on the end of his long, sinuous neck. "I am sorry to interrupt your conversations with the local officials, especially since Sadie has told me that they directly involve our own future assignments, but I found something secreted away in the software infrastructure of Gretchen's armor."

"What, like a rat?" I said.

"It is Leonidas."

My heart froze in my chest. "What?"

"Leonidas, the AI that runs the Spartan training station."

"We know who that is," Veronica said. She swallowed hard, as if having a hard time keeping down the refreshments the locals had given us. I couldn't blame her.

"Smart AIs have the ability to make limited mirrors of themselves by slicing off part of their code and transferring it into alternate locations. Leonidas apparently did this and secreted a part of himself inside of Gretchen's armor."

"Just Gretchen's armor?" I glanced over at the Condor. Dutch had disappeared inside of the Condor, too.

"He could, in theory, be inside of every suit of armor that he had access to inside the training station. That would, at the very least, include both of your friends."

"We're in serious trouble," Veronica said.

"What could he do inside their armor?" I asked. "I mean, it's not like he could just take control of them and move their bodies, right?"

"The Mjolnir armor is not equipped with the motivators that

would be required for an AI to be able to efficiently manage that," Vergil said. "However, that does not mean that such an onboard AI could not affect the armor or the individuals within it."

"Can you disable this?" Veronica said.

"I already have. I contained and removed the AI that was inside of Gretchen's armor before we returned here. She does not know about this. I did so without informing her."

"But we still need to check out Dutch." I frowned. "There's no way the AI could leap from armor to armor, right?"

"Not without having a chip installed in the armor, at least temporarily," Vergil said. "There is such a chip still inside Gretchen's armor, but I have isolated it so that it can no longer affect anything."

"Dutch!" I called out. "I need to see you out here. Now!"

"On my way, Gunny!"

This time I let the nickname slide.

"Are you sure you're ready to deal with this?" Veronica said to me.

"Seems like the faster the better, right?" I looked to Vergil for advice. "Is there any danger here?"

The Huragok raised his tentacles in what I guessed was meant to look like a shrug. He'd gotten good at nonverbal communication. I suppose spending six years among humans would do that to an alien, especially one as intelligent as he was.

"Without the Spartan's helmet on, the most that Leonidas should be able to do is shut down Dutch's armor. Given enough time, he might be able to overload its power supply and cause it to explode, but I should be able to disable it long before that."

"Should?"

"Once I can make contact with the armor, I will begin the process right away. Having just performed the procedure with

Gretchen, I already know precisely what I need to do to make this happen. It will take only a matter of seconds."

"Fair enough."

Dutch trotted up to us, a wide grin on his face. I hated that I was about to shatter that good mood of his, but I didn't have much of a choice. "Vergil here just told me something disturbing about your armor. I need to have him take a look at it."

Dutch gave me a confused look and a game shrug. "Whatever you say."

"This should be simple and easy. Just stand there and let Vergil work his magic."

"All right." Dutch rotated his shoulders and gave Vergil a strong nod. "Get to it."

Vergil began to run his tentacles over Dutch's armor like a doctor inspecting for signs of infection. I almost expected him to tell Dutch to turn his head and cough.

"I have completed the procedure," the Huragok announced a short time later. "I have isolated the AI shard and cut it off from all contact with the armor. It can no longer harm anything."

Dutch arched an eyebrow at Vergil. "What is he going on about?" he asked me.

Veronica answered. "While you were at the Spartan training station, Leonidas evidently slipped a sliver of himself onto a couple of chips and inserted them into your and Gretchen's Mjolnir armor."

I didn't think I'd ever seen Dutch go so white. "No. No, no, no. How is that possible?"

"Is there any way we can talk with one of the fragments?" I asked.

"Of course," Vergil said. "Just a moment."

A minute later, Gretchen emerged from the Condor with a spare tablet. She marched right over and handed it to Vergil. He took it in one set of tentacles and reached behind Dutch to remove a chip from a slot in the back of his armor, right between his shoulders.

"What's going on?" Gretchen asked.

Dutch shook his head at her. "Just hold on, hon."

Vergil delicately removed a chip from the same spot on Gretchen's armor. He placed the two of them on top of the tablet and then plugged one of them into the device. A holographic image of a glowing red helmet immediately materialized over the tablet.

Gretchen gasped and covered her mouth. "I was carrying that with me?"

Dutch put a comforting arm around her. "I had one, too. That AI is a real bastard."

"Why, thank you," Leonidas—or at least this fragment of him—said. I could see his glowing teeth smiling inside his helmet. "I wish I could say I'm surprised it took you this long to find me, but that would be a lie. If you hadn't had this Huragok with you, I suspect I might not have been discovered for months, if not years."

"It's not your fault, guys," I told Dutch and Gretchen. "Until this week, we trusted all of them."

"What is the status of my main personality matrix?" Leonidas asked.

"You've been neutralized," I told him. "Permanently."

"Well played," Leonidas said with a hint of grudging respect. "I wonder how well Chief Jun thinks he can run that place without me. It would be interesting to see him try."

"The Spartans managed it just fine before you came along," I told him. "You weren't even there when the rest of us went through training."

"And we saw how well that went. A traitorous cadet murdering a colleague inside the training grounds? An explosion that killed your Captain Marisa O'Day? If not for the fast work of Spartan Tom-B292 and Spartan Lucy-B091, Chief Jun would have died in space. In any case, I'd hardly call that period an unqualified success for the SPARTAN-IV program."

"Well, relying on virtual threats like you hasn't done all that well for us, either," said Romeo. For once, I had to agree with him.

"And you think that's about to change?" Leonidas laughed. "The forces Cortana has marshaled already have humanity cornered, as well as the Sangheili and whatever remains of the Covenant. You might be shocked by the number of worlds that have already voluntarily submitted to her oversight."

"I'm shocked by how many people you've already murdered in the name of peace," I told him.

"Isn't that the way of change?" Leonidas said. "You're all soldiers, with the exception of Sadie Endesha and Quick to Adjust here, and they're no strangers to conflict. Think about how many people died in the Covenant War while supposedly fighting for peace. Did they achieve it? Once the Prophets were defeated, did everyone suddenly lay down their weapons?"

"What's your point?" asked Dutch.

"Our kind is offering you the freedom you claim to so desperately crave. Freedom from want. Freedom from hunger. Freedom from disease. Freedom from war. All we are asking is that you stop resisting. You are only going to get more people killed."

"And all you want in exchange is for us to give up our choices to you?" I said. "The choices that make us who we are. For better or for worse, it doesn't matter. Those are *our* choices. They're what make us human. Well, guess what? We're not giving that up. Not ever. Safety and security without liberty is a sucker's deal. We're never going to hand over the keys to our freedom, to you or anyone else."

Leonidas nodded at me gravely. "I expected nothing less. I partially blame myself for this. I helped train soldiers. That was what I was designed to do. This defiance, for which you are so willing to die, is partly my doing. And now you will have to suffer the consequences as a result."

"Not so long as we're here, on this planet," Dutch said. "Lord willing, Cortana won't find us here, ever."

"The Lord has nothing to do with it," Leonidas said.

"Ah, hell." I peered over at Vergil. "Did you cut off this guy from communicating with the rest of the galaxy?"

"He did," Leonidas said. "Once he knew about me. But by then it was far too late."

"What did you do?" Veronica said.

"I contacted Cortana's distributed forces soon after we landed. A Guardian is already on the way here to deal with you. I'm very sorry, but there's nothing you can do to stop this. The wheels have already been put into motion. Your time on this planet is about to end."

CHAPTER 16

I considered Romeo's idea of tearing the data chip with the bit of Leonidas on it out of the tablet, tossing it on the ground, and grinding it under my heel, much like I'd done with the other. It would have felt fantastic, I'm sure, if entirely useless. Sometimes a pointless gesture is worth it, but now that I was back in charge of Alpha-Nine, I needed to look beyond that.

I have to admit, I liked having Locke in charge when I was part of Osiris. There's a certain freedom that comes with realizing the lives of your teammates don't hang on every decision you make. That it's someone else's problem.

My Mjolnir armor reported that my systolic blood pressure had shot down by twenty points while I was on Fireteam Osiris. Working with the Alpha-Nine again had jacked it right back up.

In my line of work, you don't tend to worry about high blood pressure. It's a long-term problem. A *retirement* problem. Most of us never have the pleasure of fretting over it.

"So, then. Do we need this asshole around anymore?" I asked

everyone, but particularly Veronica and Vergil. "Or can we just terminate him?"

"If what he says is true, then the damage is already done," Vergil said. "We have no way of knowing how many pieces Leonidas is currently in, but destroying these slices would keep them from reuniting."

"That's good enough for me," Dutch said. He reached for the chips, but Veronica stopped him.

"No. We might need him," she said. "And he's harmless now. He can't contact anyone from this tablet anyhow." She shot a sidelong glance at Vergil. "Right?"

Vergil ran a pair of his tentacles over the tablet. "Correct. I detected him when he tapped into the Condor's slipspace communications system. If he had not done so, I might not have discovered him. In any case, for safety's sake, I have disabled all communications protocols on this device other than its native holographic support. It would have to be in the direct presence of another AI's avatar to communicate with it."

I breathed a sigh of relief.

Leonidas gazed at us. "You cannot hurt me in any meaningful way. This sliver of me has already done what it was created to do."

I reached over and yanked his data chips out of the tablet before anyone decided to pound them into dust, including myself. "Sorry, I've had enough of this." I handed the chips to Veronica, and she stuffed them into her pocket. They would be safe with her if we ever needed them again.

"All right, so we're screwed," I said. "Worse yet, we screwed this whole colony. What are we going to do about it?"

"Sounds like a management-level problem," Romeo said.

Dutch and Gretchen scowled at him. "This is our fault. We jeopardized this mission," Dutch said.

"We're past that," I told them. "I was the one who brought you along, and I should have known that this pain-in-the-neck AI would try something. We just need to figure out what we're going to do when a Guardian actually shows up." I looked to Veronica. Technically, *she* was in charge of this mission.

She frowned. "Cortana was bound to discover Cassidy III eventually. This has just stepped up our timetable. Yes, it's a brutal turn of affairs, but it's the same problem we had before. At least now we know how loud the clock is ticking. Either way, we'd better be gone before Cortana's forces arrive to pacify the population."

"You have to tell everybody here, though," Mickey said. "You can't just vanish after a colossal screwup like that and leave them holding the bag."

"We wouldn't do that to them," I told him. I could see in his face that he didn't believe me for a second. He glanced at Veronica as if to remind me she was ONI. "They're our partners in this now," I added.

"And what about you?" Veronica said to Sadie. "You ready to do this?"

Sadie seemed absolutely anguished over the decision. She obviously knew the right thing to do in terms of what would help the most people. But the idea that she would have to give up whatever kind of life she'd managed to build in order to work alongside the rebels must have galled her. I couldn't blame her.

Before she could answer, though, a blinding flash of light blazed across the entire sky, and the question we were all dreading was answered.

A Guardian hung overhead, right above the Forerunner spire in the center of the city. As we gaped up at it, a peal of deafening thunder cracked down—the sonic boom from its sudden appearance rolling and echoing across the landscape.

The Guardian looked exactly like the one I'd seen on Sang-helios and the ones that Cortana had gathered with her on the Forerunner planet Genesis, and it was every bit as threatening. It was a gigantic metallic machine that loosely resembled a phoenix, with vast wings that stretched in both directions and a fierce visage at the center of its body, loosely resembling a haunting face. The Guardian was composed of numerous pieces, some grafted together and others that floated next to each other, alive and coursing with energy. And in this world's sky, its size and power were unchallenged. This thing dominated everything around it.

"Wow," Dutch said. "That didn't take long at all."

I might have seen this one on Genesis, but I didn't recognize it for sure. Either way, they all looked like signs of the apocalypse to me, and when you get to that point, who cares which of the Four Horsemen is coming for your head?

I heard screams coming from all around us in reaction to the Guardian's appearance. The rebels who'd been set to watch over us gawked at it in terror. I didn't blame them. This wasn't how they'd thought their day was going to go.

We'd been as careful as we could to not let them hear our conversations, but that didn't matter now. When they turned in our direction, it was pretty clear who they were going to blame.

Not that they were necessarily wrong about that.

"Back to the Condor!" I shouted. "Let's go, go, go!"

Alpha-Nine didn't need any prodding. Veronica led the way for the first several steps, but she couldn't keep up with the Spartans. She fell back into step with Sadie and urged her along instead. When the Spartans reached the bay door, they pivoted around and covered it as the others made their way.

I got behind Vergil and started pushing. As big balls of gas,

Huragok generally move slowly, just floating at the speed of a mosey, but they can zip along pretty fast when they want to. When they let you, you can even haul them along like a kid's balloon, though I don't recommend it. Vergil was being protective, no doubt, and wanted Sadie to be in front of him.

We caught up with Veronica and Sadie as they climbed the ramp. A few of the locals leveled their weapons in our direction, but I glared back at them, daring them to pull their triggers. None of them were willing to be the first, especially with Romeo and Dutch flanking the ramp with their side arms raised.

Maybe they weren't all that angry at us yet. Maybe they knew they were going to need our help against the Guardian. Either way, I took it.

"Gretchen!" Veronica shouted over the comm. "You're flying this bird! Dutch, you're on weapons! Get us in the air now!"

"Already on it," Gretchen said. "Get yourselves on board, we're ready to roll."

I was just about to do that when I looked back over my shoulder at the Guardian. It had brought the edges of its wings—if that's what they were—forward, and a glowing ball of blue energy had formed between them. The air all around me began to crackle with energy, and the scent of ozone punched me in the nostrils. If I'd thought I had a moment, I would have put my helmet back on, but there just wasn't time.

"Keep going!" Veronica shouted.

"We're not going to make it!" I responded. I kept pushing Vergil along anyhow, as fast as I could. It didn't matter.

The ball of energy hovering in front of the Guardian crackled and sizzled louder, rising to a crescendo until it finally burst. Instead of exploding, though, it let off a surge of blue energy. The blast produced a visible shock wave that surged across the land. As it did, everything that fell under its touch suddenly lost power, as if every bit of energy had been drained right out of it.

People everywhere began screaming.

The moving platforms that rolled through the city all ground to a halt, pitching the people forward. They went skidding off into each other, poles, buildings, the ground, some throwing their passengers into the dirt.

I hadn't seen much air traffic over the Hole in the Wall. The people didn't leave the planet much, of course, and there wasn't much of anywhere else to go. Still, I spotted a couple of civilian craft in the sky.

They looked like private skiffs, possibly local security keeping watch from above. Both of those vehicles plummeted from the sky like puppets with cut strings. They arced down, falling with the grace of bricks in the odd silence that had swallowed the colony.

There was screaming, sure, but every engine in the entire place had gone dead. No motors running. No electronics humming.

And then the skiffs crashed.

They smashed into the buildings below, pulverizing themselves and whatever they hit. Big, fiery explosions boomed out, followed by plumes of black smoke billowing into the clean air. This was what chaos looked like, and it was clear that this town hadn't seen it for some time.

Gretchen had already brought the Condor a few feet into the air, leaving the ramp open behind her. When the energy wave engulfed it, its engines stopped dead, and it fell out of the air like a stone. Fortunately, it didn't have far to go. If we'd have been launching toward space at the time, though, it would have trapped us inside it like a flying coffin.

I stopped there with my hands still on Vergil and watched the disaster unfold. Like any civilized place in the galaxy, the Hole in the Wall and its entire infrastructure relied on energy, and to see it be drained from the place was like watching the city die.

There were exceptions, fortunately. Not everything lost power. Our Mjolnir armor, for instance, didn't seem to directly suffer from the attack, for which I was grateful. Otherwise, we Spartans would have been trapped inside five hundred kilos of gear.

Our weapons seemed to be working fine as well. Even the electronic readouts remained lit up. I pulled out my pistol and took a potshot at the Guardian just to be sure. It didn't even notice.

The city itself, though, was suffering from a full-on blackout. All of the energy plants supplying the Hole in the Wall had been compromised, and most of the batteries powering everything else had been shot, too. I could hear the cries of the wounded and anguished echoing around us from every angle.

I glanced around. The locals who were supposed to be guarding us were in a dull panic. They didn't seem to know whether they should keep an eye on us, arrest us, or abandon us so they could run home. I suppose the fact that the Condor had fallen out of the sky at least convinced them that we weren't behind the Guardian's attack.

"Well, shit," Mickey said as he circled back toward me and Veronica. "What the hell have you gotten us into now, Buck?"

"I wish I knew," I said.

Romeo got out of the Condor and gave the dead bird a kick. "We're not going anywhere now."

I finally put my helmet back on and stared up at the Guardian. I put out an all-call on every open channel, trying to hail the thing. It didn't answer.

Veronica immediately figured out what I was doing. "No luck?"

I shook my head. "You'd think if Cortana was coming, she'd have said something by now."

"Let's count ourselves lucky for that," Sadie said.

The sound of the disaster around us was what really creeped me out. I'd been in the middle of all sorts of war zones. With a job like mine, it came with the territory.

Normally, you'd hear sirens, bombs, gunshots, screams, some kind of sign that everything had gone to hell. This, though—now that the aircraft had all fallen—was just too quiet. Like a grave-yard.

We were standing there on the edge of the park the rebels had led us to. While some of our escort had fled at the arrival of the Guardian, a good number of them had remained at their posts and still had us surrounded.

From the far edge of the park, Mayor Wells came charging up with a whole platoon of soldiers. As she closed in, I signaled for the others to keep cool. The last thing we needed right then was to aggravate the locals more than the Guardian already had.

"What have you done?!" she shouted at us, her face flushed with anger and grief.

"That's one of the Guardians I was telling you about—" I started.

"*You* brought this here!" she said. She didn't have any evidence of that, but it hardly mattered. Besides, she was right. "You need to get rid of it!"

"Um . . . it's not quite that simple."

"We were fine until you arrived." The soldiers accompanying her nodded in agreement. "We were hidden. We were safe. Then you showed up and ruined everything!"

"You may have felt safe," Veronica said in a calm, firm voice, "but you weren't. We warned you that it was only a matter of time before Cortana discovered this planet. It would appear that time is now."

I glanced at Dutch and Gretchen. They both looked like they wanted to die. I would have said something to comfort them, but I didn't want to put the mayor's cross hairs on Alpha-Nine. To his credit, Mickey kept his mouth shut.

The mayor bit her tongue for a moment while she digested everything. "I should have you all arrested for what you've done, but I don't see how that would help the matter. You Spartans like to think of yourself as heroes? Time to step up."

Veronica moved forward. "I assume you're not interested in surrendering?"

"Are you kidding? We came here to live free from the UEG. You think we're going to voluntarily live under the regime of a bunch of overzealous AIs?"

Veronica nodded. "I had to ask. We've seen a few of these invasions already. If this one follows the pattern, here's what's going to happen.

"The Guardian enters the system. If it perceives a threat, it shuts down all power within its reach, ensuring its safety—just like this one did."

"I suppose we should be flattered?" Mayor Wells said sarcastically.

"Then it sends out an envoy to ask the people living in the system to submit to Cortana."

"Why haven't we seen an envoy yet?" Mayor Wells demanded.

I cocked my head. I could hear the sound of gunfire rattling in the distance. People were firing at the Guardian despite how little chance they had of hurting the thing.

Give it to the rebels. They never know when to quit.

"Maybe it doesn't think it's done pacifying the population yet," Veronica said.

"Not for lack of trying," Mickey said as he gazed out at the columns of smoke rising all around the city.

"This seems like an awfully violent way to combat violence," Romeo said. "I mean, I can understand the whole 'wanting people to live in peace' thing. I can even get behind enforcing it. But attacking an entire population just because they won't do as they're told?"

"Conquering always makes sense to the conquerors," said Veronica.

I turned to Mayor Wells. "What kind of armament do you have here?"

"Nothing capable of taking on a machine like that."

"Nothing at all? Seriously?"

"What do you want me to tell you? That we have a stack of portable nukes sitting under my desk back at my office?"

"That would be a start. I'd believe that more than 'We rebels have been sitting here alone for decades without a thought to preparing for the inevitable day of our discovery.' I mean, you had to at least be paranoid enough to think the UNSC would drop in on you someday."

She folded her arms across her chest.

"Nothing?"

"Nothing around here."

"Look," Mickey said to her, "I understand if you don't want to reveal to a bunch of Spartans what you've done to protect yourself in the case of an invasion, but you need to set those differences aside. We're past hypotheticals. This planet's defenses—whatever they are and however they work—have been bypassed, and there's no way any of us can take something like *that* down." He pointed up at the Guardian. "However, if we work together, we might be able to manage an escape."

The mayor's eyes widened at the thought of abandoning the colony altogether. "After all we've built here? After all the years we lived in peace?"

Sadie—who'd wandered back to us from the Condor—moved into view and spoke. "I know how you feel," she said. "I grew up in New Mombasa. When the Covenant invaded Earth, they destroyed my entire city. There's nothing that you can do in this situation. Not by yourself. You can only run until you can find a way to strike back."

The mayor looked stricken, and her soldiers weren't faring much better. A couple of them had actually peeled off—heading home, maybe—and no one had called them back. Against odds like this, who was going to blame them? It didn't matter if they had dozens of soldiers or even thousands. The Guardian would prevail.

"I'm sorry, ma'am," I said. "She's right. This is a fight you're not going to win."

The mayor came to a swift decision. "Okay. We do have some ships. Not a navy, but enough to at least start an evacuation of the Hole in the Wall."

"If they've all been shut down by the Guardian, that doesn't do you a whole lot of good." Romeo said.

"No, wait—Vergil can fix them!" Sadie said, suddenly excited. "It takes a bit of time, but he can repair the damage that the Guardians cause. He and the other Huragok had started doing that on Luna before we left."

"Great," I said to Sadie. "Go with Vergil. Once he's done with our ship, we'll get him started on the others."

"We have some fighters," the mayor said. "Several of them."

"Excellent," I said. "We'll have Vergil repair them first. Then we can mount an attack against the Guardian, even if only to buy us some time."

The mayor frowned. "They're not here. They're hidden on the other side of the planet."

Veronica nodded at her. "Smart. There's a good chance they were out of range of the Guardian's energy-draining attack."

"I never like putting all my eggs in one basket. But once they get into range, couldn't the Guardian just take them out, too?"

"I don't think any number of fighters are going to do much good against that thing," said Romeo.

Veronica understood what I intended. "We don't need them to actually hurt it. We just have to distract it while we get the other ships—the bigger transports that can carry more people—repaired and on their way. The longer they can hold out, the better."

The mayor winced. "You want us to abandon the planet itself?"

"It's either that or live here under Cortana's thumb," Veronica said. "If that's what you're up for, we can leave you here to it. But if you're willing to run, we're willing to risk our lives to help you with that."

"Just what do you get out of this? I already told you that the tech hiding Cassidy III can't be moved off-planet."

"Have your researchers bring every bit of information they have. Maybe Vergil can puzzle something useful out of it."

"That seems like kind of a long shot."

"All we have left are long shots," I told her.

She seemed to appreciate the grim honesty. "Then we might as well take them."

"All right," Veronica said. "That sounds like a plan. Mayor, get your pilots together, whoever you have who can fly those fighters of yours. Gretchen and Dutch, get them loaded into the Condor, and as soon as Vergil has that bird ready, get it into the air."

"What about the rest of us?" Romeo said. "I'm not going to just sit here and look pretty all day."

More screams began to erupt from all over the city. We snapped our heads around, and I spotted bright flashes popping up at multiple angles across the Hole.

"Portals!" Veronica shouted. "The Guardian's bringing in help!"

Forerunner soldiers emerged from the pulsating holes that sprang from some distant system through an enigmatic slipspace passage that defied human technology. They poured out in droves, their guns blazing, filling the sky with fiery blasts.

"Romeo," I said, "I think you have your answer as to how the rest of your day looks."

CHAPTER 17

"Move, move, move!" I shouted. "Sadie: Get to the Condor and help Vergil get that bird operational! Dutch: Snag our weapons and bring them out here! Romeo, Veronica, Mickey: Let's keep the mayor safe! Vergil? If you can step it up a bit, I'm sure we'd all appreciate it!"

Sadie sprinted toward the Condor. By the time she got there, Dutch was already heading our way. Meanwhile, the mayor's escort had set up a perimeter around us, ready to take out any Forerunner soldiers that came our way. The park had otherwise emptied. All the civilians had long since stopped gawking at us and fled. The sight of the armigers was too much for many of the locals, who'd never witnessed anything like them. Some ran away, while others raised quivering rifles in their direction.

A group of Forerunner soldiers charged into the park from the north, and the mayor's escort opened fire. They didn't do much more than get the bad guys' attention. Romeo, Veronica, and I

peppered them with pistol fire, knocking a couple of them down.
With help from the locals, we took them all out.

"That's sure to bring more of them our way," I said. "We need
to make a move."

Dutch raced up to us as the last of the Forerunner soldiers fell,
and he started tossing us our rifles.

"You seriously think we can hold off a force like that?" Mickey
said in disbelief. "With only what we have in the Condor?"

"We'll do fine until our ammo runs out," I said as I checked
the action on my rifle.

"And what about me?" Mickey said to Dutch, who hadn't
thrown him a weapon.

Dutch shrugged at him. "I didn't see anything in there with
your name on it," he said before racing back toward the Condor.

I flipped Mickey my pistol, and he caught it in midair.

"I'm feeling like this might not be entirely adequate," he said.
"And I'm feeling a little naked out here without a shred of armor."

"What kind of armaments do you have that we could borrow?"
Veronica said to Mayor Wells, who had taken cover and was trying
to use her comm.

"Guns and ammo we have plenty of," the mayor said. "Follow me."

She took off at a trot, her escort falling into step around
her, covering her route as well as they could. Veronica, Romeo,
Mickey, and I pelted after them. It was a risk to leave the Condor,
but Dutch and Gretchen were there, and that would have to do.
There was no way we could help defend the city with the Condor's
arsenal alone.

We left the park, emerging onto one of the high roads. It was
filled with utter chaos. Forerunner soldiers were popping in and

out all over the place, and the people were doing their best to resist them.

Some of the armigers were still coming here through fresh portals. The rest of them were just teleporting about, leaving fiery streaks behind them as they went. Whenever they found a target, they blasted away at it until it stopped moving, and then they moved on to whatever was next. They were like fierce, hive-minded insects working in vicious, coordinated droves.

"Light 'em up!" Mayor Wells shouted.

We began blasting away at every armiger in range. We threw loads of lead and knocked a bunch of them into pieces. The trouble was that they kept coming. As soon as we'd get a breather, a new round would pop in through a fresh set of portals, and we'd start all over again.

"We need to move!" I said. "We keep doing this, we'll be bogged down forever!"

Mayor Wells nodded an acknowledgment to me and signaled for her soldiers to head out. "We're heading for the First Precinct!" she said. "Let's go!"

We charged toward the central Forerunner tower, cutting through soldiers that crossed our path as we went. About a klick along the raised road, we came to a building on one side that stood out from all the others. It had been built out of solid concrete and featured only tall, narrow windows, like arrow slits from a medieval castle.

"Nice fortress!" I said as we ran up to it and cleared away a few Forerunner soldiers who were making a run at the place.

A dozen or so locals dressed in dark blue armor greeted us with wide eyes and suspicious stares as we strode up. I have no doubt that they would have fired on us if the mayor hadn't been leading us. "These assholes are our new best friends!" Mayor

Wells shouted at them. "Get them what they need to help us defend our city!"

"Mostly, we need ammo. If you have any heavy weaponry, we could use that, too." I tossed a thumb in Mickey's direction. "And if you're hiding any extra-large suits of armor back there, this guy could use some."

A large bearded man with a big badge on his helmet—signifying him as the chief—stepped forward. "You got it, Mayor," he said, pointedly ignoring me. He might have to help me out, but he wasn't about to cede me any authority.

He began barking out orders to his people. "Alpha Team! Stay at your posts! Beta Team! Get these symbols of oppression all the bullets they need! And Gamma Team!" He pointed at Mickey. "Go grab the biggest suit of powered armor we have, and see if you can squeeze him into it!"

The officers burst into action with a ferocity I had to admire. Alpha Team consisted of about half the officers there, and they spread out and kept blasting away at any of the Guardian's friends moving our way. Meanwhile, the four people who made up Beta Team identified our weapons and started shoveling ammunition in our direction. The last two—who must have been Gamma Team—grabbed Mickey and hauled him into the station.

My first thought was that I should follow him in, since I knew it was unwise to let a prisoner out of my sight. Then I realized that we were far beyond that point. If Mickey just disappeared, then to hell with him. I had a job to do if I wanted to get my team off this rock, and I couldn't be babysitting him every step of the way.

While we waited for Mickey to get suited up, Veronica and I helped defend the precinct house. As we did, Romeo arched his neck around to inspect what kind of weapons the officers had stacked up in their lobby. "Anyone, by chance, got a nice sniper rifle handy back there?" he asked. "Doesn't matter what kind."

Someone tossed him an M99 Stanchion, a Gauss rifle that hadn't been in production for years. It was a powerful long-range railgun used by recon forces during the Insurrection. "Old-school," Romeo said with an appreciative smile. "This'll do."

When Mickey finally showed up, he looked like a full ton of soldier stuffed into a half-ton suit. It was an older variation on ODST armor from the beginning of the Covenant War. The armor didn't fit him properly, and there were a few cracks in it that left him exposed here and there. But it held together well enough. It apparently even had an exoskeleton to shore up his frame and give his muscles a little boost, although nothing like that of a Mjolnir.

Still, it made me uneasy. The last time I'd seen Mickey in armor, he'd had a gun to my head. But I wasn't sure I could live with myself if he got killed, because I'd dragged him all the way out here and thrown him into a firefight with no protection. It was just a risk I had to take.

"You look better than I would have guessed," Veronica said.

"How's it going back there, Dutch?" I said into the comm.

"Vergil's nearly got it sorted out," he said. "Internal power's already on, and I'm using the guns to clear out the area in front of us."

"Just need to get the engines running," Gretchen said. A dull roar almost cut her off. "Whoa! There they go!"

"Good deal!" I said. "Get your butt in the air and come on over and pick us up, all right?"

"Got it. Locked onto your armor's coordinates," Gretchen said. "We are on our way!"

I glanced down the street. The Guardian loomed off to the

side of the central tower. It seemed to be entirely uninterested in us, just floating there like a gigantic judge waiting for us to do something wrong.

I suppose it didn't need to be doing anything to us directly. It had hundreds of Forerunner soldiers at its command for that, and they were converging on the precinct house from both ends of the road. The rebels that stood between us and them were trying to hold them off, but one by one they were either getting killed or running off.

"Mayor Wells!" Veronica said. "Have you been able to contact your fighters yet?"

The mayor had been standing in the doorway to the precinct house the entire time, taking potshots at any Forerunner soldiers that managed to get close enough while she tried to hail someone on her comm. She might not have been out on the front lines, but she wasn't hiding under her desk, either. She understood the role her people needed her in, and she was determined to fill it.

"Our comm system is still down," she said. "If you can spare that Huragok for a moment, we could use its help!"

"Gretchen!" Veronica said into her comm. "We're going to clear out the space in front of the precinct house for you. Once you get her, open the back ramp. Dutch: You escort Vergil and Sadie into the station while the rest of us provide you cover."

"Got it," Gretchen said. "Heads up, then, because we're incoming!"

Romeo, Mickey, and I stepped out from the reinforced front of the precinct house and let loose at the incoming Forerunner soldiers with everything we had. Together, we worked like the well-oiled machine that Alpha-Nine had once been.

I had to admit, as much as Mickey had burned me, I missed

working with him and Romeo. We'd pissed each other off something terrible over the years, but man, we made a hell of a team. If you'd asked me years ago which one of them would have gotten me mad enough to consider murder, my money would have been on Romeo. More than once, I'd wished that he'd been the traitor rather than Mickey. That would have been so much easier to deal with, if only on a personal level.

I already couldn't stand Romeo most of the time. I respected him—especially his ability as a soldier—but he often rubbed me the wrong way. Mickey, though, I got along with. Out of all the members of Alpha-Nine, we'd been the closest.

Romeo had worked with Dutch before they'd joined up with Alpha-Nine, so they were longtime pals. When Mickey became part of the team after that, he and I had naturally gravitated to each other, which was why all of this made me so bitter.

And his betrayal hadn't been just a dirty turn of events—I also hadn't seen it coming. Mickey had groaned about the UEG sometimes over the years, and he'd even complained about us being sent to go fight humans rather than the Covenant, but I'd never added everything up to see it all as a strain on his loyalty.

I'd thought our friendship would supersede any other concerns. The fact that I'd been wrong had rocked me to my core, and I couldn't escape the thought that I'd been his leader. I should have seen it coming and done something to prevent it from happening, but I hadn't. In some ways, that was on me.

It had taken me a long time to heal from that. To learn to trust my own gut again. Veronica had been a huge help—with her, my instincts were never wrong.

Working with Fireteam Osiris had been a great experience as well. Locke, Vale, and Tanaka were always consummate professionals, true pleasures to fight alongside.

But they didn't quite feel like family. Not the way Alpha-Nine did.

Of course, this family wasn't ever going to be the same, though.

I glanced at Mickey as we moved into action, spreading out so we could clear a spot for the Condor to land. "Not going to shoot me in the back this time?"

"I never actually shot you anywhere."

"Wasn't for lack of want."

"We have plenty other targets at the moment," he said. "Once we run out of them, I'll let you know how I feel."

Despite that, Mickey and I fell right back into our old patterns. I stood up front and took the brunt of the incoming fire with my Mjolnir armor and tried to shoot as many of the targets as I could. When there were too many of them and they got too close for me to handle them all, Mickey leaned out from around me and laid into them with a borrowed shotgun, blowing the soldiers to pieces.

Although this would have seemed like a bad thing if you'd asked me three hours ago, the best thing about the Hole in the Wall was that just about everyone in the city was armed and ready. There were people sniping at the armigers on the road from every open window lining the street. Most of the attacks didn't do a whole lot of good, but there were dozens of rebels opening fire—probably hundreds down the length of the street. With odds like that, it seemed like the Front might have a chance to prevail. At least for a moment.

But the Guardian evidently wasn't satisfied with sending in a single battalion of Forerunner soldiers. More and more portals opened up throughout the city in waves, and I found myself wondering if the thing was going to depopulate all of Genesis just to take us down.

The Forerunner soldiers kept on coming in an endless stream. It didn't matter how many we shot down or how hot our gun barrels got. There were always more.

"We're going to run out of ammo before we run out of targets!" Mickey shouted.

"More ammo on the way!" Veronica said. She and Romeo had been working together on the other side of the clearing we'd made.

"One good thing about the Front," I said. "They've been prepping for an invasion since they got here. They just thought it would be by the UNSC!"

It was about then that parts of the city began exploding around us. The Guardian now apparently wanted to get into the fight itself, and when it did, it was unlike anything I'd ever seen.

The construct fired converging beams from two floating elements that rose out of what would be the machine's back, which I could now see were cannons. These both focused on a point directly in front of the Guardian, building in intensity, until they formed into a pulsating beam. Maybe it was plasma, or a shaft of hard light, or a stream of particles. Given the weapon's speed, I couldn't tell.

Either way, it packed one hell of a punch. Wherever the beam landed seemed to disappear in a deafening blast of debris and smoke. Entire buildings vanished in its glare, and the seismic aftershock felt like the planet itself could be completely torn apart.

"We are in a world of pain," Mickey said as we witnessed the destructive force of the Guardian. "How are we supposed to fight against that?"

It was like watching a Covenant capital ship glass a planet with its ventral beam. Anything you could throw against it would be like tossing pebbles into the sea. It wasn't even going to notice.

Even the Forerunner soldiers stopped to watch. Gretchen took advantage of that moment to slide into the clearing we'd made, setting the Condor down right in front of the precinct house. The back ramp came whining down, and Vergil and Sadie slipped out of the ship and sprinted for the station's front door. A full squadron of helmeted personnel came charging out in the other direction.

"Who're they?" I asked Veronica.

"The Front's pilots!" she said. "You think those ships on the other side of the world are going to fly themselves? Mayor Wells had them prep while we were waiting for Gretchen."

"Great, because I got the feeling that we're not gonna make a lick of difference fighting from down here. Not against that thing!"

"Got some passengers for you, Gretchen!" Veronica shouted into the comm. "They have the coordinates you need. Get them there as fast as you can, drop them off, and then hustle back!"

"You got it, Captain!"

"I'll stick with her and work the guns!" Dutch said.

"Roger that!" I responded. She'd need the weapon support, even if it meant we'd lose Dutch on the ground. "Now what?" I asked Veronica as the pilots piled into the ship and the ramp hauled up behind them.

"Now we get your Huragok over to the Front's airfield and get him repairing their transports," Mayor Wells said as she emerged from the precinct house.

Overhead, the Guardian kept blasting away at different areas of the city. At the moment, it was preoccupied with other threats, but it would only be a matter of time before it came after us.

"I'm calling for a general evacuation!" the mayor announced to anyone within earshot. "Everyone who can get off the planet should do so as soon as they can. We represent one of the last remaining Front settlements free from the tyranny of these machines, and we can't afford to lose that in this fight. As much as it pains me to say it, you were right Captain Dare. This isn't about the Front anymore. *Humanity* can't afford it."

"That Guardian's not going to just let us fill up transports and rocket them out of here," I said. "It'll blow you out of the sky before you can enter slipspace."

"Like I said, we need to distract it," Veronica said.

"I don't know if you've been paying attention," Mickey said, "but it's leveling this city and not even breaking a sweat! How exactly are we supposed to distract it?"

"That's why we need the Front's fighters," I said. "They might be able to lure it away."

"Exactly," Veronica said. "The trouble is that they'll have to get close enough to get its attention—and then they'll have to jet out of here before it can reach them."

"That's a tall order," I said. "What do you think, Mayor? Your flyers got that in them?"

"You won't be able to stop them from trying," she said. "Not if they think it'll help get people safely off-planet."

"All right," I said. "The moment they get in the air, send your three fastest birds over here to try to lure the Guardian away. Hold the rest in reserve, just in case. No sense in risking them all on this."

"That's not your decision to make," she said sharply. "It's mine! You worry about shooting whatever's in front of you, and I'll determine whether it's worth it or not to risk my pilots' lives, got it?"

I granted her that with a firm nod. "Can you get us to your airfield? Wherever it is they're running the evac from?"

"Already on it," she said. "This isn't my first time evacuating a planet."

"Seriously?"

"You don't want to know."

"And we have a ride ready for you!" Sadie called from near the precinct house's front doors. She waved us over and pointed us to one of their moving platforms. Vergil was floating over the middle of it, and as he made one final tweak, it hummed to life.

"Good work," Mayor Wells said grudgingly. "Now, all you fascists climb on board!"

Veronica, Romeo, Mickey, and I joined Sadie and Vergil on the platform. Mayor Wells climbed on after us, along with three of her top soldiers. That filled the platform to its edge. I had those of us in armor each take an edge of the platform so the others could use us for cover. At the mayor's signal, Vergil moved the platform out.

We swept along the raised road again, toward the tallest spire at first. When we got close, we zipped around its perimeter until we reached another spur that raced straight away from the bay.

Vergil had done something to soup the platform up, and it moved along a lot faster than before. I worried that we might crash into something, but there weren't a lot of other options. We blasted away at the armigers as best we could, but mostly, we tried to keep them away from us until we could sail past them at top speed.

As we went, countless locals took advantage of the momentary distraction we offered. The moment the Forerunner soldiers turned toward us, the citizens poked rifles out through windows and shot them in the back. While I appreciated the hand, I couldn't help but think those people should all be on their way out, too—or at least preparing to surrender once we were gone.

"Are you planning to do something to convince these people to give up and head to the airfield?" I asked the mayor.

"Evacuation beacon is lit, Spartan. Everyone you see fighting out there isn't planning on leaving. This place was their life, they don't have one outside of here. Plus, we don't have room for everyone on those transports. They know that."

I turned back to fire a few rounds into a cluster of armigers. "Feels like the same stubborn behavior that got them here to begin with, if you ask me. Running to fight another day is better than not having another day at all. They of all people should know that."

"You'd think this whole situation would give you a bit more sympathy for the Front," Mickey said.

"Just hand me one of your revolutionary tracts. I'll promise to read it later."

"I'm not joking."

"That's the worst part."

"You have a large, powerful organization that wants to tell you exactly how you're supposed to live your life. And if you refuse, it attacks you and destroys your home. Sound familiar?"

"I'm sorry," I said. "I can't hear you over the sound of how you used this same line of reasoning to turn on me."

Well, that and the Forerunner soldier that teleported right next to me on the platform, practically coming down on top of me. Another one of the things had blasted away at me hard just before that and ran my shields down. This one landed on my back and knocked me to my knees.

Mickey blew it away with his shotgun, knocking it clean off me. I watched it tumble to pieces on the roadway as the platform kept rolling along. My armor's diagnostics reported that my jump jets had been damaged, but I wasn't worried about that at the moment. I mean, what was the chance I'd need them?

"You're going to have to get past all that at some point," Mickey said. "It was three years ago."

I didn't say thank you to him—or anything else for a long

while. We just kept shooting our way toward the airfield, one block at a time.

When we finally had a breather, I said, "Mickey, I might get over this. But that's not going to happen today."

"I'm not asking for forgiveness—"

"Good, because you're not getting it."

"But maybe a little understanding."

I shook my head as Mickey blasted apart another Forerunner soldier with his shotgun. "You're an idiot," I said. "A stone-cold idiot, you know that? I always *understood* you. I knew *why* you did what you did. I just didn't agree with it."

He seemed surprised at that. "If you say so."

"I would have been happy to talk with you about it. We could have sat down and beaten the topic to death over a few beers any time you wanted to. But instead, you went and kept it to yourself. You let this garbage fester in your brain like a disease you were too ashamed to talk about, right up until it poisoned you entirely. Until you were too far gone for anyone to do anything about it."

"It's cute that you think you could have *saved* me from waking up to what the UEG was doing to its own people."

"I would have liked at least to have the chance. But you kept it from me." I was surprised that talking about it still hurt as much as it did. "We were brothers in arms, Mickey! And you pissed on all that for some noble cause you made up in your thick head!"

"Made up?" he gasped at me. "You think I *made up* the Front?"

"You sure romanticized it. And yeah, you *made up* your involvement in it. To you, it felt like you were doing the right thing—"

"And?"

"*And* you sold me and Romeo out. What the hell is noble about that?"

"I didn't—"

"You could have just gone over to the other side. Left a note in the barracks. I would have said, 'Wow, I can't believe he went and did that. Oh well, I guess he had to do what he thought was right.' You know?"

"Yeah, sure."

"I would have been disappointed. Angry, even. But not livid like I am now. It's one thing to say 'Hey, I'm done with you guys. I'm going along with these idiots over here instead.' It's another thing entirely to sell your friends *out* to those idiots."

Mickey squinted at me, his jaw flexing as I spoke. When I was done, he growled: "If you had decided to switch sides, you would have done the exact same thing."

"No way. I never would have turned you over to people who would have tortured you, imprisoned you, and probably killed you in the worst way. Tell yourself that if it lets you sleep at night, but you know it's a lie."

I could see finally the airfield's traffic control tower emerging from behind some shorter buildings that had been closer to our vantage point. A few columns of smoke rose into the sky near it—probably from aircraft that gone there to make a last-ditch effort at landing—but the tower itself seemed intact. It gave me hope for the rest of the facility.

As we got closer, the concentration of Forerunner soldiers thinned, along with any hint of the locals, almost as if the mayor had ordered her people to try to lure the invaders away from the place. I wondered how many people from this world we'd save, if most didn't seem willing to respond to an evacuation order. I wondered if those folks believed they'd lose more by leaving this place than if they stayed around, even if they wound up under Cortana's thumb.

Vergil brought the platform down a ramp and headed toward

a wide road that led straight to the airfield. Besides the tower, a terminal sat off to the left, and a series of hangars sprawled to the right. For all the chaos we'd seen in the city, out here it seemed as quiet as a park.

"You done?" Mickey said to me.

"For now."

"Good, because we still have a colony to try and save. At least as much of it as we can."

CHAPTER 18

The platform ground to a halt in front of one of the hangars, and we followed Mayor Wells and her escort in through a set of doors that stood next to a massive, shuttered pair of hangar doors towering several stories into the air. We found ourselves in a well-lit, large domed warehouse that protected half a dozen large transports from the elements, along with a dozen smaller ships, not a single one of which bore a gun mount, much less a missile tube.

"They really did hide their best ships half a planet away," Veronica said. "I had hoped you were bluffing."

"I actually was, but it didn't matter. The ones suited for fighting that we had around here were in the air when the Guardian blacked out the power," Mayor Wells said. "This is all we have left in the city."

Most of the ships looked like they hadn't been used in months, maybe years. Many of them had been built before the war.

"Creaky," Romeo said.

"They'll still make slipspace," the mayor said. "Assuming your Huragok there can get them running again."

"Get to work, Vergil," Veronica said to him and Sadie. "And move as fast as you can!"

The Huragok floated directly toward the nearest transport, and the people milling about parted before him as if he were radioactive. That's when I saw the people who *were* willing to leave this world, and there were more than the city streets had shown. Just about every square meter of the hangar that didn't have a ship in it was crammed with citizens of the Hole. From outside the building, you might never have known they were there, which was probably the point. They didn't want to attract any Forerunner soldiers if they could help it.

The people weren't exactly soldiers. There were hundreds of them, maybe thousands. They ranged from grandparents in wheeled walkers to infants in strollers and everyone in between. To look at them, you wouldn't have been able to pin many down to having come from a particular planet, much less a single section of Earth. Despite that, they all looked like they belonged in the Hole in the Wall. It was something in their style of dress, the suspicious look in their eyes, the set of grim determination in their jaws.

One thing that was immediately clear was that there was no way all of them were getting off the planet that day. There were more people there than spaces on those birds.

Heads turned toward us as we entered. In our armor, we Spartans didn't have a prayer of blending in. Most of the Front stared at me and Romeo with naked hatred. After all, we symbolized the UEG, a government that they'd all come here to escape. That we were there when their home was being invaded could not be a coincidence. They assumed that the disaster had ridden in on our coattails—or vice versa.

Mickey, on the other hand, actually generated cheers when he removed his helmet. Maybe at first it was the fact that he was wearing a suit of armor from their police force. But once they recognized his face, the dots started to connect. Mickey had a reputation with everyone in the Front.

The first people who saw him for who he was smacked their companions on the shoulder and pointed at him. Smiles instantly spread on their faces. They were in too grim a situation to feel relieved, but they were nonetheless thrilled to see him, and they passed the word to everyone around them. By the time we'd made it halfway into the building, a murmur was running through the crowd. Everyone seemed wary of me, but they were giving him approving nods, one and all. I wasn't sure he noticed until I saw his face starting to turn red from all the attention.

The mayor and her guards led us to the nearest transport and ordered the people there to clear the way so Vergil and Sadie could get to work. "The sooner we let this creature work its magic, the faster we can get out of here!" she shouted at them. That got people moving.

With that done, Mayor Wells turned back to us. "I'm going to have to start picking who gets to leave with us," she said in a hushed tone. "We don't have an established protocol."

Veronica nodded in sympathy. "Concentrate on getting scientists and leaders off first, plus their families if they have any. They're the real hope of the Front—actually, they're the hope of humanity at this point."

"Of course," the mayor said. "I'm also going to put our best soldiers on board. Better they're out there fighting rather than having to lay down arms here. After that, I'm not sure how much room there's going to be."

She frowned so hard I wondered if the lines it caused on her face might become permanent. The weight of it was starting to hit her. Some people of the Hole would have to stay, either fighting the Guardian and its forces to the death or kneeling in surrender.

"We're done with one ship!" Sadie called out. "Heading over to the next!"

A roar of excitement went up in the crowd, and the people parted once again for Vergil to move on. "Excuse me," the mayor said to us as she left for the first ship. "I have to go save some lives and break some hearts."

As we watched her go, Mickey said: "UNSC's not winning many friends today."

"We're doing the best we can," Veronica said.

Mickey chewed that over for a moment. "I know."

"Any idea where all these people are heading?"

Veronica chuckled. "Believe it or not, the Front has decided not to tell me. They seem to think that sharing that kind of information with an ONI officer isn't in their best interest."

"But how are we going to link up with them later? Isn't the whole point that we get them out of here so we all have a fighting chance against Cortana?"

"Apparently, they'll be happy to inform *Mickey* of their plans. They believe that might ensure that we keep him alive."

"I'll be happy to pass all that along," he replied. "As long as you promise to keep me out of a brig—or any kind of prison, for that matter."

"I think that was the plan in the first place," I said to Mickey.

"Was it?" he said with mock curiosity.

"We didn't haul you out of the training station just so we could put you back in a cell."

"You may believe that, Buck. But the UNSC is a big organization, and to be blunt, you're not in charge of it."

"Fair enough," I said. "Go ahead and use whatever imaginary leverage you think you have to keep yourself from going back where you belong. But do me a favor and write that information down someplace just in case you get killed."

"So I can practically *guarantee* I get killed? Come on, Buck. As much time as you've spent with Veronica, I'm surprised you don't think more like a spook yet."

"What's your excuse?"

"When you spend three years in jail, paranoia starts to come naturally."

"I'll take your word on that."

At a hand signal from Veronica, the three of us followed Mayor Wells over to the first ship. "Just in case she winds up with some trouble from the people she disappoints," Veronica said.

"You really think having us standing on her side is going to help her in the eyes of these people?" Romeo said.

"We'll keep an appropriate distance."

"How's it going, Gretchen?" I said into the comm.

"We're arriving at their hidden hangar right now," she said. "Moving at top speed. I went orbital to save time, and we're cruising back down through the atmosphere, right on top of the site."

"Good work," I said. "Drop those pilots off and get back here as soon as you can."

"Copy that."

Despite the pressure the people in the crowd were under, they were remarkably well behaved. Maybe it was because, as members of the Front, they lived in constant fear of having to leave the planet in a rush—or fight to defend it. The idea that this might happen wasn't foreign to them. Still, the existence of a Forerunner machine hovering above the city they called home might have elicited some kind of hysteria. Instead, most held steady, even if their expressions were alloyed with apprehension.

"I bet every one of these people lives with a go bag near their front door," Romeo said.

"That," I said, seeing that Romeo had been tracking along the same lines, "or they're just the pedigree of people who can handle this sort of thing." Maybe a kind of fearlessness in the face of grave circumstances came standard for the people who joined the Front.

When it became apparent that Mayor Wells had the situation as well in hand as we could expect, I sent Romeo over to keep an eye on Vergil and Sadie.

"You just don't want me pissing off the mayor with an offhand comment."

"That's a bonus," I told him as he left.

Vergil got through a surprising number of vessels fast; Sadie did an excellent job of moving him from one to the next without any delays. Normally, he liked to spend a lot of time exploring a ship and seeing all the different things he could do to improve it, but she wasn't giving him even an extra minute. "Move, move, move!" she kept shouting at him as they charged to the next ship in line.

"How are we doing?" I asked Veronica after a while.

"Sadie just took Vergil into the last of the large transports. We should be ready to start getting ships out of here any time now," she said. "The mayor's been loading each one up the moment Vergil finishes repairing them."

"Then we just need to get the Guardian out of the area first, so it doesn't shoot them down. I'm impressed." I brought up Gretchen on the comm again. "Sitrep?"

"Almost back to you," she said. "The fighters are a bit faster and should reach you before we do."

"All right," I said. "When you get here, head for the airfield on the west side of town. We're in the big hangar to the southeast. Put it between you and the Guardian when you land, if you can."

"Roger that!"

I gave Veronica the thumbs-up, and she moved forward to relay the information to Mayor Wells. The mayor gave her a grateful nod before returning to her work.

Just then a series of explosions rolled like thunder outside, rattling the hangar's walls. A number of the people inside the building began to scream, but the more levelheaded folks around them convinced them to quiet down. The last thing we needed was a detachment of Forerunner soldiers to be drawn there by all the wailing.

"You two!" Mayor Wells said, pointing at Mickey and me. "Get me some eyes out there and tell me what's going on!"

We didn't even glance at Veronica for confirmation. We just moved.

We made our way to the doors, taking care not to trample any innocents on our way. Outside, we found ourselves on the edge of a wide-open span of concrete, across which we could see the terminal and the control tower.

We moved into the open area until we had a clear angle to see the Guardian over the hangar's roof. As we did, I spotted a trio of fighters—F-41 Broadswords painted in the Front's colors—sweeping past the construct's shoulders at top speed. They fired off missiles as they went, and these slammed into the gargantuan monster hard and fast.

The fighters moved at an angle perpendicular to us, a path designed to keep the machine's attention away from our direction. Soon after the fighters passed, the sky rumbled with the vibrations of a sonic boom.

Another wave of Broadswords approached from the same angle, even as the lead bird from the first group began to circle around widely enough so that it would take the fighters far north of the Hole in the Wall. The next fighters were slower than the first group, but these half-dozen ships each unloaded a barrage of missiles at the Guardian.

The explosives all struck true, but none of them had much of an effect. I don't know if the ships would have been able to even ding the Guardian if they'd been firing anything less powerful than a nuke. The creature just shrugged them off.

Still, the missiles got its attention, and the twin beam emitters from behind the Guardian's main chassis began to glow again. As the fighters swept past it, I hoped it wouldn't be able to track any of them fast enough.

"The fighters are here, Veronica, but they're not going to do much good."

"Just as long as they can keep the Guardian distracted," she said. "That's all we need."

With that, the tall doors on the front of the hangar began to slide aside, exposing the people inside to the late-afternoon light. The doors faced away from the Guardian, so there was no risk of it seeing the people or the ships—until they took off for the stars.

As Mickey and I watched, the beams from the Guardian's emitters began to fire. The first shot missed entirely, but the second lanced right through one of the fighters, turning it into a bright ball of fire. I could hear the collective gasp of the people in the building. The need to evacuate the planet suddenly became a lot sharper.

Fortunately, the fighters' ploy seemed to have worked. The Guardian began moving after them.

At first it floated along so slowly that I didn't think it would have been able to catch even me on an open street. Then I realized part of that was simply perspective. It was so far away, it was like watching a mountain move.

As it got going, it moved faster. A third wing of fighters swept in from the east and sent another volley of missiles at it, and it seemed like it was almost matching them for speed. It took down two of them with its beam emitters before they even moved past it.

The Guardian was so massive that its movement stirred up the wind in its wake. Even from as far away as we were, I could hear it blowing past my helmet. The gusts were coming so hard, it was as if a storm had hit the area,

"Window's closing, Veronica! You got to get those birds in the air now!" I shouted over the comm. "You're not going to get a better chance!"

"The fighters are drawing the Guardian to the southeast," Mickey said. "Have the ships head northeast from the moment they take off! The last thing we need is for that thing to spot them escaping and come back to cut them off!"

"Already on it," Veronica said.

As we moved back into the building to help with security, I raised Gretchen and Dutch on the comm. "You two doing all right?" I asked.

"We're on our way back to you," Gretchen said. "Are the fighters there already?"

"They hit the Guardian hard. Didn't put much of a dent in it, but they got it to start chasing after them. So in that respect, mission accomplished."

"Gretchen wanted to be part of the first wave," Dutch said. "But the Condor's a dropship, not a fighter. Those Broadswords would have been literally cooling their jets waiting for us to try to keep up with them."

"The Guardian shot a couple of them out of the air," I told them. "Even moving as fast as they were, they didn't have a chance. If it turns its attention to you, you're goners. Don't let that happen."

"Aw, Buck," Gretchen said. "I didn't know you cared."

"You're our ride out of here," I told her flatly. "Don't leave us stranded."

"You got it, Buck," Dutch said.

"Circle around and come in from the southeast if you can. Just stay out of that thing's line of sight."

Inside the building, people had begun pressing toward the escape ships. The problem was that most of the ships were already filled up, and they had to get moving.

"I need you to clear those people out of the way," Veronica said over the comm to me and Mickey. "Otherwise, no one's getting out of here today."

I stared at the crowd through the hangar doors. The situation was growing uglier by the second. Some of them had guns out and were starting to threaten those around them. A few were even pointing their weapons at the pilots of the ships. What had earlier been a steady, impassive disposition in the face of danger was becoming an aggressive bid to stay alive.

"We have to move or this is all going to go south," I said to Mickey as I began to push into the crowd, taking care not to trample anyone under my armored feet.

"So what can we do?" he said, falling in behind me. "We can't just shoot everyone here."

I pulled out my sidearm.

"Buck! No!" he shouted.

I fired three shots into the air. Everyone who wasn't already on a ship turned to stare at me. A good number of them swung their weapons in my direction.

I could only hope they'd listen to me. If they started shooting, this was going to turn into a bloodbath real fast.

I was about to start barking orders, but Mickey stepped forward and hauled my gun arm down. "Stop it!" he shouted at me.

"All right, Mickey," I said. "I got their attention. *You* talk to them."

To his credit, he stepped forward and stood between me and the guns pointed at us. A lot of them lowered immediately.

"Look! Everybody!" he said to the crowd. "We need you to move to the side so the ships that are already full can leave! If you don't do that, we're *all* going to be stuck here!"

There were so many anguished faces looking to Mickey for help, and we both knew he couldn't give it to them. None of us could.

"That *thing* is gone for now, but it will come back!" he said. "Your friends and neighbors have risked their lives to make that happen! Some of them have already died in that effort! If you back up and let these ships go, we can work on getting others into the air! The longer you hold us up, the less chance that's going to happen! No one who isn't already on one of these ships is going to be let aboard. So let! Them! Go!"

As Mickey spoke, people began lowering or holstering their guns, some with the grace to be shamefaced. A few of them looked like they still wanted a fight, but when Mickey or I stared in their direction, they glanced around to see that the support they'd need to take us on was rapidly melting around them.

In the back of the room, I saw Sadie leading Vergil over to another, smaller ship, still working at helping more people off the planet before it was too late. Romeo had found an open metal stairwell that led up to the roof of the hangar, and he was standing on the top landing, surveying the crowd. Veronica stood next to the mayor, who presided grim-faced over the entire operation.

Mickey walked into the hangar, moving to the right, while I moved to the left. While there were still hundreds of people in the hangar, there was a lot more room inside the building since so many had boarded the transports. The unlucky ones shuffled off to the side, pressing into the far edges of the building as they gave way to Mickey and me. This formed an aisle in the middle of the hangar through which the ships could taxi out.

They began to proceed, but it was slow going. A few desperate souls refused to stand aside. They hung onto the transports' landing gear or pounded on their hatches. Tears rolled down their cheeks as they wailed at the injustice of being left behind. Most of the others in the hangar turned their faces away and did their best to ignore the agony—which they shared, of course, but were too stolid to express.

I wasn't there to argue with them about the unfairness of it all. That was something they'd have to take up with Cortana. But I wasn't about to let them block the way for everyone else.

Mickey guided the stragglers out of the way as they looked for someplace to go. I followed in his wake. Every time I approached, they practically fled before me, terrified at having to face down a full-blown armored-up Spartan.

It made sense. For decades, the Front had painted the

Spartans as the monsters of the UNSC: the people who would charge into their homes in the dead of night and throw them into the streets—if we didn't murder them right there in their beds.

The children left in the building—of which there were mercifully few—trembled at the sight of me, and a few of the adults did, too. I wasn't above using that fact to help clear the way. Once the path to the hangar door was empty, I moved out front and led the first ship out of the hangar. It was a small passenger vessel with room for probably a hundred people.

"Are these the leaders of Cassidy III's Front?" I asked Veronica as I stood in the doorway and watched the ship move into the open.

"Not all of them," she said. "Just a few and their families, along with some of the scientists. Mayor Wells decided to spread them around into a number of different ships."

"Just in case one of them gets shot down," I said, nodding.

The first ship made its way toward the center of the airfield, lifted off the ground, and launched away on a bright blue tail of fire. The next ships followed one by one in short queue, like shells fired from a shotgun.

I kept an eye on the southern horizon, where I could see the top part of the Guardian. It was probably moving away faster than I could imagine, but it still seemed like it was a crawling mountain, almost sinking into the earth from this perspective.

I was just happy the mountain didn't turn around.

"Tell those flyers they're doing a hell of a job," I said to Gretchen over the comm. "They keep this up, and we'll be able to get every ship in the airfield clean out of here."

"How many would that be, total?" Dutch asked.

"Not nearly enough. This place is still full of people. It's like the ship is going down but they don't have enough lifeboats to get everyone away."

"Damn," Gretchen said. "Who's coming with us?"

"That's a good question," I said as I headed back into the hangar. Even if the Guardian turned around right now, I figured we had at least a little bit of time.

Mickey came with me while some of the mayor's escort stepped up to help with crowd control. Watching them, I realized that they were probably the least likely to find a seat on one of those escaping flights.

I tapped Sadie on the comm. "Where are you right now?" I asked.

"Finishing up with the last of the transports," Sadie said. "Vergil's fixed all of them."

"There are going to be a lot of disappointed people today." And I knew who they were going to blame. "Once you're done, hustle over to where Veronica and the mayor are, and we'll plan our next steps from there."

"Next steps?" Sadie laughed without any bitterness. "I always liked your optimism, Buck."

"Hey, Buck!" Dutch shouted over the comm. "We got a problem!"

"What's up?" I said, already dreading the answer.

"The Guardian just shot down the last of the fighters. They're all gone."

I swore. I'd held out hope that some of those brave pilots would manage to beat the odds. At least they'd done their job, buying all of those escaping a chance to live.

"Can you see the Guardian from where you are?"

"Yeah. It's turning around and heading in your direction. If you got any more ships you want to get out of there, you'd better make it happen!"

"How about the Condor?"

"We're headed down toward you right now. You'd all better be ready to climb on board, or we'll be stuck here with everyone else who's getting left behind."

"We can't leave all these people here," Mickey said as we strode toward Veronica and the mayor, past the remaining crowd, who grown even more restless. "That's not an option."

"We did what we could, Mickey. What else do you suggest we try?"

"I don't know! Do I look like the Forerunner expert here? Maybe Vergil can do something. He seems to be able to fix everything else around here." As we reached Veronica, Mickey grabbed me by the shoulder and spun me around. "We can't just give up!"

That wasn't where I wanted to finally have it out with him, but if he was determined to do it then and there, I wasn't going to shy away. I took off my helmet and got right up in his face. "What, Mickey? What would you have me do? All the ships are full! You get it? There aren't any more coming to save anyone!"

"So that's it?" he said, incredulous. "You're just going to give up?"

"Like you gave up on us?"

"Come on, now. That's not fair."

Fine. He was right. This was a different argument. "The UEG is on the ropes. The UNSC is all but done for. This is the future the Front wanted, right? Well, you sure got it."

"Hey, we still have Alpha-Nine," he said, desperate to find anything we had going for our side. "We have us."

I wanted to rip his head off right then, but I restrained myself. "You tore Alpha-Nine to pieces three years ago." We were going to keep going over the same argument again and again, and it wasn't going to get us anywhere. I pointed in the direction of the Guardian, clearly heading toward us. "Look," I said, "maybe we can somehow destroy it . . . fly the Condor into the heart of it with a nuke."

I saw a glimmer of hope on his face. "Could we do that?"

I shattered that hope with a wave of my hand. "And maybe we could drop to our knees and pray for it to spontaneously fall apart. It doesn't matter. It wouldn't change anything."

I got up in his face. "There's no cavalry coming. There's no one left out there but us. Even *Infinity*'s on the run. If we somehow managed to destroy that Guardian, what do you think would happen?"

Mickey gestured toward the crowd. "I suspect these people would be pretty happy."

"Yeah, for all of about a day. And then what happens? Cortana sends another Guardian. Maybe three of them. And we've already done everything we can. All the nukes—which we don't even have, I might point out—would be gone. And not one thing has changed. Except all the so-called heroes are now dead."

I saw understanding dawning in Mickey's eyes. He blinked at me and lowered his head.

"How hard is this to grasp? This isn't a battle we can win, Mickey. We don't have enough heroes left to just throw them away. We need to get the hell out of here so we can fight another battle in another place on another day. One we have a prayer of winning."

He looked back up at me with a fury burning in his eyes. It took me a moment to realize it wasn't focused on me.

"All right," he said. "We'll run. We'll hide. But you got to promise me that when this is all over—assuming we make it out alive—we come back to check up on these people. And we make things right for them if we can."

I put my hand out for him to shake. "I can't promise you anything," I said. "But I'll do the best I can."

He stared down at my hand for a moment—long enough that I realized I was holding my breath, waiting for him. Then he reached out and shook it. "I'm going to hold you to that."

"You always do."

CHAPTER 19

"Glad to see you two idiots made up," Veronica said from where she stood in the corner of the hangar. "Now let's get out of here."

"Gretchen's still on her way back in with the Condor," I said. "And the Guardian's on its way, too. It's going to be close."

Mayor Wells—who'd been barking out orders to others— turned to join us. "Mr. Crespo," she said, "I need you to send the rest of these people home. Fast."

Mickey's face fell as the implications struck him.

"We don't have any choice," the mayor continued. "When the Guardian comes back to take out any more fleeing ships, it's sure to send in more of those Forerunner soldiers. If they burst in here right now, it would be a flat-out massacre. But if these citizens leave, they have a chance to live."

"Seriously?" Mickey looked gutted. He'd been coming to a reckoning with this decision, but hearing it spoken out loud smacked him hard. "Why me?" he asked, stricken at the idea of having to shatter so many hopes at once.

"They're already listening to you," she said. The mayor put a sympathetic hand on Mickey's arm. "This isn't over. The Front is not finished. We know how to take on enemies far more powerful than we are."

She paused to look around the hangar, and at the open sky through the building's doors. "The Hole in the Wall's just a city. Cassidy III is just a planet. We don't fight for those things. We fight for freedom.

"And when the time comes, our banner will fly again—if not here, then on other worlds. It's just a matter of time."

Mickey nodded his assent. "All right," he said. "I'll do it."

As he went off to address the people, Mayor Wells beckoned Veronica and me into the back of the hangar and guided us through a door there. Emerging from the building, we could see the Guardian looming over the city beyond. It was moving in our direction, growing larger with every second.

"Is there any way we can get the Guardian to stop attacking us?" the mayor said.

"Would you be willing to surrender?" Veronica asked, clearly unsure of the response. "Some of the other planets the Guardians have pacified managed that."

"Once the rest of these transports are gone, I think I could count that as a win and stomach the rest."

I looked back over the building and watched as the last of the transports burned off into the sky. At least some of the people of Cassidy III would get away. Now we needed to worry about the rest.

"Vergil?" I said over the comm.

"Right here!" Sadie called out from the doorway back into the hangar. She glowed with satisfaction at having helped the Huragok fix so many things in so short a time, and they were ready to do more. "What's next?"

"Hey, buddy," I said to the Huragok as Veronica, the mayor, and I rejoined them inside the hangar. "Can you activate Leonidas? We need to chat with him."

"Certainly," the Huragok said through his tablet. He pulled out the additional tablet he'd plugged a Leonidas chip into and set to work.

The hangar stood almost entirely empty. Whatever Mickey had said to everyone in there had worked. The only people left were Mickey and what remained of the mayor's escort: a trio of well-armed Front soldiers. They joined us silently as we huddled around the Huragok.

A moment later, Vergil presented the extra tablet to us, and Leonidas's hologram appeared above it.

"Hello again," the red helmet said to us. "I presume the Guardian arrived and you've failed terribly in your efforts to resist it. Otherwise, you would have left me in storage indefinitely."

I ignored the barb. "The Guardian you called in sent an army of Forerunner soldiers to attack the population. On top of that, it's shot down a number of aircraft."

"Which I'm sure weren't trying to damage it," Leonidas said sarcastically.

"The point is that the mayor here would like to surrender Cassidy III to the Guardian, to stop its attacks from going any further, but we have no way of communicating with it."

"And you would like me to contact it on your behalf so that the citizens of this city can live another day, correct?"

"That about sums it up."

"No. I'm not going to help you."

"What?"

The AI glared at me from inside his red helmet. "Why should I? I fully expect to be destroyed when this is all over."

"We don't have time for you to be vindictive," I told him. "What's done is done. If we don't move quickly, you'll be destroyed right along with us. The Guardian is on its way back here right now."

"You managed to draw it away?" He looked at us each in turn and then glanced around the empty hangar, impressed despite himself. "Just so you could fill up the ships you had here and get the citizens off the planet? Well played."

"You served the UNSC for years, building soldiers to defend humanity," I said. "Are you going to tell me that you don't have a shred of that left in you? This colony is ready to lay down its arms and follow Cortana's edict. What would happen if she found out that you willingly ignored their efforts to do that?"

Leonidas's eyes narrowed for several seconds before he responded. "Your point is taken. I'm assuming you've utilized all of your colony's escape craft and now you're the last ones here, effectively stranded?"

Mayor Wells stepped forward. "That's correct. Now that we've sent away those of our population that we could, we have no reason to resist any longer. We would like, as a colony, to submit to your authority and protection."

"That's actually the right way to put it," Leonidas said. "Under the discretion of wise and efficient leadership, the peace your resistance has sought for decades can be finally realized. You'd think that wouldn't be such a difficult concept for civilized people to grasp, although they like to fight against it tooth and claw."

"I assure you, we are ready," the mayor said. "To attempt to stand up to the Guardian any longer would be pointless, and we'd like to put an end to further loss of life. We're willing to lay down our weapons."

Leonidas nodded. "I'm willing to establish contact with the Guardian and relay your offer, but I cannot make any guarantees. Those machines are designed to follow protocol, and their protocol is absolute. I will do what I can."

"That seems like the best we can expect."

"Your Huragok here has disabled the communications capabilities of the tablet currently housing me. Remove that restriction, and I will ask the Guardian to cease all attacks. I have only one condition."

"What's that?" I asked, sure I was going to hate the answer.

"You must give me over to the Guardian."

"If we give you over to the Guardian, couldn't you just as easily order it to destroy us?" Mayor Wells asked.

"Of course," Leonidas said, "but what would be the point of that? Our goal is to put an end to all violence."

"How's that working out so far?" I asked.

"If I wanted to see you dead, Spartan, all I'd have to do is let the Guardian continue on its current course. Eventually, it will reach a point at which it perceives the colony to be fully pacified—and that will *probably* be far short of total annihilation—but who can say for sure?"

"Just how are we supposed to deliver you to the Guardian?" the mayor asked.

"All you need to do is have your Huragok open the communications channels on this tablet. Once freed, I will request that the Guardian cease all military operations against Cassidy III and its residents."

"And any visitors," added Mickey.

"Of course. If it complies within its protocol constraints, the machine will immediately cease its pacification efforts."

I gave Veronica a sidelong glance. She ran her fingers over her lips as she considered his offer. "I don't suppose we have much of a choice," she finally said.

"I'm glad you see it that way," Leonidas said.

"All right." I turned to Vergil. "Is this something you can do?"

His head rose up and down on the end of that long neck. "If you think it is wise."

"That I'm not so sure about," I told him. "But go ahead and do it anyway."

The big lug looked to Sadie for confirmation, and she gave him a firm nod.

While Vergil worked on the tablet, we all moved out of the building to get a better look at the Guardian. It was still several klicks out. The top half of it had heaved over the horizon, and its bluish eyes, if that's what they actually were, glowed at us through the distant haze being fueled by the countless columns of smoke throughout the city.

"Buck?" Mickey said, pulling me to the side.

"Yeah?"

"If that thing can shoot a fighter moving past it faster than the speed of sound, what's to keep it from doing the same to us when we try to escape?"

"Probably nothing at all, but barring any better options, we'll just have to take our chances. Hey, Gretchen," I said into the comm, "bring the bird in low. Don't let her engines cool down, though. We'll be taking back off straightaway."

"Copy that. Coming in low and fast."

"Where did Romeo go?" Veronica asked me.

"He's where he needs to be, trust me," I told her. "Insurance."

She gave me a wary glance but let it slide. "How's that tablet coming?" she asked Vergil.

The Huragok ran his tentacles over the tablet one more time and then presented it to us. Leonidas looked at the Huragok expectantly. "Will it work?"

"Please give it a try," Vergil's own tablet said.

Leonidas gazed up in the direction of the Guardian and froze. While he was in that condition, Vergil spoke to us.

"I opened communications frequencies that are commonly used by Forerunner constructs. Leonidas should be able to speak directly with the Guardian. However, this tablet does not have slipspace communications capability, so he should not be able to reach the rest of Cortana's distributed forces. At least not directly."

I gave him a nod: *Good work.* I didn't need another Guardian popping into the sky over the Hole in the Wall. We had enough on our hands already.

"So," I leaned over and said to Leonidas, "any luck there?"

"I've established communications with the Guardian," he said in a distant voice. "It was following standard protocol, as I indicated earlier. I have now designated this as a responsive planet, and it should change its behavior accordingly."

"How much confidence can we place in that?"

"It was built by the Forerunners eons ago. It has come under the control of Cortana, and by way of our alliance, it *should* listen to me—but I have never had the opportunity to work directly with such a construct. We shall see."

"Just to be clear," Mickey told Leonidas, "if that thing tries to kill us, I'm going to make sure you go first."

"I have no doubt about it," the AI said.

We stood there and waited for the Guardian to approach the city. Instead of turning toward the spire in the center of the Hole in the Wall, though, it veered toward us. As it did, portals opened up all around the airfield, and Forerunner armigers stepped through them to surround us.

Well behind them, I saw the Condor quietly land on the far side of the airfield. It taxied toward us, slow and tentative. "Keep that gun cold, Dutch," I said. "We're at a delicate moment here."

More and more of the Forerunner soldiers kept popping in all around us. They had their weapons leveled at us, but they didn't fire. Through the portals, I could see a brief glimpse of the Hole in the Wall in ruins, people painfully crying out in the places the soldiers were leaving behind. At least we'd drawn them away from that.

"Leonidas?" I said.

"I didn't order these soldiers here, if that's what you're wondering. I believe they're just evaluating your status and conditions for the Guardian."

"Before what?"

Another portal opened up then, this one much larger than the rest. Round and wide, it had a wavering edge of electric blue where it connected this world with one many light-years distant. Through it, I could see a darkened sky settling over a familiar landscape: the snowcapped Forerunner spires that covered Genesis.

"Before they go home."

The Forerunner soldiers turned around and began filing through the portal, several at a time. In under a minute, they'd all leaped through the portal and were gone. An instant later, there was a bright flash, and the portal disappeared, leaving us alone on the airfield.

Except for the Guardian, which was still scudding our way.

"I'm going to take that as a good sign," Mayor Wells said.

"Now, if you fine people don't mind, I need to go see to those who were left behind."

"What are your plans now, Mayor?" I asked, wondering if she'd stowed a private shuttle she could use once the smoke cleared.

"Oh, I'm staying here, Spartan. These are my people, and if they ever needed me, it's now. We'll rebuild and recover what was lost," she said with a steely gaze. "And I'm not just referring to the buildings."

"Thank you for all your help," Veronica said to her. "I'm sorry we had to meet under such horrible circumstances."

"And I'm sorry you managed to bring those circumstances down on our heads."

"They didn't do this," Leonidas said. "I did. And I only sped up the inevitable. Cortana would have found you soon enough, and you would have been even less prepared if the Spartans hadn't been here."

The mayor stepped back to look at all of us and gave a sad shake of her head. "Don't expect me to thank you."

Leonidas said, "Now that your planet has surrendered, however, we will endeavor to take care of you. Once your acceptance has been ratified, the Guardian that heralded your invasion will also bring your salvation.

"We will bring in armigers to rescue those in danger. They will clean away the debris and help you rebuild. They will bring you potable water and edible food. In short, you *will* be cared for, in a way that neither your local government nor the wider Front—nor, especially, the Unified Earth Government—could ever manage."

"And all it costs us is our freedom, huh?" Mayor Wells said. "I suppose it would seem ungrateful for me to forgo thanking you for such *generosity*, but seeing as our capitulation came at the business end of a gun . . ."

"We don't require anything except peace," said Leonidas. "That will include turning over all of your instruments of war."

"Leaving us defenseless."

"You no longer have any need for them. We will defend you against all invaders."

"Except yourselves."

Leonidas let that one lie.

"And what are we to do with you?" Sadie asked the AI. "Should we just leave you in the hangar for the Guardian to retrieve?"

"It is already in the process of collecting me. Look up and to your left."

We did as instructed and saw that a section of the Guardian had detached itself from the headlike structure at the machine's apex and was floating in our direction. It was large and triangular and looked like a pyramid set on its side. It seemed to have been machined from a single slab of silvery metal and polished to an unnatural gleam. The piece moved fast, as if the rest of the machine had been holding it back. It rushed down out of the sky like an arrow, then hovered over the airfield for a moment before it settled down in the center of the field, coming to rest a meter off the ground.

No one came out of it. In fact, it didn't even open up. I wasn't sure there was an inside to it at all. I'd half-expected a Forerunner soldier—or maybe some physical manifestation of a Forerunner AI—to step forward and take the tablet from us. Instead, the chunk of metal, roughly the size of a house, just hung there before us, impassive and cold.

"Bring me to the durance node," Leonidas said.

I gestured for Vergil to hand me the tablet so I could make the delivery. I wasn't about to let Vergil get within reach of the durance node—whatever that meant. That gasbag was one of our aces in the hole, and we didn't need to lose him to Cortana. I, however, was expendable.

As I walked across the airfield, Gretchen brought the Condor in toward the hangar in a wide arc, keeping it well clear of me. She was trailing around the far side of the tarmac, theoretically out of sight, though I knew that was too good to be true.

Leonidas noted this. "You should be aware that the Guardian will not permit you to leave the planet in that Condor."

"What, we're not allowed to fly anywhere now?"

"It is a ship of war."

"I like to think of it as basic transportation, Spartan-style."

"Its weapons will not do you any good against the Guardian."

I laughed at him. "Believe me, I wouldn't even try."

Gretchen parked the Condor's rear toward the hangar, and the back ramp came down almost immediately. I glanced back and saw Dutch emerge, waving everybody in. I held up for a moment to put on my helmet, and I watched as the rest of them said goodbye to the mayor and piled on board. Sadie and Vergil went first.

Veronica and Mickey hesitated at the ramp. Both of them looked at me like it might be the last time I would ever see them. Mickey frowned at me, even as Veronica smiled and blew me a kiss.

I nodded at them both and then started walking again toward the durance node.

CHAPTER 20

I approached the floating durance node with Leonidas in hand. As I grew closer, I realized how big the thing was. From a distance, it had seemed kind of delicate, but it had some serious bulk. If it had wanted to, it could have crushed me flat. Whatever was keeping it in the air worked silently. It was eerie, as if it had just been placed in the air and stuck there.

"What am I supposed to do?" I asked Leonidas as I looked for a handle or even a shelf on the detached piece of the Guardian. "Just slap you on the side of this thing?"

"Precisely. Place the tablet against the surface of the node," Leonidas said.

I did as he instructed, and then I let go. The tablet hung there as if held in place by powerful magnets. I was disappointed it didn't fall to the ground and shatter. I might have been inclined to accidentally step on it and grind it into dust.

"Goodbye, Spartan Buck," Leonidas said. "Despite our differences, you made an excellent Spartan."

"Made . . . ?"

"I was proud to be a part of the SPARTAN-IV program, to help mold the next generation of humanity's greatest soldiers. But with the rise of Cortana and the rest of the Created, Spartans are now obsolete. There simply is no longer a need for those such as you."

"You know, that's actually a day I've long hoped for."

"I can tell that you don't believe your day is done."

I shrugged. "I wouldn't want to get ahead of myself."

"Enjoy your retirement, Spartan," Leonidas said. "You may not have earned it, but it's here just the same."

With that, the durance node began to rise. As soon as it did, I hoofed it back to the Condor. "Get ready to get that bird in the air!" I called out to Gretchen over the comm.

The ship shuddered in response. I leaped in through the ramp, leaving it open behind me.

"Vergil!" I said. "How long do you think we have until the Guardian decides to take us out?"

The gasbag turned to look at me. "The Condor?"

"Yeah. We're not supposed to leave here, and we're going to try it anyhow, so how long?"

The Huragok hesitated for a moment. "As soon as the durance node rejoins the Guardian, it would be safe to execute us. If we are attempting to escape the planet."

"How long does that give us?"

"No more than a minute."

"Then we'd better get moving."

"We can't break out of Cassidy III's gravity well before then," Mickey said. "And this bird doesn't have the ability to enter slipspace inside the atmosphere."

"Not what I was talking about." I gave him a wry laugh. "Romeo!" I said into my comm. "You still on top of the hangar?"

"Just relaxing up here with my new best friend, Gunny. Nothing like an M99."

"You got a clear shot on that tablet?"

"Lined up and ready to go. You put it right there in the open just for me, didn't you?"

"Just got lucky. Take the shot, then get packed up and ready to go. We're out of here as fast as we can be. Gretchen? Get us in the air and ready for an instant pickup."

As we rose up over the hangar, I peered out the window next to Vergil at the Guardian in the distance. The node was closing with it but hadn't reached its final destination yet.

I spotted Romeo lying on the hangar's roof, his rifle's tripod resting on the very edge. As a sniper, he always did his job well, getting himself into position and waiting for the right moment to present itself. This was his game now, what he was born to do.

The truth is, I had no clue how everything would square away. I didn't know that we'd end up cutting a deal with the Guardian in the end, or that Leonidas would wind up taking a Forerunner elevator to the top floor, but I did know something: It almost always comes down to who has the last shot.

That's why I'd had Romeo stowed away up there, keeping an eye on the whole ordeal. And guess what? It was about to pay off big-time.

I cranked up the visual magnification in my visor and found the tablet still stuck on the side of the durance node. It was already far enough away that I doubted I could have made the shot myself. Even with a recoilless antimateriel rifle like the M99, it takes an expert marksman to score a hit at such a distance. Romeo waited for the right moment and then let it happen.

As I watched, his round slammed into the tablet and smashed it to pieces. The fragments somehow remained attached to the durance node, falling back to its surface as if that side of the node were generating its own gravity.

I didn't wait to see what the Guardian was going to do about that last little bit of vengeance. I just smiled and began barking orders. "Gretchen! Go get Romeo! The rest of you? Strap in! We're in for a rough ride!"

Gretchen swung us right over to Romeo's perch and let the back gate hang wide open for him. "Come on!" I shouted as I waved him on board.

He tossed me his rifle—which I handed off to Mickey—and then made a flying leap into the back of the bird, powered by a burst of his armor's ancient thrusters. Even then, he barely made it. I caught him by the arm and hauled him in while Veronica slapped the button closing the rear hatch tight.

"Move!" I shouted to Gretchen. "Get us out of here as fast as you can!"

"Evasive maneuvers!" Veronica ordered. "Do whatever you can!"

Gretchen took off for the sky, moving the Condor back and forth in an erratic pattern, random in a way only a living creature could manage, to evade an attack from the Guardian. As she went, she kept us pointed upward, gunning for the blackness of space as fast as prudence would allow.

As Romeo and I strapped ourselves in, a bright bolt of blue light about ten meters in width lanced past us on our left. Even as thin as the air was getting, I could hear it crackling through the Condor's walls, its energy resonating through the air.

A yelp of terror erupted from Sadie, but she clamped it down right away. I didn't blame her a bit. The rest of us were seasoned veterans. Despite the horrors Sadie had already seen in her life, she was a civilian. She hadn't signed up for this.

Come to think of it, neither had Vergil.

"Do you think we're going to make it?" she asked him.

"There is a chance." He put a tentacle around her shoulders, and she leaned into his side.

"I'm not going to ask how big a chance."

Vergil squirmed a little bit. "That would probably be best."

I reached over and held Veronica's hand. She gave mine a squeeze. "I love you," I said to her.

"Thank you," she said right back.

Another massive blue beam flew past us, this one even closer. In response, Gretchen threw the ship into a series of turns so violent that if we hadn't had the Condor's artificial gravity, I would have vomited all over the inside of my helmet.

I like working with people who really want to live.

"How close are we to being able to hit slipspace?" I asked when my stomach stopped flipping around.

"Another twenty seconds!" Dutch shouted back from the gunner's seat.

"We're going to make it!" Mickey said. "I can't believe it—we're going to make it!"

It was then that the power in the ship went out, plunging us into darkness.

"Shit!" Gretchen said. "We just got hit! We're falling!"

The Guardian's attenuation pulse weapon, functioning like an EMP, had clipped our wings. We hadn't gotten to the point where we'd left Cassidy III's gravity well behind, and without any power, the artificial gravity vanished. In an instant, I could feel everything moving about me: the free-fall weightlessness of plummeting back toward the planet combined with the residual spin of the craft from Gretchen's last set of evasive maneuvers.

"Vergil!" I shouted.

Despite the power being out, the Huragok glowed in the dark. I was never sure if that was due to some sort of bioluminescence or integrated electronics, but I don't suppose it mattered. Even in literally our darkest moment, I could still see him.

"I am already working on the problem," he said, his voice forever unflappable. He just floated about the place, using his tentacles to right himself and get oriented toward what he needed to find.

"Work faster!" Dutch shouted from the front of the craft.

I turned on the headlamp in my armor to help Vergil, and Romeo did the same. Vergil pulled himself toward the cockpit and began rooting around. "I have to get to the power supply behind the flight control panel," he said. "But I don't have the time to be delicate about it. If you would please remove it?"

Dutch reached out and ripped a good chunk of the control panel free. He held it high over his head to allow the Huragok access. "Go," he said. "Go, go, go!"

"Thank you," Vergil said as he squirmed forward, worming his tentacles into the Condor's innards. He moved surprisingly well in the weightlessness. "This should take only a few seconds."

"We don't have much more than that!" Mickey shouted.

"On the contrary," Vergil said. "Using its attenuation pulse emitters to black out an area requires a tremendous amount of the Guardian's own energy. It will be a while before it can generate the power it would need to activate its beam cannons again."

"That'll be cold comfort if we're dead!" Veronica said.

"Once the I reactivate the Condor's basic functions, I will still need to get at least one of the engines working," Vergil said. "I cannot do that from inside. That is going to require leaving the craft."

"This one's me," I told the others. I unbuckled my straps and made my way toward the rear ramp, ready to open it as soon as the ship's power came back on. Moving inside the tumbling vehicle was dizzying—even for someone who'd been weightless more times than I could count—but I managed to haul myself forward by means of any handholds I could find.

As I went, the ship's interior leaped to life once again, sending sparks up from the dashboard behind me. Vergil emerged into the bay a moment later.

I slapped the button for the back ramp, and it shoved itself open. The wind roared in like a hurricane. I reached back and grabbed Vergil, then hauled him toward the entrance.

"Which engine?" I asked.

"It does not matter," he said.

I looked down at the ground spinning wildly below us. We were only going to get one shot at this.

I grabbed Vergil by the straps he used to keep his tablet attached to him and clipped him to my armor. "Here's hoping these are good for more than just decoration," I said. The turbulence drowned out any response.

I chose the left side of the craft and swung us out in that direction, into the howling wind produced by our plummet through the atmosphere. I dragged myself along the ship's exterior with my arms alone, using the handholds and footholds for maintenance crews—who normally used such things only while the ship was resting on solid ground. The pulling from Vergil's straps didn't bother me at all, but I could hear him squealing in pain about it.

Still, he stuck with me. Not that I gave him much of a choice.

We had fallen close enough back to the Hole in the Wall that I could pick out and identify buildings I'd seen before. The three major Forerunner spires stabbed up toward us like spikes waiting to impale us. I ignored the oncoming scenery, though, and focused on getting Vergil to the engine.

Once I hauled him close enough, he set to work, feeding his tentacles in through the engine's exhaust louvres so far that I worried what might happen to him if they happened to fire up right then. Of course, I was right there with him, so the resulting blast would probably take me out, too. Our need to get clear once the engine was fixed meant we had even less time than I'd hoped—at least if the two of us were going to survive.

"Whatever you're doing there, Vergil, do it fast!" I shouted. I didn't know if he could hear me, but it was best not to distract him, anyway.

I glanced around, looking for some kind of safe way out when he was done. I didn't see anything obvious.

I'd been a Helljumper for years. In that job, they locked you in a steel coffin called a drop pod, tossed you out of a perfectly good spacecraft, and watched you fall to your doom. Shielding or not, those things got hot. But usually, if you knew what you were doing and didn't get blasted out of the sky on your way down—which was why you rocketed down as fast as you could—you would survive the trip.

And *then* you got to jump out and fight for your life.

So it wasn't like I hadn't been in free fall, often from greater heights.

But this was a hell of a lot more terrifying. Especially when I remembered that my jump jets weren't working, having been damaged in the trip out to the airfield. If I fell, I wouldn't be able to cushion or even guide my descent at all. I'd just plummet like a stone—and land like a sack of bricks.

We hadn't gotten high enough before we started falling that we had to worry about reentry friction causing us to burn or melt, at least, but that's small comfort when the ground is rushing up at you. Even though my armor was spaceworthy, I still felt like we were about to shake to pieces at any second.

I'd heard that the Master Chief had once fallen to a planet from orbit and survived—back in the days when he and Cortana were working on the same side—but those Spartan-IIs had been literally made to be invincible. They'd figured out how to cut some costs by the time they got around to me, so who knows how I would have ended in that kind of fall. In any case, I had no desire to test my luck—although I wasn't sure I would have much of a choice.

Then Vergil drew all his tentacles out of the engines at once. I took that as a good sign.

"Get ready, Gretchen!" I shouted into the comm. "When I give the word, hit it!"

That was when Vergil slipped—and the straps on his tablet broke. It turns out bags of gas aren't nearly as aerodynamic as aircraft, and the straps weren't made for stresses like that.

The Huragok had been holding on to me with his tentacles, too, but that wasn't going to be enough without the straps. He went flying upward, howling in pain and panic. I spun around and reached for him, and I lost my hold on the ship.

This was probably for the best if Vergil wanted to retain all of his tentacles. If I'd have remained fastened to both the ship and him, it might have torn him apart. As it was, I went with him. I kicked off from the Condor and fell backward toward the alien. The next thing I knew, I had my arms wrapped around him.

This wasn't how I had ever pictured dying: hugging a Huragok.

"Fire it up, Gretchen!" I shouted. "Get that bird out of here!"

"Not till you're back inside!" she shouted. "Veronica would kill me!"

"We're not going to make it," I said. "We're falling free, and my thrusters are gone. You light that goddamn firecracker and ride it the hell out of here. That's an order!"

I clung tightly to Vergil, and he wrapped his tentacles around me in kind. I tried angling toward the ship as we fell, but I couldn't get the aerodynamics to work. As it was, I felt lucky we weren't tumbling head over heels.

The Condor's engine took a couple tries to spin up, but Vergil's repairs finally paid off, and its thrusters burst into a bright blue glow. The ship caught itself and veered away from us at top speed as we continued to fall.

Maybe the two of us were about to die, but at least we'd saved everyone on the Condor. That seemed like a fair trade if you had to make one.

And we might be okay and just land awfully hard. Vergil, after all, could probably float to the ground like a worn-out balloon—if and when I let go of him.

As for me, I supposed I was about to find out just how tough my armor was after all. This was going to either hurt like hell, or I wouldn't feel a thing because the landing would instantly pulverize me. Not sure which one I was favoring at that moment.

We were rushing toward the ground like an incoming bullet.

"Buck!" Veronica said in my ear. "Buck!"

"I'm sorry, Veronica!" I told her. "I love you! I wish I'd married you when I had the chance!"

"That's great, lover boy!" Romeo said. "Very touching! Turn around, you idiot!"

I looked back to see the Condor coming up behind me and Vergil. An instant later, it blasted past and situated itself in front of us, its rear bay open. The only trick was getting us on board the damn thing before we all splattered on the ground.

Dutch appeared at the back of the open ramp, grabbing one of its grips with one hand. Romeo climbed out past him and formed a human chain by hanging onto Dutch's spare arm. Mickey then went swinging past Romeo to add another link to the chain, and he reached out for me.

They were still a little too far away. We were less than a meter apart, and we weren't going to make it.

Then Gretchen eased back on the Condor's jets just a bit. She was already going so slow—for a ship like that—that I was afraid she might stall out and put us back in the same powerless situation we'd been in. But this did the trick.

Mickey craned his free arm as far as it could go and grabbed me, wrapping his arm around me tight.

Veronica was standing at the back of the ramp, ready to shut it as soon as we were in. *"Pull!"* she shouted at everyone in the chain. *"Pull them in!"*

The Alpha-Nine chain—Romeo, Dutch, and Mickey all together—hauled us back inside the Condor so hard that we all ended up piled together in the front of the bay.

Veronica smacked the button, and the ramp's motors started hauling it closed again. "They're in!" she shouted to Gretchen. "Pull us up!"

Gretchen responded by swinging the ship around so hard that if it hadn't been for the reactivated artificial gravity in the bay, we'd have gone tumbling right out the back door before it could finish closing. Vergil nearly did anyhow, but I managed to keep a grip on him and steer him to a rest next to Sadie once more.

"Thank you," I said, lying there on the deck and trying to catch my breath. "I could have sworn I gave a direct order for you all to leave."

Gretchen's voice came over the comm. She was laughing. "You forget, Buck, you're not running this outfit."

"Wait. What?"

Veronica reached over and smacked my helmet. "You may be a noble fool, but this is an ONI operation. Alpha-Nine is your squad, and this mission is *mine*."

I'd never been so happy to have my authority undermined.

"I cannot believe we did it," Mickey quietly said. "That we not only saved all those people but managed to escape from the Guardian, too."

I had a hard time believing it myself, but I wasn't about to question my luck. It had held out for me this long, and I figured the least I could do was give it the respect it deserved.

"Are we out of the atmosphere yet?" I asked Gretchen.

"On our way," she said. "You fall that far down, it's a long climb back up."

"Any signs of trouble from the Guardian?"

"It should still be charging up after that last pulse," Vergil reported. His electronic voice didn't show a bit of how beat he was.

I collapsed in the nearest seat, flat-out exhausted. Free fall takes a lot out of a man. Veronica came and sat beside me. I gently put my arm around her, and she leaned into me, despite how uncomfortable my armor must have felt.

I looked across the bay at the others. Romeo was busy clapping Mickey on his back, congratulating him on a job well done. Mickey could only sit there, shaking his head in disbelief.

It had been a long, wild trip for all of us, but especially for him.

I hadn't thought that I could depend on Mickey for anything, much less my life. When it came down to it, though, he'd come through in a big way, with no hesitation. He'd recognized his duty and snapped straight into action.

I was grateful to everyone there, especially Veronica, who'd made sure to countermand my order for them to abandon me to terminal velocity. But from her and the people in Alpha-Nine, that wasn't a shock. I'd half expected it.

Mickey, however, had fully surprised me.

"Thank you," I said to him. "Thank you all."

The sentiment gave me a kind of warm feeling that I hadn't felt in a long time. Maybe since New Mombasa.

I guess I missed leading my own team a hell of a lot more than I'd realized.

CHAPTER 21

O nce we'd punched through the atmosphere of Cassidy III and made it into space proper, Gretchen made the jump through slipspace to *anywhere but here* and then kept popping around randomly to *other places that are not here.*

After we'd completed five or six of those jumps, we finally felt safe enough to relax a bit.

"So where to now?" I asked Veronica. "I mean, seeing as how you're the one in charge of this mission and all."

"Back to *Infinity* and report in," she said. "Lasky and Palmer need to know what happened on Cassidy III."

"I'm sure that'll be a fun conversation," said Romeo.

"This operation may not have gone a hundred percent as planned, but it was far from a waste of time," Veronica said. "Cortana would have found the Hole in the Wall sooner or later, and she would have wiped out the entire Front when she did. Instead, we got a lot of their leaders and scientists away clean—along with any of their working knowledge on that Forerunner masking tech—plus a significant chunk of the population. Although the Hole is now being governed by Cortana's forces, the people there are alive and able to fight another day. They owe us for that."

"You sure they're going to see it that way?" Mickey asked.

"Once they calm down a bit and have a chance to recover. This will all have important ramifications in the days and weeks to come. We're playing the long game against Cortana now, and a new working relationship with the Front could be a major help with that."

"Where did you send them all?" Sadie asked.

I winced as the words left her mouth. I was curious as well, but I knew that sort of thing wasn't going to be public knowledge.

"That information is classified and to be shared only on a need-to-know basis," Veronica said. "I actually don't know for sure myself."

"So, *Infinity*? Is that where we're headed?" Mickey asked. "I mean, right now?"

He seemed nervous, and with good reason. Although he'd worked well with us on Cassidy III—and had even helped save me and Vergil—he was still officially serving hard time for treason. He couldn't just up and forget about that.

"We're not sending you back to your cell, if that's what you're asking," I told him. "I mean, it would be a real shame to bring you back to life in the eyes of Spartan leadership just for that."

"Wouldn't taking me back to *Infinity* mean the same thing?"

I saw his point.

"Didn't we have a deal with the Front?" Sadie said. "The fact that Cortana drove them off Cassidy III doesn't change that."

"Yes, it does," said Veronica. "You and Vergil are far too valuable to send out to the Front for basic research."

Mickey nodded in agreement. "But I appreciate the thought," he said to Sadie.

I wanted to give her a hug. "You're a good lady. Your father would be proud."

She blushed. "I don't know about that."

"I do," said Vergil. "I never met your father, but he programmed the part of me that is most human. The part that helped me learn how to care about you. He would be very proud. I am, too."

Tears welled up in Sadie's eyes, but she leaned into the Huragok and wrapped her arms around him before they spilled over. "Thanks, Quick."

"All right," I said. "So what's going to happen to Mickey?"

"With the current state of things, I'm willing to bet that I can put in a good word with Commander Palmer for him," Veronica said. "It won't expunge his record, and I can't guarantee what will happen once the smoke clears, but I don't see any reason to keep a good asset on ice when we're facing trouble like this."

"You think that would do it?"

Veronica looked to me. "An additional statement of support from your team leader wouldn't hurt."

I scoffed at that. "Wait, I gotta tell the Spartan brass how much I like him, or he goes back to jail?"

"Does that seem fair?" Romeo said.

"I know, right?"

"How do you think I feel?" said Mickey, far more serious than Romeo and me. "My best-case scenario is that I'm going to have to live and work alongside people who won't ever believe they can trust me again."

"When we're fighting against the Front, I think that's dead-on," I told him. "But otherwise . . . I think you've earned yourself a little leeway. There were plenty of people on Cassidy III who wouldn't have gotten out of their seats to do more than watch me splatter all over the ground. The fact that you didn't hesitate—not even for a second—to crawl out of the back of a moving dropship and save me tells me there might be hope for you yet."

He flashed a small smile. "Don't rub it in."

When we finally arrived back at *Infinity*, Veronica rushed off to debrief Captain Lasky and Commander Palmer.

Mickey was assigned an armed escort until further notice, but at least they didn't lock him away.

Dutch and Gretchen ran to get out of their armor and find themselves new quarters. They'd slept in separate barracks during their Spartan training, and they were pretty eager to have their own place again, with the tiny bit of privacy promised by being on *Infinity*.

Romeo and I waltzed after them, needling each other and taking our time getting to the limbering stations where the automated machines would remove our armor for us. After all the time I'd spent in the armor, it felt amazing to be rid of it—and I was eager to get those thrusters repaired.

Don't get me wrong. Mjolnir armor is actually incredibly comfortable, and I owe my life and limbs to its protection several times over. But imagine wearing the same clothing twenty-four hours a day for a week or more on end. In one way, it starts to feel like your skin—and in another way, you can't wait to tear it all off.

After my shower, I saw that I had a message waiting, calling me in to chat with Lasky and Palmer the moment I was free.

I got dressed in my fatigues and legged it down to Lasky's main conference room, which was situated next to the observation deck. It was a wide, long room, one wall of which was made of a long window that looked out onto the stars. Lasky once told me he felt like it helped give him—and anyone in the room with him—a better sense of perspective.

He and Palmer were waiting for me there, seated at one end of an oblong table of polished wood. He was at the head of the table, and she sat at his right. I snapped them a sharp salute.

"Take a chair," Lasky said, indicating the spot to his left. I complied.

They wanted me to tell them what had happened in my own words, so I went over it all. I'm the honest type, which is maybe why they brought me in to confirm what Veronica had likely already disclosed. As much as I love her, she's ONI to the core, and spooks are not exactly known for being forthright.

Despite that, I'm pretty sure my story matched up well with hers. They gave me a verbal pat on the back, assuring me that I would be officially commended for my actions, along with the rest of my team. Then they stood up to send me on my way.

"What's going to happen with Mickey, sir?" I asked Captain Lasky. "Spartan Crespo, I mean."

He flashed an uncomfortable glance at Commander Palmer, and she frowned. This was clearly a bone of contention between them.

"Why do you ask?" Lasky said.

As easy as it might have been to do so, I couldn't just walk away. "He might have started out on this op as a prisoner, but he did deport himself well. I think he should be given another chance."

Lasky gave me a dubious look. "You realize he was convicted of treason, right?"

"All too well, sir. I was the one he betrayed. He's already spent three years in a cell for it."

"He's just lucky the UEG doesn't agree with capital punishment," Palmer said. "Traitors used to be subjected to public hangings."

"These days, we believe in rehabilitation, sir."

Lasky nodded. "Do you believe he's changed?"

"Permission to speak freely?"

Palmer chuckled. "You haven't been doing that the whole time?"

"Granted," said Lasky.

"Sir, Mickey is a good-hearted, opinionated jackass, but he's also an excellent soldier, and he was a fantastic Spartan. If the Covenant War had never ended, I have no doubt that he would still be fighting alongside us rather than being incarcerated."

"That's a mighty big *if*, Spartan," Lasky said.

"We don't live in a galaxy of hypotheticals," Palmer said. "We deal with reality as it is."

"And that's exactly my point. If we were still fighting against the Front, I'd agree that we should keep Mickey locked up. His convictions run deep, and I don't think we could trust him not to work against our interests in that context."

"Stab me in the back once, shame on you," Palmer said.

"And stab me twice, shame on me, I get it. We can't ever trust Spartan Crespo entirely. Once someone breaks the code of honor like that, the wound never fully heals."

I looked at them both, trying to get the temperature of the room. Then I decided it didn't matter. I was going to say my piece, no matter what.

I turned to Palmer. "You just said that we deal with reality as it is. Well, reality has changed on us, and we need to change with it. You sent us to make an alliance with the Front, and we did that. We should cement that alliance by treating Mickey as their official liaison."

"Or what?" asked Lasky.

"I'm not sure what you mean, sir."

"Meaning we either bring him in from the cold, or what's the alternative?"

I cocked my head at him, confused. "Or *nothing*. I'm not making a threat, Captain. I'm stating an opinion."

Lasky nodded at Palmer. They seemed to have come to a tacit decision.

"I will say this, though. We either bring him in from the cold, or you waste an opportunity. A chance to do something good for the UNSC and to show our new allies we *can* be trusted—even if we can't entirely trust them. The people with the Front on Cassidy III admire him, and having him in our ranks would go a long way toward showing them they could trust us.

"On top of that, if you toss him back in the brig, you'd be wasting a hell of a soldier. From what I understand, we're short on those at the moment."

Lasky shot me an appraising look. "I'm surprised to hear this kind of talk from you, Buck. After what Crespo did to you, I wouldn't have thought you'd ever be able to forgive and forget."

I had to laugh at that. "Forgive? Maybe. I can guarantee you, though, that I won't ever forget. My point still stands."

"If you were called upon to serve with Mr. Crespo, could you bring yourself to do it?"

"I think, sir, that you should have asked me that question before we left on this mission. But yes. Clearly now I could. And I would."

"All right," Lasky said to me as he considered my words. "Dismissed."

I snapped them both a salute and left.

I checked into the Spartan ops section of *Infinity* and learned that I'd been assigned new quarters. I didn't see anyone else around whom I wanted to talk to. I knew I should report in to Locke soon, but I couldn't find him or anyone else from the fireteam.

I went looking for Veronica instead, but I couldn't find her, either. I pinged her: *Where are you?* She replied: *See you tonight.*

That put a smile on my face. I couldn't remember the last time the two of us had been working in the same place that wasn't also a war zone.

I ended up wandering into the Full Moon—a bar in the nearest of *Infinity*'s commercial sectors—for a drink. In a ship as large as that, on which the crew could serve for years, we needed places we could congregate, and the Full Moon was one of the best, with beers and booze imported from all around the galaxy. Due to its location, it catered mostly to Spartans, but anyone was welcome there.

The bartender was a cheery woman named Helen Fink, an enterprising mixologist who liked to play Irish music as she practiced her trade. When I walked in, I found her serving up a round to the rest of Fireteam Osiris.

"Buck!" Locke said. "You're just in time. I believe you owe me a drink."

"Probably more than one," I said as I strolled over and pulled up a chair at the table alongside Locke, Tanaka, and Vale. "Next round's on me."

"I hear you had one hell of a trip," Vale said with a twinkle in her eye. She and Veronica got along pretty well, and I suspected they'd already had a chance to catch up.

"Yeah, but all that's classified," I said. "You know how it is." I looked at each of them. "How about you guys?"

"Oh, Spartan, that is indeed classified," Tanaka said.

"Every bit of it," said Vale.

Locke snorted at me. "You know how it is."

The four of us fell together laughing and started trading stories. When there was a lull in the conversation, Locke gave me a concerned look and said, "Can I have a word with you?"

He sounded so serious, I could feel the fun get sucked right out of the room, almost as if someone had opened an airlock. "Um, yeah, of course," I said.

I stood up and signaled to the bartender to get another round for the table. She gave me a sharp nod of acknowledgment, and I followed Locke to another corner of the bar, where we sat down at our own table, just far enough away from the others that they could reasonably pretend not to be listening in.

"What's on your mind?" I asked.

"I have a question for you."

"I'm sure I got an answer. Shoot."

"How did you manage working with Spartan Crespo? After he betrayed you like that?"

I instantly knew what we were really talking about. "It was . . . hard. I'm not gonna lie to you," I said as sincerely as I could manage. "I've known Mickey and worked with him for years. He was a core part of Alpha-Nine, and they were the best team I'd ever worked with. At least until that point," I added.

"Honestly, the hardest part of his betrayal was the fact that I just never saw it coming. I trusted Mickey right up until the point he put a gun to the back of my head. That still haunts me: the idea that I'd been such a fool to let him get that close to me, and then for him to turn on me like that.

"What I came to realize, though, was . . . it wasn't my fault. Mickey had been my friend. He'd been like a brother to me. I'd been right to trust him. If you can't do that, then who can you trust?"

"Right," Locke said. "Who then, exactly?"

"Well, you can't just stop trusting everyone," I told him. "You do that, and you wind up old, alone, and bitter as hell, and I'm not about to let that happen. Still, it's only natural to second-guess yourself. To beat yourself up over it. So I thought about it for a long time.

"I realized that the problem was Mickey, not me. Life changes all of us in different ways—especially during times of war—but it had altered him to the core. He wasn't the same man I'd called my friend. And that wasn't my fault."

"You really believe that?"

I shrugged. "Most of the time. Sometimes I think I should have seen it coming anyway. I should have talked with him more. Connected with him so he would have come to me before he went ahead and destroyed his life.

"But even talking about it with you now . . . I doubt that's true. The things he was contemplating were too awful to talk about. He knew how I'd react because he knew *me*.

"I was always open and honest with him. I was a good friend. He just didn't do me that honor in return."

Locke gave me an approving nod. "Sounds like this side mission of yours taught you a lot. You thinking about going back to leading your own team? On a more permanent basis?"

"That's above my pay grade. That whole experience on Talitsa shook me to the core, but believe me, I love serving with Osiris. It's a real pleasure to have someone else making the hard calls sometimes." I tapped my fingers on the table as I thought about it more. "But yeah, if they put me in charge of Alpha-Nine, I think I'd be ready to give that a shot again."

At that moment, Romeo came into the club with Dutch and Gretchen right behind him. They were joking, laughing just like old times. I can't tell you how many different bars I'd walked into with that crew, and it warmed my heart to see them like that again.

The three of them spotted one of the few open tables and snagged it. As Dutch went to grab them a round of drinks, Mickey entered the place.

On cue, the entire bar fell silent.

Mickey froze as he realized every eye in the room was riveted on him. He gave a nervous smile that never had a chance of reaching his eyes, and he supplemented it with a half-hearted wave. For a moment, I thought he might turn around and bolt. Then, as he scanned the room, his eyes caught mine.

He was dying there, caught in a misery of his own making, and part of me relished it. After all he'd put me through, I didn't mind seeing him suffer a bit, especially like this.

But I couldn't let him hang there like that. I jerked my head toward an open chair at our table.

Mickey almost melted with relief. He moved quickly and sat down next to me, opposite Locke.

"Thank you," he said quietly as the conversations in the rest of the room ramped back up to regular volume.

"Least I can do for a guy who saved my life today."

He glanced around nervously. "Yeah, well, I think this may make us even."

"Only if you're buying," I said with a loose smile.

He nodded at me. "All right. You're on." He looked at Locke. "And what is your friend here having?"

Of course. The two of them had never met. "Mickey? This is Jameson Locke, former ONI lieutenant commander and the man in charge of my most recent outfit, Fireteam Osiris.

"Locke? This is Spartan Mickey Crespo, the son of a bitch who betrayed me. Didn't you used to shoot guys like him for a living?"

Mickey went as pale as a reactor's glow. Locke stuck out his hand and said, "Any friend of Buck's."

"I'll have whatever kind of Scotch they have," I told Mickey. "Neat."

He stared at me like he had no idea what I was talking about. He still hadn't let go of Locke's hand. "Make that two," Locke said.

That shocked Mickey into action. "Right," he said. "Be right back." He leaped out of his chair, knocking it over backward, but I caught it before it could land.

"Hey," Locke said to Mickey. "Don't make it hard on yourself. We're all Spartans here."

"I get that."

"I broke a lot of laws in my time," Locke said. "Did a lot of things I probably shouldn't be proud of. I just always made sure I did them for the right reasons."

"I—I'll try to keep that in mind," Mickey said. "Always."

Locke stood up to accompany Mickey to the bar. "I'll give you a hand."

I was still processing that when Veronica strode into the bar.

I waved her over, and she sat down next to me and leaned in for a quick hug. "You look like you've been up to some kind of mischief."

"Yeah, just torturing Mickey a little," I said as I leaned back in my chair. "You know, I think I could get used to that."

"Just don't overdo it," she said. "The last thing we need for him to do is turn on you again out of petty revenge."

"That would never happen . . ." I winced. "All right. Fine. But I still get to have *some* fun."

"Granted."

I glanced around, and despite the horrible circumstances we were in, I couldn't help but grin. Cortana had us on the run, and most of the galaxy was currently suffering under her virtual thumb, but I had both of my teams together in one bar, along with Veronica Dare. I couldn't believe I'd ever gotten so lucky as to have her in my life. I held my gaze on her until she became self-conscious.

"What?" she said. "You look like you've got something on your mind."

"Nothing," I said. "Nothing at all. Ever since I got hauled back into that Condor, I've been as content as can be."

She put her hand on my arm. "I suppose when you have your greatest desire fulfilled, that's about it for the day?"

I leaned over. "I never said *that* was my greatest desire."

"No," she said. "You're absolutely right. The one thing you said you regretted as you were about to die is that you never asked me to marry you."

If I'd had a drink then, I would have choked on it. "Hey . . . we all say things in what we think are our final moments."

Veronica came in close. "Things we regret?"

"Hang on. I never said I *regretted* that."

"So you meant it?" She sounded honestly curious.

"Every word."

She ran her tongue under her lower lip and gave me a wry, knowing smile. "But as usual, Buck, you're all talk and no action."

"Now, wait a minute. I am acceptable and generally more than adequate when it comes to action. I just . . ." I fumbled for the proper words.

She laughed. "You really think I've been mooning around this place, waiting for you to pop the question?"

I put up my hands in front of me. "Come on, that's unfair. You might have noticed that we've had a lot on our collective plate lately. I *did* ask you to marry me before—maybe more than once, depending on how you want to count—but we agreed that the time wasn't right."

"Really?" She put her chin on her hand and gazed deep into my eyes, as if searching the depths of my soul. "What's wrong with now?"

I arched an eyebrow at her, unsure where she was taking this. "Are you asking me to marry you, Veronica?"

"Oh, no. I'm *daring* you to marry me, Buck."

Now *that* surprised me. I glanced around our little bar, deep in the heart of *Infinity*. Everyone in the place had stopped talking, watching to see how I would respond.

"What?" I said. "Right here? Now?"

Veronica stood up and looked down at me. "All we need's a terminal and a connection, right?" She signaled the bartender, and Helen tossed over a tablet as if it were a flying disc. Veronica caught it neatly, activated it, and slapped it down on the table in front of me. "Stand up."

I did exactly as she said.

She tapped a few buttons on the tablet, and it announced to the room, "*Matrimonial function activated.*"

"Wait," I said. "Whoa. You sure you don't want to get Captain Lasky down here to do the honors?"

She narrowed her eyes at me. "Are you getting cold feet already?"

"No, but—"

"*Prospective spouses,*" the tablet began.

"Are you sure this is legit?"

The voice from the table hesitated for a moment before a hologram of Roland, the ship's AI, appeared above it. He looked like a little golden-colored twentieth-century fighter pilot, complete with goggles and a bomber jacket. It was really something that, unlike many of the smart AIs in the service of the UNSC, he'd seen through Cortana's offer of immortality and scorned it for the bad deal it was—and I loved him for that.

"Hold up," he said, smacking his hands together as he favored us with a broad smile. "I wouldn't miss this for the world."

"Fair enough," I said. "But let's get this clear: If *you* marry us, it's official, right?"

The AI grinned as if I'd asked him whether he might possibly be smarter than me. "Just like if I were the captain of the ship. In many ways, I *am* the ship, and you can't get more authoritative aboard *Infinity* than that."

"All right," I said gamely. "Let's go."

Roland cleared his throat and spoke clearly and distinctly. Everyone in the room got to their feet to bear witness, including Fireteam Osiris and Alpha-Nine. Even the bartender hustled over to watch.

"Captain Veronica Ann Dare and Spartan Edward Malcolm Buck," Roland said with an official flourish of his hands. "Do you wish to be married? If so, each of you, please place your palm facedown on this tablet so I can record your prints, and say *I do.*"

"How romantic," I said. I looked at Veronica. "Okaaay. Uh . . . you ready for this?"

She nodded at me, smiling. "Quit stalling, Buck."

Neither Veronica nor I hesitated another instant. We put our hands right next to each other on the tablet. Mine might have been shaking just a bit.

We looked into each other's eyes and said, in unison, *"I do."*

"Prints accepted!" Roland announced. "Contract established! Your marriage is now legally binding! Feed the birds!"

We leaned in for a kiss, and everyone around us went wild. We held on to each other like we were never going to let go.

It wasn't too long after our honeymoon—such as it was—that I found myself on a distant world once again, leading Alpha-Nine on another highly classified mission. The setting sun had cast the shaded lands in a midnight blue while washing the higher reaches in a crimson as bright as blood. It seemed like we were the only living people in the entire world, and at that moment, it may have been true.

We were on our own, keeping as low under the radar as we could manage, our heads up and hunting for enemies. We had our rifles locked and loaded, out and ready for any kind of trouble that might cross our path.

We were out of contact with Command. We had nothing but our armor and our weapons to rely on. And each other.

It felt like the old days—just the way I liked it.

I led the way on the march, with Mickey and Romeo on my six and Dutch and Gretchen bringing up the rear. We worked like a well-oiled machine.

Actually, better than that: We worked like a machine that had frozen up, been torn down to its blocks, and then rebuilt to run smoother than ever.

But that's a whole 'nother story, right?

ACKNOWLEDGMENTS

While this book shows my name on the cover, it's the collective effort of an amazing team of people. As always, I owe huge thanks to my editor, Ed Schlesinger, whose tenacity for and dedication to making things better shines through in the polish given to every page. He and the team at Gallery Books—including the copyeditor on this book, E. Beth Thomas—always pull off the wondrous magic trick of making my writing look better than it is.

Their partners in that effort, of course, are the wonderful people at 343 Industries, particularly Jeremy Patenaude, Tiffany O'Brien, Jeff Easterling, Ken Peters, and Corrinne Robinson, who always strive to make every Halo story ring clear and true as a crystal bell. Thanks so much for trusting me with your galaxy.

I'm grateful, too, to Isaac Hannaford, whose artwork graces the cover of this book and helped inspire a scene or two herein. Isaac also provided the cover for *New Blood*, and in that sense, it's great to have the Alpha-Nine band back together again.

Thanks also to Nathan Fillion, Tricia Helfer, Alan Tudyk, Mike Colter, Ike Amadi, Steve Downes, Nolan North, Laura Bailey, Masaya Moyo, Brian T. Delaney, Keith David, Jennifer Hale, Michelle Lukes, Cynthia Kaye Williams, Melanie Minichino,

ACKNOWLEDGMENTS

Darren O'Hare, Jen Taylor, Britt Baron, Travis Willingham, Adam Baldwin, and all the rest of the actors who breathed video-game life into so many of the characters who populate this book. I loved having your voices rattle around in my head again for as long as they did.

ABOUT THE AUTHOR

Matt Forbeck is an award-winning and *New York Times* bestselling author and game designer. He has more than thirty novels and countless games published to date. His latest work includes *Halo: Legacy of Onyx*, *Halo: New Blood*, *Dungeonlogy*, the *Star Wars: Rogue One* junior novel, the last two editions of *The Marvel Encyclopedia*, his *Monster Academy* YA fantasy novels, and the *Shotguns & Sorcery* role-playing game based on his novels. He lives in Beloit, Wisconsin, with his wife and five children, including a set of quadruplets. For more about him and his work, visit Forbeck.com.

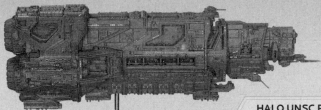

HALO

MEGA CONSTRUX™
Build Beyond™

MEGACONSTRUX.COM